Praise for
LAID BARE

"It's impossible not to love this story. The sex is sizzling, the emotions are raw. Lauren Dane has done it again. *Laid Bare*, quite simply, *rocks*!" —Megan Hart, author of *Deeper*

Praise for Lauren Dane and
UNDERCOVER

"Lauren Dane deftly weaves action, intrigue and emotion with spicy, delicious eroticism . . . a toe-curling erotic romance sure to keep you reading late into the night."
—Anya Bast, national bestselling author of *Witch Heart*

"Sexy, pulse-pounding adventure . . . that'll leave you weak in the knees. Dane delivers!" —Jaci Burton, author of *Riding on Instinct*

"Exciting, emotional and arousing."
—Sasha White, author of *My Prerogative*

"Fast-paced action, steamy romance."
—Megan Hart, author of *Stranger*

"Scintillating! . . . A roller coaster of emotion, intrigue and sensual delights . . . I was hooked from the first sentence."
—Vivi Anna, author of *Veiled Truth*

LAID
BARE

LAUREN DANE

HEAT | NEW YORK

THE BERKLEY PUBLISHING GROUP
Published by the Penguin Group
Penguin Group (USA) Inc.
375 Hudson Street, New York, New York 10014, USA
Penguin Group (Canada), 90 Eglinton Avenue East, Suite 700, Toronto, Ontario M4P 2Y3, Canada
(a division of Pearson Penguin Canada Inc.)
Penguin Books Ltd., 80 Strand, London WC2R 0RL, England
Penguin Group Ireland, 25 St. Stephen's Green, Dublin 2, Ireland (a division of Penguin Books Ltd.)
Penguin Group (Australia), 250 Camberwell Road, Camberwell, Victoria 3124, Australia
(a division of Pearson Australia Group Pty. Ltd.)
Penguin Books India Pvt. Ltd., 11 Community Centre, Panchsheel Park, New Delhi—110 017, India
Penguin Group (NZ), 67 Apollo Drive, Rosedale, North Shore 0632, New Zealand
(a division of Pearson New Zealand Ltd.)
Penguin Books (South Africa) (Pty.) Ltd., 24 Sturdee Avenue, Rosebank, Johannesburg 2196,
South Africa

Penguin Books Ltd., Registered Offices: 80 Strand, London WC2R 0RL, England

This is an original publication of The Berkley Publishing Group.

PRINTING HISTORY
Heat trade paperback edition / August 2009

Library of Congress Cataloging-in-Publication Data

Dane, Lauren.
    Laid bare / Lauren Dane.
        p. cm.
    ISBN 978-0-425-22971-2
1. Stalking victims—Fiction.   2. Bereavement—Psychological aspects—Fiction.   3. Triangles
(Interpersonal relations)—Fiction. I. Title.
    PS3604.A5L35   2009
    813'.6—dc22   2009001331

PRINTED IN THE UNITED STATES OF AMERICA

10 9 8 7 6 5 4 3 2 1

This one is for Tracy

ACKNOWLEDGMENTS

Thank you always, first and foremost, to my wonderful husband. Thank you for loving me despite my being a horrible housekeeper, especially around deadline time.

Laura Bradford, my friend and a fabulous agent, thank you for always being there and for believing in me.

Leis Pederson, you're as shiny in person as you are via e-mail. Thank you so very much for being such a great editor.

Thanks to the Berkley art department, because this cover rocks my world, like, whoa!

Megan Hart, there are very few people in the world who *get* me and still love me. Thank you so very much for always being there and for making me laugh more than a girl ever has a right to. Your advice is always good, your eye is always keen and you're a dork just like me.

Anya Bast, you're awesome. Thank you so much for being you. Ann Aguirre, thank you for those countless hours on IM! Renee and Mary, thank you so much for all the wonderful beta reading, thank you for moderating my message board and thank you for always being such wonderful, supportive friends!

And of course, thank you to my girls and those guys on my

Vixenreader board! Heck, all my readers, new and old and those in between. Thank you for taking the time to pick up my books and read them. Thank you for reviewing them and talking about them! And thank you for all the lovely notes you send. You all make this gig so much more enjoyable.

LAID
BARE

1

Seattle, The Off Ramp
Ten Years Ago

Music, raw and hard like sex, pulsed through the speaker stack, caught the people in front of the stage, as much as it had her, in its grip.

The bass line throbbed through her like a second pulse as the scent of beer and sweat settled into her system. Sweat slicked her forehead and slid down the line of her spine. The muscles in her forearm corded as she played, her fingers finding their way as they had time and again. A secret smile marked her lips as her half-lidded eyes focused on something not visible to anyone else.

Yes, it was a man's world up there, but she'd kicked down the door with her Doc Martens and she wasn't giving her spot to anyone else. She loved making music, and it fit her like a second skin. It made her alive.

Her dreads swung forward, partially obscuring her face—adding, she knew, to the overall effect. Her belly, glistening with sweat, slid against the back of her bass where her shirt ended and her low-slung jeans began.

Up there, under the blue lights, she didn't have to work at it.

She *was*. She was exactly where she wanted to be, a guitar strapped to her body, calluses on her fingers from playing. The muscles in her upper arms were well defined because she hauled equipment around for gigs. There wasn't any doubt, any self-consciousness. She lived the life she wanted.

Erin Brown had stopped apologizing for wanting things. She grabbed experiences with both hands and gobbled them down.

Even if the band never made it beyond small, local rock clubs, she'd be happy to just keep playing. There wasn't much more you could ask for in life, and Erin accepted her blessings quite happily and graciously.

Todd took a pull from his beer, one leg bent as he leaned against the windowsill, looking out toward the street. There she was, getting out of her beat-up van. He had no idea why the hell he did it, but since he'd moved to the day shift he found himself at his window every night at six-fourteen to watch her make the walk from car to door.

She was so *not* the kind of woman who usually caught his eye. Still, his fingers gripped the sill as he greedily took in the way she moved. Like she couldn't care less if people watched. Or worse, got off on it.

Long and lean, her gait ate up the walk, her dreadlocks swinging to her ass. A fine ass it was in those faded jeans. If he looked close enough, he saw the threadbare spots just beneath the pockets. Reflexively, he tightened his hands into fists as tension hummed through him. Anticipation and a sort of need filled his gut as he watched her.

He snorted at what an idiot he was being. *Dreadlocks*. What woman wore dreadlocks? Not his sort of woman, that was all there was to it.

Time stopped, along with his heart, when she turned at her door

and met his gaze with a smile. A smile that told him she'd known
he watched. Surprised but rooted to the spot, he raised a hand in
greeting. She paused a moment before tipping her chin at him.
Briefly he relaxed as she turned back to her door, but that slid away
when she paused again, dropped her bag on the porch and turned
back toward his place.

Shit.

She was already on his doorstep by the time he'd put his beer
down and opened the door to face her.

"Officer Keenan, how are you today?"

Her voice did things to him. Unwilling things. Low and smoky.
It went with her eyes, a sort of brownish green, full of promises.
Damn it, she was not what he wanted. And still he couldn't keep
his eyes from dropping to take in her nipples straining against the
front of her shirt.

"Erin, I've told you, it's Todd." Yanking his gaze back to her
face, he stood in the doorway, fighting the urge to invite her in. She
put a hand on her hip and he caught the taut expanse of her belly
exposed with the movement. And the glimmer of the ring she had
there.

"I know, but I like calling you Officer Keenan. It's sort of sexy.
Very in-charge and authoritative." She winked. "Anyway, I wanted
to let you know we were having some people over later tonight. It
shouldn't be loud. You should come over if you're going to be
around."

"Thanks for asking, but it's really not my thing." He shoved his
hands in his front pockets before he did something stupid like
reaching out to trace around the ring in her belly button or to test
the texture of the dread hanging nearest to him.

She smelled of something unique. Heady, smoldering and sweet
all at once. Every time they came in close contact he had that scent
in his nose for days.

"If it's too noisy, come by and pound . . . on the front door." She
drew out the last bit and his cock jumped in his jeans.

He cleared his throat. He took scum down on the streets every
fucking day and this woman had him on the ropes. What was up
with that?

"I have a date. I won't even be here. But thanks. Have a good
time." He stepped back and started to close the door and she actually smirked before moving away down the walk.

"Okay then, Todd. Have a good time."

Damned if he didn't watch the captivating sway of her ass as she
went back to her own door and inside. And damned if she didn't
stop and wink at him before she disappeared from sight.

Erin Brown had been his neighbor for a year. She and her
brother had moved in next door, and even through he tried hard not
to judge on looks alone, he couldn't help but wonder if they'd be
trouble. Adrian, the brother, had hair nearly as long as hers and
neck tattoos. He rode a motorcycle and the group of people in and
out of the place looked like they came from an episode of *America's
Most Wanted*.

Happily, they'd proven his initial wariness wrong. They'd been
great neighbors. They kept up their small front walk and yard.
They weren't loud. Hell, the brother took the trash cans out for the
elderly woman across the street on Friday mornings. Long hair, motorcycle and neck tattoos hadn't stopped the Browns from being
really nice folks.

He knew they played in a band. He'd seen Erin walking in and
out of the apartment with a guitar case, and her brother often had
black equipment cases as well. And a woman couldn't get away
with looking the way she did without being in a band or something
equally unconventional.

Still, it worked on her. The dreads, the tattoos and the piercings
didn't make her look hard. They made her look exotic and raw. She

was a walk on the wild side and he'd always avoided that sort of thing.

He was a cop. He listened to country music and drove a big truck. She had belly tattoos and played guitar. He went out with nice, quiet women who wore pink dresses and let him open the door. Women who responded gently in bed. Todd bet Erin fucked like the rockstar she embodied. He bet she was loud and demanding. Pushy, probably.

Not that he thought about what she'd be like in bed. Much. It was taboo, that had to be it.

Erin went inside, slamming the door in her wake. God, why did that cop have to look so damned good? All masculine and clean-cut in his jeans and snug cotton shirt. He was so earnest with his big, white smile and his good manners. Not her usual type at all, but he sure did fill out the aforementioned jeans. Right into her masturbatory fantasies.

The guy watched her every night when she got home from work. Sometimes she thought she saw interest in his eyes. Other times she thought he was just making sure she didn't steal anything.

Tonight as he stood there in bare feet, his dark brown hair looking soft and sexy, still wet from his shower, she was pretty sure it was the latter.

In fact, he'd looked practically panicked when she impulsively invited him to their party. Stupid. It *so* was not his scene, but she wanted to talk to him. To hear the smooth and yet rough voice; to see that slight afternoon beard shadowing his jaw. There was something about him, just beneath the surface. An edge she was dying to expose and rub herself against like a cat.

"Oh for fuck's sake! God, Erin, just do the man already. Watch-

ing the two of you circle each other pretending not to be interested
has ceased to be amusing and now chaps my ass."

"Evening, Adrian." Ignoring his comment, Erin sauntered into
the living room, where her younger brother sat re-stringing her
guitar. A bottle of ginger brew sweated at his right hand, as Tool
played in the background.

"I tuned it for you while I was at it." He put her beloved Fender
P-Bass back in the case and flipped the latches closed. "And I'm
serious. What's stopping you? If this guy was some dude at any of
the clubs we played or the coffee shop, you'd have turned the full
power of your magic on him and bagged him by now. What's so
different about the cop?"

"I don't think he's interested, Aid." She plopped into a chair
across from him.

"He think he's too good for you?" His deep green eyes narrowed.

Erin laughed at how protective he sounded. "I think I freak him
out. I invited him tonight and you'd have thought I asked him to
eat kittens in puff pastry."

Adrian shrugged. "Maybe so, but the dude watches you every
night when you get home. And not like a stalker. Believe me, I've
checked. I'd squash him like a bug if that were the case, cop or not.
No, he likes to look at you because he's interested. You want him,
you take him. He should be so lucky to have a woman like you."

"Aww, thank you." For a man who had spent most of his life until adulthood and then some tormenting her, he could really be a
sweetie pie sometimes. She stood again. "I'm gonna shower and get
ready. Brody is due by with food and drinks in an hour."

Adrian shook his head sadly and then raised his eyebrow in challenge. "I've never thought of you as a quitter."

He knew her vulnerable spots. She'd never let him call her a
punk and a quitter. It was on.

2

For the next week Erin tried to ignore the eyes watching her every night, but it was futile. Adrian knew exactly what to say to push her buttons. Quitter indeed! She wasn't a quitter, damn it.

Finally, Friday night she took off her bra, smeared on some cherry red lip gloss and stomped downstairs, condoms tucked into her pocket.

Adrian waited for her at the bottom with a six-pack of beer in one hand. "Finally. Took you long enough." He handed the beer her way. "Take it. An ice breaker. Invite him to the gig tomorrow."

"You're weird. I thought brothers were supposed to pretend their sisters were sexless." She took the beer and kissed his cheek.

"I'm your brother, not an idiot. If he hurts you, I'll crush him, but I want you to be happy. You want him and that's enough for me."

Warmth settled inside as she hugged him quickly. She'd lucked out with both her brothers. Good men. They'd saved each other after their parents had died. "Thank you."

"Go on now. Let's not spoil this by making me think about any details." Adrian winked and she left.

Erin slid into her stage persona. Pulled it on like a costume and felt the confidence roar through her as she sauntered over to Todd's front door and knocked.

He opened up and started a moment before catching himself. But not fast enough that she didn't catch the perusal from toes to eyes.

She gestured toward him with the beer. "So, you know what? I'm thinking we live next door, and other than the few times we've spoken here and there around the neighborhood, we've never shared a beer and hung out."

He opened his mouth to speak and settled for nodding. *Ha!*

"Are you alone, Officer Keenan?"

He nodded and she pushed past him and into his apartment. Clearly one of them had to make the first move or she'd be at the front door forever.

In the middle of his living room she turned to face him as he closed the door. "Want a beer? I brought a few."

"Make yourself at home." His lips twisted in a sarcastic smile and she liked it. He had spirit.

She put the beer on the table and bent at the waist to untie her boots before taking them off. "I wish we had hardwood floors." She sashayed past him and put her boots next to his at the front door. Instead of moving back into the living room, she leaned against the wall in the entry hall where he stood.

"Why are you here?" he asked. Not hostile. Wary. Curious.

"I'm a very blunt woman." Her reply was a challenge, and he barked a quick laugh, deep and husky. *Lord.*

"I've noticed."

"I know. Every night when I get home from work." *Take that.*

The air thickened with tension as they took each other in. He wore a cotton T-shirt—*ugh* Toby Keith. Still, her revulsion tempered as she meandered south and saw the taper of a slim waist and thick thighs covered in worn denim. Dirty denim. She'd always thought the term was stupid until she looked at the nearly thread-bare spot over his fly and never felt dirtier. His cock strained at the material and it was her he stood at attention for. A particularly vivid impulse to drop to her knees and suck him off right then and there sped her pulse.

"So?"

His voice brought her back, her gaze moving to his face. That sexy evening stubble gleamed in the low light from the lamp in the other room.

"I'm here because I want you. I think you want me too." She toyed with the button on her jeans as her nipples pressed wantonly through the material of her own T-shirt. PJ Harvey. Probably gave him the same mental lip curl Toby Keith gave her. Good god, if they did fuck, it was going to be all teeth and nails and feral action.

A shiver worked through her at the thought.

She what? Todd drank in the sight of her. Leaning indolently against his wall, her breasts offered toward him with the arch of her stance, she shouldn't have been so ridiculously hot but she was. Presented like a gift.

He couldn't find fault with the tight nipples on what appeared to be braless breasts, high and proud. What healthy man could look away?

Her belly was flat and he caught the tip of a tattoo that had to cover her just above her pussy. Dizzily he tried to tell himself porn stars had those tattoos. That wasn't sexy, right? A laugh nearly escaped him at the thought. She was ridiculously sexy.

Fuck. His cock was hard enough to drive nails with.

"So this is what? A booty call?" He tried to sound casual,

disinterested, but her eyes flicked back to his cock straining against his jeans and that smile, her *I've got a secret* smile, broke over her lips.

"Tell you what, Todd. Let's have a beer and we can go from there. Unless you aren't interested and that cock is hard for someone else. In which case, I can leave and we can pretend this never happened." One of her brows rose slowly, the one with the ring in it.

He contemplated telling her he wasn't interested. For like a third of a second. Instead he nodded and walked into his living room.

"I'll put the beer in my fridge." He pulled two out before disappearing with the rest. In his kitchen, he desperately struggled to get a handle on his rioting hormones as he tossed the bottle caps.

When he got back, he found her kneeling backward on his couch, looking at the CD rack behind it. Her sweet ass canted in his direction.

"Country, huh?" She spoke without looking back as he walked around behind the couch to face her, handing her a beer. Better not to be back there with her ass presented that way. He loved to fuck from behind with a woman in just that position. It didn't happen very often, but he craved it nonetheless.

She took a long pull from the bottle and he watched as her throat worked. A visual of how she'd look as he fed his cock to her shocked through him a moment.

"Yeah. I take it you don't like country." A smile threatened until she put her beer aside and reached to grab the belt loop on his jeans and pull him closer.

"I like some country." Her voice was little more than a hoarse whisper. An involuntary shiver worked through him as he watched her hand move from the loop, nails scoring his cock through the thin denim.

He hissed, arching toward her, and she smiled.

"I like Patsy Cline and Loretta Lynn. The Dixie Chicks are good. I just heard them the other day. My mom raised us on Conway Twitty and Tammy Wynette. I love music of all types."

Her fingers traced down the line of his zipper as she looked up into his face—waiting for him to refuse. Yeah, like that was going to happen.

He flexed his hips instead and watched, rapt, as she slowly pulled his zipper down, the metal rasp loud over his breath.

Gentle, cool hands pulled him out.

"No underwear. My. Surprise, surprise."

"I like it when my cock rubs against my jeans this way." He'd never spoken like that to a woman before. It made him harder.

She angled him and the air shot out his mouth as her tongue circled the head, the tip digging into the sensitive spot just beneath.

He did what he'd wanted to do for the last year. He ran his palms over her hair, wondering at the texture of the ropes. Not hard or wiry, not fragile. Unique and unexpected, a lot like she was. A wisp of tenderness wafted through him briefly.

He grabbed it in his fist as she swallowed most of his cock, taking him as deeply as she could.

"Holy shit," he muttered, sliding his hips forward to meet her mouth. She hummed her satisfaction and it vibrated up his cock.

She shoved his jeans down farther and cupped his balls. He thought he'd jump out of his skin when she licked down the shaft and tongued his sac.

"Yeah, oh fuck, yes, like that," he whispered.

She opened her eyes and looked up at him, her lips swollen and wet. "Tell me. What do you want, Todd?"

He panted as the words threatened to break through. He wanted to say them, but the darkness in them wasn't something he was used to letting free.

"Shall I go first? Should I tell you that when I'm done sucking your cock and you've blown down my throat, I want your face between my thighs? That I want to feel your mouth on my pussy, licking and sucking my clit? What do you say? Hmm? Is there a dirty talker in there waiting to break free? Trust me enough to tell me what you want and I'll give it to you."

He swallowed hard. Erin Brown made him want things he'd been fine not wanting. On one hand, it felt marvelous; on the other, it scared the hell out of him. He let his tongue free because she'd demanded it of him with her own uninhibited behavior.

"Suck my cock, Erin. Take me as far as you can into that sweet, hot throat. I want to fuck your mouth and control you by your hair." As the words unfurled, the tight ball in his chest eased for the first time in years. His spine relaxed even as his balls drew tight against his body.

Controlling her by her hair. God. How many times had he imagined it over the years when a woman sucked his cock? He'd had to grab the sheets to keep from reaching out to put her mouth just where he wanted it. But he hadn't. He told himself it wasn't gentlemanly to grab a woman by the hair.

Watching Erin down the line of his body, he caught her smile right before she bent over him and swallowed his cock just the way he told her he wanted.

Her mouth kept even pressure, kept him nice and wet as he began to roll his hips, fucking into her while he grabbed a handful of her hair, tight, in his fist, holding her head just the way he wanted it.

The way he wanted it. Not gentle, not nice, but hard and dark. Emotion rushed through him as she sucked him into her mouth. Her hair in his fist felt right, so right he had to stop thinking about it because it overwhelmed him. Instead he watched her. She was so beautiful.

Each time he pulled out, the stalk of his cock was deep red and shiny from her mouth. Her eyes stayed closed, but every once in a while she'd open them and look up at him, shocking him down to his toes.

Her ass swayed as she held on to the root of his cock with one hand and lightly scored his thigh and balls with the blunt, neat nails of her other hand.

Orgasm rushed from the tips of his toes and his scalp, barreling toward his cock at hyper-speed, until he clenched his jaw to hold back the roar as he shot down her throat just like he'd wanted to. Like he rarely ever did with a woman.

Pulse after pulse, he continued to come. She never stopped her rhythm on him until he softened and let go of her hair.

He stumbled back against the CD rack and panted to catch his breath. He kept his eyes closed to try and gather himself, to rein in his rioting emotions. It was powerful to have let go that much, to have given in to what he wanted. Getting it was even more so, and the floodgates opened a crack. He could see himself shoving her to her knees when she walked in his front door every night. Ordering her to suck his cock to start the evening off but not make him climax. Still wet from her mouth, he'd fuck her right then and there in his hallway. Pump his cock into her cunt over and over while she was on her hands and knees. Erin. Just for him.

Fine tremors worked through him for long moments. He'd never allowed himself to be so specific with fantasies. Stayed away from the BDSM porn. He didn't want to hurt a woman, and for him, fear that he'd cross the line and become a deviant kept him far away.

When he opened his eyes after a deep breath, she still knelt on his couch, drinking her beer, watching him with that smile of hers.

He'd wondered briefly, as he'd begun to come, if she'd run out the door afterward. After hearing his coarse words. But hers were just as coarse, and fuck, it wasn't like he was some fragile dude. He wore a gun to work!

"You"—she tipped her chin toward him—"have some pussy to eat."

He didn't stop the smile this time. "You're a very dirty girl." And it worked. It worked for her and it *really* worked for him.

"I am. Please feel free to tell me more."

He jerked his chin toward his bedroom. He wanted to spread her out as he ate her.

Erin let him lead the way down the short hall to his bedroom. His place was smaller than hers and Adrian's. No second floor, which was too bad because she'd love to be bent over and fucked from behind on the stairs.

She'd actually planned to drink a beer and slowly seduce the man, but he'd eroded her control. As he stood there with his cock in her face, she'd had to taste him. And she really liked the way his breath caught when she told him what she wanted. There was a thin veneer of control over his emotions. He didn't want to be turned on, but he was. Part of her thrilled at being the one to flip that switch, but the other part went wet and gooey at the idea of him dominating her.

His bedroom was cool and dark until he flipped on the light next to the bed, casting a yellow glow around the space.

He stood there in his doorway, staring at her. She watched the war on his face. She'd seen the women he dated. Unless they were all the kind to be very prim and sweet on the outside and hoochies in the bedroom, he probably either scared them off when he laid the dirty talk on them or he held back.

"Tell me," she whispered. *I won't judge you. Just be yourself.*

"Strip. I want to see you naked."

"That was easy." She smirked as she drew her T-shirt up and over her head, tossing it aside.

Gasping, he took a step forward and then another until he stood within touching distance. His eyes locked on the twin rings in her nipples.

"Touch me, Todd." Oh, how she needed him to put his hands on her!

With an impatient growl, he brought his hands to cup her breasts as he bent to look at the rings. Carefully, he traced her nipples with a fingertip and she arched into him.

"You won't break me. Harder. I *like* it hard, Todd."

It was like she'd thrown a switch as his teeth caught the ring and tugged. Shards of pleasure skittered through her. The tip of his tongue flicked the underside of first one nipple and then the other; the weight of each ring as it slid and moved with his mouth added to the sensation.

"So sensitive." His voice was low, rough. "I've wanted to do this for a long time now." He fell to his knees, fingertips tracing over her tattoos until he got to the waist of her jeans and made quick work of them, yanking them down.

Bracing her weight on him with a hand on his shoulder, she stepped out of her pants and panties, kicking them to the side.

He rocked back on his heels and looked up at her, taking in every detail.

"Turn around. I want to see your back."

She did, bending and bracing her hands on the bed, hoping he'd get the hint.

"Amazing." His body heat blanketed her as he leaned in to look at the intricate inkwork on her back.

"My older brother is an artist, isn't he? That one took six months to finish."

Rustling alerted her he was getting naked too. She saw the flash of his shirt and jeans out of the corner of her eye. She had to see his body, so she stood and turned.

"Oh, well, that's far better than I imagined." He radiated masculinity and a sort of feral sexuality he'd either hidden with the clothes or had been repressing. Either way, it sent a thrill straight to her cunt.

"I'm glad you approve." He hesitated for just a brief moment before continuing. "On the bed, spread your legs. Knees up, feet flat."

She swallowed hard and moved to obey. His comforter was soft and cool against her back, relaxing her a bit. The room smelled like him. But the wetter she got, the more her own scent added spice to his.

He moved between her legs and knelt, looming over her. "I haven't tasted your lips yet."

Before she could give a sassy reply, he'd crushed her mouth beneath his. He slid his palms over her arms and held her hands as he plundered. He held her wrists and she wished he'd hold them harder, wished he'd pin her down so the play struggle would be sweeter. He held back. There was a part of him she sensed he kept tightly reined in and she wondered why. Wanted him to break the control on her. Ached to see the full extent of what he truly wanted.

Step by step, tongue, teeth and lips worked together to devastate, to own and control, to make every part of her body hard but her pussy, which bloomed and slickened for him.

She arched her neck as he started to pull away, not wanting to lose his taste. He chuckled in that arrogant male way as he broke from her mouth.

"If I don't stop kissing your mouth, I can't lick and suck your clit like you wanted."

Her breath caught. Like she'd argue with that logic?

"First your nipples and those sexy fucking rings again." He let go of her hands and began to play with her nipples and the rings, tugging and teasing with his mouth and fingers until her hips churned. It felt so good she wondered if she could come just from that alone.

The rasp of his stubble added another layer of sensation to the experience as her head began to slowly move from side to side.

She saw enough to know it made him hot too. His cock was heavy and the slit gleamed with a bead of semen. She unconsciously licked her bottom lip, recalling how he'd felt as he'd pressed his cock into her mouth over and over. Remembering the hot, salty taste of him.

Finally, he broke away from her nipples and continued downward, over her belly button, pausing to take that ring between his teeth.

"What is it with you and the piercings?"

"I told you I like it hard," she breathed out. "It hurt for a moment but then the sting felt good."

His knuckle slid between her labia and against her clit.

"I like the way it—*oh god, yes, more*—feels when my nipples brush against things. I think it looks sexy."

"You like it hard?"

She arched up, crying out when he pulled her open and flicked his tongue over her clit several times, then backed off.

"Yes. I do. Hard. Dark. Uninhibited. I like it rough, Todd. I'm too old for apologizing and I don't want to. I like sex and I like it dirty."

He swore under his breath and moved his mouth back to her cunt, tasting her like he was starving.

Those women he dated hopefully let him work this magic, because the man's mouth was fucking gifted. He swirled his tongue through her pussy, fucking into her with it, licking and sucking on every part of her until she didn't even have words.

Bursts of pleasure, feeling, emotion, colors, sounds and scents buffeted her as he ate her pussy. His thumbs teased her gate, dipping in slightly and sliding 'round and 'round as he abraded her clit with his teeth, just before sucking it into his mouth as he feathered it with his tongue.

The deep moan she heard was her own, but she didn't remember making it. All she thought of was the orgasm that boiled through her, taking over everything in its wake until she managed the strength to push his head away because she couldn't take it anymore.

Todd struggled to take a deep enough breath, but when he did, he pulled her essence in deeper. Jesus God, he was in deep.

Her cunt tasted like spicy honey. Her scent teased him from his hands and mouth, and she lay before him like a buffet.

I like it hard.

He was fast losing perspective; the reins he kept so tight had begun to get away from him and he wasn't so sure he wanted them back.

She opened her eyes and stared at him as he looked her over. The intricate tattoo on her belly connected to the one covering most of her back. The tree of life. On her belly lay roses and ivy. They embodied her. Sharp, barbed and yet beautiful and essential. Sweet and intoxicating.

"That was magnificent."

Her velvety voice sounded lazy and satisfied, and he smiled. He'd planned to order a pizza and watch a baseball game. Eating Erin's pussy had been far better.

"Glad you enjoyed it." He only barely resisted the urge to fist his cock a few times. There was something about her that removed his normal inhibitions. He wanted to fuck her tits, wanted to come all over her pretty skin, wanted to eat her again. He wanted every-thing, and that rawness made him shake a bit.

"Your cock is hard again. You gonna do something with it?"

"Turn over."

She moaned then and flipped to her belly. "Condoms in my pocket."

He lay across her back, sliding his cock between the cheeks of her ass while he reached the top drawer of his nightstand. "I've got it."

Unable to resist, he pressed a kiss to her back before getting to his knees and rolling the condom on.

"Ass up, Erin. I'm going to fuck you from behind." The more he gave voice to his desires, the better it felt. The easier it became.

She got to her knees, her upper body still on the bed. She was going to kill him, but it'd be worth it. The long line of her spine led him past the sweet, high cheeks of her ass and down to her pussy. Her thighs glistened with her honey as the scent of her hung in the room.

He nudged the head of his cock down the line of her ass, the heat of her cunt guiding him as he pressed into her body in one hard thrust.

Her inner walls fluttered around his cock, but it was the soft sigh she made when he seated himself completely that nearly did him in.

"More." She pressed against him, her ass fitting in the cradle of his hips.

So he gave her what she asked for. Hard and a bit rough. In-creasing his speed, he grabbed her hips to hold her in position, placing her just the way he wanted as he fucked into her body with deep, feral digs of his cock.

She received him, rolling her hips to take him as deeply as she could each time he thrust. The sounds she made buffeted him, soft moans, whimpers of entreaty—all because *he'd* made her feel that way. He'd controlled her responses.

The embrace of her pussy intoxicated him, drew climax closer each time he pushed into her body and the wet clasp of her took him in.

"You feel so fucking good." He said it because it was true. He wasn't sure he wanted it to be, but it was.

"Yes. God, you do too."

He was surprised, although he shouldn't have been, when she slid a hand up to finger her clit as he fucked her. Goddamn, she was sexy.

Her movements were less rhythmic as she met his thrusts, and he knew her orgasm must be close. Her pussy spasmed around him as she caught her breath and gave a strangled cry.

It was all too much. He threw his head back and fucked her, loving the way his balls slapped her cunt and then drew against him, loving the wet sounds of fucking, loving her sighs and moans.

When he came, he tasted it on his tongue, felt it in his scalp and his toes as wave after wave of climax took him away and he let it.

3

Erin drank a bottle of water and tried to get into the right head-space for the show. After a fairly sleepless night, she still had to be up and out for the early shift at the coffee shop attached to her older brother's tattoo parlor.

She'd left Todd's place after several more hours of wicked, mind-bendingly hot sex. He'd blushed when she invited him to the show, and mumbled something about not being sure if he'd be able to make it.

The man was hard to pin down. He was ridiculously sexy and he totally owned it when he wanted to. The trouble was, Erin wasn't sure he really wanted to. While they were naked and sweaty he seemed totally behind the idea of letting his freak flag fly, but af-terward he'd distanced himself from her again.

Whatever. She knew who she was and what she was. There was no escaping it even if she wanted to. And she didn't. If Todd Keenan wanted a woman comfortable with her sexuality, he'd come back.

He pushed his way to the front, near the stage, and watched her. She was magic up there. Unexpected and unique. Total rockstar in a short skirt with fishnets and black Docs. Instead of a T-shirt she wore a vest with no bra beneath. He highly approved.

His cock throbbed in time with the music as his eyes caught a trail of glistening sweat between the exposed curve of her breasts.

He shouldn't be there. He'd argued with himself even as he'd driven through downtown on his way to the club. He was turning into someone he didn't recognize. He'd begun to lose hold on what he'd considered normal.

That morning he'd woken up with a sex hangover. He'd never actually had a sex hangover before, and he liked it. He loved the way his muscles hurt in all the right places. Loved the musky scent on his sheets and the way his skin smelled like Erin.

Never, never had he felt so charged after sex. And it wasn't as if he hated sex. He loved it and he had it often with the women he dated. Just not the kind of sex he'd had with Erin. He'd never let the words bubbling in the back of his brain free, much less actually *done* some of the things he'd wanted to. His dates were sweet and feminine. He couldn't imagine what any of them would have done if he'd yanked them by the hair and jammed his cock, still gleaming with their pussy juices, down their throats. And, god help him, he wanted more. And he shouldn't. Real men . . . good men didn't want that sort of sex. Right?

Because Erin had looked up at him and licked her lips after she made him come yet again with her mouth. She wasn't fragile, wasn't sweet. She was hot and wet and demanding in bed. She made him laugh too.

Combing his fingers through his hair, he continued to watch her, enthralled by the puzzle of this woman fate had shoved into his life.

"Your cop is here," Adrian said in her ear as they finished up.

She looked down and saw him there, looking sexy and totally out of place. Smiling, she knelt and beckoned him closer.

"You made it."

"Yeah. You were . . . wow. I don't know what I expected, but you're a really good bass player."

His compliment made her warm inside. "Thanks. Are you busy or can you hang out for about half an hour? I have to put this all away."

He took a deep breath and she wondered if he'd beg off. Instead he nodded slowly. "I'll get a drink. Come get me when you're done. I can drive you home if you'd like. Or can I help?"

"I'll get you when we're done. It'll be quicker if we do it."

They broke everything down and loaded it into the van. She ran into the joke of a dressing room and toweled off a bit, trying to clean up. Changed her top, ignored Adrian and the other guys' curious looks and sarcastic comments and headed out into the bar, where he waited.

"Hey."

He turned and devoured her with his eyes.

"Hi. I'm parked out back."

"We can walk through backstage then. There's a door out there."

The hand he put at her back burned against the sliver of bare skin between her shirt and skirt.

"I like the miniskirt," he murmured as they started through the alley toward the pay lot at the other end.

"I'm always hesitant about wearing them on stage so perverts can't look up and see my pussy. But the way this stage is set up and where I stand, it's safe."

He turned and she found herself pressed against the wall adjacent to the army/navy surplus store, his body caging hers.

"I don't think you're safe now."

Her heart pounded and honey flowed into the well of her pussy. She moved from side to side across his chest, loving the feel of her nipples against his muscles.

"Good. But I smell like cigarettes and sweat. Or is that part of what you like? Does it get you off that I'm dirty just now?"

He paused, swallowing a groan. She'd gotten to him. She wanted more.

"Do you, Todd? Do you like it when I'm this way? Just for you. Waiting and wet for your cock?"

"I do." He whispered it, the words pulled from him taut and reluctant but genuine nonetheless. "I like that you smell like a woman who needs to be fucked."

Her mouth opened and she had to gulp in air before replying. "Yes. Oh, god, yes, I do. Are you the man to do it? Right here? Right now? Have you ever fucked a woman against a wall when you could get caught at any moment, Todd?"

"You're bad for my self-control, Erin. You make me want things I shouldn't want."

His lips hovered just above hers; she saw the need etched into his features as his pupils nearly swallowed his eyes.

"Or maybe I make you want things you've always wanted and only now have a safe place to express them," she challenged. "Why shouldn't you want them? Why shouldn't you get off on what gets you off?"

He pulled out a condom and tore it open with his teeth. One-handed, he rolled it on after he'd freed his cock, and then ripped a hole in the crotch of her fishnets, shoving her panties aside.

He froze a moment, his fingers buried in her pussy. "Wet. Fuck."

"That's the idea. Isn't it?" Erin laughed and then groaned as his middle finger slid from her cunt and drew upward to circle her clit, spreading her lube around it.

He looked from side to side, checking to be sure they were alone before stepping closer. She hiked one leg up over his thigh and all the air whooshed from her as he thrust into her cunt.

The pace he set was hard and fast, and his lips found the sensitive place just below her ear. One hand held up her thigh, fingers reaching to brush against her clit from behind. The other burrowed under her shirt, finding a nipple. He pinched and then tugged the ring.

"Yes. Fuck me, Todd. Out here, where anyone could find us at any moment. Does it feel good deep inside my cunt? Does it feel good knowing I got wet the instant I saw you tonight?" She caught the lobe of the ear she'd been whispering in between her teeth for a moment as he groaned.

"Yes. God help me, yes, it does."

Erin couldn't tell if the anguish in his voice was because he was nearly ready to come or if he was fighting the moment. She didn't want to know right then.

All she wanted was to feel him inside her.

Todd could not fucking believe he had his cock in a woman in public! And it felt good, damn it. He felt *alive* and turned on. Erin was his own personal siren.

He licked the column of her neck, taking in the salt of her skin as her honey seeped down his cock to his balls. The woman was on fire. Need throbbed inside him, making his skin feel too tight over his bones. Images flashed through his mind; he wanted to hold her wrists high against the scrape of the wall at her back, wanted to sink his teeth into her shoulder.

She began to writhe against him, grinding her swollen clit against his fingers. He heard her breath catch and a soft moan as she came around his cock, squeezing him with those muscles until he wanted to weep with how good it felt.

Instead it was as if all his organs shot out his cock when he came, pinning her to the wall as she quietly sobbed her own release.

Catching his breath, he rested his forehead on her chest as he pulled out, tied off the condom and tucked his cock back into his pants.

He didn't know what to say, but when he looked into her face, she winked and leaned in for a quick kiss. "That was incredibly hot."

He shook his head and tugged her toward his car, disposing of the condom in a nearby Dumpster, wondering what magic she possessed to make him want so very much the things he should not.

4

For the next two months their contact remained at a fever pitch. Any time they were alone for more than five minutes, they had sex.

Standing up, sitting down, on the kitchen table, on the stairs at her place, in the shower. He was on fire for her, and the freedom made his blood sing. Erin was good for him in so many ways. He truly believed it. Enjoyed her company, loved being around her. At the same time, he battled his guilt and shame over his desires and he didn't quite know what to do about it. He was raised to believe men didn't harm women, even if the woman liked it. Raised to see that the union between the genders was about gentleness and kindness, and when those dark urges of his had bubbled up before, he'd tamped them down.

Only, with Erin, those urges were encouraged. She reveled in them, and in doing so, he found himself craving more. He distrusted the rawness in that, distrusted his behavior, because it was far from what he'd been led to believe was good and true.

On one hand, when he was with her, he felt as if he were coming into his own, growing into the man he wanted so badly to be. But at the same time, he struggled with the belief that the man he wanted to be was wrong. If she made him feel that way, didn't that make her bad for him? In the end, feeling good also felt bad, and who the hell was he going to talk to about it? Not his parents, that was for sure. His friends? How would he broach that he liked to leave little bite marks on her shoulder so he could look at them while he fucked her from behind? If it wasn't shameful, why would he be afraid to talk about it?

One afternoon, at lunch with some friends, he'd seen her come into the small restaurant and he lifted a hand. His stomach warmed at the sight of her.

She saw and smiled, approaching them.

"Who the hell is that?" Ron Dyson, his old partner, mumbled. Dyson was old school. A lifelong beat cop, a man in his early sixties with very set opinions. A good cop, great instincts, but not the most open-minded man around.

"Hi, Officer Keenan. What's doin'?"

Todd couldn't help but return her smile. She looked so beautiful there, her dreads back in a bandana, her long, lithe body wrapped in some funky blue dress thing.

"Just having lunch." He wondered if he should invite her to sit down. Wondered if their worlds could ever accommodate each other. "And you?"

"I'm picking up a to-go order. I'll see you later. Have a good day."

She grabbed several large bags and waved as she left with another woman and headed up the block. He knew her older brother's tattoo shop and the adjoining coffee bar she ran weren't very far away.

"Um, she's not your usual type. Where'd you meet her? Did you arrest her or something?" Ron snickered.

"She's a friend. She lives a few doors down. Her name is Erin."

"Don't get your boxers in a bunch. I was just askin'. It's not like I thought you were marrying her or anything."

Todd looked up the street and back to his friends, sighing.

Erin knew something was up when she got home from a show and he'd left a note asking for her to come over. She showered quickly and changed before going to his place.

Rolling her eyes inwardly at the music he played, she plopped down on his couch. The scent of pizza hung in the air.

She smiled her thanks when he handed her a plate with two pieces of hot, melty pie. "You're a god. A genius in bed and pizza too. Why are you single anyway?"

He looked at her, surprised.

"I'm not kidding. I'm curious. You're like, incredibly, unbelievably handsome. You have a steady job. You're responsible. You make sure I come before you do. You have a good car. You're intelligent, funny when you're not trying to pretend you don't get off on the wild sex we have, and you're hot."

"I don't know how to talk to you." He scrubbed his hands over his face.

"Why do you make simple things so complicated? Maybe you should stop worrying so much and just talk to me. Be yourself. Why don't you tell me about yourself? We've been, um, dating for a few months now, but you don't talk about yourself much."

He took a bite of pizza and watched her carefully. "Not much to tell. Seattle born and bred. Being a cop runs in the family. My dad, both brothers and my sister are cops. I'm single because I broke off an engagement about a year and a half ago. I'm dating around right now. It's hard to find a woman who accepts the whole cop's wife thing."

Erin looked at him and thought over what she'd heard.

"Maybe you're looking in the wrong place."

"What do you mean?" He shifted uncomfortably. "Look, Erin, I like you and all, but this . . . thing between us is just fun. No offense but we're not suited at all."

It shouldn't have hurt, but it did. He was delusional. "Bullshit." She finished the first slice and leaned back. "I'm not asking you to marry me or anything. But we connect, Todd Keenan. You spend so much time trying to just be fucking normal, you get tripped up in it. Just be yourself. Yes, you like dirty talk. You're kinky, big deal. Why do you fight so hard against what you seem to really like? I like it, I'm willing. You come hard. Why do you deny yourself this way?"

"It's not who I am!" He stood and stormed into the kitchen. She heard the plate clatter and she wiped her mouth.

"Is it so fucking awful? It's not like you want to wear a chicken suit while you fuck someone wrapped in plastic wrap or something. You don't, do you?" She laughed but stopped when he growled and stomped back into the living room.

"It's not who I am, damn you! Look, it's you and me. I'm not like this with other women. I'm gentle and the sex is nice. I don't know what comes over me when you're near. It's not *right*. I wasn't . . . I'm not supposed to like it."

She shrugged. What else could she do? Beg him to be who he was? When he thought being who he was, who *she* was, made them some kind of freaks? "The last thing I want to do is force you into talking dirty and begging me to suck your cock with my fingers in your ass, stroking your prostate."

He winced and petty satisfaction settled in. He liked it. Got off on it. And it was *her* fault he was so damned repressed he hated himself over it?

She grabbed her bag. "I'll spare you the *it was fun* talk and you can spare me the *it's not you, it's me* stuff. Okay?" Hesitating, she sighed and tiptoed up to kiss him quickly. "I hope you find a place in your life when you can let go and be happy. But I'm not a dirty secret. I'm not bad and wrong for being comfortable with myself, and I won't let you make me feel that way."

He slammed a hand against the wall next to her and then grabbed her around the waist, pulling her flush against his body. "Damn it, Erin, I don't lose control. I'm a controlled man. I make good choices. I don't fuck women against alley walls. It's off-putting."

"Really now? So who fucked me in that alley, Todd? Your doppelganger? Who shoved my mouth down on his cock in his truck three nights ago when we got back from the grocery store? You *like* it rough. You *like* it dirty. Why are you so ashamed of it? You didn't hurt me. I was there with you every step of the way."

"I don't want to like it, damn it. Can't you understand that? I don't choose to like it. I don't want to be the man who likes to fuck rough! I choose not to be him." He shoved a hand through his hair.

Pain sliced through her. "I get it. You think being with me is a bad choice."

"It's not . . . I didn't plan for you, Erin. I like you."

"But you don't like who you are when you're with me. You blame this on me and I'm not having it. I won't be responsible for your life. You're a big boy."

"No. Oh fuck, I don't know. This is very intense. I have an intense job. I'm not sure if I need an intense personal life too."

"I see." She looked into his eyes, wishing he'd wake up and see her. See them and what they could have together.

"You keep saying that, Erin. But how can you see? I don't even see."

"All I see is a man who can't face himself. And it makes me sad, because you're alive when we're together and you're not hiding who you are. You're playing a game with this, a stupid game. Why I don't know, because I like who you are. I won't play this game with you. I'm worth more and so are you." She leaned up, pressed her hand over his heart and kissed his chin. "Good-bye, Todd. I wish you well, I really do. If you change your mind, give me a call. Maybe I'll be available."

He watched her walk out the door and told himself it was for the best, but he knew he was lying to himself. Just like she said he was.

5

Present Day

Todd pulled his truck down his street and smiled when he saw the house. *His house.* He'd been driving for three days. Escaping Boston, a broken marriage, a waste of a job and eighteen months of physical therapy that had enabled him to walk without a limp. Mostly.

Into his new life, back to Seattle and into his new job with some old friends from the Seattle Police Department.

Coming back to the Northwest seemed a lot less like escape than leaving it nearly ten years before had. He'd spun out of control, run from what could have been a great relationship and into a job he'd started out loving and that had ended up nearly killing him.

That didn't even address the ex-wife situation. He'd tried; she might have for a few more years, but it just fell apart. She wasn't who he'd truly wanted, and he wasn't the person she thought she'd married either. A mess of epic proportions, and the shooting had been the final burden that had simply torn the last bit of the foundations apart.

Sheila was a nice woman and all, but he didn't ache for her at night, didn't think about where she might be at any given time. In truth, it was as if the past eight years of his life had been an uninteresting interlude punctuated with a coma, painful PT and mediocre sex. He had no one but himself to blame.

She'd filed for divorce when he came out of the coma, but had hung around to be sure he was all right. He'd give her that much. Not six months after that she'd gotten married to someone else, and last he'd heard she was pregnant with the child she'd wanted but that he'd been too busy to give her.

He'd had a lot of time to examine his life, his mistakes. He'd looked at himself pretty unflinchingly and he'd admitted he lived half a life out of fear of expressing just exactly who he was. So he'd accepted it, and during his physical recovery he'd had the time to make plans for a future doing what he wanted to do. A future being who he was instead of who he thought he should be.

Once he'd gotten the green light to go back to work, he'd handed in his resignation and begun to figure out a business plan with some old friends of his in Seattle.

So here he was, opening the front door to his new house and ready to take on his new life.

The house was typical of the Greenlake neighborhood: big bay windows, hardwood floors, small bedrooms but large common rooms and a good-sized kitchen. The basement had been converted into a mother-in-law flat, so he would use that as his office.

The furniture and boxes had been delivered the week before, and he smiled when he noted that his mother had not only put linens on the beds but had taken the time to leave a note telling him she'd left him dinner in the freezer.

He turned in a big circle. This was his. His life, his future, loomed ahead of him, and for the first time in a very long time, he couldn't wait to see what was next.

Erin finished stirring the soup for that day's lunch special and turned around to check the progress of the pasta for the salad. Another two minutes should do it.

She checked the readerboard above the coffee counter and made sure it had been updated with the specials before returning to drain the pasta, cool it and toss it with the dressing and veggies. The work was a ritual; it soothed and connected her to her life when at times she felt like just floating away.

Running the café gave her tangible goals. She started and finished tasks every day. It marked time in a positive way. She needed it.

Brody, her older brother and the owner of the other half of the building—his tattoo shop—ambled in, and she turned to get him something to drink.

"Hit me with some caffeine, sister," he said as he slid onto a high stool.

She made him the latte he preferred, very hot with extra foam. She even made a foam design in the shape of a leaf for him and popped in a curl of shaved chocolate.

He sighed happily as he drank it. "Awesome. Thanks."

"Late night?" She grinned at him.

"You know what it's like when Raven's in town. We went out late, saw a show. She doesn't have to be up and at work, so it wasn't a thing for her to roll in at four."

"You didn't have to be at work until eleven! Admit it, you're too old. I know I am."

Absently, she made an Americano with room for a customer,

followed by a mocha. Her staff consisted of herself and two part-timers, which suited Erin just fine. They handled the early coffee rush during the week, and she took the weekends. The café closed by two p.m. and she had the rest of her day free. Not a bad deal.

She liked her employees enough to consider them friends. Especially Ella. The other woman was young, vibrant and funny. She was working to try to finish a degree at the University of Washington, so she worked at the café to pay for books. Erin admired that, especially in light of some of the personal problems Ella had been going through.

"You're thirty-four years old, Erin. That's not exactly an old-timer."

"But you're thirty-seven. Tell me you can go on two hours' sleep like you could at twenty-seven, huh?"

He laughed. "No shit. What's for lunch today?"

"Pasta salad, three-bean soup, tuna or veggie panini sandwiches. It's Thursday."

"Tomorrow is clam chowder day, my favorite." He grinned as he sipped his latte.

"You're lucky you got the good genes from Mom, because all that cream would kill you otherwise."

She heard the chimes over the door sound and finished her greeting to a customer at the counter before looking up.

And into the sleepy brown eyes belonging to Todd Keenan. She froze a moment at the unexpected emotions welling within her, but they wisped away. That Erin had been another person, in what had been an entire lifetime ago.

Still, she took a quick look to the left, where a large mirror hung. Not bad. Thank goodness she'd put on earrings and some makeup before she'd left the house!

She realized, as he moved toward her in what felt like slow motion, that he hadn't recognized her yet, and a horrifying thought that he wouldn't remember her assaulted her gut with a cramp.

His eyes slid down her body and back up again. The way his expression went half-lidded and sexy made something low tug and spark after being dead a long time.

Her nipples beaded against the thin shirt she wore, and he stopped there for several moments of appreciation before meeting her eyes again. He hesitated a moment and then smiled.

It was then that recognition hit his gaze. "Erin?"

She hadn't known how she planned to greet him, but the beautiful, open smile he gave her and the way he stepped around the counter brought her into his hug and against his body.

Her arms moved to hug him back, every cell in her body reacting to being touched again. Not as a sister, not in grief or mourning, but as a woman.

The unexpected beauty of it, the bittersweet sensation of sexual attraction after being dead inside for years, made her want to grab a pen and start writing. Crying could wait.

For that moment she reveled in it, in feeling something so lovely.

Finally, after a hug long enough to let her know he enjoyed the attraction between them still, Todd kissed the top of her head and let go enough to lean back and look into her face.

"It's so good to see you. You look damned good. I like the pink hair."

She laughed and only barely managed to catch herself from playing with it. "Thank you. You look great too. Are you visiting?" Oh yeah, he was married, wasn't he?

"No. I just moved back to the area. I'm starting a security consulting business, or rather, buying into part of it with some friends of mine."

She noticed people waiting and stepped back. "Hang on. Let me get these orders filled. Do you have the time to visit a bit?"

"I do, and I'd like a bite too."

Todd watched her move with the same effortless sensuality she'd had ten years before. Noted how she worked quickly and efficiently, ladling out soup and sliding sandwiches onto plates.

The soup he'd ordered was rich and spicy, and the veggie sandwich served on dark bread satisfied his hunger quite nicely.

What the heck was she doing running a tiny café in Ballard? He knew she and her younger brother had gone down to LA roughly about the time Todd had gotten married. They'd made it big sometime after. Not his kind of music, so he'd only seen her in passing on MTV, on his way to CMT.

She'd disappeared from the limelight—some sort of legal trouble, he thought he recalled. But he'd been so busy with his own life and career, he hadn't followed the entertainment news at all, outside the country music he liked.

Drugs, perhaps? Although he doubted it. Erin had been a very strong and self-possessed woman. Plus, she and her brothers were very close, so they'd have been a good support system. Still, there was a hesitancy in her she hadn't had before. He supposed that was only natural. They hadn't parted as enemies but certainly not on the friendliest of terms either.

She hadn't been far from his mind over the time they'd been apart though. Not that he'd pined for her, but a wisp of memory would come and fill him with the sense of longing, of loss. And she'd played a part in many of his fantasies over the years too.

About an hour later, after the eight tables and the counter had filled up and then emptied out again, she brought over a bowl of soup and sat with him.

"Sorry it took so long. Lunch rush. You want a refill on the tea? Or some coffee?"

"I want to sit and talk with you." He put a hand on her arm, gripping to stay her, and their gazes locked. That familiar darkness wafted through him, taunting him.

She swallowed and eased back. Obeying him just like that, and he remembered all the times he'd closed his eyes and thought of her. Of her arching beneath him, taking all he had to give and wanting more. She'd been his, and he'd been too scared to take what she offered. All because he'd been worried about what his desires made him look like.

No longer.

"When do you get off?"

She snorted a laugh and he joined her, adjusting in his seat. "You know what I mean."

"I'm the boss. I close up at two and then it takes me about an hour to close out the till, clean up the back and prepare for tomorrow."

"Oh, this is yours now?"

Those hazel eyes of hers took him in carefully. There were shadows there that hadn't existed before. "Yes. I came back to Seattle three years ago and wanted something to do. Brody had someone else running this place, but it wasn't doing much. I bought it and I run it how I like. It works to keep me out of trouble."

"You used to like trouble." He looked her over again. The hollow of her throat called to his lips. His fingers twitched with a need to touch the soft, warm skin there again. "Are you free when you close up?"

She blinked, and slowly licked her lips, but before she could answer, the bell on the door jingled and she got up to deal with customers.

Erin didn't know what to think. No one had ever gotten to her as deeply as he had. Not even Jeremy had touched that spot deep within her, let it uncoil. At one point she'd just figured it was that memory thing where you tend to make the past better than it was. But Todd did that to her then, and he affected her still.

Her hands shook a bit as she steamed some milk and absently made small talk with a customer. But when she looked up, she saw him watching her.

Their spark hadn't been her imagination. His invitation was more than just a *hey, let's hang out and grab a beer*. While she was on board with a little reliving of old times in bed with him, it wasn't going to happen if he was married.

She ladled soup, poured out tea and coffee until everyone had been served, and there he was again, waiting patiently, his eyes moving over her body like a caress.

Erin hadn't been so sexually on edge or so needy and out-and-out horny in years, it seemed. He hadn't propositioned her. He hadn't even touched so much as a breast, but her body thrummed with excitement and anticipation. It seemed wrong to hope he was divorced, but she did anyway.

He sat in the corner, drinking his tea while she worked. She said a few words here and there, but it had been busy, as it sometimes was so near to closing. All he'd said to her was "I'll wait."

He'd wait. *Lovely.* The tension inside her was nearly painful, something she poked at as she worked, like that spot inside your cheek you bit earlier that day. She examined it, stroked over it, thought about it, enjoyed it even.

Finally at three she moved through the place toward the door, and he'd simply stayed like a stray cat she'd made the mistake of feeding. When she locked up and flipped the sign, he finally moved, standing to his full height.

She stood, rooted to the spot as she looked up his body. The width of his shoulders seemed to blot out the light. Erin was tall; at five-eight she didn't often get the experience of looking up and then up some more at a man.

"Erin, I'd like to know you again. Can we do that?" He brushed the back of his knuckles down her cheek.

Once the sensual shivers subsided enough that she could find her words again, she swallowed hard. "Are you married? Because if you are, we can know each other but we can't *know* each other. I don't do that."

He smiled, one of the most genuine smiles she'd ever seen from him. "I'm not. Not for the past eighteen months. I'm glad to know you don't do that, because I sure as hell don't either. You're not married or with anyone?"

She lost her train of thought for a moment when he slid those same knuckles down her neck and into the hollow of her throat. *God, that felt good.*

"No. Not for a long time now."

"So, we're both free." He looked at her. *Into her.* She felt bare to her bones. His scent rose from his skin, heady and warm. He smelled different than she remembered. This was . . . She leaned in just a bit, giving in to her needs . . . deep and dark. A man who worked with his body; clean sweat, sex, alluring, something she wanted to lick.

He waited as she watched his pulse jump at his throat. So close that if she moved just a bit more, she'd touch his skin with her lips. Suddenly she wanted that so much, it hit her in a wave, bringing a slight disorientation in its wake. Instead she reached out, sliding her palm up his arm, over his biceps. "Looks that way."

His pupils enlarged, the color of his irises deepening. "I have a few errands to run. Why don't I come to your place. Or you to mine, I don't care which. Would six work for you?"

She loved his voice, had forgotten how sexy it was. Erin grabbed a pad of paper and wrote down her address. "I'll let the doorman know you're coming. Use that code and you can park inside the garage."

They stood very close in the quiet café. Neither spoke, but they both looked at each other. The tension thickened, tautened until Erin wanted to groan.

Finally it was as if he'd made some sort of internal decision. He slid his palm around her neck, cupping it at the nape. "I'm going to have to kiss you."

She smiled up at him, raising a brow. "You never used to need to ask."

His face hardened and his mouth found hers. The taste of him bloomed through her, opening her up, softening her in the right places, hardening her in others. The seam of her jeans pressed with delicious friction against her sensitized clit, even better when he rolled his hips and ground his cock into her.

Oh, they still fit and he still had it going on. Only now he seemed more confident with it. A delightful thrill coursed through her at the thought of a confident Todd, a man who owned his dominance.

On the surface, the kiss was exploratory. He tasted her easily, his tongue sliding back into her mouth like it hadn't been over a decade since he'd done this last. But beneath that, there was no angst, no guilt or hesitance. The kiss was sure. He knew he wanted to be there and, god knew, she wanted him there too.

When he caught her bottom lip between his teeth and nipped, her knees buckled and she held on to keep standing.

He chuckled then and pulled back slightly. "You still taste like sin, Erin. I can't wait for more." One more brief kiss and he headed to the door. "See you in a few hours."

She nodded, her fingers pressed against her lips, her heart beating wildly.

6

Erin looked at herself in the mirror as she dried off from the shower. Not bad. The last time he'd seen her, she'd been twenty-four years old. The years hadn't been too bad on her outside. Her belly wasn't as flat as it had been then. But genetics had spared her stretch marks and, despite nursing for nearly a year, her breasts were still in good shape.

The thought of Adele's downy little head snuggled to her made her pause as the familiar pain passed through her belly. Phantom pain, like she'd lost a limb. But she'd lost so much more.

Erin sat on the side of the tub and just gave in to the tears for a time. If she didn't fight it, she'd feel better sooner. When she'd finished, she washed her face with cold water and then wandered into her bedroom to get dressed.

She may not have had a regular sex partner in a few years, but that had not stopped Erin from possessing sexy underthings. Like she'd told Raven, Brody's on-again-off-again girlfriend and Erin's best friend, she had boatloads of dough, and there were worse things to spend it on than panties.

The evening was warm for late spring in Seattle so she chose a flattering camisole with a corset fit and the skirt to match. A handy-dandy push-up bra and some cute boyshort undies and she was good to go.

After deciding to leave her hair loose, she contemplated cutting it now that it had reached the middle of her back. With a shrug, she put on a bare bit of makeup and tucked some condoms under her pillows before heading out to the kitchen.

Todd wasn't due for about forty-five minutes, so she poured herself a margarita and went out to sit on her balcony with her pad and guitar. She looked out over downtown and a bit of Puget Sound.

It had been an emotional day, full of beauty and sadness, and the words came quickly, as they sometimes did. She heard Adrian's voice in her head as she wrote and she lost track of time until she heard her doorbell a few times.

Todd would have wondered if the apartment number was wrong, but there were only three on this floor and the funky folk-art knocker clued him in.

She opened the door, looking surprised and slightly harried. "I'm sorry! I was on the balcony writing. I was so in my head I lost track of time. Come in."

He followed her inside and when he closed the door, he noted the locks. Four of them. In a ridiculously secure high-rise building.

His question about the locks died as he entered the loft and got a look at the place. Floor-to-ceiling windows fronted the living room, giving a grand view of downtown and a slice of the water. Light, natural woods marked the cabinets and built-ins and also warmed the floors.

He kicked his shoes off and left them near the door.

"You don't have to take your shoes off. Come in, make yourself at home. I made margaritas. You want?"

He looked at her, her hair loose to where the sway of her back began in earnest, big hazel eyes staring back through arty little glasses. She was even more beautiful in her otherness than she was ten years ago.

"Damn, you're something else to look at. You know that?"

She smiled and he noted the lines next to her mouth. Not from age, but the kind of lines only life can put there. He wanted to thumb across them, smoothing them out, sliding away whatever pain had etched them there to start with.

"Is that a good something else or a bad something else? Because it's pretty ridiculous that a man only looks better as he ages, but women not so much."

With two strides he was there, just inches away from her in that sexy top and short, flowy skirt of hers. Her legs were still sexy, as were her bare feet.

"Good." He traced a fingertip over the curve of each breast where it heaved out the top of her shirt. From his angle he caught the shadow of her nipples and the memory of the rings shot straight to his cock. "You look amazingly sexy, Erin. Beautiful."

"Mmm. Good answer."

The silence between them wasn't awkward; it was fraught with sexual tension, and he let himself revel in it. He'd be inside her that night, so why rush? Why not just enjoy it?

"Margarita sounds good."

She licked her lips and turned, the skirt flaring enough that he got a good view of her pert ass in some pink boyshort-style panties. God, he loved those.

"Are you hungry?" she asked as she salted the rim of the glass and poured the margarita over ice.

"You remembered."

"What?" She smiled at him, putting the glass on the bar before him.

"That I like margaritas on the rocks."

"Of course." She shrugged.

"Yes, I'm hungry. You're quite the cook, by the way."

She put a covered pan in the oven. "I wish I could say I'm usually more on the ball, but when I'm writing, I lose track of time. I put together some enchiladas earlier. They just need to heat. Why don't you sit down there and keep me company while I pull together everything else?"

He hopped up on a stool and saw her guitar in a case near the open doors to the balcony.

"You mentioned writing. Writing music? I heard you made it big out in LA. Are you still doing that?"

"Yes. 'Big' is a matter of perspective, I suppose." She shrugged. "I write for Adrian; he's still in the biz. He has a house on Alki with a studio. We record together there."

"Do you still tour and stuff?"

Her face froze. He was a cop for many years, enough to know when someone had been shaken by a question. She licked her lips and then breathed out. "No. But Adrian does. He gets groupies camped out at the end of his driveway and stuff. I just write music and do studio work. I like it better that way. No groupies camped out. I can walk down the street without being recognized. I like my privacy."

There was a bigger story there, but he'd wait to hear it later. He'd only been back in her life for hours. "So the café is like a sideline?"

"It's a nice way to keep myself working, leaving the house every day." She shrugged as she began to shake a bottle of dressing for the salad she'd just prepared. "We can eat on the balcony; there's a table out there, but it's getting a bit windy. Or in here, where it's not."

He laughed, and she cocked her head.

"What?"

"I'd forgotten how much I liked your laugh."

"As compliments go, that's a good one. How about in here? You have some view." He helped her carry plates and silverware to the table she'd indicated.

"I like it up here."

She sashayed off and returned with a plate of fresh fruit and cheese. He'd liked to watch her ten years ago but had always told himself to stop. Now he sat and openly ate her up with his gaze.

That afternoon when he'd left her café, he'd run around town finishing up his errands—stopping by to check in on his parents, going to the hardware store. The whole time, he'd come to grips with his situation. He wasn't going to run from what he felt anymore. From what he was.

All those years ago he'd walked away and left what had made him joyful—when he wasn't miserable that he liked it. He'd denied his sexual need to dominate women ever since, had starved a whole side of himself and lived half a life.

Although she had no idea, she'd given him small respite in the dark when he'd closed his eyes and fantasized about her. Erin, her hair in his fist as he'd held her in place and done whatever he wanted to her beautiful, willing body.

Here, now in her condo with the evening sun dancing over the water, reflecting up to her windows, he could admit it was all about Erin. His need to finally open up and admit he liked to dominate and control women in bed had been kindled by this amazing woman. She was the key to the lock he'd kept on his secret urges and he would finally own up to it all.

What a fantastic coincidence that he'd found her again—even better, found her unfettered and still attracted to him. He'd never been one for believing in things like fate, but looking at where he sat just then eroded a lot of skepticism he might have had. It was meant to happen, and he wasn't going to dance around what he really wanted ever again.

She slid the hot casserole dish onto the pad on her table and sat. "That's some look you have on your face. Wanna share?" She made him a plate, surprising him even as he loved how it made him feel to be taken care of that way.

"Erin." He took a sip of his drink before speaking again. No more dancing. Just say it. "I was just thinking about how much I loved dominating you." Once he'd let it out, he felt a thousand times better.

She looked up from what she was doing, locking her gaze with his. "I loved being dominated by you."

"If I told you to get on your knees and suck my cock, what would you say?"

She leaned back in her chair, raising a brow. "I'd say a real dom doesn't ask. But I'd also say you're not my top; not yet anyway. I'd also remind you that you left me a decade ago because you were ashamed of that part of yourself, and I'd want to know just exactly what's changed before we went there again."

He grinned and forked up a mouthful of food, pleased she took him seriously. "Okay. We can talk more about that after we eat. Christ, were you this good a cook before?"

She quirked a smile. "Not really. I took some classes when I landed in LA. Or rather, I waitressed in this fancy restaurant and the owner liked me and she let me hang out in the kitchen and learn. She told me if I ever gave up music, I should open a restaurant. My café is nothing compared to her place, but at heart, I love good, simple food made with fresh ingredients. The Market is just blocks from here, so I shop for fresh food pretty much daily."

"Why did you come back here, Erin?"

"Why did *you* come back here?" she countered.

He took a deep breath. "Everything about my life had been a lie. I married a woman I enjoyed but didn't love. I hid part of myself from her because I was ashamed. I worked in a division I wasn't suited for. I missed my family. I missed Seattle. My wife grew, not to hate me, but to not care about me one way or the other, and it was my fault. She wanted kids, but I couldn't see myself having children with her. Then I got shot. Several times. And was in a coma. Three days of being just shy of death is not an experience I ever want to repeat. But I'll give her credit, she stayed until I recovered, and then served me with divorce papers. I went through some pretty nasty surgeries and then physical therapy. Last month when I finally got my papers saying I could go back to work, I accepted the offer of an old friend to buy in as a partner at his security firm here in town."

"Are you okay now?" She brushed the sensitive skin at his wrist, a butterfly of a touch with alarmed fingers.

Moved, he took her hand, drawing it to his mouth and kissing her fingertips. "I am now. Here with you. I came back here to live a full life. When I saw you today, it made sense. It was right for the first time in more years than I can remember. Pink hair." He smiled. "I like it. I like you, Erin, and I know I was a fool for walking away before. I'm the same in many ways, but different in all the ones that count." He exhaled. "Can I be honest with you?"

"I insist." She shrugged. "Tell me, Todd. I told you then and I'll say it again—I won't judge you."

No, she never had. And it gave him the courage to say it, to tell her what he wanted most. "I want to top you. I want you to submit to me." He nipped her fingertip. "And only me."

A smile hinted at the right corner of her mouth. The corner where her dimple made a sweet dent. "Only you, huh? And would I be the only woman you topped?"

"Of course." He felt as if he were in a job interview or something. He was supposed to be in charge, but right then she held
it all in her hands. Which, given what he was prepared to ask—
demand—of her, he supposed made sense.

She shrugged with a small, feminine sound and went back to
eating. He wanted to laugh—hell, he wanted to spank her ass—but
he just shook his head at her, amused.

Once they'd eaten, and Erin noticed he'd had three platefuls, he
helped her clear the dishes and start the dishwasher.

Her body was on fire and she wasn't quite sure how to handle it.
She'd very nearly dropped to her knees to suck his cock when he'd
suggested it before. But while she wasn't looking for marriage or
even love, she *was* looking for a man who was serious about the
business of D/s. She and Jeremy had edged around it, but he'd
never really gotten into it. She'd craved it, and his disinterest and
halfhearted gestures had only left part of her unsatisfied and empty.

No one, in the time since Todd, had ever mastered her the way
he had. He hadn't even known it, which had frustrated her to no
end. He hadn't understood his own power because he was too busy
running from it. But in those times when they were in sync, it was
fucking marvelous. She'd never felt anything like it before or since.

She'd been in love with Jeremy, yes. Love for the man whom
she'd had a child with. Love for the man who'd joined his life to
hers. But that love hadn't lasted the pain and tragedy of losing
Adele. Although he remained a dear friend, she'd never burned for
him, yearned for his touch, for the feel of his body against hers the
way she had for those short two months with Todd ten years before.

And here he was, telling her what she wanted to hear, and from
what she'd seen, he meant it. D/s wasn't a game to her. It wasn't
something she played at. In the last few years she'd been able to
admit her sexual submissiveness was integral to who she was. She
hadn't been with anyone since she'd left Los Angeles, and she'd

never really thought she'd want anyone again. But now that her libido had sprung into action again, she wasn't going to accept half measures. If he could admit the same, they might have a very fine time together. She just needed to know he meant what he'd said about being okay with his desires.

7

"Music?" she asked, moving toward the sleek media system in a cabinet near the far wall. Her walk was sure and graceful, feminine. He'd noted that she seemed more at ease here, less hesitant.

"Sure. And then how about a tour? This is really a beautiful place."

Something smooth and female slid through the very swank surround-sound-style speaker system. She turned with a smirk. "No PJ Harvey today. This is Tegan and Sara. "

"Not bad." And it wasn't. He got up to check out the media center. "Damn, Erin, that's some fucking sound system."

She laughed. "It's a far cry from the piece of crap we used to have back in the day." She held out a hand. "Come on, let me give you the tour."

He moved to her and took her hand, the connection singeing up his arm.

"You've seen the living room and the kitchen. This is my balcony; it wraps around the front here." She walked him outside. The wind had kicked up, but it wasn't overly cold. Still, he used that to put an arm around her, pulling her into his body, sliding a palm up and down her upper arm and shoulder.

The view was gorgeous. Clearly her music career had left her with some money in the bank if she could afford this place. Her furnishings and lifestyle didn't seem ostentatious from what he'd seen so far, which was an important indication she'd not let fame or money go to her head.

They went back inside, and she led him around to the kitchen through a wide hallway.

"This is my office." A big table with a large computer monitor on it dominated the back corner. A small area near the windows had a comfortable club-type chair and a table next to it, and across the room music stands, various electronic equipment and a variety of guitar cases completed the look.

"*Holy shit!* Erin, is that a Grammy?" He walked into the room and stared at the case holding several trophies. "*Two* Grammys. Wow."

She blushed. "Yes."

He turned to her. "I'm sorry I'm such a dork and I didn't know. You were a lot bigger than you led me to believe. That's awesome. Those are gold records too, right?"

She nodded.

"Why did you give it up?"

"Something very bad happened." She put her fingers over his lips and shook her head. "I really, *really* don't want to talk about it. But I'm happy now. I write music. I record it. I'm in the studio. It's my bass on all Adrian's studio tracks on his CDs. I just don't need all the rest. I don't want it. I like my quiet, safe life here in my condo. I like my café. I like my family and I don't need the rest." She indicated the room with a sweep of her hand. "I have enough money. I don't need the fame part."

"Okay. I'd like for you to share it with me sometime, but we've only just reconnected. I understand. I'm glad you're doing something that makes you happy."

She nodded and led him out and pointed to a guest bedroom and a bathroom. At long last, at the end of the hall, she pushed open large double doors, exposing the master suite.

It was her, utterly. The walls were saffron yellow. Framed art lent beautiful explosions of color to the space. The hardwood floors were dotted with pretty area rugs, and her bed sat on a platform facing the wall of windows.

"Wow."

She turned to him, sliding her palm up the wall of his chest. Her nails scored over his nipple, and a wave of pleasure echoed through him. He took her glasses off and kissed each eyelid.

"Erin, I want you to take your clothes off. I want to see you."

There was no hesitation; she simply unlaced the shirt and pulled it over her head. Her tattoos were still there; her nipples, hard and dark, each bore a ring, and it still nearly brought him to his knees. How sexy she was. Nearly breathless, he couldn't tear his eyes from her as she slipped her skirt down her legs, tossing it to the side. Her panties were the last to go and then she stood there, totally naked to him, the sight of her burning into him.

"God, how are you still so beautiful?" he murmured as he moved around her body, taking her in from head to those pretty toes. The tree of life still marked her back. He'd seen that tat in his mind's eye so many times it was almost like a dream to be looking at it in the flesh again.

"I'm older."

He laughed and then swatted her ass. It'd started out playful, but the sound shot straight to his cock, and her soft sound of surprise wrapped around him, lodging in his gut.

"You're beautiful," he repeated and kissed her shoulder near her neck. "Undress me, Erin."

She turned to him and tiptoed up to kiss his lips quickly. Then with determined, slow movements, she unbuttoned each button on his shirt until she slid it open and down his arms.

"I'm not the only one who's beautiful." Her nails dragged over the sensitive skin below his belly button, bringing gooseflesh. "You're still so very *big* and feral." Leaning her head toward his body, she breathed him in and made a low, needy sound that tore at his control. "You still smell like the best thing I've ever tasted."

He continued to watch as she unbuckled his belt and then unbuttoned the front of his jeans, *pop, pop, pop, pop, pop.* He had to swallow hard as she pushed his jeans and shorts down, getting to her knees to help him out of them and his socks.

"Before you suck my cock, *and you will, Erin,* I want to kiss you. Come here." He led her to the bed and lay down with her. The bedding smelled like her—spicy, saucy, free.

She looked up at him and he was slammed by a sense of déjà vu so strong his hands trembled.

"I know. I feel it too," she whispered.

The darkness at his edges smoothed a bit as tenderness rolled through his system. He trailed fingertips down her neck, loving the smooth, warm skin there. All the feeling he'd had for her and abandoned, that he'd shoved far away except as jerk-off fodder, came back to him.

She waited, watching him carefully, he realized, letting him lead, and damned if that didn't make him want her even more. He lowered his mouth, brushing it over hers, but it was her dimple he sought first. Then down to her jaw. She arched her neck, giving him access, which he took quite greedily. His teeth grazed the hollow of her throat and her hum vibrated against his mouth.

She nearly passed out when he rubbed the whole of his body against hers to get back to her mouth to kiss her. He was so *male,* hard and predatory; his skin was hot, and the wiry hairs on his thighs abraded her skin just right.

Until that moment when his cock stroked up and against her cunt, it hadn't felt totally real. But it did now as his tongue slid into her mouth, boldly taking what he wanted.

If she'd been standing, her knees would have buckled at the gesture. It was nearly too much and yet not enough. She had to have more. But if she pushed for it, demanded it, she'd lose the edge. It was that very thing that made her crave being dominated so much. That delicious choice every time, to want satisfaction so badly and to put it aside and let someone else give it to her the way she needed.

Erin realized this was an audition of sorts for him. Could he do it? Submission wasn't simply taken—it wouldn't be submission then. Submission was *earned*, and Todd needed to be the kind of man who deserved her on her knees. If not, she'd fuck him a few times and move on.

Todd tasted her mouth, took what he wanted as he slowly gave back. He'd been a good lover before but this man knew what he was about in a way only years can teach.

He broke the kiss, breathing hard, and stared into her face. "It's been so long. I can't quite believe this is real."

How could she not be touched by such a declaration? She glided the pad of her thumb over his bottom lip and he turned, nipping the fleshy part sharply.

He zeroed in on her face, on her reaction, and a smile broke over his face. "I see."

Todd moved down her body, kissing to her nipple, and she nearly jumped from her skin when he took the ring between his teeth and tugged just right. Not too hard but just hard enough to take her to that place hovering near pain. And when he took the nipple into his mouth and fluttered his tongue, she couldn't help the groan or the way her nails seemed to dig into his sides where she'd been holding on so tight.

She'd forgotten how much he loved the rings, and it was clear they still did it for him. What he was doing sure did it for her.

When her nails scored into his side, he hissed, not from pain but from the sharpness of sensation. Unable to stop himself, he bit the fleshy side of her breast, holding back only for a moment and then realizing if he listened to her body and her responses, he'd know how far to go. When she moaned, arching into his mouth, he knew where that line was and tucked it away.

He licked across the place he'd bitten and moved down further, drawing his tongue over the tats on her side and belly. She still had a ring in her belly button, and he still thought it looked hot.

"Shall I lick your cunt?" he asked, surprised by the roughness of his voice.

"Please, ohgod, please," she whispered back.

He wanted her to suck his cock, wanted to fuck her, wanted everything at once, but he reined himself in. He'd have her; they'd have each other. There was time.

He settled low on the bed, his face right above her pussy, and spread her open with his thumbs. Her scent teased him, drove him to want to dive in. Instead he inhaled, having missed her more than he'd allowed himself to admit until that moment.

The way his fingers dug into her skin, the way she arched up into his mouth, taking what she wanted—within limits—turned him on beyond all measure. How he loved to eat a woman's pussy as she lay spread open for him this way.

Each fold, each furl of her cunt brought him back to that place when she'd offered herself to him ten years before and he'd not understood, not totally, what a gift she'd been.

Instead he'd run, choosing to continue walling off part of his soul. Denying what he yearned for, and now, full circle, he'd torn down those walls and embraced all she offered. Which, in such a simple way, was acceptance of who he was.

If she could accept it, why not him?

Todd nuzzled her, pressing lips and then teeth against tender, sensitive flesh. Possession floated into his consciousness. He wanted her, had always wanted her, and this pussy, this precious gift, wasn't something he planned to share. Or give up ever again.

He kept from laughing but only barely. She might be submissive sexually, but Erin Brown was one of the strongest willed individuals he'd ever known. It would be about proving to her that he was worth it, that he deserved her.

Stabbing his tongue deep into her gate, as deep as he could, he concentrated on making her feel good even as her taste rode him. Goddamn, the woman tasted right.

Her pleas, her whispered moans and entreaties brought him back to her clit, swollen and hard against his tongue as he pressed the flat of it against her, sliding it from side to side until she practically vibrated, just before she flew apart against his mouth.

Erin struggled for breath as Todd kissed the inside of each thigh where it met her body, back up her belly, over her breasts, and then his mouth was on her, claiming it as her taste hit her system.

He spoke through the kiss. "Suck my cock, Erin. You remember how I like it? Don't make me come though. I want to fuck you too."

Her eyes slowly opened until she stared right into his. His lips were glossy from the kiss, from her honey, and she leaned up, licking them. He groaned and she smiled, liking the power to turn him on.

Pushing him back against her bed, she scrambled atop him with a laugh. Soon enough her mouth found his frantic pulse, right at the base of his throat, and tasted it with an openmouthed kiss.

His fingers in her hair tightened and she shivered, loving that pleasure/pain. His chest was still hard, although she kissed over the scars. Several of them that must have been from the shooting he'd told her of earlier.

She could have lost him and not even known it. There'd been enough loss, damn it.

He yelped and then groaned as she nipped him just above his left nipple. Each flat nipple was so sensitive he writhed up as she licked over it and then traced it 'round and 'round with the tip of her tongue. And down further still, licking over his breastbone, down the center of his belly.

Erin loved that he had some hair. So many men had taken to "manscaping" that it was rare to find one with a hairy chest and belly. He wasn't *woolly*, that would have been distasteful. No, he was just—she shivered—so masculine. Repeated sharp nips just below his belly button brought her to his cock. Right where she wanted to be.

"Damn, Erin. Looking at your back, with that gorgeous tat and your ass, I may not last."

If he looked close enough, he'd see her very own set of gunshot scars, which Brody had inked over and around to disguise.

Still, she smiled at the compliment before grabbing his cock firmly and swallowing it as deeply as she could. Sucking cock was sort of like riding a bike, she supposed as she breathed through her nose and kept her swallow reflex working so she wouldn't gag.

He was warm and hard, so hard, and she remembered back to that first time when he'd been standing behind his couch and she'd totally caught him off guard.

She palmed his balls, pressing the pads of her fingers against the spot right behind them. He rewarded her with a surprised gasp. Even better when she slid her middle finger just a bit farther, circling it softly over the pucker of his ass. He made a deep, feral sort of sound and her pussy bloomed.

All the way down and back, slowly, she sucked him deep and then pulled up. Her grip at the base of his cock was firm, but her mouth was looser so she could tongue the length of him as she came up.

He'd buried his hands in her hair, holding it tight to guide her up and down on him. She let herself fall into that space, the soft place where she just gave him pleasure, where she reveled in the way she must look to him right then, her ass in the air, swaying back and forth, the line of her back with her tattoo so visible, the shock of color her hair must have made against him. She wanted him to objectify her in the best sort of way, to hold her out as beautiful and desired.

"Wait." He tightened his hands, pulling her hair taut. "Climb up there and fuck me. I want your cunt around my cock."

She pulled off him and laid a kiss on the crown before scrambling up. Leaning over him, she retrieved a condom from under a pillow and tore it open quickly before rolling it down over his cock.

It wasn't more than two breaths before she'd moved back and driven herself down against him, his cock slicing into her cunt, filling her in ways she'd wanted desperately for ten years. She froze, just letting herself revel in how good it felt to be there. How good his cock felt so deep inside. So good it scared her a bit—the thought of not having it again. It wouldn't do to get attached.

She let her hair fall over her face as she rose and fell, wanting to hide a bit of herself from him. The intensity of the moment was nearly overwhelming and she didn't want it to be. She wanted it to be hot and satisfying but not emotionally involved. Erin wasn't the same inside as she was before. Before she'd given him everything— her heart, her soul, her submission. Now she'd give her submission, but her heart wasn't going anywhere and she wasn't sure how much soul she had left to give anyway.

He looked up at her, at the sway of her breasts as she fucked herself onto his cock over and over. A sheen of sweat seemed to make her skin glow. He'd always found her otherness to be incredibly alluring, exotic. Just the sight of her body made him ache deep inside, not just sexually but emotionally.

Her cunt was like hot heaven, grasping his cock as she undulated over him like a fucking siren. She was magic, always had been and still was. Maybe more so because time had passed and yet here she was again, riding his cock like ten years hadn't elapsed since she'd been wrapped around him last.

"Damn but your pussy feels good." He traced a fingertip up her body to flick the hair from her face. He wanted to see her eyes when she came. "Open your eyes." Todd let the words come, not holding them back, the freedom of it intoxicating. "I want your eyes on me when I'm fucking you."

Slowly, her gaze found his, like the unfurling of a flower, and he felt it to his toes when her attention was fully on him. Like he'd commanded.

"Tell me, Erin. Tell me what you want." His voice was deep, nearly fuck-drunk.

Her breath caught twice before words came from those sweet lips. "I want to come."

He'd always thought her voice was sexy, scratchy, whiskey rough, but now, blurred with sex, Todd was sure he'd never heard anything that made him harder.

"Touch your nipples for me. I've got your clit handled." He traced the line of her lips and she sucked his fingers into the wet of her mouth. His balls drew tight against his body as he struggled for control.

She knew it and a smile edged up one corner of her mouth. He wanted to laugh, but it died in his throat when she began to roll and tug on her nipples and the rings.

His fingers, still wet from her mouth, found her clit. He squeezed gently and then slid his thumb and forefinger back and forth around it. There was so much to look at, he simply cruised from his fingers in her cunt to her nipples and up to her face, where she looked at him intently.

Deep inside her cunt he felt the telltale flutters of her oncoming climax. When it hit, her internal muscles grasping and fluttering around him, his own followed. The pleasure of it rushed up his spine, his back bowing as she ground herself down, pressing hard to keep him deep even as she came.

Her mossy eyes blurred just momentarily, but she kept them open and focused on him. He couldn't tear his attention away as something big passed between them, linking them in a way he felt all the way to his toes.

Surprise marked her features and she blinked several times. No matter. It was there, the bond between them, and he liked it just that way. Had no plans whatsoever to do anything to dislodge it. In fact, he wanted to strengthen it.

Erin dragged air into her lungs as she dropped to the mattress. Todd pressed a kiss to her lips and got up. She listened to his movements as her heart's galloping beat slowed down to normal. The water turned on, the toilet flushed and his footfalls came back toward her.

"The bathroom is a hedonist's dream," he said, flopping next to her, taking up space. She liked it when his hand found hers, took it in his and squeezed.

"It's been a while since I've had to live in a shithole with not enough hot water and nicotine stains on the walls. Money has brought a lot of luxuries to my life, like the view and a bathtub the size of a Volkswagen." It couldn't buy happiness, but it certainly could make life a hell of a lot easier. People who insisted the opposite usually had a lot of it.

He laughed and, without realizing it, she snuggled into him. He smelled so good. "What's your cologne?"

"Um, something my mom gave me for Christmas. Black, Ralph Lauren, I think. Mmm, feel free to do that anytime you like," he murmured as she pressed her nose into the place where his neck met his shoulder.

"I like it." She licked him, tasting salt.

"I'm glad." He groaned. "Even when I've just come you make me want to fuck you again."

She leaned up to see him better. "Is that a bad thing?"

His eyes found hers, locking in, and disorientation struck for a brief moment. "Not at all. C'mere, I want to kiss you."

She stretched her neck to give him her lips, and he gave a satisfied near growl as their mouths touched.

For the longest time they traded lazy kisses, until she heard the trilling of a cell phone.

"That's not mine." She pulled back, amused at his annoyed look.

He rolled away, giving her an excellent view of his ass as he did.

"Keenan." She wanted to laugh at how annoyed he sounded.

She got up, pulling on a nearby robe and wandering into the kitchen for another margarita.

Todd ground his teeth together. Of course he had to get a call to deal with a client *now*. But he was the new partner and he needed to meet existing clients, even if he had been settling in and getting ready to fuck Erin again.

He sighed as he splashed water over his face and combed his hair back into something resembling a man who hadn't just fucked for a few hours.

Despite his need to go, he stopped as he came out into the living room and caught sight of her standing in the open door to the balcony. The breeze had blown open her short robe, exposing her breasts and her cunt. Her hair had swept back from her face and her eyes were closed.

He wished he could paint or even that he had a camera nearby, because she looked so soft and beautiful he wanted to capture it forever.

She turned, a smile on her lips. "Is everything all right?"

"No." He frowned. "I have to go. One of our clients is having problems with his security system and wants us to come in and consult on how to use it. Again, apparently. But he's some big-shot attorney here in town and he's used to snapping his fingers and getting results. Frankly, he's paying for it, so"—he shrugged—"there you go. Anyway, I haven't met him yet and I'm the new guy. I'm sorry."

"Your job is important of course. Thanks for coming over."

He moved to her, not liking how nonchalant she sounded. "I'll be back. What are you doing tomorrow?"

"I can't. I'm working with Adrian for the next few days. He's been out of town and we need to lay down some stuff for his new CD."

He realized as he stood there how much he wanted her. Not just for sex, but Christ, he liked her. Had liked her before but was too cowardly to really admit it. Todd wanted to know her and wanted her to want that too.

"Okay, when you're done, why don't you come to my place? Do you paint at all? I could use a hot assistant to help me paint my living room."

"All right. I can do that. But you have to feed me and I like Popsicles too. Painting is hot work, you know. I need sustenance."

"It's a date then." He handed her a card. "My home and cell numbers are on the back. Call me when you're done with Adrian or when you know you'll be free. I'll save the work until then."

She put the card in a colored glass bowl and then reached into his pocket to grab his cell. Quickly, she punched in a series of numbers and handed it back to him. "My numbers are in there."

"I enjoyed tonight." He banded her waist with his arm, hauling her to him, liking the way her breath caught and her pupils swallowed the irises of her eyes. He captured her breathless sigh as he swooped in for a kiss and she merely held on to his shoulders, letting him sample her mouth.

Breaking away, he rested his forehead on hers a moment.

"I'll see you soon, Erin."

He didn't stop smiling until he finally fell into sleep many hours later.

8

"You're distracted." Adrian put a bottle of water in front of her and sat back down.

"Huh? No, just busy. Between the café and here, I'm running around a lot."

He peered at her, suspicion in his gaze. "Everything okay?"

"I'm fine. I promise." After she took a swig of water, she picked the guitar back up and ran through the end of the song. "How's that?"

He hummed a moment, finding his voice, and began to sing as she played along. Adrian's voice was a thing of beauty. He could growl better than Chris Cornell and hit the high notes too. It didn't hurt that he was handsome either. It had made him very marketable, even when Erin had stopped touring and Adrian went solo. Their drummer still went out on tour and did studio work, so really, in all the important ways, she hadn't lost a whole lot when she'd "retired" from the band.

She paused a moment, making a note, and then went back to it and they picked up where they'd left off. She and Adrian had made music together since she'd been fourteen to his eleven. They'd started Mud Bay when she was seventeen. A long time. He knew her better than most anyone on the planet, which she found comforting most of the time.

"Goddamn, you did it again." Adrian sat back and lit a smoke.

She waved a hand in front of her face and moved back a bit. "You're going to ruin your voice with that shit."

"I only do it so you'll correct my lax morals," he said dryly. "So tell me what's going on in your life. Are you really okay? You need something more than this and pulling lattes. You're meant for more, Erin."

She looked at her baby brother with a smile. "Aww, thanks. I think. Anyway, yes, I'm okay. I'm actually . . . I think I'm dating someone. Seeing him. Something like that."

"Really? Who? Why didn't you tell me?" He leaned in, stubbing out his cigarette like she'd known he would.

She snorted a laugh. "You remember that cop who used to live next door? Todd?"

"I thought he moved back east. Didn't you dump him? Do I need to send goons over to kick his ass? Now that I'm a star and stuff, I have people for that." He winked.

"Yes, I broke up with him, and yes, he moved to Boston. He's back in Seattle for good and we had a date. We've been talking on the phone and e-mailing every day of the past week. He's not that guy anymore, or not the part I dumped him over."

Adrian narrowed his eyes. "You're not that girl anymore either."

She choked back her emotion. No, she wasn't. "No. But he makes me smile and he's a nice diversion."

"Just a diversion?"

"Good lord, it's been a week! I don't want to marry him or anything."

"You were gonzo for him back then. He rang your bell in a major way. You sulked for months. Then again, I suppose I have him to thank for pretty much every song on our first CD, huh?"

She shrugged. "He listens to country music. He has no idea." It amused her that he didn't know how big they'd made it. At least she knew he wasn't a starfucker. He liked her for Erin, not because Mud Bay had dominated MTV for four years nonstop and Adrian still did.

Adrian snorted. "Like, good country or . . ."

"Or, I think. I'm going to his house day after tomorrow to help him paint. He's promised me Thai food and good beer as payment. Oh, and Drumsticks. Chocolate *and* vanilla. I'll check his CDs then. Maybe I'll be pleasantly surprised."

"This guy totally has your number with the Drumsticks. Lemme know about whether he needs a beat-down. Don't let him get too fresh."

"Ha!"

They went back to work, noodling around on the last two songs until way past midnight.

"Why don't you stay over?" He walked with her back upstairs from his basement studio.

"I'm past panic attacks, Adrian," she lied. "My building is totally on lockdown and I'm just a regular citizen these days."

For a solid year after she'd come back to Seattle she found herself having panic attacks. Anyone looking at her funny, any sudden, loud noises and she was transported back to that day. Back to that day when she'd been lying in a doorway, dying, helplessly watching as her baby was shredded to ribbons in the cross fire as *he* tried to escape, using Adele as a human shield.

"God, Erin, I'm sorry, I didn't mean to make you think about it."

He'd held her hand often enough since that day—hell, since the letters and calls had started. He and Brody sat on either side of her all through the trial, had helped her pick up the pieces and had supported her when she wanted to come back home to Seattle.

She shook her head. "Stop feeling guilty. I'm fine. You're fine. I'm going home. I'll see you tomorrow." Erin kissed his cheek when they got to her car door.

She looked inside before getting in because that was something she did. The drive back to her building was quiet. The streets were pretty much empty by that hour.

Once the gate slid closed behind her in the parking garage, she sighed, feeling very tired. Her spot was very near the elevators, which was a lovely favor done because the building manager's daughter had been a huge fan and Adrian had even shown up and introduced himself. After the manager's wife had heard what had driven Erin back to Seattle, she got a spot even closer, right beneath a light and in full view of the surveillance cameras.

Her place was quiet but for the noise from the fish tank where the jellyfish undulated, ghostly white in the pale light coming from the partially shrouded moon.

Once she'd changed into a cami and some sleep shorts, she pulled a bottle of juice out and headed to her bedroom. Sleep would come fast, as it often did after she spent so much time in the studio.

Big brown eyes flecked with amber were the only things she thought of before drifting off.

9

Todd grinned when she pulled her Outback into his driveway. He wasn't surprised by her choice of vehicle, or that it had purple metallic paint. He ambled out to meet her, pleased to see she'd pulled her hair into twin braids and wore faded, low-slung jeans with a thin, snug vintage T-shirt.

"This is a great neighborhood," she said as she got out.

"I like it. I like you in it." He swept her into a hug, burying his face in her neck.

She laughed, wrapping herself around him. "Hi there."

"Come inside." He took her hand and she followed him, looking around.

"Decent front yard. You should plant some flowers and stuff to add color."

"That's on the list. Wanna help?"

One of her eyebrows rose and he saw the small scar. "Hey, what happened to the ring?"

She touched the spot. "It closed up and I didn't bother to get it done again." Her shrug wasn't defensive, but it seemed closed somehow, and he thought, not for the first time, that the flighty, carefree Erin had been edged away, smile lines replaced with those resulting from enduring emotional pain.

He led her inside and she turned in a circle. "Pretty! I love these big front windows."

He joined her, standing very close, and she leaned back into him. He had to close his eyes at how good it felt.

"It's nice that the trees and the shape of the lot actually give you some great privacy."

His hands slid down her belly and up under her shirt. "No bra. You're playing with fire," he said as he nipped her shoulder.

"Yeah? As a former cop you're close enough to a firefighter, right? Show me."

He spun her so she faced the wall. "Hands on the wall."

She obeyed immediately, canting her ass back at him. One-handed, he unbuckled his belt and opened his pants, freeing his cock. He leaned over her, caging her there with his body. One hand played with her nipple, pulling it, playing with the ring while the other hand headed down into her jeans and panties.

He groaned when he found her hot and slick. "Ready for me." That she was so responsive to him drove him crazy. His teeth gripped the back of her neck and she bucked back against him with a feral-sounding cry. Her honey rained on his hand, easing his way as he pressed two fingers up into her gate while his thumb stroked over her clit.

He fingered her slippery cunt until she breathed out one long exhale and came. He could have lied to himself and pretended he hadn't remembered how quickly she came, how often and seem-ingly effortlessly—but it was unnecessary. He was simply relieved she still came for him so easily.

Within moments he'd sheathed himself and she'd helped him

shove her jeans down and off one leg. He nudged against her ankle, urging her legs apart.

"This is the best assumed position I've ever had the privilege of seeing," he grunted just as he found her gate and thrust up and into her in one hard flex of his hips.

She hissed, and he saw her fingers curl into the wall. He'd ached for her for the last week, not getting enough from their phone calls and e-mails. He'd fucked his fist over and over and it had not been enough. Right at that moment he had to have her. Right then. It wasn't the time for long, slow lovemaking.

She thrust her ass back, taking him deeper.

"Yes, baby, that's it. Give me your pussy."

He held her hips tight, keeping her forward and where he wanted her. His fingers dug into her skin. He knew he'd mark her and it only made him harder.

She kept making small, needy noises in the back of her throat, urging him on. He let those noises guide him as he fucked into her with short, hard digs.

He let it all go, let the walls he'd built around himself fall away. Their first time had been raunchy enough, but this was hard. Hard and rough and at his whim.

She moved one hand down and began to play with her clit as he fucked her. Christ, this woman was a fucking goddess.

"Mmm. Make yourself come again," he said into her ear right before he bit it. He knew she liked it when her cunt rippled around him.

Harder and harder, he continued to thrust until he let his head fall back. So close. It barreled up from his heels as he came so hard he saw spots. Her muted cry and the way her honey coated his cock, sliding down to his balls, told him she'd come too.

A few more thrusts and he finally pulled out slowly, holding the condom in place. He pressed a kiss to her neck. "I'll be right back. You can get dressed again." At the end of the hall he called out, "For now." And heard her laugh.

That was fucking hot. Her right hip was a bit tender and she knew there'd be a bruise or two there. In truth she loved to be marked that way. It had scared Jeremy to mark her at all, no matter how much she'd told him not only was it okay, but that she liked it.

That Todd, so powerful and strong, had just fucked her, used her the way he wanted but hadn't actually harmed her, showed her just how much control he had. She hoped he didn't feel like he'd lost control when really he'd shown incredible restraint.

She looked around the front room they'd been in. Things were arranged in a feminine way, but not in the way a woman does when she's a lover. Not in the way of a woman who has marked a space she was a regular part of. No, this spoke of mother or sister. She knew he had both, or he did before anyway.

A knot of tension loosened at that realization and then agitation rolled through her. She shouldn't care one way or the other. Only that she wasn't *the other woman*.

"There you are." He came back into the room and moved directly to her. She liked that he sought her out, liked the way he kissed the back of her neck.

"Like I'd run away? You promised Thai food and beer. Can't run out on that. Now is this the room you wanted to paint? If so, dude, you haven't even moved the furniture. And, not to be nitpicky or anything, but um, shouldn't you have more than this?"

He dragged her down a hall into another room. This one had drop cloths down, and painter's tape had been put around the windows and at the ceiling.

"This is the room. I used to have more furniture, but the divorce, you know." He shrugged. "She'd bought most of it anyway. I let her have it. I need to start over, I suppose."

"Ah. I understand." And she did. She'd come back to Seattle with very little that had decorated the home in LA she'd shared with Jeremy and Adele. "Sometimes you just need to make a clean break."

He bent, prying open a can of paint, pouring it into a pan. The back of his T-shirt rode up, showing a work-hard, sun-kissed swath of skin. A shiver went through her at the sight, like a secret between them.

When he turned, she'd put a bandana over her hair. She took the roller brush he handed her way.

The windows were open and she heard birds chirping, children playing, lawn implements buzzing and whirring. Normal, everyday life went on, comforting her and making her feel inadequate all at once.

"You know about clean breaks?" he asked before taking his own roller brush up and putting it through the paint.

She followed suit, the wet-swish sounds of the brushes distributing paint on the walls a surprisingly warm combination between orange and yellow.

It wasn't like she'd never told anyone what happened. But the telling was like pulling an organ out, ripping it from her flesh and nearly dying from the pain.

"Yes," she murmured as she worked.

"You had someone in LA?"

"Yes."

He waited awhile, as they painted. After a time he began to speak.

"When I met Sheila, she was everything I wanted in a woman." He paused. "Everything I *thought* I wanted. Soft. Feminine. She went to church on Sundays. We had dinner with her family every other weekend. She was—*is* beautiful in that "magazine spread for *Family Circle*" sort of way. Perfect. Blonde, big pale-blue eyes. Her voice is so soft and sweet."

Erin knew he had a point to make, but whatever it was, the lead up was making her want to run this Sheila bitch over with her car a few times. And kick him in the junk for telling her all this.

"Anyway, I thought once I married her, I'd feel better. I'd be doing what I was supposed to. I'd have this pretty wife, I'd be a cop, have a career, a house in the suburbs, kids in a few years maybe. I should have been happy. But I wasn't. I came home every night to a perfect house. Dinner on the table. She was good to me, Erin, but I did not hold up my end of the bargain. After a while she sort of gave up. I can't blame her. She wanted kids and I put her off. I think she was considering leaving me long before the shooting. Anyway, I guess sometimes what we think we want isn't what we need, and until we admit it, we're fucking lying to ourselves."

She sighed. "I haven't painted a wall in many years. I'm going to be sorry tomorrow." She paused and looked at him sideways. He raised a brow and she admitted defeat. "Fine. I had a lot of things I'd dreamed of. I *was* ridiculously happy, I can't lie to you. But something so singularly horrible happened to me that it broke me. It turned me inside out and I will never be the same. Jeremy had a different way to process what happened. Our romantic relationship didn't make it through. He's still my friend, you should know that. He'll always be a part of my life if for no other reason than that he's Adrian's manager. Anyway, sometimes things happen. Things you dream of as your worst nightmare but you simply can't imagine the horror until you're living them. And you're so bent, so broken and changed that you have to walk away or you'd . . . die."

She blinked the tears back as she painted, letting the rhythm of the work soothe her.

"Jesus God. What happened to you, Erin?"

"I lost someone. I can't . . . I really just can't talk about it right now. Are your parents happy you're back home?"

Todd's hands trembled as he pushed the roller up and down the wall. Her voice, her demeanor—she'd changed and he wanted to comfort her, but he didn't know how and it was clear she wasn't ready to reveal more at this stage in their relationship. Whatever it was, it had stolen the joy from her eyes, taken the edge of free-spiritedness from her and put lines around her mouth.

"They are. My mom has been making noises about meeting you, by the way." He wanted to make it clear to her that he'd been talking about her to his family. Before he'd done the wrong thing, but now he'd rectify that. Now he would put her where she belonged.

"Tell me about your business." She bent and rolled the brush through the paint before setting back to work again.

He allowed her the space to steer away from the other topic. "Ben and Cope started it four years ago. Both did bodyguard work on the side and finally figured out security consulting was a good idea up here. Loads of rich people who need help with not just personal security like bodyguards, but home security as well. We do office and home security systems and consultations like safety plans when our clients travel. We hook people up with safety training like martial arts and self-defense courses as well as providing bodyguards and security forces. Essentially whatever the client needs."

"And what do you think? Do you like the work so far?"

"I like it a hell of a lot more than being out on the streets in a squad car every day. I like helping people take charge of their own safety. Speaking of that, do *you* have a safety plan? I'm not asking as BCT Security Solutions but as Todd to Erin. It's clear something horrible happened. I want to be sure you're safe."

She smiled at him as she stretched to get the top of the wall painted. "Yes. The label hooked me up when I came back to Seattle. My condo has state-of-the-art security and the building is very secure too. They offered me a bodyguard but I don't want that. I just want to write music, to make coffee and to be left the fuck alone." She turned to face him. "But it means a lot that you'd ask. Really. Thanks."

They painted in amiable company for another two hours, until a ruckus at the back door made him groan.

"That'll be Ben. You may as well meet him now or he'll just keep on. He's that way. I wouldn't have even told him you'd be here today, but he wanted to go golfing and I told him why I had much better plans."

She looked startled for a moment and then softened. He liked that. Liked when he could tell he'd touched her in some small way. But they couldn't discuss it, because in moments Ben's boots sounded as Todd's best friend shouted out a greeting.

"Hot damn, it *is* Erin Brown. I was wondering if Todd had made you up to keep his mother from fixing him up with the single daughters of her church ladies." Ben, well over six and a half feet of burly, used to play football in high school, grinned as he burst into the room. *Holy hotness, Batman.* This hunk of homegrown Northwest man gave Todd a serious run for his money in the mouthwatering department.

Erin blinked a few times, blushing. "You'd be Ben, the 'B' in BCT Security Solutions, then." She wiped her hands and held one out for him to take. She wasn't small by any means, but Ben dwarfed her anyway.

"Hands off now. Why are you here?" Todd put the lid back on the paint after he'd poured the remainder back into the can.

"Room looks good." Ben turned to look and then bent to help gather the drop cloths.

"Excuse me a moment, gents. I'll be back." Erin ducked out, heading toward the bathroom at the opposite end of the hall.

"I should have known you'd come by. Nosy bastard." Todd took the painting stuff out to the garage and disposed of everything properly, cleaning up while Ben helped.

"Of course you should have. This woman is someone you talk about constantly and in a way I've never heard before. Not afraid to get her hands dirty, I like that. She blushes and she didn't seem to get that I meant Erin Brown the rockstar not just your girlfriend. After Sheila, god knows someone needed to keep an eye on your choices."

"I still have a hard time believing she's a rockstar. Or was. Whatever."

"Did she tell you what happened? Why she came back here?" Ben lowered his voice.

"She's hinted around the edges. It sounds awful. She says she lost someone. I gather it was someone close. I want her to tell me, but I have to admit I'm dying to look it up. Do you know?" He kept his eyes on the back door to be sure she wasn't coming toward them.

"I told you, I'm a huge fan. I have all Mud Bay's CDs, the tour DVD and now Adrian's stuff too. Yes. I know." Ben hesitated, and both men smiled as they caught sight of the pink hair through the kitchen window. "In person she's less fierce than her onstage persona was. I hope you don't mind my saying she's really fucking hot too. Intelligent I already knew through her lyrics. She's an amazing songwriter. Listen to a song called 'Absence'. I've got the CD in my car, you can borrow it. She lost a child, Todd."

Ben would have said more, but she ducked her head out and saw them. Todd shoved the disorientation away, his sadness at what she must have experienced, but also a gulf beneath his feet that she'd made a baby with someone else.

"This is my hungry face," she said simply. "If you two are finished swapping stories about me, you need to make good on that promise of Thai food."

Ben laughed. "I'll go get it. You two hang out and I'll be back in a few."

Before Todd could tell him he wasn't invited, Ben jogged off to his car and drove away.

"He's pushy. You two must have known each other a long time."

He kissed her first, just because he craved her taste. "Mmm, you have such delicious lips," he murmured. "And yes, we've been friends since the second grade. His dad and mine are cops, his younger brother was too. Cop families." Todd shrugged. "They're close-knit. Anyway, he's like a brother to me. My best friend and a big pain in my ass. Cope is his little brother and the closest friend I have after Ben. I'm closer to them than to my own brothers. Maybe it's because we're all the rebels who quit cop work." He shrugged. "As for Cope, I'll give *him* about half an hour more before he shows up. He's got an uncanny ability to know when food is available."

She laughed. "I like that. Family is important. Are you okay with your friends knowing me?"

He grasped her face, cradling her cheeks in his hands. "I need you to understand something. You're important to me. Ten years ago I was stupid. I didn't know what you were to me. I didn't understand what I was myself. I want them to know you. They're important to me and so are you."

Her gaze held his for long, silent moments until it slid away. She held herself back, and while he understood he'd hurt her back then, he wanted her to give herself to him now. He'd have to earn her trust again. He wanted her to tell him the story. But losing a child wasn't something you talked about when you were about to be invaded by your boyfriend's buddies. And he was her boyfriend. Period.

"Let me set the table then. I see you've got it set so you can eat and still see the ginormous television. Not enough furniture but a big TV. I suppose the essentials are taken care of." She smirked as she spun from him, but he caught her again, pulling her back, her ass fitting in the cradle of his hips.

He leaned to her ear, nipping it. "I didn't say you could leave my arms."

Her breath caught and he couldn't help but notice her nipples pressing against the cotton of her T-shirt.

She didn't spit back a flip remark and he wanted to bend her over and fuck her then and there, but as luck would have it, Cope's truck pulled into the driveway and the engine cut.

"Yes, you like that, don't you? God knows I do." He pressed a kiss to the side of her neck. "Cope is here and I have a hard-on the size of that television. The dishes are in the cabinet next to the fridge." He let go and she leaned back against him for one more moment before flitting off into the kitchen.

Holy shit. Erin pressed the back of her hand to her mouth as she tried to get herself under control. He'd just pushed a monster button. In a good way. A button she hadn't even known she had apparently. But all that big, hard, strong maleness against her, holding her tight, telling her he hadn't given her permission to leave his arms? Christ on a cracker, that was hot. Hot enough that her panties were wet and her nipples throbbed. She was sure she still bore the flush of arousal when the other one of the guys stomped into the house and all that male noise rose to a pitch as backs were thumped and insults were traded.

She smiled as she got herself together enough to reach for plates. Todd and his friends were a lot like Brody and Adrian. That kinship showed, and Erin felt that if Todd trusted these men enough to love them like brothers, they were indeed worthy men.

If Ben Copeland had been overwhelmingly large and very handsome, his little brother was downright sinfully gorgeous. He was
Todd's size, with black hair and striking blue eyes. She also knew
him.

"So Cope is actually Andy Copeland, huh?" She put the plates
on the table and moved toward them.

"Oh my god! You're the café hottie! Your brother has done my
inkwork." Cope turned to Todd, whose eyebrows had slashed down,
his face darkening into a scowl. Cope laughed. "I sneak into your
girlfriend's café at least once a month to drink coffee and to check
out what color her hair might be next. Back with Mud Bay you had
dreads, and then your hair was very short and black. Hot." He waggled his brows. "I can't believe I didn't recognize you. I should have
recognized your voice though. You should have sung more often.
That smoky sex voice thing you do on 'Lashed' is hot stuff."

She laughed. "Um, thanks."

"I can't believe you and Ben know her stuff and I don't. I feel
like an idiot."

She reached up, sliding her hand up his neck, wanting to soothe
him. "You know *me*. That's better. It's okay, really."

He turned like his friend wasn't there and kissed her, hard and
fast.

"I blame Waylon Jennings and Toby Keith." Cope shrugged.

She wrinkled her nose. "It's only half as bad as I imagined. Waylon kicks ass," she teased.

"What do you have against Toby?" Todd asked.

"It's my belief that men who are aggressive and always threaten-
ing to beat people up are overcompensating." She grinned, knowing
she and Todd were not close politically at all. Good thing the sex
made up for it.

Just then Ben came in with several bags of takeout and the space was filled with so much testosterone a girl could have gotten drunk from it. Instead, she ordered them all to sit, and they popped open lids to the various containers. She sighed happily, putting spoons in things and passing around plates.

Without thinking, she made a plate for Todd and put a beer down for him. His eyes, when he looked at her, burned with some inner light. She hadn't meant it to be provocative; she just took care of him. Not because he was her master or anything, but because she liked making him happy.

Which scared her. She couldn't take anyone else into her heart, damn it. It was too much and she'd already lost him once. It had hurt a lot after only a few months when she was very young. What would it be like now? What would the emotional cost be if he walked away again? She sure as hell didn't have the currency left to pay for it.

She played a stupid, dangerous game with him and she knew it. If she was smart, she'd walk away now. Telling herself she could keep it friendly was a lie and she knew it. Not because she wasn't capable of fucking casually; she totally was. Erin wasn't the type of woman who equated sex and love. But this was different because *he* was different. He got to her. No one had made her want to serve them simply because she wanted to please. God help her. She wasn't strong enough to deal with the emotional devastation if he walked away, but she wasn't strong enough to run now herself.

He leaned in and kissed her cheek. "You're thinking, Erin. It's like a movie, watching your face. Don't run from me. I'll come for you. I want you and you want me. Let yourself have it." His whispered breath was hot on her ear and it sent a shiver down her side.

She nearly dropped her beer from fingers gone nerveless. How did he get her so well?

"I wanted to tell you how much I loved Adrian's latest CD. He's really growing into that voice of his." Ben's big blue eyes found hers and she latched on to the lifeline he tossed her. She liked his face. It was open and honest as well as gorgeous.

"Thanks. I think so too. He's just put the finishing touches on the new CD this week. I've been in the studio with him."

"Do you ever sing anymore?"

"On the tracks I do. In the studio. When he goes out live, he has backup singers. His tour bassist is almost as good as me." She grinned. She may not have been able to handle being on that stage anymore, but she still loved what she did, was proud of it, in fact.

"I saw you back at the Off Ramp. A million years ago it seems." Ben laughed. "I still have some bootlegged, home-pressed CD you sold out of the trunk of a car in the parking lot."

She burst out laughing. "Oh my god! Really? Adrian and I sold plasma to afford that pressing." Shaking her head, she tipped the last of her beer into her mouth.

"I've seen them live too. Twice as a matter of fact, back in the day. But Ben, bring in that CD. I want to hear it." Todd sat back in his chair.

Erin felt the heat build up her neck. "Gah! Listen to it when I'm not here. I'm hypercritical and it's sort of masturbatory to listen to your own music with friends." She wrinkled her nose.

"Masturbatory?" Cope raised a brow and then winced when the cap from a beer bottle glanced off his forehead when Todd tossed it at him.

"I should be going soon. I've been away from the café more than usual because I've been working with Adrian. I need to get some bread in the ovens for tomorrow. I usually bake on Sunday evenings."

"Do you need help? I can help in the kitchen." Todd's lips curved into a smile that told her his "help" would be of the shoving-his-cock-into-her-cunt type and not the kneading-dough type.

"I'm sure you can. But it's sort of my alone time." She rolled her eyes at his pout. "Oh goodness gracious, don't pout. It's not like I'm half a world away. I'm only three miles from here. You know my number."

"I'll walk you out." He grabbed her bag and put an arm around her waist.

"It was nice to meet you both."

"Definitely. And we'll see you soon I'm sure." Ben nodded and Cope winked. Lord, what a mischievous little boy he must have been.

She let Todd walk her out. She'd chosen the alley behind the garage, where he'd suggested she move her car earlier, and she was glad. They were out of sight when he pressed her against the side of her car and shoved his fingers through her hair, tangling with her braids. His mouth came down on hers, his tongue seeking entry right away.

She gave it to him, melting into his touch.

Without thinking, she stroked him through his jeans, and he made a strangled sound she eagerly swallowed.

When he broke away, he looked down into her face, chest heaving. "I wanted to be with you this afternoon. In my bed. Let me tell them to go."

"It's okay. I liked meeting them. They're very nice."

"You and me, dinner on Tuesday night."

He hadn't exactly asked, but she nodded anyway.

"I'll pick you up at your condo. We'll walk to get dinner."

"Wow, like a real date and stuff?" She winked, but she wasn't being flip, she liked the idea.

He nodded. "I told you, I'm serious about you, Erin. Now go on and bake. I'll call you later."

10

She drove to the café and breathed through the panic when she saw the darkened front windows. Erin had wanted to tell Todd yes, to come with her because she hated the fucking fear. If he'd been with her, she wouldn't have had a damned panic attack at the very thought of going into her own business at five in the afternoon on a Sunday in full light.

The neighborhood was safe. She knew everyone in it and they knew her. Her feelings were irrational; she knew it, and yet they were there. She had to make herself do this every Sunday, even if she would have to change her shirt once she got inside because she'd become so sweaty from the panic. But she did it because she would not let Charles Cabot steal any more of her life.

"It's daylight. Stop. You are an adult. There is nothing to be afraid of," she muttered as she walked toward the café's front door. It seemed as if the short block lengthened, darkened.

Two sort of scary-looking guys, albeit—*hello*—her brother's bread and butter at the tattoo parlor—and her people really—stood near the alley on the other side of the café.

Her heart sped, making her dizzy. So dizzy she had to touch the window of the shop to keep her bearings. Damn it, she would not, *would not* allow a fucking panic attack right now. She wasn't a pussy. She wasn't a coward. She could open her own door without falling into a weepy puddle just feet away.

"Erin? Honey, are you all right?"

She looked around, blinking, and saw Brody standing in his doorway, wearing concern on his face. She'd seen it so many times she nearly burst into tears of frustration.

"Fine. Fine!" she spat out and forced her legs to take the next steps to the door.

"Shut the fuck up about fine." Brody caught up to her, putting an arm around her shoulders and taking her keys. "I've told you to call me when you're pulling up and I'll meet you to unlock and let you inside. Why you do this to yourself every week is beyond me."

He jammed the key into the lock and then two more before the door swung open. She stood near her brother while he turned off the alarm and flipped on the lights.

At last he faced her, holding both her hands. "Baby girl, I love you so much. Let me help you. It's not necessary to be superwoman, you know? Why don't you call me? I'm just next door. You know I'll come with you. I don't judge you, because there's nothing to judge. You're not a burden. I like to do things for you."

She blinked, but the tears came anyway and he simply hugged her, sliding a hand up and down her back.

"I hate being this person," she said softly. "I used to be brave. I used to climb mountains and yell at hecklers. Now I jump at shadows."

"God, Erin. You *are* brave. I wish you could see yourself, I wish you could see the woman Adrian and I see every day. Beyond strong to survive this goddamn mess." He stepped back enough to look into her face. "How long has it been since you've been to therapy?"

"I should be better! How long will this last? I can't go to therapy for the rest of my life."

"Honey, you experienced something so horrible it would take any person years to get over. Why do you hold yourself to such a ridiculous standard? *I* needed therapy after it happened and it didn't even happen to me. For a year and a half I went every two weeks because I was terrified of losing you. Do you think I'm a loser for needing that? Adele was your little girl, you loved her. Adrian and I loved her too. You nearly died and you're my heart. That doesn't come with a 'heal by' date like a carton of milk."

She knew he was right. But therapy sometimes made it worse. Stirred up things best left alone and forgotten, or at the very least, pretended to be forgotten. Still, she couldn't keep living this way.

"I'll call her. It's coming up anyway . . . the anniversary. I'll probably need it."

"We could go away. Me, you and Adrian. Head out to the coast. Go to New York, Vancouver—hell, Amsterdam even."

"No. I can't run this year. But I want you to know I would have died without you and Adrian. You guys throw me life preservers. You must hate being my lifeguard so much. Without me you'd have been able to go to art school. Instead you had to raise me and Adrian. That's fucked up."

He walked her back into the kitchen after locking the front doors and resetting those alarms. She started to pull out all the ingredients she'd need, all her pans and things, and he watched for a long time before he spoke.

"I'm your brother, Erin. I love you. When Mom and Dad died, of course I stepped in. Not because I had to, but because that's what family does. That's what you do when you love people. I didn't go to art school, but I have my own business. A successful business with a damned fine reputation. People come from all over to get my inkwork. What happened to me was supposed to happen. I don't hate being your lifeguard. I'd be so sad if I couldn't be there when you needed me. Just like you've been for me when I needed you. Adrian and I love you, we want to help you. We both feel a heck of a lot better when you reach out instead of suffering alone."

She began to fall into the ritual of measuring and mixing by hand, of flouring and kneading. Her panic smoothed after a few minutes.

Brody flipped on the CD player and PJ Harvey growled through the speakers.

"I'm leaving the connecting door open. If you want to sing, you know I'd love you for it." He kissed her forehead and looked her over. He knew the storm had passed and so backed away.

She worked as *Dry* played. Played until "Fountain" came on and she stood near the door and sang part of the lyrics, ending with the line about what to do when everything's left you.

The noise from the room next door had stilled to utter silence until Brody cleared his throat.

"Thanks, baby girl. You know I love that one."

She did too.

11

He pulled into her parking garage and headed up to her condo. The doorman let him straight up on her orders. Standing orders apparently. Todd liked that a lot.

He'd spent the last three days listening to her CDs. Christ, her voice on those few songs she sang lead on was burned into his brain.

There's a hole where you used to live
Dead inside and I can't hide
I smoke and I drink and I still can't stop
Thinking of you
Absent and there's no going back
Absent and I hurt
Can't hide from the hurt

Ben hadn't been wrong about the song he'd recommended. Listening to Erin's low, smoky moan as she poured her grief out, the gasp at the end where her tears were close to the surface, had nearly driven him to his knees.

He'd wanted to do some Internet research on the incident, but he'd been called out on one client meeting after the other, stumbling home to fall into bed, calling her or texting her if it was too late and he didn't want to wake her.

He knocked, and when she opened up, she stood in a short, pretty dress, flowy at the leg and tight at the breast part. Perfect.

"Pink Floyd." He smiled as he went into her place and heard "Wish You Were Here" in the background.

"Thank god. I was worried, you know. This Toby Keith thing has been keeping me up at nights."

Laughing, he swept her up into a hug, craving more of the way she felt pressed to him.

"Hello there, my gorgeous little freak."

She paused for a moment and then snorted laughter, kissing his nose. "Only you could get away with these things."

He could. Which is why, he supposed, he liked to do them so much. She made him feel special even when she did something as silly as making him a plate of food or laughing when he teased her.

"How hungry are you?" he asked.

And then she dropped to her knees, looking up at him after setting her glasses aside. Her hands rested in her lap, her back was straight as she waited.

He had a fleeting thought that she had no idea what she looked like kneeling there, how she moved him, but he knew she did, and that made her actions undeniably arousing. She did it on purpose because she knew what it did for him.

"Suck me. You know what I like."

She murmured, licking her lips as she slowly unbuttoned his jeans and pulled his shorts down to free his cock. She breathed deep, sliding her cheek along him, the cool of her skin a contrast to the heat of his.

She palmed his sac with one hand and gripped his root with the other before sucking tightly on him, inching down, bit by bit, until she'd swallowed a good portion of his cock, her lips touching the top of her fist where she held him.

Her hair was down, leaving him free to run his fingers through it, gaining enough purchase until he grasped tight and guided her—up and down, up and down—over his cock.

"Are you wearing panties?" His voice had lowered, neared a grunt as her mouth surrounded his prick with wet heat.

"Mmm," she said, shaking her head with him still in her mouth.

"Christ," he hissed as the image of her wet, sweetly pink cunt flashed through his head. "Take that hand off my balls and finger yourself. Don't come yet. That's mine. But I want you primed for when I shoot down your throat."

Each time he gave the words up freely, each time he did what he wanted, what he craved, it got easier the next time. It wasn't as if there was a manual for all this stuff, but with her it wasn't necessary. With Erin on her knees before him, Todd knew they'd work it through, find ways to pleasure each other, keep each other wanting more, without pain, without disrespect, with . . . love.

There hadn't been a single moment, a time when the clouds had parted and the angels sang that he loved her. He just knew he did. Maybe he'd loved her a long time, tucked away in his mind for all these years. Maybe it had been when she leapt into his arms moments before. What mattered was that he felt it, and even better, he knew it.

Thought skittered away as her left hand slid between her thighs and she gasped around him. Her fingers were touching her cunt, he knew. He wished he could see more, but at the same time what he could see only forced him—*ha, forced*—to imagine it. Which, actually, was just as good.

He heard the wet sounds of her fingers playing through the juicy folds of her pussy; the scent of her arousal teased him as he continued to fuck into her mouth.

She pressed the tip of her tongue down the center of his cock each time she swallowed him, a line of pleasure, something new and entirely delightful.

He was close to coming, and the increasingly jerky movement of the hand between her thighs told him she was as well. He let go, coming in a hot rush, filling her.

"Don't come yet," he warned as a needy sound echoed around him. He pulled out and knelt before her. She swayed a bit, her eyes wide, face flushed. Her chest heaved and he knew she was a hairsbreadth from coming.

He touched her gently, his palms pushing the hem of her dress upward, exposing the vee between her thighs. Bare, wet—the scent of her honey tightened his gut and he leaned down, breathing her in.

Her fingers still curled there, shiny with her juice. Fuck. Fuck, he was in so deep with her. She moved him when he imaged himself quite beyond being touched in such a way.

"You want to finish, don't you?"

Erin focused her gaze on him, the tendrils of climax still holding her close, beckoning. She'd never actually let another person hold her orgasm before. It was ridiculous and yet beyond intoxicating to hand him that power.

One twitch of her fingers and she'd fall. She thought of it, holding her hand still. Their gazes locked. His taste rang through her system; his cock was still out of his jeans, partially reviving. He was so near, the heat from him radiated across her skin.

She swallowed hard, trying to find words. A nod was all she managed.

He took her wrist, gently moving her fingers away from her cunt. Her breath caught as he lowered his face, on his hands and knees now, to her pussy.

Nothing at first, just the soft waft of his breath against her thighs. She had to fight the urge to strain upward to his mouth. He hadn't said she could. So she remained still, waiting . . .

"Good god, what you do to me," he said, his lips just barely brushing her labia. The subtle sensation sent a shock wave of heat through her. "You can touch your nipples or me," he said right before the slick of his tongue slid through her cunt.

She didn't think to touch her nipples; all she could do was brace herself with her hands on the floor behind her ass where she knelt, her back arched, her thighs widening.

She wanted to watch him, but bright stars painted her vision with each small flutter of his tongue against her pussy, so she closed her eyes and felt. Her muscles began to burn from kneeling; sweat broke out on the back of her neck and she licked dry lips.

One more flutter of his tongue and a gasp wrenched from low in her gut. Orgasm rocketed through her body, rolling in waves until she had to beg him to stop.

He kissed her while her eyes were still closed, and they tumbled back to the area rug.

When she opened her eyes again, he looked down and she saw the tenderness in his gaze. Inside she knew what would happen and before she could stop him, he said it.

"I love you, Erin."

She could not love him. Would not. The price was too damned high! She had to close her eyes again because tears welled up. Too late, too late, because she knew she loved him too, had for years, and it had lain dormant in her heart until she saw him in her café just weeks before.

Shit.

He kissed each eyelid. "I know it might seem sudden but it's not really. We've known each other ten years. You fit in the empty spaces just right. There's a spot in my life that's your size. Don't say anything just now. Let me take you to dinner. Let me love you. The rest is what's important. Not words, but deeds."

If he'd been harsh or hurt, if he'd demanded an answer, she could have resisted. But this gentleness was not something she could deal with.

So she nodded and allowed him to help her up.

He insisted on holding her hand as they walked over to Fourth and Virginia, to Lola.

He pulled her chair out for her, then moved his next to hers instead of across. His arm rested at her back, at the top of the chair, and he smelled so good she wanted to eat him up.

"What's good here? The only place Tom Douglas had when I lived here before was the Dahlia Lounge." He grinned at her before brushing a strand of hair back that had stuck to her lip gloss.

"Most everything. First of all we have to get fresh pita. It comes with all these different spreads and it's really delish. I'm having a tagine, but the kabobs are yummy too. It all is, I promise."

They ordered, and when the bread arrived, she automatically made him a plate, laughing and asking him what he liked and didn't. When she placed the plate in front of him and looked into his eyes, she jolted a moment.

"Are you mad?"

He brushed a thumb over her collarbone, ever so softly as he shook his head. "No. I love when you do that. When you take care of me. It's," he licked his lips, searching for words, "it gets to me."

"Th-thank you. That's a lovely thing to say." She didn't say more, because she liked taking care of him. A lot.

She couldn't love Todd Keenan. Period. The cost of loving people was losing them, and she could not bear it again. It was too late not to love her brothers, but she needed to put the kibosh on this love thing for Todd right then.

Fucking—hell yes. Loving—hell no. She didn't have the time to love anyone else. Her love bill was full. He needed a woman who was whole and not fucked up. She was not that woman.

12

Todd walked back with her, loving the way the breeze ruffled the bottom of her dress. Her hair, so shockingly pink, looked like soft cotton candy. He nearly laughed aloud at the thought that he'd ever find such a description romantic, much less beautiful, but there it was.

On her it all worked. Because she was simply one of a kind. One of a kind and nervous as the shadows had lengthened into night.

She'd jumped several times as sudden laughter or talking drifted from a doorway, from the fronts of the cafés and stores marking their route back to her building.

Her eyes cut left and right and her spine vibrated with tension.

This was not the woman he'd fucked in an alley ten years ago. That woman had been totally fearless and he ached for whatever had happened to her to rob her of that.

"Why don't you tell me what happened?" he asked gently as he led her into her house and helped her out of her sweater.

"What do you mean?" She toed out of her shoes and set them on a wooden rack near the door and he followed suit.

"I know a little bit about the attack. Not a lot. I know you lost a child. Tell me what makes you jump at shadows."

She turned. He noted her knuckles on the hand holding her bag had gone white.

"I don't want to talk about it. Yes, I lost a child. I nearly died. You can imagine the rest."

She had no fucking idea. Todd worked to keep himself relaxed, even as his body wanted to go and pick her up, force her to tell him and hold her forever. "I can, and it scares the shit out of me. Share it. You can trust me to catch you when you fall."

She took a step back and dropped her bag on the table. "It's not that. I just don't like talking about it. And I don't mean any offense, but I trust three people. Me, Adrian and Brody."

He thought of what he'd say in response. It hurt; there was no denying that not being included with her brothers sliced through his gut. But he understood. He loved her and he saw her pain. He got why it would be hard to trust. And he'd show her she could add his name to that short list. There was no small amount of irony that their situation had flipped from where it had been before. Back then she'd been coaxing him to open up to her and he'd been scared shitless.

A sickening thought occurred to him. "At least tell me *he* didn't do this to you. Jeremy, the guy you loved before."

Total surprise washed over her face and he relaxed a bit. No, it wasn't the ex. The ex who had made a child with her, with the woman Todd loved.

She shook her head, hard. Her hair spilled into her face. "No. God, no. Jeremy loved Adele. Loved me. He never would have hurt either one of us." Her voice caught, and he was wrapped around her before he even thought about moving.

They remained there, just hugging, until the tenor of the moment changed, deepened, thickened, and he had to step back because his cock hardened against her.

She looked up into his face, her eyes lost. "Help me feel alive," she whispered.

He nodded.

Erin watched his face change and her cunt bloomed at the sight of the birth of the very potent dom he was becoming. She didn't think in terms of "dom" being capitalized and "sub" being lowercase. To Erin, D/s wasn't about one person being worthy of a capital letter and the other not. It wasn't about unequal worth; it was about two equals *sharing* power, sharing sex and emotion. She didn't submit to him because she wanted to be debased or harmed, because she needed to be lesser than anyone. She was aware some people got off on that, and hey, whatever floats your boat. But when he dominated her, she felt cherished and adored, cosseted in those perfect moments between them—in a way she never achieved with anyone else.

She liked that he looked her over carefully. She knew to be sure she was ready for whatever he planned to dish out, and god help her if she didn't want to fall to her knees right then.

He nodded once, apparently having decided she was on board with his plans, and jerked his head toward the living room. "Naked and bent over the arm of the couch. Now."

Blinking rapidly, she reached for a calming breath even as a flush worked through her body at his command. Trembling hands managed to get the side zipper on her dress down so she could step from it. Her bra followed. She walked over to the couch, then bent forward, bracing her hands. The air in the room was cool against her bare skin; the slight nub in the fabric on the couch abraded her belly and thighs.

Would he use his hands on her ass? Would he fuck her hard? What was his purpose?

The questions wisped through her brain idly as she sought to find a quiet spot in her head. Waiting.

"Mmm. I do love looking at you like this. No panties either, just the way I like it." She heard the jingle of his belt buckle and the slither as he pulled it from the loops. Her pussy softened at the sound combined with raw desire in his words. He looked at her and saw the beauty there. She pleased him, and in turn, that pleased her.

He drew the thin but sturdy leather over her bare back, leaving shivers in its wake. Her breath caught at the soft/rough caress.

"I've never used my belt on a woman—hell, on anyone but my-self. I've craved it for so long."

She swallowed, trying to wet her mouth enough to speak. "On yourself?"

"I . . ." He hesitated, his thigh against hers, denim against bare skin. "I used to wrap it around my hand when I jerked off."

Her heart skittered in her chest a moment at the very powerful image he'd just given her. But even more that he'd shared such an intimate detail.

"Todd, please use it on me. I need it." She noted the slight slur in her words. God, he made her pleasure drunk.

His shirt fluttered to the ground in the corner of her vision, and she heard five pops of the buttons on his fly. Those *pops* had become a potent aphrodisiac. Each one, knowing it went lower and lower, exposing the front of his boxers, made her wetter and wetter. An-ticipating his touch, what he'd do to her next, her body burned. It was like this only with him. There had never been another who'd done this to her body. And soul.

The first crack of his belt over her thighs was more a caress than an outright strike of leather against tender flesh. He stood close, at her hip, and his cock nudged ever harder against her.

"You won't hurt me," she whispered. "Do it again. Please."

He groaned and another strike fell, this one a bit harder, and the sting built into warmth. Hormones surged inside her, endorphins responding to the pain. She'd never felt anything like it and she craved more, arching back to him.

Another fell as he experimented with the strength of the strike and how to hold it, where to use it. She closed her eyes and let herself fall into the place where feeling became everything. Each successive strike of his belt—on her ass and thighs, sometimes the bite of the belt flicking against the tender, swollen lips of her pussy— pushed her farther and farther away, until she felt like she floated.

The fire on her flesh brought her nerve endings to vivid life. Her senses were fine-tuned. She felt everything—the cool air on her skin, the warmth of his body behind her, the breeze that preceded each stroke of his belt.

She heard the strangled moan he made and then the belt dropped to the couch in front of her, in her line of sight, where it could taunt her.

His fingers drew over the heat on her ass and thighs and she wondered what it looked like, what he saw. She knew how it made him feel. His cock seeped pre-come against her hip; his movements, though gentle, were slightly jerky.

His instincts where her pleasure was concerned were scarily accurate. Somehow this made sense to her, as she'd always felt such a deep connection to him.

His fingers found her cunt swollen and wet, blooming just for him. He trailed a finger over the flesh of her thigh, her own juices cool against that heat. "You don't know how hard it makes me to see your pussy so wet for me. To know your cunt is hungry for my cock." His voice was thick and hoarse.

He licked a trail from the back of her neck all the way down her spine. His fingertips traced the design of her tattoo. Pressing gentle kisses over her ass and down her thighs, he pushed her legs open wider with his hands. She gasped as his mouth opened over her pussy.

"I love looking at you this way." Tongue and lips, he devoured her for several long moments and pulled back. "Damn, so sweet. Your clit is so pretty there, peeking out of its hood, wanting attention."

The flat of his tongue pressed over it, moving it around against his taste buds. "And this." He tickled his pinky over the puckered star of her anus. "This little hole. How is it that every part of you is so damned beautiful and sexy?"

All she could do was moan.

His middle finger teased around her gate as his mouth found her clit again. He tormented her that way for a very long time, until he finally stood up. Dimly, she heard the crinkle of a condom wrapper in the background and he was back, pushing into her body with inexorable strength.

She arched, taking him as deeply as possible. He reached around, grabbing a nipple in one hand and sliding down to her clit with the other. He *tug, tug, tug*ged the ring, sending bright shards of pleasure through her when she wasn't sure she had any left to give.

But he continued to fuck into her, slow and deep, while he played with her clit. All it took was a few gentle squeezes between slippery fingers and the orgasm he'd been carefully crafting over the last minutes exploded through her.

Writhing helplessly as he thrust deep into her body, she continued to come, cunt clasping around his cock. But he held on, continuing to stroke deep into her. His hands had moved back to her hips, where he gripped her, keeping her at precisely the angle he wanted.

She lost herself in receiving him, in her body making way for his over and over until he finally thrust one last time, deep, and came.

He stumbled away a step to get rid of the condom, pressing a kiss at the small of her back before he left.

In the bathroom he splashed water on his face and stared at his reflection. His pupils were large, his skin flushed with sex. With something more. He'd never used a belt, or anything other than his hand, on a woman. The high of it rode him, surged through his senses. He'd loved it, loved watching her skin turn pink, loved the slight welts he'd made. He worried at first that he'd hurt her, but he listened to her sounds, watched her body language, and if the slickness of her pussy had been any indication, she enjoyed it too.

He went back out to her, knowing she might need a bit of snuggling. He wanted her to understand that what had happened, despite its roughness, was tender on his part. He hoped it hadn't been too much, so soon after she'd told him that little bit about her daughter. Hoped he hadn't made a mistake.

She was in the kitchen, singing as she dug through the fridge. Still naked, her ass and thighs still bore welts, and he felt awful even as the sight hardened his cock. She turned to him, smiling.

"Thirsty?" She drank deeply from a bottle of water, holding a spare one his way.

"Are you all right?"

She set the water down and moved to him, sliding into his arms like they were made just for her to be in them. "I'm more than all right."

"I just never, ever want to harm you. I don't want you to fear me. You're precious to me."

She looked up into his face. "I'm not afraid of you, Todd. I wouldn't have allowed you to do any of this if I hadn't trusted you not to harm me."

"I don't know how to do this. I'm sure you're more experienced with it."

She laughed. "I know what I like, but I wouldn't say I was experienced. I've played over the years." She put a hand on his cheek as he began to blush, thinking about her with other men. "But never what we've had between us. We'll learn together. There's no 'Big Rule Book of Bondage' or anything. It's about what works for us. And the belt works for me." She fanned her face and his angst lifted.

He grinned at her. "Works for me too."

13

She saw him enter the café and placed a plate with a turkey sandwich extra-loaded with avocado and bacon on the bar. She'd tried to
get him to sit at a table, to give her some space, but he'd ignored
the suggestion and crowded in. So she'd given up and let herself be
happy with making him lunch every day, even as she refused his
invitations for dates.

Ella had been there the morning after Erin's last date with Todd.
She'd come through the door shell-shocked by the depth of what
they'd shared. Her friend had just put a cup of coffee and a huge
blueberry scone on the counter. Erin hadn't spoken for long minutes until, finally, she'd given up a little bit to the other woman. A
bit of her fear, a bit of her hesitation at becoming so deeply involved when she wasn't back on her feet emotionally.

In the end, Ella had just wiped the counter, taken the cup and
plate away and looked Erin right in the eyes. "This guy *is* your way
back to your feet. You've had love before. This is different and you
know it. Don't let fear chase your potential for happiness away."

Erin knew Ella understood the difference between love and

obsession; knew her friend was trying to get on her own feet again after a long, harrowing relationship. The irony that it was Erin who usually offered advice wasn't lost on her, and she'd truly taken it all to heart.

But it had been a lot to process and she still struggled.

That night when they'd gone to dinner and he'd come back to her place had moved things inside her. She wasn't comfortable in her skin because she wanted him. She wanted to see him, to be with him. Damn it. The second and third round that night had been just as powerful as the first. It wasn't just fucking as he'd held her wrists, the leather of his belt chafing her skin just right. He'd looked her in the eyes the entire time. In the morning he'd laughed and praised her simple toast and eggs. He'd sucked down her coffee, and as he'd left, he'd told her he loved her.

So she'd tried to dodge his calls, but he'd simply shown up at the café every day at lunch. She told herself she wanted him to give up and go away, but mostly she knew it was a lie, even if she did think it would be better for both of them if he found a woman who didn't jump at shadows and sleep with the bathroom light on.

"Mmm." He took in the plate with a happy sound. Before she could dodge, he'd grabbed her and kissed her, bold as you please. "That's even better." He plopped his gorgeous, hard-as-steel ass down and dug in.

"Why, hello there," she said, unable to stop a smile.

"Good salad. Is this pasta or rice or what?"

"It's orzo, rice-shaped pasta."

"Ah. Okay then. It's good. Mint is a nice touch. Unexpected." He leaned forward and said quietly, "Is it just me or is my sandwich on steroids?" He looked around. "It seems bigger. Is that because you're sweet on me or something?"

She rolled her eyes and moved to help a customer. "You'll do," she said over her shoulder.

"Good. I guess that means you'll go to the movies with me to-night. Or I can grab a pizza and we can rent a movie."

"I can't tonight. I'm working with Adrian." Adrian was sick of her coming over; she was sure of it. But he hadn't said much other than to tell her she was being a pussy for not just talking to Todd and telling him what happened.

"Lots of that going around lately."

He finished his food and tried to pay. She gave him a dirty look; he told her he'd call her later and that he'd see her tomorrow. The same as he'd done every day for the last week.

She wished her feelings for him would just wear off, but she looked forward to seeing him walk through that door every day just the same.

He hadn't seen her alone in two weeks. He'd called and they'd e-mailed, but she'd put him off and he knew she was avoiding him. He still showed up at her café for lunch every afternoon. At first much to her consternation, but now she had a plate of something tasty waiting for him every day when he arrived. They'd had that much progress at least. But she wasn't alone with him and she continued to plead busy if he asked her to dinner or to spend time with him after work.

That last night he'd seen her, he'd slept over. He'd used his belt to strap her wrists and tie them to the headboard of her bed. He'd knelt over her, feeding her his cock as she sucked it eagerly.

They'd made love, they'd fucked, and he'd gorged himself of her body and soul. They'd connected, and when he'd left the next morning, he knew with total certainty she loved him too.

Which was why she was avoiding him, he knew. She was scared of losing him. Given what he'd done ten years before, he understood. Despite that knowledge, he was annoyed.

"Sit down and use your damned computer to look it all up," Cope said, standing up and pushing Todd into his chair and sitting next to him. Ben manned their main office just south of downtown Seattle but Cope had set up shop three days a week with Todd in his basement turned home office.

The place had turned out very nicely. They'd spent a lot of time painting and laying down new flooring. There were still plenty of windows set high into the walls, but they'd installed good lighting as well. It was brightly lit and comfortable, with several computer terminals, multiple phone lines and other office equipment, including the not-so-standard gun safe in the back corner under the stairs.

"Fine," he growled, swiveling toward his computer. He'd been putting it off. He wanted her to tell him and then when she'd started avoiding him, he'd kept it off his mind the best he could, thinking up ways to get her ass by his side permanently.

Two hours later he felt sick. All the pictures, all the news coverage, the media circus of the trial. No wonder she'd returned to Seattle. No wonder she'd worried about losing anyone else she let into her life. No one should have to endure what she had.

"That's just fucked up. Your woman is even more awesome in my eyes now. Go talk to her. She's afraid, dude." Cope moved back over to his desk from the chair where he'd sat next to Todd as they surfed the Internet.

Todd stood, gut still roiling, and headed out. "I'm gone for a while."

"Take the time you need, man. I've got things covered here." Cope waved at him as he left.

It was still early, earlier than his normal lunchtime visit, but the café was dark and her purple sparkly car wasn't anywhere near the area; he'd driven around to look. So he decided to go into the tattoo parlor.

Brody Brown was a big man. Where Adrian was lively and a bit smaller, not quite six feet tall, Brody was watchful, menacing even. His black hair was close-cropped, and his eyes had clapped onto Todd the moment he'd walked into the shop.

"I was wondering when you'd come around."

The two men had only met briefly ten years before. Brody had been in Erin's café several times in the last two weeks when Todd had stopped in for lunch. They'd achieved a somewhat civil relationship and Todd liked how Brody seemed to take care of his sister.

"Come around back," Brody said before grabbing his bottle of soda and leading the way out the back door.

"I tried to respect her space. I care about Erin. I love her. But she's holding herself back and I hate it. She won't tell me about what happened in LA."

Brody stiffened.

"Yeah. Two weeks ago she told me I could guess the details. She wouldn't give me specifics. I've tried to be patient. I tried to let her come to me with the story, but I looked. Okay? I looked and now I know. And I'm sick at heart for her. More sick at heart than I was before I knew the details."

"You love her? What's different now than before? When you broke her fucking heart? You tell me now, and I better like your answer." Brody crossed his arms over his chest, his muscles bulging. Todd and Brody were roughly the same size, but Brody had the righteous indignation of a big brother to a little sister done wrong. Those odds were *not* in Todd's favor.

"I was young before. Stupid. And so very wrong. Not ready to face what I was, who I was. She was smart, knew it and didn't want to apologize for what she liked." He shrugged, really not wanting to be much more specific than that. "But I am not that confused boy anymore. I know what I want, I like it, and I'm pretty sure I've been in love with Erin all these years anyway. I can stand here and shout that I love her. I want to marry her. I want to have kids with her, but I know it may not ever happen because of Adele and I am okay with that. I want Erin and I want her to be happy and safe."

Brody remained silent for a while before speaking again. "She's broken inside. Not as much as she thinks, but what happened to her, the months of terror at being stalked, the kidnapping, the attack, Adele's death, her near death, the trial, god, it was unbelievable. She drank too much just to get through the day, took pills. She was a mess and we were too. She was just . . . *not there*. But we managed to get through the trial. Thank god that fucking bastard got twenty-seven years, although he should have been killed for what he did to my sister and niece. Her relationship with Jeremy was over, that was obvious. We packed her clothes, her guitars, her awards and stuff and we brought it back here. She's slowly been coming back to life ever since."

Brody began to pace, lighting a cigarette as he did.

"Don't tell Erin I was smoking or she'll kick my ass. I'm supposed to be quitting." Brody flashed a guilty smile. "I haven't seen her so happy in years. Because I fucked up my share of times with a woman I love, I'm going to cut you a break right now. You tell me, one last time, are you in this? For real? I need to know, because if you're not, if you have any doubts, just get out now."

"Where is she? Why isn't she here today?" Todd finally remembered to ask. Jesus, his fucking adrenaline was riding him now.

"Are you in or not?"

"Yes! I'd die for your sister. I love her. I've said that to one woman in my whole life and that's Erin. It's the only time, other than my mother of course, that I've meant it enough to say it." He hadn't even said it to Sheila, he'd just done the *you too* thing. Another reason she'd left and another reason he hadn't blamed her.

"She's not here. She won't be here tomorrow either. Probably not Friday. Tomorrow is June sixteenth, the anniversary of the attack, of

Adele's death. She goes into lockdown every year for a few days. She wasn't too bad yesterday. I'd begun to think it wasn't going to be bad this year, but Ella, her assistant manager, got a call saying Erin wouldn't be in for a few days and could she just open for two hours in the mornings for the coffee rush."

"Why are you here? Is Adrian with her?"

"She's alone. Holed up in her fortress of solitude. I can get into the building, even past the doorman who knows me. But I can't get in her front door. I tried." Brody held up a key ring attached to the chain at his waist. "It didn't work. She gets new locks a few times a year." He exhaled, pinching off the end of his cigarette and tossing it into the trash. "Adrian tried, same deal. We went to the doorman, but he shined us on."

Todd's heart raced at the thought of her all alone and suffering. "I'm going over there. My business partner is quite handy with picking locks. Is she all right? Should we just call 911? She wouldn't harm herself?"

"No. She knows the pain of losing someone; she wouldn't do it to me and Adrian. But she'll be in rough shape I'd wager."

"I'm going over there right now. Thank you."

"Call me." Brody handed him a business card. "So Aid and I know she's all right."

Todd nodded as he jogged back through the shop toward his car. On the way, he called Ben and told him to get his ass down to her building ASAP.

14

"Okay, here's the deal, I know the codes to get upstairs and also her internal code on her alarm." Ben held up a hand. "Don't ask how. I just do."

Ben punched some numbers into the pad on the elevator from the lobby and they rose skyward.

"I brought you an overnight bag." Ben held it out. "I had Cope shove your toothbrush and some underwear in it. A few T-shirts. Don't get mushy. We just figured you might need them."

Todd smiled his thanks. When they exited the elevator, they went to Erin's door and knocked. She didn't answer. There was no noise from inside and Todd shielded Ben with his body as his friend made very quick work of all three locks.

"Get her to put a chain lock on, will you? I like her, she sucks at cards, but she never gives up. Strong." Ben opened the door and stepped inside, where he punched numbers into an internal keypad stationed behind a pretty wall panel. "Go. I'm out of here. Call me if you need anything."

Todd took a deep breath, sent a thank-you to Ben and shut and locked the door behind himself.

"Erin?" he called out. He tried to calm himself enough to walk slowly, but his fear, the fear born of walking into more than one crime scene and finding disaster, made him jog into the main room.

A mess. Not her normal level of artsy-fartsy chaos—scribbled song lyrics, colorful batik-patterned scarves, bags, books and bass and acoustic guitars. No, this was disquieting. Takeout containers left on countertops. Empty soda cans. Clearly her descent had been happening for several days. Even as she'd been working and smiling to his face, she'd been aching inside.

He walked through and a stack of photographs caught his eye. He picked them up and saw Erin with short, inky-black hair, holding a chubby, cake-faced one-year-old. The baby had her mother's eyes, and mischief as well as frosting on her face. Erin in the picture was the Erin he'd met ten years ago. Fearless because she held the best thing on Earth.

"Erin? Goddammit, where are you?" He put the picture down carefully and stepped over a pile of stuff to head back down the hall where the bedroom was.

Her office was empty, but thank god it wasn't trashed.

He heard something in her room and rushed inside. She was there, lying on her bed. An empty vodka bottle lay on the floor to one side.

Her shoulders shook and he moved to her, his heart breaking to see her like this.

"Erin? Honey, it's Todd," he said softly as he moved to her. He'd yelled her name loud enough that she should have heard him, shouldn't be startled or scared by his appearance. But she had to be on edge, more so than usual, so he took it slow even though he wanted to dive on her and hold her now that he saw she was all right.

She burrowed her face deeper into the covers, still crying. "G'way," she slurred quite loudly, around a snuffle.

"We both know that's not going to happen." He moved to the bed and got on it next to her. "Honey, let me in. I want to be here for you."

"I canhanle it," she stammered, her head still beneath the blanket.

He pulled the blanket back and pushed the hair from her sweaty face. She was pale, clammy and three-sheets-to-the-wind drunk.

"Bright!" she squealed and dove back under the covers.

He got up and pulled her curtains closed. The room closed in, dark and cool. "Okay, let's get you cleaned up. It's dark now. I'm going to turn on your shower to get the water heated up."

"G'way!"

He laughed, even as he hurt for her. "Told you, that's not going to happen."

He cleaned up her bathroom enough to get to the bathtub and tossed the towels and dirty clothes into a washing machine he'd seen on an earlier visit.

Divesting himself of his clothes, he moved back to the bed and grabbed a foot and pulled her free of her cocoon again. "For a pretty thing, you do *not* smell good," he muttered as he peeled her tiny tank top off before picking her up carefully.

"Gonna puke."

"You'd better not, missy. That's an order."

"Canorder me."

He managed to lever her to get her panties off and took her into the shower stall with him. She sputtered and jumped from his arms to scramble out and to the toilet, where she did indeed puke.

Stepping out of the stall, he pulled her hair away from her face and let her get it all up. No doubt she'd feel better.

She curled into a ball on the floor, crying again, and he simply picked her back up and returned them both to the shower.

"It'd be a lot easier if you stood so I can get you clean," he said. "Hold on to me if you have to—hell, even if you don't. I like you holding on to me."

She sighed, but held his hips once he set her on her feet. She stood still while he lathered her hair and soaped her body, all the while trying not to think about how beautiful she looked there, even as she cried.

"Don' need you here. I'm not the grr fuh you. Can't protect anyone."

He paused at the raw grief and guilt in her voice. With a bracing breath, he rinsed the last of the soap from their bodies before getting out to towel them both dry."

"Brush your teeth, you'll feel better." He pointed her in the direction of the sink. "And then we'll talk. Where do you keep the sheets? Clean ones."

"Why?" she asked, trying to get toothpaste on her toothbrush but getting it on her hand instead.

He sighed, taking the toothbrush and paste from her to do it himself. He wiped her hand off and gave her the brush back.

"Because your bed smells like puke and vodka. Not a nice combination."

She groaned and he left the room. He looked through several drawers and found spare bedding in a closet in the hall. Quickly he stripped the bed and remade it with clean, cool sheets and blankets. While he was at it, he put a pair of boxers on. Even with her so upset, his cock responded every time she came near him.

When he'd finished, he looked up to see her standing in her bathroom doorway, staring at him, looking lost.

He went to her, gathering her to his body, and guided her into bed, snuggling down after her.

"Do you want to sleep?"

"Ever' time I close my eyes I see it."

"The day when you lost Adele?"

She flinched, but he wanted her to get it all out. She nodded. "I didn't do my job. I didn't protect her." Her slurring had cleared a bit after the shower, but tears had made her words thick.

"Do you have super powers? You had a fucking bodyguard, Erin. You had a bodyguard and you never went anywhere without him. It was Adele's well-baby visit at the pediatrician. Were you supposed to stop living altogether?"

Erin wanted so badly to just sleep and not think on it anymore. She wanted a day where the mere thought of her child didn't make her want to sink to her knees and howl.

"I see you did your homework," she said, feeling sullen, annoyed and yet comforted by his presence all at once.

"I asked you to share, you told me to use my imagination. My imagination had you dying in the street and I hated that vision, so I used the Internet instead. And *fuck*, you nearly did die in the street." His body radiated tension and for a moment she was able to focus on his distress instead of her own.

She felt a wave of something—safety, yes, that was it. Against his body like an anchor to keep her from drifting off into oblivion.

He must have sensed that, because he stroked a hand over her hair gently. "Sleep. I'm here to catch you."

When she woke up, she had a horrible headache from crying and from booze. She smelled coffee and Todd.

"Hey there," he said, nuzzling her neck and kissing her. "Feeling pretty shitty? I made coffee. You'll need to eat. Then, you'll need to tell me."

She looked at him and the world shifted because she loved him, and there was no going back to not loving him. Maybe there'd never been.

"I've got to brush my teeth. I'll be out in a few minutes."

He watched her go; she felt his eyes on her, not as a weight but as a cloak, protective.

She took in her reflection in the bathroom as she brushed her hair. She wasn't twenty-two anymore, that was for sure. She'd gone past the age where she could binge drink for an entire day and a half and not look it.

Pink tufts of hair stuck up every which way from going back to sleep with it wet. She ran a brush through it and used a headband to keep it out of her eyes. He'd seen her puke; she may not have looked like a magazine ad right then, but if he'd stayed after puking, he must have been telling the truth about loving her.

She came out and he looked so good it hurt. Closing her eyes against it didn't help. He was there, in her mind's eye, his scent layered on her skin, letting her know he'd slept against her.

When she opened her eyes, he smiled and indicated for her to sit at the table. "Toast, coffee and fruit. Let's start there and see how it goes. Once you've eaten you can take something for that headache you must have."

"Why?" she asked, sitting down and sipping the coffee.

"Why do you have a headache? I'd take a guess and say hours of crying interspersed with that giant bottle of vodka I found next to your bed."

She picked up the sunglasses on the table and shoved them over her eyes, and the broken glass in her eyes seemed to stop hurting so much. "You know what I mean."

He took her hand and kissed it. "You know why."

"You love me." She said it but left a bit of question in the words.

"I do. I think, to be honest with you, that I've loved you since the first day I saw you. And I ran because I was afraid of you. Of how fearless you were in embracing who you were. It only made me cowardly by comparison. I didn't see that it simply would have given me the freedom to be as fearless." He snorted a derisive laugh. "I love you and I'm not leaving. I love that you see me, all of me, and you embrace it. I'm free to be what I am. You get me, Erin. In a way no one ever has. I love you, all of you. I want you to share with me because you trust me to protect you, to take the pain and bear part of it. Not because I can possibly know what it's like to have endured what you have. How could I? But because in telling, you lighten your load just a small bit. I'd like to . . ." He hesitated. "I'd like to hear about Adele. I saw the pictures you left out. She was beautiful."

God, he knew just how to get to her.

"So about a year or so after we got to LA, we got that big break everyone hopes for." She ate slowly, sipping her coffee and the water, feeling her body respond. "Anyway, it was big right out of the gate. Our first CD just blew up. We lived in the worst little shithole apartment in Hollywood. Junkies in the alleys, hookers turning tricks in the scraggly bushes outside. And I was never afraid. That's how stupid I was. Anyway. We went on tour. We stayed on tour for nearly two years except for the time when we were in the studio making the second CD, which also hit big. In the midst of this, Jeremy, our manager, and I, started seeing each other. Secretly at first but then I got pregnant. It was a surprise, but not one I was regretful of.

"We bought a house near Griffith Park. Big. My god. He wanted to marry me, but I didn't think I was ready. I liked Jeremy, I loved him even, but not in that way I thought you should love someone you married." She shook her head and looked at Todd, thankful for the sunglasses.

"It was good. Fame, so much money. They let us have a lot of freedom in the studio. Adele came and it was like a dream. And then the first letters began to arrive. It seems that along with the money and the house, I'd acquired a stalker. And as Adrian pointed out, I never did anything halfway, so my stalker wasn't just *sort* of crazy, he was fully homicidal. We got guard dogs and they ended up being shot. Other dead animals were mailed to me, left outside the studio. It kept escalating. And now I had real fear because I had something precious to lose."

She'd thought she was out of tears, but no. Todd handed her some tissues and she took the sunglasses off to use them.

"The label got a bodyguard for me. Two actually, and they worked on twelve-hour shifts. The cops were on it; they did really truly try to find him. And it sort of died down. The letters stopped, the phone calls stopped. But I still kept a guard with me at all times.

"On that day, yes, Adele had her two-year well-baby visit and, damn it, I wanted her to have as normal a life as possible, so we headed out in this ridiculous SUV Jeremy insisted on."

Her hands had begun to shake, so she put her coffee down. Instead, Todd reached across to take them in his hands.

Erin took a deep breath and continued. "So about three miles from the doctor's office, there was an accident at a stoplight. Our car was hit, but two others were too. John—that was our guard— saw the lady in the car in front of us in the intersection. She was hurt really badly; you could see it. I told him to go and help. I called 911 on my cell, and I guess that's what enabled them to find us because the phone had a satellite chip in it. Suddenly someone jumped in the car and drove off. It took all of like forty seconds. I can't even remember it all at this point. It's all feelings. Terror.

"The cell phone fell and slid back under the seats. He drove so fast. I tried to get around the seats to Adele. She was screaming." Erin still saw that face, Adele's eyes wide, scared, her cries. "He— Charles Cabot, my stalker—hit me on the side of the head with something. I don't know what it was, but they think it might have been John's coffee mug, this big porcelain thing he carried around with him everywhere. I knew I had to stay conscious, but I saw stars and blood kept getting in my eyes. I remembered what the self-defense people said about not letting a kidnapper take you, no matter what. Adele was in her car seat. I didn't know what to do, but doing nothing was wrong, so I kicked him. I levered up and kicked him in the head, and we ended up on the sidewalk. The SUV was already damaged, and he couldn't get it restarted.

"I'd managed to get over the seat into the back with Adele. I put myself between them. He jumped over, on me. He kept hitting me and kicking me and"—she burst into full sobs—"he pulled her from her car seat and dragged us both into the lobby of this building we'd essentially crashed into. People had scrambled. I heard sirens, but he kept hitting me and then he shot me. He shot me and I begged him to let Adele go. I told him I'd go with him anywhere. On my knees, slipping in blood, begging him, and he still held her. He shot me again in the back as I slipped and fell forward. I couldn't breathe. I was failing her; she needed me. I heard sirens and I prayed and prayed that they'd save her. He ran from the building, holding her and shooting. I crawled; people tried to help me, and I got to the doorway. I knew I was going to die. I felt it, you know? Just my hold on things was slipping, and that's when I saw him drop her. She was bleeding and I couldn't scream. I couldn't work my arms, and she died and I wasn't there. She wasn't with me. She was scared, and I wasn't there to protect her. I failed."

He fell to his knees and pulled her to him; they both cried.

Through sobs so hard she had to run to the bathroom to vomit again, she told him the rest. How her relationship with Jeremy had fallen apart because she'd distanced herself and he hadn't known how to reach her. The horror of the trial and finally moving back to Seattle and trying to start over.

And when she'd told him everything, she did feel lighter. The pain was still there. She still had a hole in her heart Adele should have filled with laughter, but it wasn't an ugly secret weighing on her heart every moment anymore.

Even if he hated her after the telling or couldn't deal with her baggage or whatever, she'd unburdened herself and she could breathe.

Todd had of course read the newspaper accounts, but hearing her tell it, watching her sob at helplessly witnessing her daughter's death as she nearly died herself—it tore him up.

"Erin, honey, I— There aren't words. I'm sorry. Tomorrow is the anniversary?"

She nodded as he helped her to sit again.

"Is she up here?"

Another nod.

"Let's go then. Tomorrow we'll take flowers and go. That is, if you'll let me go along with you."

She touched his cheek. "Okay."

"Your brothers are worried about you. I want you to know I did call Brody while you were sleeping. Would you call them now? So they can hear from you that you're all right? Or as all right as you can be anyway?"

She blinked. "You did? You spoke to Brody?"

"I'm sorry if you think it's interfering but . . ."

"No, it's not that. I—well, thank you. It means a lot to me that you'd call him." She briefly put her head on his shoulder before picking the phone up.

While she spoke to her brothers, he cleaned her kitchen and changed over the clothes from the washer to the dryer. Earlier, he'd watched her sleep and then gotten up to call Brody. While he was up, he'd cleaned up the clutter and done her laundry, before setting her coffeepot for some hours later. The circumstances were not so sexy, but, in truth, they meant a lot. Yes, he'd had to essentially break into her place, but she'd finally turned to him and let him help.

15

Erin looked up at the chiming of the bells over the door of her café and smiled. "I wasn't expecting to see you until later tonight."

"I thought I'd come by and see if you wanted help closing up." He held up a small shopping bag. "And to bring you this. I want you to wear everything in this bag tonight."

She raised a brow but took the bag.

"No peeking yet."

"Hmpf. All right, joykiller. I'm fine, you know. I can close up without being scared. It's still daylight, Brody is next door." After placing the bag on the counter, she crossed her arms over her chest and glared at him.

He wore that grin of his and she couldn't stop her body from responding.

"Stop being so defensive. I know you can close without being afraid. I just thought you'd like the company."

"I need to do this stuff on my own. I appreciate this, I do." She softened because she knew he did it out of concern for her. Out of love. In the weeks since she'd told him the whole story about

Adele, they'd gotten much closer. "But I told you, I need to get my life back. These baby steps may not seem like a big deal to you, but they are to me. This place is concrete proof that I can have a life."

He turned and locked the door, flipping the CLOSED sign, and then was on her in two steps.

"I love you."

"I know." She hadn't told him she loved him yet, even though she knew she did. It wasn't as if she held it back to punish or reward him. She just kept trying to find the perfect time. She realized there was no perfect time. None more perfect than simple, everyday stuff. "I love you too," she said into the front of his T-shirt.

He froze and took a deep breath. She felt his lips press the top of her head before he leaned back and tipped her chin to look into her face. "You do? You're not just saying it?"

She laughed. "Yes, I do, and no, I'm not just saying it. I love you, Todd. But if you leave me, if you get hurt or dump me, I will kill you myself." She held on to his belt loops and snuggled her body into his.

"I'm not leaving you. I told you that. The sex is really good and you're a rockstar in the kitchen. Oh, and in general." He grinned.

"So go. I'll see you at your house at seven. I suppose Ben and Cope will be there too?"

"Not Cope, but Ben. Does that bother you? He likes you. He likes to hang out with us, but he won't stay super late. Now that Cope is seeing this new woman, I think Ben is sort of feeling odd man out."

She did like Ben, a lot. Since he was around so often, she'd become friends with him as well as his brother. They clicked in a way she didn't with most other people. He often cooked with her or hung around outside when she worked in Todd's garden. She had the sense that he stayed out there if Todd wasn't around, simply to make her feel safe. Which made her feel exactly that. He shared her intense love of music. She liked his easygoing manner, she liked his sense of humor and he'd taken on the gargantuan task of trying to teach her to play cards. She sucked at cards and most people just considered her a lost cause, but he kept at it and never lost patience with her.

He and Todd were close, really close, and they brought her into that bond they shared. There was this *something* between them sometimes. Nothing either would act on, but sometimes it felt like it was a relationship of the three of them because he was there so often and they'd all assumed such an intimate and close friendship. Todd never seemed bothered or uncomfortable and she always kept an appropriate distance.

"It's fine. I like Ben. It's not like I can complain about spending the evening with two very fine male specimens. I'm bringing the pizza, fully loaded, so don't fill up on crap."

"Speaking of you talking like my mother, don't forget Saturday."

Saturday was Independence Day and they had plans to spend it with Todd's family. Erin was nervous as hell. But she'd spoken to his mother on the phone twice now, and Lorie Keenan seemed like an incredibly nice woman who cared a lot about her children.

"I won't. I'm even going to the hairdresser's Friday morning."

"Why? You getting a cut? I like it long." He sort of pouted, and yet he still looked hot and menacing too.

"No, silly. I'm having the pink stripped out and going back to my natural color. I can't meet your family of cops with pink hair, Todd."

"The hell you can't! You will *not* color your hair any which way unless you want to. My parents know about you. My brother and his wife are big fans I've recently come to find out. I love you and you're a free spirit. If you want pink hair, you'll have pink hair. I don't want you thinking you have to change yourself." His eyes darkened and she realized this was about more than just pink hair.

"I didn't think they'd hate me. I just didn't want to scare them or have them think I was wrong for you. I want them to like me." Which was sort of scary for her. She hadn't worried about Jeremy's parents liking her, although they had. But Todd meant too much to her, and she knew he was close to his family so that was important. Being part of them was necessary. She'd gladly go back to dark blond if it meant easing the way.

He kissed her hard. Fiercely. "No one else in the universe makes me feel so at home with who and what I am. Do you know what a gift that is? I love you. I love your tattoos and your funky hair and your artsy-fartsy clothes and attitude. I don't want you to change who you are. I *love* who you are and I want you to be comfortable with that. If I ever thought I made you feel ashamed of that, I'd hate myself."

Oh. That was so sweet. "You're going to make me cry. Stop it."

"Keep the hair?"

She nodded. "Okay."

"See you at seven. Don't wear panties."

With that little missive, he let himself out and stood there while she locked up and turned on the alarm for the front of the shop. She looked at the bag but left it there. Obeying him was hard sometimes, but he always made it worth her while.

Todd opened his door to meet her as she walked up his front steps. He took the pizza from her and noted the flush on her face. "You wearing them?"

She nodded and he chuckled. "Good."

Ben was there already, drinking a beer and watching television. His gaze went to Erin and the long expanse of leg she showed in the skirt she wore.

For some reason, it turned Todd on to see it, to see his best friend attracted to Erin and to know Erin was his. How could a man not look? She looked ridiculously sexy in what she wore. That Todd knew what she had on underneath made it all even more delicious.

"Be right back," he called out after he put the pizza down on the table. The remote fit nicely in the pocket of the cargo pants he wore, and he gave the knob a pulse of power, smiling to himself as he imagined what her face must have looked like.

When he came back around the corner, she was bent over, putting plates on the table. Nothing indecent showed, but the fine, pale expanse of upper thigh made his fingers twitch.

"You've been very busy," she said in an undertone as she moved to grab the red pepper flakes he liked so much.

"Not as busy as I'm gonna be, making your cunt nice and wet as I play with the vibrator all night long. I can't wait to watch you squirm. Like now." He turned it on, knowing the vibe was inserted deep in her cunt. With his free hand, he reached under her skirt and felt the rubber attachment that fit over her clit. The soft hum let him know it was working.

Her breath caught and her eyes cut to the doorway where Ben leaned. He probably heard and saw. Todd moved his hand away and turned off the vibration. The scent of her cunt filled his nose, made his heart beat all the harder. He wanted to fuck her right then and there.

"Dinner ready?" Ben asked in a slightly teasing tone. Yeah, he'd heard.

"Everything is ready," Erin answered as she sat and took a pull of her beer. Automatically and with her own grace, she put two slices of the pie on a plate for Todd, even shaking on the red pepper just how he liked it. "Ben? Two slices?" she asked, holding another plate. It wasn't the same as it had been for him, but she was being nice to his friend and Todd liked that. Liked that Ben and Erin got on so well.

Todd watched her, knowing she wore the weights on her nipple rings, wondering if they throbbed yet in just the right way. He toyed with the remote, watching her face flush as pleasure rolled through her cunt.

Her fingers flexed on the table's edge; her eyes went glassy. There was no way Todd would be getting up from the table any-time soon; his cock threatened to burst through his jeans.

He eased back and she blinked. Her nipples stood hard against the soft material of her shirt, and he saw the shadow of the weights hanging from the rings. He'd gone a little retail crazy at a few places online. Then he'd finally gotten out of his truck and gone inside The Crypt, a sex toy store in Capitol Hill. The name made him sigh, he didn't really envision himself as the kind of DOM who spoke in all CAPS and made his sub call him MASTER and all that stuff. He supposed his mixed feelings about what he'd come to real-ize was a very wide variety of people involved in BDSM was one of the biggest things that had kept him from really investigating without shame.

But once inside the store, he'd begun to relax. There weren't black candles and people in ball gags, although they certainly sold ball gags and enough porn to supply the entire state of Washington quite happily. The gear went from mild and silly to items that gave him pause and even a wince or two once he'd looked at them care-fully.

In the end, he'd carried out a large bag of different items and was satisfied with the realization that he wasn't a freak for liking what he liked.

Erin's thighs trembled and her nipples throbbed. She needed to come and badly. Todd had used that damned remote on her, ramp-ing her up and then pulling back over and over all through dinner.

Ben knew what was going on, watched her, slowly drinking his beer and talking with Todd. It should have embarrassed her, but instead it turned her on. Ben was incredibly hot and she'd be lying if she denied some attraction. She wondered though too about the way Ben looked at Todd sometimes. Todd never seemed to notice or comment on it. Ben oozed sexuality in a way that sometimes seemed to catch Todd in his radar. It was hot, she had to admit it, and *hello*, how could people not look at Todd and think he was gorgeous and fuckable?

"I'll be right back." She stood. She was going down the hall to get a bit of relief, damn it.

Todd looked at her as she walked by, taking her wrist as he did. "Don't do anything I wouldn't do."

Did he just tell her not to make herself come? Without specific instructions, she couldn't really read it that way and so fuck that.

She smiled at him. "I can't pee standing up."

Ben laughed, and when he looked at her, she wondered just what Ben got up to when the doors were closed and the curtains were drawn.

Todd raised a brow and stood up, weaving an arm around her waist. Without a word, he walked with her back toward the bathroom just off his bedroom.

"You were going to finger that hot little cunt and make yourself come, weren't you?" he asked once they'd gotten to his doorway. He'd left the door open and she examined his face. He knew Ben could hear. Heat flushed her face.

"Yes, I was. You can't leave me this way! My nipples are throbbing, my clit is hard, I'm so wet it's on my . . ."

He dropped to his knees, shoving her skirt up. His breath was hot on her thighs, against the slickness there.

"Your cunt is so pretty this way," he murmured, removing the harness holding the egg and the clitoral stimulator onto her body. The egg came out easily, and her inner muscles fluttered at the sensation. So good but not quite enough to come.

He licked his fingers and she groaned, leaning back against the wall next to his door.

"Hold your skirt up. I want to see all of you as I eat your pussy."

She swallowed at how much his words, how much what he *did*, turned her on.

"Widen your legs," he said, his gaze gone dark, focused on her body. She obeyed, readily.

She looked down her body, watched that caramel-toned head move to her, and then she felt it, his thumbs pulling her labia apart, the cool air against hot flesh and then the slick of his tongue sliding through her, up and around her clit.

She choked out a strangled cry, her free hand seeking the softness of his hair, cradling his head to her.

Her head moved from side to side, her hair a breath over her face as he put his mouth on her and slid his fingers up into her gate. She'd already been on the verge, but the way he'd teased her over the last hour had built like a storm inside her until it exploded and her knees nearly buckled.

He surged up her body, his mouth finding hers as he kept her pinned to the wall. Her taste still coated his lips and she groaned, trying to get closer.

"Fuck me," she said into his mouth.

"I will." He stepped back, chest heaving. "But not now."

"*Why?*" she nearly wailed.

He laughed. "Because it's my job to make you come and you tried to do my job for me." A shrug and she narrowed her eyes at him.

"This is like what? Punishment? Because you just licked my pussy until I came. The only one hurting now is you." She motioned toward his cock.

"You want my cock, don't you? You're hungry for it? You want me to pound you right here, right now, against the wall? With the door open so Ben can hear it?"

She swallowed again, not sure what to say.

"Tell me, Erin. I want you to tell me." His eyes glittered and she wanted to fall to her knees to suck him off right then and there. She wanted to worship what he'd become, who he was to her. He held her desires in his hands.

"Yes." She stepped closer to him and ran her palm up his chest, up his neck. "But I want *you*. Always you. I love you." She needed him to know the last bit about Ben wasn't anything that would displace him or even hold the slightest threat of that.

He kissed her again.

"You have no idea what you do to me," he said against her mouth. "I want to fuck you where everyone can see it. I want every man and woman in the room to know how beautiful you are. To know you're *mine*."

He ripped open the front of his jeans, his hands shaking. Hell, her knees were still rubbery from orgasm and how intense he was. But when he pulled his beautiful cock out, she couldn't help but lick her lips.

"Christ. Hold on, honey, I'm gonna fuck you right here and right now." He rolled a condom on quickly, leaving his jeans around his ankles. She tossed her leg up, wrapping it around his hip, opening herself up to him. "You're so fucking wet." He traced around her gate with the head of his cock, teasing with small thrusts and pulling out again until she whimpered.

"Please," she begged. "Fuck me."

One flex of his hips and he shoved his cock in deep, straight to his balls with a feral groan. "Pull your shirt up, I want to see those nipples and the weights."

She obeyed quickly and he groaned—hell, she groaned too. Her nipples throbbed in time with her pulse as the beads on the chain running between her breasts swayed merrily.

"Oh honey, how does it feel?" He grunted, fucking into her body furiously.

"Hot. Hard. So good. The weights are like tiny tugs on my nipples. Oh god," she wailed softly. It felt so good it nearly hurt. The wet slide of his cock deep into her over and over was an intimate lick of flesh against latex, and she knew she'd need to talk to him about testing. She needed to feel his cock, naked inside her.

She moaned and he swallowed it with his kiss.

In the mirror on the far wall she watched the muscles of his ass flex and hollow as he pushed his cock deep, watched her eyes, the eyes of a woman fucked to near mindlessness.

Her nails dug into his shoulders and he groaned.

"Wet your fingers and play with your nipples. You can take the weights off if you need to."

No need to tell her twice. In two movements the chain slid loose; the small sound of it hitting the ground was followed by his moan as she wetted her fingers in her mouth and began to tug on her nipples as he fucked her.

"Damn that's so good. So pretty. Hot. God you're so fucking hot."

Pinned to the wall like a butterfly, she received his cock over and over, loving the way he burrowed into her flesh and came out. Inside her, a fire grew. She was sated enough from his mouth on her just moments before that she was happy to feel his cock slide deep.

But he managed to find her clit with one long finger, stretched around them both, just a light touch, but it was enough as she ground down, her nipples pinched between her fingers, her breath short, desperate now to take her pleasure. His cock seemed to swell inside her until she came and then, within the maelstrom of her climax, she heard and then felt him follow.

Slowly, he lowered her to the ground and kissed her before pulling out and straightening her skirt back down her thighs.

"Be right back," he murmured.

By the time she'd readied herself he had returned to kiss her and
walk back out to the kitchen, bold as you please, where Ben waited,
a smirk on his face and a hard-on so big she worried for him.

16

"It's been a long time since I've seen you this at ease and happy," Adrian said as he sipped his cup of coffee.

"It's been a long time since I've felt it." She shrugged. "I am happy and at ease. Things are good."

"I want to talk to him."

She looked at her brother, all broody and handsome. For someone with so much privilege and luxury, he wore it well. He appreciated what he had and hadn't forgotten where he came from. After Adele died, he'd come back to Seattle with her, set up a house and a studio. He'd never made her feel guilty for leaving the band.

In a lovely bit of karmic justice, he'd remained a star, had become even bigger without the rest of them.

"Why?" She shot a look at the two girls who'd been edging closer. This was her place, a haven for Adrian and their friends. No little groupie girls would change that. They tried to ignore her. She touched Adrian's hand to shush him and then moved to the girls.

"You two have a problem?"

They blinked up at her, but she narrowed her eyes. They shoved their hands in their pockets. "We just wanted his autograph," one of them said sullenly.

"He's having a cup of coffee. Leave him alone. If you're at a show, that's when he's working. Show some manners, girls."

Muttering, they shuffled out and her regulars chuckled.

"My valiant protector," Adrian said with a wink. "Back to the subject, I have his number. I'm not asking your permission or anything. I just thought I'd let you know I was going to get in touch."

She frowned. "All right. But don't be a dick."

"He's the dick, Erin. He broke your damned heart ten years ago and I don't like that." He held a hand up to stop her from speaking. "I know and I agree, he's making up for that now. He seems a stand-up guy and all. But Brody and I are your family and we deserve to know what his intentions are."

She snorted, moving to pour a cup of coffee for a regular who'd just walked in. It was sweet, this protective thing her brothers did. Todd could handle himself, she knew that much.

"Fine. Just be nice or I'll let the girls get at you." She winked and he laughed, pushing the hair from his face.

"That's low. By the way, Jeremy called me this morning. Studio loves the new material. They want me to tour. This will be the first big one without you up there with me."

She took a deep breath. Inside her the craving to be on stage warred with the fear, the fear of the public eye and the horrors that came with it.

"Would you consider doing a few shows? We'd open and close at the Gorge. Hometown crowd. And then Madison Square Garden. That's just three shows."

She wiped the counter down just to have something to do with her hands. "How long do I have to answer?"

"First show would be next May. They'd obviously want to pimp it if I told them. But we don't have to tell them. You could just show up. Whatever. I'm not asking to boost ticket sales."

"I'd never think that. I need some time. I'll let you know by August. Is that okay?"

He took her hands, grinning. "That would be awesome. Thank you."

She shrugged. "This is our baby. I'd like to do a few shows. You know, if I can." Not a whole tour. Not ever. But a few shows, maybe.

"You may not have to call Todd after all," she said, smiling toward the doorway, where Todd had just stepped through with Ben and Cope.

Todd's gaze went right to her and he smiled. She'd had to leave early the morning after their, um, thing with Ben, and she hadn't seen him for the rest of the week around their conflicting schedules.

He approached, bold as brass, and dropped a kiss on her lips. "Hi, honey. Take pity on some guys in desperate need of caffeine?"

"You remember Adrian, right?" She indicated her brother.

Todd nodded and the two of them did that guy handshake thing and then began to talk, heads close.

"Let's see, Americano with room for you and an iced mocha for you, right?" She turned back to Ben and Cope with a smile, her hands already at work on their drinks.

Quickly, she slid a refill to Adrian, an iced latte to Todd and then finished up the drinks for Ben and Cope.

"You two want anything else? Since tomorrow is a holiday I only have soup and bread for lunch. It's good though, Indian veggie. The bread is focaccia from the bakery a few doors down."

"Yes, please." Ben paid for everyone's drinks and food and went to sit down.

Without needing to ask, she put two big bowls out for her brother and Todd on her way to take lunch to Ben and Cope.

"Let me know if you guys need anything else, okay?"

"Delicious stuff, Erin. I can't wait to see what you bring over to the party tomorrow." Cope grinned.

"I grew up in Seattle and I've never known anyone who had a boat. I'm so excited to watch the fireworks from the lake that way. Todd put in a request for this Thai noodle salad he likes so much. I'm making that and some enchiladas. Nothing fancy."

"Our families are all about the outdoors. Boating, fishing, hiking, camping. His dad and ours bought that boat. God, we were just kids." Ben pushed a chair out. "Sit with us if you can. Looks like your brother is making sure Todd's on the up-and-up."

It *was* quiet. A lot of people were on vacation, and the café closed early that day. She sat, pleased they liked her enough to ask.

She relaxed, catching Adrian laughing at something Todd said. Erin was glad they liked each other, really glad Ben and Cope liked her. Todd's people liking her was very important.

Brody pounded on the wall as he sometimes did when he needed some caffeine but was too busy to run over. She stood. "My other brother," she said by way of explanation. "Cope knows him. Anyway, I need to run something over there. Be right back."

Todd and Adrian were still speaking quietly when she made a leaf pattern on Brody's latte foam.

"Adrian, I'll be right back. Keep an eye out, please?"

He looked up and nodded before going back to his conversation.

Brody gave a satisfied sigh when she stepped through to the shop. The hum of the tattoo guns and the smell of ink and the shop in general greeted her. Brody had opened this shop nearly fifteen years before and she'd spent a lot of time there. It was a place she felt totally comfortable in.

"You're the best little sister I've ever had," he said as she handed him the drink.

"Mmm hmm. Adrian is interrogating Todd. How come you're not being bad cop?"

"I had my bad cop moment with him already. I'm good. Aid wanted to see for himself. Todd's a punk if he can't handle it. But I doubt he'll have a problem. He seems to love you, and as long as he doesn't revert, things are copacetic."

"Good. I brought you soup too." She handed over a container with the soup and some bread as well.

The guy on the table looked up at her and then to Brody. "Jeez, how come *my* sister doesn't do stuff like that?"

"Yeah, well, does your sister call you while you're out on dates and ask you to bring home feminine hygiene products?"

"Oh god, let it go! I was fourteen. I'm leaving now, Brody." She waved over her shoulder as he laughed at the telling of that old story.

Still smiling, she'd just walked through, back into the café, when a loud cracking sound came from somewhere. Panic ate her insides and she fell to the floor, her hands over her head.

Todd heard what sounded like gunfire outside and stood, looking toward the front of the café and the street. Ben was on his feet already, running out the door, and Cope turned and ran toward the counter.

Adrian had jumped the counter, knocking shit everywhere, and that's when Todd saw Erin and his heart nearly stopped.

Adrian gathered her in his arms. Brody came through the door and joined them, skidding to them on his knees.

Ben ran back in. "Fucking fireworks. Everything's okay, folks," he called out to the few people in the café and then turned toward where Erin huddled.

"Shit," Cope said.

"Get back," Brody said calmly. "Crowding around her will only make it worse. Adrian, can you get people their tabs or whatever? It's closing time."

"Shhh, come on, gorgeous, it's just fireworks. You know what it's like this time of year," Ben said, dropping down to sit, looking up at Todd.

Todd reached out, touched her hair. She turned her head, tipping her chin to see him as he sat on his haunches to be at eye level and not tower over her. "Is that what you want, honey? Do you want to close up and we can go home? Have a nice quiet afternoon?"

"No!" Erin shoved at them and sat up. She shook so hard her teeth chattered, but Todd recognized the determined look in her eyes. "Help me up," she ordered Brody, who obliged, standing back after she stood.

Ben nodded at Todd with approval and though it felt odd, Todd was proud.

"I just n-need to drink something and I'll be fine. I'm not closing an hour early just because of f-fireworks."

She let Todd take her hand and walked to the coffee bar where she hopped up on a stool. He barely resisted the urge to gather her to him and comfort her, but he knew they'd both fall apart if he did. She needed normalcy, so he tried to give it to her.

"Sorry 'bout the mess," Adrian said and began to clean up. Cope joined him, and Brody saw to the last few people still inside. All friends, it appeared, because they delivered small touches and a kiss to Erin's cheek as they cleared out.

"Leave it. I'll get it in a minute," she said.

Adrian glared at her as he swept up the broken glass and wiped the coffee and soup off the floor and walls.

"I'm . . ."

"Don't you even fucking apologize for that," Brody said fiercely. "It's fine and it's over, but *you are allowed* to be upset. Do you hear me?"

Todd had liked Brody before, but he really liked the man now.

Erin nodded and gave a wan smile. "Ever the big brother."

"It's my job. Now, I was having a delish bowl of soup and my customer is probably wondering where I ran off to." Brody kissed her forehead. "You all right?"

"Yes. I will be."

"Okay. Why don't you come out with me and Raven tonight. Both of you." Brody looked to Todd. "Pool, beer, pizza. Who can say no to that?"

"Sounds good. We'll see you later then." Todd looked from Brody back to Erin, catching her smile. They needed to integrate their families into each other's life. Her brothers were everything to her; he knew that and he wanted them to understand he was there for good.

"I'm coming too," Adrian added.

"We invited?" Cope asked.

"Yeah, of course," Brody said.

"Okay then, that's settled. Now everyone go." Erin heaved herself off the stool and slowly began to clean up and put things back into place. Her color had returned and the shaking had stopped.

"Don't you have a job?" she asked Todd when he inquired after dessert.

"You're my job, honey."

She rolled her eyes but some minutes later brought them out plates with some cookies. Ben just shook his head at Todd.

"She spoils you."

Todd heard the envy there, not covetous, but he realized his friend must want that too. Who wouldn't?

"I know. It's pretty awesome."

She sang in the back as she worked.

"And she can quote Pearl Jam too. I need to tell you that if she wasn't your woman I'd steal her away." Cope shoved an entire cookie in his mouth.

"With manners like that, how could any woman resist?" Ben said. Todd laughed as he stood and went to the counter.

"We need to get going. I have a job site to visit this afternoon. I'll meet you at your place later on. You gonna be okay?" He dropped a twenty down to pay for lunch and she just looked at it before shoving it back at him.

"This is such a tiresome thing you do."

"What? Paying for service?"

She sighed. "It's some soup and bread. I love you. I like taking care of you. I have a bit of money in the bank, I think I can afford to buy you lunch."

"I find I really like hearing you tell me you love me." He kissed her fingers and dropped the twenty in the tip jar. "I love you too, and I'll see you tonight."

Erin watched him leave, nearly as much a pleasure to do as watching him come in. The man had a very fine ass.

She moved to lock up and saw Ella sitting in her car at the curb and waved her in.

Ella wiped her face and Erin realized she'd been crying.

"Hi. You closing up?" Ella said as she came inside.

"Yeah, lock the front, please. Have a seat while I clean up and tell me what's making you cry."

She wasn't close to Ella like she was to Raven, but she liked the other woman and enjoyed her company. Erin really didn't like seeing her upset.

"It's just stuff at home."

Erin wiped the counter and cleaned up the pieces to the espresso machines as she listened.

"Are you okay? Safe? Can I help at all?" Erin tried to keep her voice light. The last thing Ella needed was any more anger or upset. Erin knew Ella and her boyfriend had broken up recently. At least Erin could focus on this instead of the way she'd nearly lost her shit when someone set off a stupid firecracker outside.

"I got a protection order today."

She looked up at her friend. "Okay. That's a good first step. Do you have multiple copies of the order? Not photocopies but all originals? I want you to keep one here at work and also one at home and on you too. That way if he violates it you can show the police the order with the original signature on it. It helps." Sadly, she had a bit of experience in this area.

"Oh, good idea. And you listening helped. I'm staying with my parents right now. They just live a few doors down."

"All good things. Family support is important. We're going out for pizza and pool tonight. You interested?"

Erin bustled around, filling the dishwasher and starting it, wiping down counters while Ella mopped up.

"Thanks, Erin. But I'm going to the beach with my family for a few days."

"Oh, that's right, you have vacation. Good! Have a nice time and you've got my cell number if you want to talk. I'm your friend, you know that, right?"

Ella hugged her as they walked out together.

"I do. I'll see you in a few days. Have fun tonight." Ella waved, and when Erin turned to go to her car, Brody leaned against it.

"Are you all right?"

"I'm working on it. Every day I work on it. A year ago I would have lost my shit. Two years ago I would have had to go home for the day. Baby steps."

He hugged her and she let herself be comforted.

"Not baby steps at all. You don't give yourself enough credit. Still, I'm going to kick your boyfriend's ass at pool. You should wear a tight shirt or something to distract him."

She burst out laughing, thankful for his presence in her life, not knowing what she'd do without him.

"I'll see you later."

17

"Wow, this is some place," Erin said as they pulled into his parents' driveway a few days later. The large two-story house sat on about an acre filled with trees and all sorts of plants his mother had planted over the nearly forty years they'd lived there.

"Lots of love here," she said softly as he parked behind DJ and Renee's minivan.

He looked at it, trying to see it through the eyes of a kid who hadn't been able to run all around the large yard, climbing the trees and watching the stars from the roof, but he couldn't. It was simply his home.

He glanced at her as he pocketed his keys. She wore a pair of shorts and a sleeveless shirt that buttoned down the front. Her hair was tousled but not spiky and at that particular moment, he realized she'd played down her otherness for his family. She still had her sense of unique style—she wore it like a second skin—but for all intents and purposes, she could have been a cop's wife any day of the week instead of a woman who'd won Grammys and headlined Bonnaroo and Lollapalooza.

"Don't you dare get out." He sent her a warning look as he slid out on his side and moved to open up the door to help her from the truck. "Now then." He kissed her quickly and she blushed.

"Don't be all grabby in front of your family or I'll neuter you."

He laughed. "Spunky."

"Yeah, that's me all right. Should we leave the ice chest with the food here in the car since we're going to be driving to the boat?"

"Good idea. Ah, there's my sister Liz peeking through the front windows. My mom will be hopping around in there, so let's go before she bursts." He took her hand. "You look beautiful and they're going to love you."

"Hope so," she mumbled as he tugged her toward the door.

"Todd! There you are. Come on in and bring your lady. Your mother is about to pass out in there," Todd's dad called out as he walked around toward the porch.

"Dad, this is Erin Brown. Erin, this is my dad, Dean Keenan."

Erin smiled at his father as he took her hand in his. "It's very nice to meet you finally. Todd's spoken of you a lot. Even Cope and Ben sing your praises. You put a smile on my son's face. I like that."

"I like that too. It's good to meet you. Todd speaks of you all so much, I feel like I know you already."

"Is that you, Todd?" a voice called from inside and Todd and his father both laughed.

"Come on then, honey."

Holy moly was this nerve-wracking. His dad had a crew cut and had cop written all over him. More than Todd ever did. But his eyes had danced when he'd taken her hand and he'd been very kind to her.

Now she had to meet Todd's mother. Oy.

"Hello! Oh, you're Erin, I'm so glad to finally meet you."

No hand-holding this time. No, Lorie Keenan pulled her into a hug and kissed her cheek.

"I'm Lorie, Todd's mom. Look at you! You're every bit as pretty as Todd has told us. I saw you on a DVD, you know. Mercy, that's our oldest granddaughter, she brought it over a few weeks ago when she got home from college for the summer. Just finished her first year down at Evergreen. She may come out today. Not, of course, to be with her grandma, oh no. But you're something worth the visit apparently."

"Mom, slow it down, you're going to scare her to death."

Erin looked to the woman standing beside Lorie.

"I'm Renee, DJ's wife. The other Dean, that is. Junior." She laughed. "Mercy's my daughter and apparently you're the coolest girl rocker ever."

Erin laughed and shook Renee's hand. "I do try. It's very nice to meet you, Mrs. Keenan, Renee. Thank you for inviting me today."

"And Liz is my sister," Todd said.

"And she can say hello if you give the woman some space." Liz, looking very much like her mother, grinned. "Hi, Erin. Welcome. I hope you took a Xanax this morning. The rest of the boys are out back."

More noise as the house filled with people. Ben and Cope both gave her a hug and a kiss before DJ, Todd's oldest brother, said hello, followed by Joe, the next youngest son.

"Mom and Dad are out at the marina already," Ben said, explaining his parents' absence.

There was a hell of a lot of testosterone in the living room and Renee laughed. "I know, it's stunning, isn't it? Lorie, Liz and I are grateful for you to hopefully even out the estrogen levels around here. Now that Mercy, our oldest daughter, is off at school and Marianne, our youngest, has declared hanging out with family to be the worst thing for her social life ever, we're outnumbered big time."

They were all so normal. So happy and robust and filled with that connection you have to people who've seen you at your worst and love you despite that. Erin envied them their whole family but realized how lucky she was to have it with Adrian and Brody, despite losing their parents.

She looked at the pictures on the walls as they all swirled around, chattering, loading things into cars. She stopped at a photograph of who she figured would be Mercy or Marianne and her stomach cramped. Probably all of a year old, toddling, fat little knees, one tooth in her smile, drool on her chin.

Erin was transported to Adele's first steps. They'd been visiting Maryland, where Jeremy's parents lived. She saw her granny and wanted to be there, so she'd just walked right over. Erin had clapped, laughing and crying, and Adele simply took the cheers and clapping as her due for existing.

"That's Mercy. My goodness, to look at her now you'd barely see this little sprout." Lorie stood next to Erin and her smile turned to concern as she caught sight of Erin's face. "Are you all right?"

Erin shook her head, trying to shake the empty spot searing through her chest. "I'm sorry. Sometimes it's hard to look at baby pictures. She was a beautiful baby and Todd says she's an amazing young woman now. You should be very proud."

Lorie nodded. "We are. We're lucky in our children and grandchildren." She paused a moment. "I hope you don't mind, but Todd told us a bit. That you'd lost your baby girl. I'm deeply sorry. I hope the pictures didn't upset you."

She turned to Lorie Keenan and smiled through tears. "Thank you, Mrs. Keenan. But no, it's beautiful to see these pictures. For a long time I couldn't have pictures of Adele—that was her name—up in the house. I'd sneak into the drawers where I kept the snapshots and stare at her like a guilty secret. In the end, I gave in and put them up. I miss her but I can look at that perfect thing I had in my life for just two short years and I can be grateful."

She'd taken the pictures down for a while right when Todd had come back to town, but after she'd told him about losing Adele, they'd put them all back and she'd started to go to therapy again.

Lorie cupped Erin's cheek and smiled. "That's good to hear. Something like that would be hard to get over. Anyway, please call me Lorie. I have a feeling we'll be each other's family from now on. My son seems to have set his cap for you."

Erin blushed, relieved and touched.

"I'm the lucky one here. Your son is a keeper."

Lorie laughed then. "He is now. But not so much before he moved back here. I think you're a good influence."

"Everything okay over here?" Todd slid an arm around Erin's waist and looked into her eyes, noting the tears. His concern made her want to cry even more.

"Fine, fine. We were just talking about you." His mother winked at him and he backed off, much to Erin's relief. It was bad enough that they'd had to have a discussion about whether or not she'd be okay with the fireworks going off. She realized in the aftermath of the incident at her café that he'd be worried. But she could look at baby pictures and she could sit under the open sky and watch fireworks. She wasn't fragile. She was just a bit broken.

"Let's go then. Dad's already in the car."

"Lord Amighty, he'll start that blasted honking if we don't move it. It's a wonder the man hasn't had a stroke. He's the most impatient person I've ever met." Lorie grabbed her sweater and turned back to Erin once they were on the porch. "Do you have a sweater? It's hot as blazes now, but it'll be cold on the water tonight. I can grab something for you if you'd like."

"I've got long pants and a sweater too. Todd reminded me earlier today. But thank you."

True to Lorie's prediction, Dean hit the horn three times and she sighed. "Let's go then."

Todd kissed her, smiling, and she knew he was pleased they

seemed to all like each other. Erin knew she was relieved herself, that was for damned sure.

On the boat, Todd watched her as she laughed with his other women—his mother, sister and Renee. She was right there among them. Her laugh fit with theirs, occupied the empty spot in the spectrum.

His brother Dean, or DJ as most everyone called him, sat next to him, handing over a soda. "I like her. More importantly, Mom likes her."

Todd nodded, relieved his brother was right. If his mother hadn't liked Erin, it would have made things very difficult. She hadn't liked Sheila. It wasn't that Sheila had been a bitch or anything. But she just never fit, which was hard for her because she was family oriented and wanted them to like her, and hard for his family because they were too. But Sheila had been pretty and fragile, and the Keenans were loud and boisterous, and there just wasn't a place for Sheila in that. They hadn't been mean to her; they'd made every effort to include her and make her comfortable, but it just hadn't worked.

And here Erin was, his gorgeous little freak, fitting in like houses with his mother and family. He laughed to himself.

"She fits. Makes me happy." Todd watched Joe fall under her spell as she grabbed a soda for him from the ice chest and told him some story about something or other.

"It's been years since we've all been out here on a holiday!" His mother began to pass around plates. "All these cops, at least one of them had to work, more often more than that. This is the first year in about fifteen that we've all been together on the Fourth."

"If we were firefighters we'd never be home on the Fourth," Joe said.

"Now that Ben, Cope and Todd are in the private sector and Dad and Ben and Cope's father are retiring, the odds are better." DJ took a bite of Erin's noodle salad and nodded. "This is really good."

"Erin is a great cook in addition to being a wonderful musician. Heck, she's so good even *I* listen to her stuff." Which Todd knew was a brag, yes, but totally true. He'd never been one for much rock music or alternative stuff, but Adrian was really good and their stuff together was amazing. He had to give her props for that. Plus, damn it was sexy.

Erin blushed and sipped her soda. "Enough—gah!" She slid sunglasses over her eyes and rustled around in her bag until she pulled out some sunscreen.

Todd jumped up, giving Cope a glare because he'd started to offer too. His friend just snickered.

Todd settled on his knees before Erin, and one corner of her mouth canted up slightly. Now would not be the time to get wood. He squeezed the lotion into his palm, the summery scent filling his nose as he began to massage it into her legs.

He watched her swallow hard and part her lips to breathe. Good—she was as affected as he was.

"Wanna go swimming?"

"Dude, that water looks freakishly cold."

"'Course it is." He laughed. "You jump in, it's cold, and then you warm up because it's hot out here. That's how it works."

"I'm expecting you to roll your eyes and say, *Girls*, or something. This behavior of yours when you're around your brothers and Ben and Cope is so male, but extra cute."

"You know you want to," he taunted.

"I think you just want to see me in my bathing suit."

"You're wearing a bikini under there?" He swallowed, trying to will away the images sending all the blood in his body straight to his cock.

"Yeah. I mean, not like a thong or anything—sheesh, we're with your family and I can't carry that off—but a two-piece. You said there might be swimming and all."

"Can't carry it off, my ass. You'd look so hot." He looked and caught his mother watching them, clearly amused. "Take off your shirt so I can get sunscreen on your back and shoulders."

"That was subtle." Erin's voice was dry.

"I'm all about subtle."

"Mmm hm. My favorite quality in you." She unbuttoned her shirt and he watched her graceful, nimble fingers exposing more and more of her skin beneath.

Her bathing suit top was blue. Nothing too revealing, nothing fancy, but *hot damn* did she look good. He slathered the sunscreen on her back and shoulders and she made a sound. A sound very similar to one she made when he slid into her.

"Stop that," he said quietly.

"Sorry, it felt good."

Looking over her shoulders, he saw the press of her nipples through the material of the swimsuit.

"You're going to kill me."

"Jeez, let Cope put it on then."

"Ha! He's just as bad as I am."

She turned her head to look up at him, pulling her sunglasses down to show her eyes. "Oh no, he isn't, Todd. *No one* is as bad as you are." Her voice was quiet, low and so starkly sensual he stopped for a moment to gather his control again.

With a laugh, she tossed her sunglasses to the deck and followed Liz into the water, surfacing all wet and glistening in the sun.

"Yeow! Cold."

He peeled out of his shirt and down to his trunks and jumped in after her. Before long, pretty much everyone had joined them, laughing and swimming.

She moved through the water, sleek and graceful as he caught glimpses of her tattoos through the blue green.

He swam to her, gathering her in his arms as they treaded water. "Every time I think you can't be more beautiful, you prove me wrong." He kissed her.

"I see you're not experiencing any shrinkage," she said in a whisper, as he pressed against her.

"Not around you. Not even in this freezing water."

She pulled away, doing a lazy backstroke to the ladder, and got out of the water and back onto the boat.

Lord he got to her. Even in a situation where she was nervous that his family would like her, he still made her gooey inside.

The sun dried her off, warming her up on the outside. It was unseasonably warm for the Northwest, in the nineties easily. Her eyes were closed as she lounged, but she knew when Todd had come to lie next to her, knew it when he reached out and took her hand. Like knew like—they belonged to the other.

"I like belonging to you," she said quietly and he squeezed her hand.

"I like it too."

They ate on and off over the afternoon and into the evening. Todd's sister and Erin made margaritas, virgin and non, and they all settled in on blankets and chairs, waiting for the fireworks to start.

They played cards. Ben patiently taught Erin canasta and she laughed as she screwed it up over and over.

This had been part of Todd's life for as long as he could remember. Either they would go to the park and watch, or later, after they got the boat, they came out. It had been etched into his memories and now she was there too.

Erin, his love, snuggled into him as she sat on the ground at his feet, her body resting in the cradle of his thighs. She rested her head on his leg as he played with the tips of her hair.

He caught his mother looking at him with a grin several times. He was sure she'd already started making a quilt for new babies in her head. That thought led him to the look on Erin's face earlier at his parents' house, looking at the baby pictures on the wall. He wondered if she'd ever be able to get past what had to be such deep grief.

He'd always wanted children. With Sheila it had been the idea he liked, but he supposed deep down he'd known they wouldn't last. But he wanted them with Erin. Wanted to see her with their child in her arms, wanted to hear her sing lullabies, wanted that laughter only children can make when you blow raspberries on their bellies.

When the first colors exploded into the sky, they all settled in and watched. There was nothing like the Fourth over Lake Union. He'd been in Boston, had loved hearing the Boston Pops playing along with the fireworks show, but Sheila's family was different than his own. This was what he was made of, where he was meant to be.

He wanted Erin with him forever. Wanted her to be part of all his new memories.

18

Erin stretched, walking up the front steps to his doorway. She let herself in, knowing he'd be downstairs, most likely with Cope. It was afternoon and while she was off for the day, he still had work until six.

She dropped some food off in the fridge and then took her overnight bag into the bedroom. The place had her stamp on it, she noticed. Her clothes hung in his closet, her toiletries took up space in his bathroom. It made her smile.

It was the end of July and she needed to talk to him about the tour dates. She'd pretty much decided to do the two dates in Washington, at the Gorge. The venue was spectacular, outdoors overlooking the Columbia River. The sound was amazing and she had a sentimental attachment to the venue because it was the first hometown show they'd done back when they were Mud Bay and they had their first big CD.

She wanted Todd to work with the label on security though. Only he could make her feel totally safe in public like that again. And there was the matter of Madison Square Garden. A hella fabulous venue, prestigious, and to be honest, she knew Adrian wanted her there not just to share it with him, but because it would make for a really special show and MSG was a place where they'd always pulled out all the stops before.

But it was New York City. NYC was big and loud and chaotic. She wasn't sure she had it in her to do it. Talking it over with Todd would help her figure things out. He'd be honest with her, she knew that.

"I thought I heard someone up here."

She turned and caught sight of him in the doorway, leaning as he ate her up with his gaze.

"I was just dropping off some clean clothes and putting dinner in the fridge. I made enough for Ben and Cope, by the way." She walked straight into his arms and really came home, laying her head over his heart, listening to the reassuring beat.

He kissed the top of her head and they walked into the kitchen. "I came up for a soda. Cope's out on a call, but since you're coming over, I'm sure he'll be here. Ben's downstairs; he stopped by to drop off some stuff."

"Okay. I need to talk to you about something, but it can wait until you're done for the day."

He tipped her chin with his finger. "What is it? I've always got time for you."

She told him then. Told him about the invitation to play the shows, told him about her excitement and her fears. Told him about why she wanted to do the Washington shows and the MSG show but also why it scared her. He just listened, leaning against the kitchen counter.

"Of course I'll consult with the label about your security. I'll speak with Adrian and we can get it written into the rider for the shows at the specific venues. In fact, I'd feel far more comfortable being in charge of your personal security. We have personal security—bodyguards—we contract with, but between Ben and I, we can be your personal detail and Cope can handle the logistics."

He kissed her softly. "As for the other stuff? I'll be by your side the whole time. I'd love to see you play, be it just the two shows here or the shows here and in New York. It's up to you. I respect your decision either way."

"What do you *think*? I know you respect my decision, but I'm asking your opinion."

"I think you'll kick yourself if you don't play the MSG gig." He shrugged. "I know you, honey. I hear the way your voice changes when you talk about it. You're scared, yeah, but you're excited. Wistful. I say do it. We'll be your personal detail. We'll work with the label, get things set up. I'm sure Jeremy would want to do whatever he needed to in order to keep you safe."

She tried not to smile, but the way he said Jeremy's name was cute. "I don't love him, you know. I love you."

"Of course you do." He raised a brow. "But he has something with you that I want very much. He's lived with you; he's had a child with you. It's hard not to resent him just a bit. And I'm sure he has some swank house in Holmby Hills and shit and wears three-thousand-dollar suits."

"Benedict Canyon, actually. And yeah, it's pretty swank. He likes suits too. Flies to London twice a year to buy custom stuff. He drives a Bentley. He spends four hundred dollars to get his hair cut and he gets manicures. He's a nice man who cringed at the very idea of me wanting him to hold me down. Of me wanting the bruises from his hands holding my arms or wrists. He never bit me. He never made me feel even a shadow of what you do every time you look at me like I'm the most precious thing to ever breathe. You are everything to me, Todd. I don't care what you drive or where you live. You have horrible taste in music, but I'm willing to overlook it. Thank god I exist to cancel out your vote on Election Day." She grinned.

"I want *you* to protect me at these shows. I want *you* to"—she swallowed hard as emotion swamped her—"be with me and to have babies with me in the future. I never thought I'd want that again. I love you."

He pulled her close, his hands sliding up and down her spine.

"And you were *married*! I've seen her picture you know, at your parents' house, although I know your mom didn't like her. Your wife is gorgeous and perfect."

He snorted and set her away from him enough so that they could see each other's face. "How did you know my mom didn't like her?"

"She said, when I was there a few weeks ago, 'I have no idea what in god's name Todd was thinking when he married that girl. She had no spine, she didn't give him what he needed and she was more worried about what fork went where than whether or not she made my boy happy.' I asked her why she had the wedding photo up and she said," Erin paused to laugh, "she said she looked really good in the pictures."

"She thought Sheila did?"

Erin laughed harder. "N-no, your mother thought she, your mother, looked good in them. She said she lost ten pounds just dealing with Sheila's snotty attitude about the wedding and how much was being spent, and she was sure she'd never be that size again. She asked if I thought it would be bad form if she just cut herself out and left that part."

Todd laughed then. "What did you say?"

"I said I had scissors in my purse."

He laughed until he had to wipe away tears. "You fit with my family, you know that? And yes, Sheila is pretty, but she's my *ex-*

wife and she's now happily married to someone else. You aren't pretty, you're stunning. You make people turn and look when you walk into a room. It doesn't matter that you might have pink hair when you do it, or that you're wearing a torn T-shirt. You're magnetic and you're mine. Even if you have shitty taste in music, except for what you create, which I freely admit is amazing. Even if you are a bleeding heart liberal." He winked. "I love you too, and thank you for saying that. About babies. I want that too. I just didn't want you to hurt more. We'll take our time on that."

"I should think so! We've only been together since May."

"Pshaw. We've been together for years, Erin." His posture changed. He transformed from sweet and loving to something else. Intense sexuality washed over her just looking at him.

"Mm hmm," she managed to say as a flush built inside her.

He eyed her from head to toe, a slow, sexy perusal. "On your knees. Suck my cock right now. I want to come in your mouth."

She knew the door behind her was open. The door leading down to the office where Ben was. He'd be able to hear everything.

She sank to her knees and unbuttoned his jeans, thankful he wasn't having a client-contact day where he'd have been wearing zip-up khakis or something.

His cock readily sprang from the confines of his boxers, and she took a moment to inhale, loving the warmth of him, loving the way he felt in her hands, loving the way his body smelled.

The floor was hard beneath her knees, but for whatever reason, it only added to the experience.

"Suck me. The head first." His voice had gone rough and deep, sending a shiver down her spine.

She took him into her mouth, sucking hard against the slick of pre-come on the slit, straight to the crown and then stopped. Suck and draw, suck and draw. She licked around the crown, sucking against the ridge of sensitive flesh there, moving back up to suck the head again. His balls were hot in her palm, slowly drawing up against him the closer she brought him to coming.

"Now take me deep. I want to feel the back of your throat."

She took a steadying breath through her nose and sucked him down, back as far as she could, keeping her breath even through her nose and concentrating on staying relaxed. When she pulled back, she swallowed, to mollify her gag reflex.

In and out, over and over, the floor digging into her knees, his hands tight in her hair as he guided her mouth on him. He made low sounds, growls and moans of her name, gave her instructions on what he wanted, told her what he'd do to her later that night. All the while fucking her mouth, all while Ben was just feet away.

Could he hear them?

Erin's pussy bloomed and slickened as she knelt there, sucking Todd off in his kitchen, the late summer afternoon sun flowing over his shoulder and down her back.

"Oh, honey, yes. I'm going to blow right down that pretty little throat of yours."

His fingers tightened and he pressed deep as he came, filling her with his taste over and over until she was nearly drunk with it. Finally he pulled back and she licked across the head before tucking him back into his jeans.

Strong, big hands took her upper arms and brought her to stand as his mouth crushed over hers. She held on, reveling in the way he felt against her.

"I love you, honey," he said softly, kissing her once more, this time on her forehead.

"You'd better, buster."

"I should get back to work. You gonna be okay?"

"Yep. I'm going to make some calls. To Adrian to tell him yes about the shows, and then to Jeremy to have him start getting this all in the works. I may work for a bit; I have a song I'm trying to finish."

"I owe you one." He waggled his eyebrows at her.

"Yes you do."

He headed downstairs, where Ben just looked at him with a smirk.

"You're a right bastard for teasing me like that. Twice now I might add. I'm beginning to wonder if we're not all playing a game together in some sense."

"Teasing *you*? I guess you could look at it that way. I thought I was teasing *her* with knowing you could hear." Todd grinned.

"She seemed more than okay with it."

"Yes." While sharing in depth with Cope was fine, Todd had been initially unsure of how much Ben knew or wanted to know. He hadn't heard much about Ben's sexuality, but Erin had made a mention of Ben being kinky under the surface, and ever since, Todd had been intrigued with the idea. And then he'd been sort of uncomfortable that he'd been intrigued. He was still a work in progress he supposed.

"Too bad there's only one of her." Ben shrugged, but the air changed.

"Ah, it's like that?" Todd hoped he wasn't blushing. His buttons were being pushed in a big way. There was just one Erin, but could he live that fantasy of sharing her, of seeing her with someone else he trusted?

Ben laughed. "What? You think you're the only guy who gets off on kink? Seattle is a kinky town . . . or so I hear. Certainly seems that way when I'm out and about." He paused before continuing. "My ex Caroline and I had a triad, a relationship with another man, for nearly four years. I'm pretty sure I'm a poly kind of guy."

Todd just stared at Ben, dumbfounded. Erin had known his best friend better than he had.

"I can't believe you never said."

"That what? I'm bi and lived in a threesome? You lived in Boston and until you came back here you seemed very straightlaced about sexuality, so I didn't think it was something you'd want to know."

Todd wondered what that tug low in his gut meant, but then only felt shame that he'd not been open enough for a friend to come to. "I'm sorry, Ben. Sorry you didn't feel safe enough to come to me or to be open around me. I don't care that you're bi. I don't care that you're kinky. God knows I'm not one to judge; I get off when I bite my girlfriend and when I think about watching her have sex with other people." He shrugged. "I only care that you're happy. What happened? With Caroline, I mean."

Ben grinned. "She got a transfer to Austin and I stayed here. I loved her and Greg, our third, but we all sort of went our separate ways. It was time to end it, I suppose. As for you, you kinky bastard, who'd have guessed? If you ever . . . Well if you're ever looking for a third, let me know." Ben blushed a bit and suddenly the front of Todd's jeans seemed a lot tighter.

"Really? I mean, if she was up for it, you'd . . ." Todd sent a questioning glance at Ben.

"Would I love the chance to see Erin naked? To see her nipple rings and hear her gasp around the cock in her mouth?" Ben raised a brow in his direction. "To quote the kids these days: duh." He hesitated but then continued. "Uh, if you were interested in more, I'd be good with that, too."

A flush worked through him at the image of Ben's mouth on him.

"Okay. I'll think about it." He cleared his throat.

19

Erin had settled herself into the big overstuffed chair in a corner of the living room and was strumming the guitar, breaking to scribble something down occasionally, when the workday finished and Todd came back upstairs with Ben.

She stopped when she noticed them both smiling.

"Hey, you two." She moved to put her guitar down and Ben put a hand on her arm.

"Wait. Will you play something?"

She blushed.

"Please? I love your voice."

"I'd love that, too." Todd sat across from her and Ben joined him.

She licked her lips and pulled the guitar back to her lap, dropping her legs to the floor. "Any requests? Covers? Sometimes playing my own stuff is odd." She shrugged and Todd realized a lot of the stuff she sang on the Mud Bay CDs was about Adele and then about losing her.

Ben moved forward and touched her leg. "Yeah, I get that. How about 'Untouchable Face'? I love your cover of that one."

She smiled and started to play and Todd loved the magic she made. The song was sad but playful and her body language changed when she got to the title punch line.

When she finished, he and Ben both clapped and she laughed, putting the guitar in the case.

"Thanks. Stop now! I'm better on the bass, not singing, but I do love that one."

"You write using a guitar, though? Not a bass?" Ben asked and then looked shy. "Sorry, I don't want you to feel like I'm nosy. I just love your music."

Erin leaned out to drop a kiss on his cheek. "Nothing to apologize for. Really, I'm flattered you'd actually care."

"Good. I do care. I find the whole process fascinating." Ben stood, clearing his throat. "I'm grabbing a beer. You want one? That is, if I'm welcome for dinner. I do smell something really good."

Erin laughed and a rush of love poured through Todd for her. For Ben too. How fortunate was he to have such people in his life?

"Of course you're welcome. I always make enough for you guys too. And I'd like a beer."

Ben brought back a beer for everyone and sat back down again.

Erin took a drink and then wiped her hand off, tracing a fingertip across the strings of the guitar before picking it up. "This Gibson was a gift from Adrian after our first CD went platinum. It's very earthy, it fits me right. But Adrian is the real guitarist. I can plunk around enough to write songs though."

Ben snorted. "Puhleeze. Adrian is really talented, no doubt. But you're no slouch."

"He and I have complementary talents. Which is why working with him has always been such a joy. Don't get me wrong; we're siblings, and there have been plenty of times when our fights would clear a room." She laughed. "But in the end, we're family, we share a vision and that simply works out even if I want to punch him sometimes."

She stood, grabbing her beer. "Okay, I'm going to toss the salad for dinner. You two need to set the table. Just three, Cope's got a date." Erin laughed when they looked surprised.

"How do you know?"

"He came by the café earlier to ask my opinion on places to take her to dinner. Why do you act so surprised? It's not like he and I had a mad tryst in the four minutes I wasn't rushed off my feet today."

She began to shuffle around in the kitchen and Todd snorted. Of course Cope would seek her out to talk to her. She was his friend too, and Cope was outgoing and friendly.

"I like that he sought you out." Todd shrugged and began to put plates on the table. Ben followed up with silverware and began to ferry in food Erin handed him.

"What's this?" Todd forked up something lovely with tomatoes and ribbons of something green.

"Tomatoes I got fresh from my favorite stall at The Market earlier this week, with some fresh mozzarella, aged balsamic vinegar and basil I grow on my balcony."

"Holy crap, is this eggplant parm?" Ben mowed through his food with gusto and Erin smiled at him, clearly pleased he enjoyed it.

"My condo is air-conditioned, and I had all this fresh mozzarella and tomato. It seemed a good way to use it, and if you have a nice cool kitchen it's not too hot to bake. I made strawberry rhubarb crumble too. It's cooling."

Todd looked at her. "You're the sexiest woman to ever draw breath."

She laughed. "I also brought vanilla ice cream."

He sighed happily and continued to eat.

After dinner they retired to the TV room to watch a movie. They all collapsed onto the big couch.

Erin tried not to be aware of the building sexual tension in the air, wondered if perhaps she was just imagining it after the episode earlier when Todd ordered her to suck him off so Ben could hear.

Maybe she was projecting. Ben probably hadn't heard at all, and even if he had, there was no reason to think anything sexual was building between the three of them.

No, she was being horny and stupid.

So of course the movie Todd rented had to be one with lots of sex in it. She drank her beer and tried not to squirm too much. He hadn't yet made her come. That was it. She was tipsy and sexually frustrated. Damn that alcohol and sexual frustration!

She snuck a look at Todd, who was already looking at her quite hungrily. *Well.*

"What?"

He slid his fingers through her hair. "Just looking at you. I like to, you know, in case you hadn't noticed. Looking at you and fucking you are two of my favorite things."

She blushed. "Um."

Ben laughed and she realized how close they were all sitting. Ben's arm was hard and very warm against her side.

Something passed between Ben and Todd then; Erin *knew* it as she caught the interplay.

"So, anyone want to share with me what's going on?" She meant to sound pissed, but instead her voice came out breathy and aroused.

"Funny you should use the word *share*," Todd said as he moved closer, banding her waist with his arm. His lips hovered just barely above hers. "Because sharing is what's on my mind. What do you think about that?"

She blinked. Ben had moved so she rested, her back to his chest. His broad, muscley chest. Todd couldn't possibly mean what she thought he meant.

"What do I think about sharing what?" Her voice was breathless.

Ben laughed but didn't touch her any more than his chest to her back.

"Sharing our bed with Ben."

The breath rushed from her lungs. Cope was hot. Of the two brothers, she'd often watched his tight belly and ass more, because he was more in your face with his sexuality and attractiveness. And also, she knew it was harmless. He wasn't her type.

But Ben was something else altogether. A total package of guh-inducing looks, but he was also smart and thoughtful. He didn't say something unless it needed to be said. He was tall and imposing and had a sort of smoldering hotness she instinctively responded to. She'd developed a friendship with him, but she'd been very careful not to flirt the way she did with Cope. Because Ben *was* her type. She'd often thought, the way Todd was in Ben's presence, that the two of them played a sort of sexual game with each other without coming out and actually saying so. But fantasy was not reality. Reality had consequences.

She took a deep breath. "I think we should tread carefully here." Erin pushed Todd back and scrambled to sit on the low table so she could face them both. Christ, they were like sexy bookends.

"Why?" she asked Todd.

"I want to give you that, to share that with you and with him. I see how he looks at you."

"Would you feel more comfortable if I left?" Ben asked her.

She shook her head. "No, I think since Todd brought it up in your presence it's important to include you now." Erin looked back to Todd.

"Our relationship isn't a tourist destination, Todd. Inviting someone in takes a lovely fantasy"—she looked over Ben slowly and fanned herself—"and makes it reality. Reality is complicated. Reality has consequences you can't begin to understand until it's already happening. I love you, Todd. I'm attracted to Ben, yes. Lord, look at him, how could you not be? But are you going to be able to handle it? Seeing me with someone else?"

He nodded eagerly and she wanted to laugh.

"I know I am, and that's why it's so fucking hot. I can't explain it; it just makes me hard every time a man looks at you and wants to fuck you. I want to see you with another man eating your cunt." He blushed and she licked her lips.

"You're blushing. Just when I think you can't surprise me anymore, you blush. We can do this in ways that don't involve your best friend. We can fuck when people can hear, or even see. Like this afternoon. There are clubs, things like that."

"I don't want you to fuck a stranger. I want you to fuck someone I know and trust. I know and trust Ben. I know and trust you. If it's too much, it's okay. I understand. I just wanted to be honest with you. To share that fantasy."

"You don't know how much it makes me want to crawl up your body and impale myself on your cock right now just hearing that. Since we're discussing particulars and all, let me say I don't want to see you with another woman. I'd have to hurt someone, you too." She shrugged. "It's not fair, I know. But I don't want you with any woman but me."

"Good. I don't want any other woman but you. But I'm not talking about me being with another woman, and now that I know you don't want it, we've gotten that out of the way. But what if Ben and I . . . if we were together too?" He paused, waiting for her to speak again.

A flush bloomed over her at the idea of her man and Ben all over each other. "I can't lie and say it doesn't turn me on to imagine myself sandwiched between you and Ben. Or um, imagining you and Ben. But what does this mean? Have you been together before? Do you envision this to be a one-off or what? What do you think, Ben?"

"I haven't thought it all out down to the combination of sexual positions. To be honest, I haven't really had fantasies about men before, but I'm not ruling out a kiss or a touch. Three people naked in a bed, it's only natural that people would touch. I just want to know what you're okay with."

Erin did like that answer a lot. Showed her he wasn't just all *whee—three-way*, but was really thinking on what may happen and how to keep it okay for everyone.

"You've done this before?" Todd asked her.

She burst out laughing. "No. Why would you say that?"

"Aren't threesomes like communion to rockstars?"

She snorted. "The whole rockstar thing—that's *dude* rockstars, or so I hear. But I'm not a dude. I did suck a guy off in full view at a club in Amsterdam. That was before fame. Once I got famous I had to be very careful. And in truth, I'd only want that with someone I felt very secure with. I like being watched." Now it was her turn to blush. "I used to finger myself in the tour bus when I knew Jeremy could see me but couldn't do anything."

Todd made a desperate sound and Ben groaned.

"He didn't like it. He was always too worried. It was his job though."

"Did you finger yourself like the way you did at the tavern playing pool the other day? Feel free to finger yourself anytime you want in my line of vision. Or anyone else's vision as long as I'm with you. I don't want you unsafe. You like being watched, honey, I like watching. You're perfect. My perfect little artsy-fartsy freak."

She wasn't offended by his words; it pleased her that he felt comfortable enough to tease her, and she liked that she was an artsy-fartsy freak.

Ben cleared his throat. "You asked what I thought? I've been attracted to you since day one. I love that Todd loves you. He's my best friend, which makes me care about you all the more. But I adore you independent of that too. Todd and I have never been together like that, but I can't lie and say I don't find him attractive that way. You should know I'm bi, so I'm certainly not against a true three-way between us. But I don't think Todd is ready to jump into sucking cock."

Erin laughed and Todd rolled his eyes. "And you envision this as?"

"Let's take it one step at a time. It could be horrible." Ben laughed. Erin sincerely doubted that part. "I lived in a triad for several years. I enjoyed it. I know it's possible with a great deal of negotiation and communication. But that may not be what you two want. I think it's important to talk about it but to keep our expectations minimal for the time being. I want to fuck you, Erin. I can't lie."

She licked her lips, unable to deny how much the idea appealed to her. God how it appealed to her. "All right then."

Todd nodded. "Go in the bedroom. Take off your clothes, get on that bed and wait for me. I need to talk with Ben a bit more."

Todd turned to Ben once she'd left the room. "Did I make you uncomfortable?" Todd asked carefully as he opened another beer. "You seemed to be into it; it was pretty clear you knew what was going on."

"Uncomfortable in that my dick is so hard I can't walk. Dude, your woman is on-fire hot. I like how she confronted this head-on. Any good D/s relationship—hell, any relationship, period—won't work without communication. I just wanted to be sure she was into it and not just saying yes because you topped her into it."

Todd took a deep breath and nodded. "She and I had it before but I ran. I'm not running from what I am anymore. I'm lucky to have her, lucky she loves me."

"You are. I'm into it; I've said so. I just want to be sure this isn't something you've ordered her to do."

Desire, like a fever, heated Todd's skin. "I'd never do that. I like to dominate her. I don't want to humiliate her or treat her like a thing. It's something I'd like to give her. Something I'd like to share with you."

"And you like to watch."

He had to admit it, he supposed. Ben had been his friend for a very long time—if not to him, then to whom? "Yes. I like to watch. She likes to be watched. It works out, I guess. I don't know what this will be like when all is said and done. But I want to say up front I don't think you're a tourist in my relationship. You're my best friend." He wanted Ben to understand that.

"Is there anything you don't want? Ground rules?" Ben's eyes glittered as they shifted toward the bedroom.

"You wear a condom when you fuck her. She can suck your cock, if she wants, but you can't come in her mouth. That's mine. You can't . . . Nothing sexual if I'm not there. Maybe later, I don't know, but for now I'm not okay with it."

Ben shook his head. "Dude, I'd never do that to you. That's why I'm asking up front. What's more? That woman in there loves your ass; she'd never do that either. The rest of your rules are fine as long as I can eat that pussy. I take it you have condoms? I have a few on me if you don't."

"Eat it to your heart's content." Todd grinned. "She loves it when I go down on her. And yeah, I know she's mine. It's why I trust you enough to share."

"Can I top her too?"

Todd wanted to groan at the very idea. "Yeah. Yeah." His hands shook as he stood and held one out to Ben. "Shall we?"

Ben took the hand and stood. "Hell yes."

20

Erin had arranged herself three different ways while she waited for Todd and Ben to come in.

Nervous energy had led her to light some candles and turn off all but the lamp next to the bed. Holy crap, she was going to have sex with two men. Two beyond-hot men, and her boyfriend was the guy who had suggested it.

The day just got better and better. Or she hoped. Ben was hot and hard and totally in shape. Much more than she was. Lord. Okay, she needed to stop. She was Erin Brown, damn it!

Todd came through the door first and took her in as she knelt on the bed, her hands clasped behind her, resting at the small of her back. He stopped and took a deep breath.

"Christ." He stood over her just moments later. "You're so fucking beautiful this way. Every way really, but this . . ." He swallowed and ate her up with his gaze.

She looked at him, smiling. It had been a last-minute thing, deciding to do that, but she remembered the time in her condo when she'd knelt for him; it had done a similar thing to him then.

Ben shadowed the doorway and she moved her gaze to him. The two of them stood side by side, and butterflies settled low in her gut.

"Pierced nipples . . . gorgeous." Ben's voice had gone thick and low.

They both seemed to wait for Todd's lead, which was funny to Erin but still made sense in its own way.

"It's one of the hottest things I've ever seen," Todd said, brushing a forefinger over each of her nipples, which were beyond sensitive by that point. She moaned, arching into his touch. "Don't just stand there, Ben, my girl needs some attention." Todd spoke, but he never took his eyes from Erin.

Ben moved with a sure grace, pulling his T-shirt off as he did, and she blinked. She'd seen him on the Fourth when they all swam in the lake, and she'd seen him working around the house. She knew he was nicely built, but she'd held back from looking super closely, because he was her boyfriend's best friend and a girl just didn't do that. Free to look her fill, she did, gazing from the broad, wide chest to the flat belly and narrow hips.

Her cunt spasmed, still slick and swollen from an evening of erotic torture.

"I'm going to put my mouth and hands all over you, Erin. Is that all right with you?" Ben asked, the bed dipping as he got on. His jeans slung low on lean hips.

She nodded and Todd's hand slid up to fit around her neck, collaring but not tight. It was enough to sweep pleasure through her like a brisk fire. She gasped and so did he. Each new thing they found together was hotter than the last.

Ben's thumb traced over a hip bone and then over the tats on her belly.

"Would you like it if both Ben and I topped you?" Todd asked, his lips just barely above Erin's.

"Yes," she gasped as Ben's thumb roved lower, over her labia but not into her pussy.

"Ben, in that box there at the foot of the bed there's another red box inside."

Erin couldn't see what Ben was doing, but she knew what was in the red box and shivered in anticipation.

"Ah, very nice." Ben brought the chain and weighted beads over to her and he and Todd slid them all into place. The thin, silver chain hung attached to the weighted beads on both nipple rings, with one heavier bead in the center of the chain to unite it all. It was beautiful and erotic all at once to be adorned in such a way.

"Perfect." Todd flicked a finger over her nipple as Ben had gone back to sliding his thumb back and forth over her labia, teasingly. "Undress me." Todd stood back and she tore herself away from Ben's touch to follow.

Todd ducked to help her get his shirt off and she leaned in, breathing in the scent of his skin before licking over a nipple and sucking lightly. His hips jutted forward so she moved to the other nipple, scraping her teeth over it while she played her nails over the one she'd just left.

He made a low sound and she kissed down, her hands moving to his jeans and that beloved popping sound.

To her knees where he leaned on her while she helped him from his jeans and boxers. She pressed a kiss at his ankle and then up the sculpted muscle of his calf, at the indentation of his knee, up the hard bulk of his thigh, until she looked straight at his cock.

"Mmm, here I am again," she murmured, leaning in for a lick.

"I'm not complaining." Todd smoothed a hand over her hair a moment.

Ben had moved around to watch, and he groaned as she took Todd into her mouth. Each time she pressed forward, the chain and heavier beads on it swung, sending rolls of sensation straight from nipples to clit.

Her gaze snagged on Ben as his hands went to his waistband and slowly undid his jeans. When she caught his eyes, he looked back with a mischievous upturn of his mouth.

"Ah ah ah, keep your eyes here on me, gorgeous." Ben shoved his cargo shorts and boxer briefs down and his cock sprang free. Her heart sped at the sight of it.

He gave his cock a pump, three times in quick succession and then stepped forward. "Me too." He tapped her cheek with the head of his cock and she looked to Todd, who seemed pleased she'd checked with him before moving forward.

Two cocks sliding against each other, heads glistening. It was enough to make her want to sigh wistfully at the beauty of it.

Todd nodded and she gave his cock one last swirl of her tongue and moved to Ben's. His taste was different than Todd's, the geography of his body different. Alluring, yes. But Todd was preferable. Something about her man called to her in ways no one else ever had.

It was Todd's hand in her hair, tightening, guiding back and forth on Ben's cock. She held Todd's sac in one hand and Ben's in the other. His dick was short and fat, easily swallowed as she sucked him off. She wondered how it would feel inside her as a wave of excitement hit her, making her slightly dizzy.

Todd pulled back on her hair, stopping her. "Not yet and never in your mouth," Todd said, his voice taut with desire. If he had any jealousy over what he'd just seen, his cock sure didn't show any evidence of it. He was hard, so hard his cock tapped his belly. The head glistened with semen, the veins stood out in harsh relief against the skin. Cocks weren't pretty like breasts, but Erin loved how his looked just then. Utterly masculine and ready to provide the fucking she really craved.

She pulled back with a slight *pop*, looking up at Todd. Waiting.

"What next, do you think, Todd?" Ben asked him.

Maybe they'd start in on each other. Erin could so go for that!

"I got some restraints yesterday. I've been hoping to try them out." Todd held a hand out to her. "Stand up, honey. Lie on the bed while I get this all ready."

She obeyed, lying on her back and watching as Todd moved to the head of the bed and brought up a tie, attaching a wide cuff to it. Her body shivered.

"An under-mattress rig to attach the cuffs to. One of my favorites." Ben watched Todd work.

"I thought so." Todd took her wrist gently and stretched her arm up to where he was.

"Oh," she whispered faintly as the leather encircled the sensitive skin of her wrist. He tightened it, but the inside of the cuff was lined. The edge of the leather dug in, but not painfully, just enough to remind her she was bound.

"How's that feel?" She could hear the tension, the excitement threading Todd's voice.

"Really, really good." She managed to speak, but it was a close thing.

Ben moved to the other side of the bed and did the same with her other wrist. "I can tell, gorgeous. Your pussy smells so good my knees are rubber."

Her body arched, arms high above her head. Experimentally, she tugged, but there was very little give. Bound and entirely at Todd and Ben's mercy. Being bound like this did it for her in ways she hadn't anticipated. There was a total sort of exhibitionistic sense, being bound there, stretched and displayed to be looked at and desired. Her pussy responded, her nipples tightened and she writhed just a moment.

Todd climbed on the bed, straddling her chest, teasing her mouth with his cock. Erin rocked her hips, seeking *something*, anything. Her cunt needed sensation, needed to be filled. His cock in her mouth, even for teasing thrusts where he let her taste the head for mere seconds before pulling back, was good. But not enough.

Frustrated, she moaned, and both men laughed in that entirely male way.

"Need something?" Todd asked, his voice commanding. He meant to make her beg.

"A cock in my pussy. A mouth on it. Something." She waited a few beats, but he teased around her lips with his cock, the spice of his pre-come painting them.

Ben knelt next to Todd, their cocks touching as she licked them both. She strained to reach more, but they held back.

"Maybe we should just leave her like this and go get some more ice cream. Watch the game. She doesn't seem to want it bad enough to say please." Ben shrugged his shoulders and he and Todd moved off her.

"Please!" she burst out.

"There we go. Ben, eat her pussy. She needs to come and she did ask so very nicely." Todd's fingers nimbly removed the weighted beads from the chain between the nipple rings and then the chain itself. "Don't want to hurt you." He winked, but his eyes darkened as he turned, both of them watching Ben slide on his belly and push her thighs open.

"Such a pretty, pretty pussy. Slick and hot." Ben pushed first one finger and then two into her gate. "Tight. Todd, your cock is pretty big. Have you not been fucking this pussy enough or is she just naturally this way?"

Todd chuckled. "My cock is in there every chance I get. Her tight pussy is one of her charms." He swooped down and kissed her,

his tongue feathering her lips right as Ben's tongue burrowed
through the folds of her sex, sending bright bursts of pleasure from
mouth to pussy.

Ben ate pussy much like he did everything else—with total
commitment. He got about his job, taking it very seriously. She
strained, pulling against her cuffs to get more from him, from his
mouth.

"Do you know what it does to me to watch you here like this?"
Todd's words puffed into her mouth as he kissed her. "Arms above
your head, bound for my pleasure. Your nipples dark and hard because you wore the beads and chain I bought for you. Does Ben's
mouth feel good?"

He made her feel so beautiful. Adored. No one had ever come
close to making her feel the way Todd Keenan did. She tried to
speak but couldn't. Instead she breathed *I love you* into his mouth
and he groaned.

"Take it. This is just the first in what will be many orgasms."

She struggled to keep her eyes open as she rolled her hips into
Ben's face to get more. "Yes," she gasped.

He broke from her mouth and went to her nipples. She watched,
rapt, as he circled first one nipple and then the other with the tip of
his tongue.

Her thighs trembled and she gasped as Ben's thumb, slippery
with her honey, slid back and forth across her asshole.

He sucked her clit into his mouth as he gently pressed his
thumb into her and she arched up, pulling against the bonds holding her wrists, feeling the edge of the wide leather cuff dig into her
wrist. She needed the sharpness of that sensation to hold on as orgasm drowned her senses in pleasure.

In the background she heard the crinkle of a condom wrapper.
She struggled to get her eyes open just in time to see Todd moving

between her thighs, his cock in hand as he lined himself up and thrust into her cunt with one strong push.

Erin was relieved her ankles weren't bound, so she could wrap her legs around Todd's waist as he fucked her, giving her exactly what she wanted and needed.

He settled into a slow, deep rhythm, and she knew he'd be at it for some time, simply taking pleasure in their union for as long as he desired. With a smile she moved her gaze from his, settling it on Ben, who knelt nearby, watching the two of them with a smile of his own.

"That must be in dire need of attention." She indicated his cock.

"If you insist." He laughed, getting himself situated near enough that she could take him into her mouth without straining too hard against her cuffs.

Todd watched as her tits bounced prettily each time he pressed deep. Felt as if her cunt hugged him all too tightly, not wanting him to leave as he pulled back to retreat, just barely staying inside. He loved the little sounds she made as he did it. Sounds she made around Ben's cock as his friend slid himself in and out of her mouth.

He had to admit, he had a bit of curiosity about what it would be like to be with Ben in some way. To touch and be touched by another man, one he trusted and loved as he did Ben.

"Whatever you just did to get her to make that sound, do it again," Ben said, his voice tight. He cradled Erin's head, holding her so she could get to his cock without straining.

The sight, god, the sight of his woman there, open to his cock, sucking another man off—it churned low in Todd's gut. He'd never have imagined such a thing would get him off, never could have admitted it to himself, but the beauty of Erin was that she simply accepted him and through that, he accepted himself.

Ben's fingers tugged at Erin's nipples and the rings and she squirmed with a whimpering moan. Her inner walls fluttered around Todd, her honey overflowed, coating his balls.

With a groan of his own, Ben pulled back, holding the root of his cock tight. "Shit, I'm too close. Sweet, sweet Erin, that was marvelous."

Todd pulled out and Erin gasped, trying to hold on with her legs around his waist, pulling against the restraints. "No! Don't stop. Please."

"Ben, take over here." Todd smoothed hands down her legs and pried them open. "Shh, he's going to fuck you now. I'll be back inside you soon."

Ben rolled a condom on and quickly moved to between her thighs. "Unhook the cuffs from the straps, I want her from behind."

Right then, they were very close, Ben's breath fanned against Todd's shoulder. Tenderness for his friend washed over him, that they could share this. Silly as it sounded, he felt closer to Ben at that moment than ever before.

On impulse, Todd leaned in and brushed his lips over Ben's. It seemed right. And he didn't regret it as fire consumed him when Ben cupped the back of his neck and slid his tongue into his mouth.

The kiss was sure, aggressive and totally unlike kissing a woman, even one as confident as Erin. Ben had his own unique taste. His lips were firm against Todd's. The rasp of an unshaven chin against his own was an entirely new sensation.

They broke and Ben licked his lips. Todd's heart pounded against his rib cage. *Wow, how unexpectedly and ridiculously hot.* Erin must have agreed, because she made a sound, a deep, desperate sound as she pulled against the cuffs. He looked at her, just to check in to be sure she was still on board.

Apparently, yes. Her eyes gleamed with the light of desire and she nearly panted.

Ben petted a hand down her hip. "You all right with that, gorgeous? He tastes mighty fine. Will you share him with me?"

"Yes." Erin gasped. "It was beautiful." She meant it and Todd only loved her more for it as he quickly unhooked the cuffs, helping her turn over.

"Ass up high for him," he murmured as he reconnected the cuffs to the straps so that she was once again bound.

"This work is gorgeous," Ben said just as he slid into her pussy. "Give her a hand, Todd. She needs to come again, don't you think?"

"Mmm, yes, and she does it so beautifully too." He stretched out beside her, her face turned toward him, her gaze locked on his.

He kissed her, nipping her bottom lip, before reaching up and tracing the line of her spine, bent as she pressed back to take as much from Ben as she could.

When his fingertips brushed her clit, she moaned deep and low. He felt the rumble through her flesh. 'Round and 'round, he circled the hood, knowing she was too sensitive to want a direct touch on her clit.

Ben groaned as Todd's fingers stroked against his cock, moving to bring Erin's slick lube back up to her clit. Todd slid the pads of his fingertips along the slick line of Ben's cock as he fucked Erin. They'd been friends a long time. Touching Ben's cock didn't freak him out any more than kissing him had. It was hot, in the sum of what they were all doing together, that they could freely touch each other without worry.

Erin made that low sound Todd loved so much, a needy sort of groaning gasp, edged on a whimper, as he kept the movement around her clit steady. She'd come soon, and by the looks of Ben's face and the way his thrusts moved Erin up the bed, he wasn't too far away either.

Erin caught part of the blanket beneath her in her teeth as climax hit her so hard it felt as if her bones turned to pudding. Ben continued to plow into her cunt. She'd begun to fall back into that dreamy rhythm when the sharp nip of Todd's teeth as he bit her back, just below her shoulder, sent her into an aftershock climax. An orgasm so deep, it brought her breath in short gasps of pleasure.

She didn't know what it was about the biting, but it did something to her. Maybe it was that it was an indicator that normally controlled, well-mannered Todd Keenan was so moved by her he had to take a bite. It didn't really matter; the pain of it sent a rush of endorphins through her, much like when she got inked or when she'd been pierced. It made her drunk with him, and soon she fell into a place he'd taken her only a few times before, most recently when he'd tied her ankles to a chair in his kitchen and tied her upper arms with his belt. A soft, dreamy place where she floated on sensation and the world felt like honey, slow and sweet.

"Whatever you just did, she's gone all soft." Ben looked to Todd.

Todd grinned at his friend. "She's so sweet, I had to take a bite." And he sure as hell couldn't deny it made him want to shove Ben out of the way to put himself inside her now. He'd look at the mark tomorrow and know *he* made it. Know she allowed him to make it if for no other reason than that he wanted to. Christ, that was hot.

"Here we go," Ben said through a clenched jaw, pushing in deep. His head fell back as he gave a strangled moan.

Erin moaned, low and sexy, her eyes glassy as she smiled at Todd like she'd just woken from a nap.

Ben bent and kissed the base of her spine before getting up to take himself into the bathroom.

"You ready for me? Or do you need to rest?" Todd stroked his fingers up and down her spine and she moved into his touch like a cat.

"I want you in me," she said, her words desire-soft.

Lickety-split, he had a new condom on and he'd unmoored the

cuffs from the straps. He rolled them, bringing her astride him. "Fuck me."

She blinked and moved slowly, sensually, rising enough to reach between them and to guide him to her. As she slid down onto him, engulfing him with her body, he watched the sway of her breasts, the flex and play of her thigh muscles and the curve of her lips as she watched him watching her.

Ben returned, settling in behind her, kissing across her shoulders. She leaned back against him and rode Todd, wearing a smile just for him. The hasps on the cuffs she still wore on her wrists made a slight metallic sound as she moved, and the scent of new leather mixed with sex and heat and skin. Todd hoped the room kept that scent for a very long time. Then again, if it lost it, they could make it anew.

"What's that smile for?" she asked, humming her pleasure when Ben's fingers found her nipples.

Todd laughed. "You, honey."

"Good answer." She added the swivel he loved so much, circling her hips on each down thrust. He felt her clit, hot, swollen and wet, as she ground it against his pubic bone.

"That's it, take your pleasure." He slid a fingertip against her, letting her provide the friction and level of pressure. He was close, really close, but he wanted her to go off again at least once more before he came. "Give me one more."

She nodded and undulated, moving her hips in a slow forward-and-backward motion more than up and down. It felt so fabulous he dug the fingers he held her hip with deep into the muscle, and her breath caught, in a good way.

"You're so fucking hot," Ben whispered against the skin of her neck. "Gorgeous. Sexy. Come for us again."

Her internal muscles tightened and loosened in rolling waves, her eyes blurred, her lip caught between her teeth and she came all over Todd in a hot rush. Her nails dug into the skin of his belly just above his hips where she'd been holding on for purchase as she fucked him.

Freed now that she'd come, Todd surged up, as deep as he could, meeting her movements. Her tits bounced, delighting both Todd and Ben, and at last, with a gnash of teeth and a rush of pleasure, he shot, coming deep inside her for so long he sweated and it nearly hurt.

When he got up, she fell laughing to the mattress in a tangle with Ben.

21

Erin woke up early, as she had done for years. She snuggled back into bed for a moment, aware two men bracketed her body. They'd all had a very good time the night before and she hoped things would be okay in the light of day.

Quietly, she made her way into the bathroom and started the shower. It was Saturday for the guys, a lazier day than a weekday, but she still had the café to get to.

Her muscles ached, but in a good way. Together they'd made her come a grand total of six times. Each time she came she was sure she would not be able to again, but they'd kept at her, coaxing her body to new heights.

When she finished dressing and went into the hall, she smelled coffee and saw Ben sitting at the table. He was truly beautiful with the sun streaming in, casting him in a golden light. He wore little more than his jeans and her mouth watered just a tad.

"Morning, gorgeous. Gotta go to work?" He smiled easily.

"Yeah. Duty calls. Um, I don't know what the next-day eti-quette calls for after a three-way, but thank you. It wasn't just hot,

it was, I don't know . . . I feel closer to you now on a totally different level, and I don't just mean that sexually."

He got up and hugged her. "Good. I feel that too. I want you to
know I respect what you and Todd have. I'd never do anything to
harm that. I care about you both."

"Thank you for saying that. And I know you wouldn't. I trust
you, and not just because Todd trusts you. I'd love to stay for coffee,
but Ella—she's one of my part-timers—has had a rash of trouble
with her ex this summer and I don't want to stress her out by being
late."

He took her arm, looking very serious. "You're safe? Do you
want me to come with you?"

She smiled. "It looks like he's obeying the order. She has a protection order, fat lot of good it does really, but so far, he seems to be
heeding it. Probably because he knows Brody would kick his miserable ass if he didn't."

He relaxed a bit but eyed her through narrowed lids. "Okay
then. Please let one of us know if you need anything, all right? I'm
your friend too, right?"

Nodding, she hugged him. "You are, truly. I don't have a lot of
friends. Trust doesn't come easy for me, but I know I can trust you
and I want you to know I appreciate that."

"I'll see you soon, I'm sure." He walked her to her car and she
drove off wearing a satisfied smile.

When she arrived, she noted the stress on Ella's face but waited until after the rush to talk to her about it.

"What's got you so upset?"

"I had to call the cops last night. He tried to break in."

Erin turned to face Ella. "Are you all right?"

Ella nodded. "I am now. They came quickly and arrested him. I just hate that he won't let go. I hope that because I called he'll get it into his thick head that I'm not interested anymore and leave me alone."

Erin had her doubts about that, but she was relieved Ella had stuck to her guns and called the cops on the protection order violation.

"Would you like to stay with me for a while? My building is really safe. He can't get inside."

Ella burst into tears and hugged her. "I am so glad you're my friend. But I'm good. I won't let him chase me away. My apartment manager replaced the locks on the outer doors. I called that place you told me about, the domestic violence advocacy place. They were so nice, Erin. I'm going to go to a support group they have."

"Good for you! I hope you can meet some friends there. It seems like a good organization."

She smiled for the rest of the afternoon, thrilled Ella had taken so many really positive steps in her life. If only the asshole would finally leave her alone.

A week later, Todd strolled in at closing time looking better than any man had a right to. She smiled as she took a slow tour from head to toe and back again. "My, you're very pretty."

He laughed and gave her a kiss.

"You should have woken me before you left."

"You were sleeping so deep you were snoring. I didn't want to wake you."

"Are you free for the afternoon? Wanna go to a movie or something? I just found out I have to go back to Boston. I'm sorry, it's all the disability stuff. There's an administrative hearing I need to be at. My dad is going along; he wants to go fishing afterward. DJ and Joe are meeting us in Yellowstone. I'm taking a road trip from Boston to Montana with my father, god help me."

She laughed. "So you're taking me to a movie to assuage your guilt?" She wiped off the counter and set the dishwasher as she came back out into the main room. "I'm kidding, jeebus, don't look so guilty."

"I hate leaving you. I won't be seeing Sheila or anything."

"I should hope not." Erin laughed. "Todd, I don't suspect you of trying to cheat on me with your ex. And I like that you're going to do something with your dad and brothers. It's a good thing."

"I don't want to be gone for two weeks. But Ben will check in on you. I expect Cope will too."

"Two weeks?" She pouted. Just a little bit. "I suppose it's a good time of year and all. And I have work to do at Adrian's that I've been neglecting. I like to tend to his yard in the back."

She paused and looked at him. It was the perfect time to do something she'd wanted to do for a while now.

"When are you leaving?"

"Tuesday."

"All right then. Don't make any plans Monday night. But you and I need to have lots of sex before then."

He caught her, pulling her close. "That's not a problem. What do you have planned?"

"I'd like to get my clitoral hood pierced. You're not supposed to have sex for three days, and then there's a two-week healing period. My nipple piercings healed really fast; I have a superquick metabolism. I had to do it twice, you know. I took them out when I was nursing Adele, and they closed up, so I did it again."

His breath caught and his cock pressed against her belly insistently. "Did it feel good?"

"The nipple piercings? Yes. I like a little pain. You know that. I feel a bit more worried about the hood piercing pain-wise, but there's always ibuprofen. And you'll be gone, so there won't be any action in that area anyway. I want a vertical piercing so the ball sits right on my clit. Raven says it's amazing."

He scrubbed a hand through his hair. "Christ. If your brother wasn't next door, I'd fuck you right here." He pulled her hand, drawing her to the front door, and she grabbed her bag.

"Hang on there, speedy. You can't fuck me if you yank my arm out of the socket."

He laughed. "My place is closer and currently empty. I'll meet you there in a few."

When Erin walked through his back door he was lying in wait, grabbing her around the waist, pulling her shirt off before they'd even made it to the living room, where he promptly bent her over the couch arm.

His mouth met her shoulder, hot and wet as he laid a kiss there, then a bite. He kissed down the line of her spine, pulling her pants off as he did.

Todd pressed the pad of his middle finger over her clit. "Here? Is this where the jewelry will touch?"

She arched into his touch, undoing him completely.

"Yes. It makes me wet just thinking about it," she murmured.

He groaned. "Touch yourself for me. I want to watch." He sat back on his haunches, at eye level with her ass and pussy and watched her fingers questing between her body and the couch arm. The breath shot from him when her fingers disappeared into her pussy and came back out, glistening.

He loved to watch her masturbate. She was fearless in taking what she wanted, from him and from herself. He didn't know anyone who had as much self-assuredness as she did about sexuality.

"I want to hear you."

She turned her head to the side so her sounds weren't swallowed by the couch cushions. Low, deep moans slid from her lips, buffeted by her breath, which came shorter and shorter. Greedy thing, she made herself come in moments usually, never dragging it out.

She wriggled her perfect ass, fucking her fingers into herself while she worked at her clit with her thumb, until she gasped and he knew she was coming. He surged to his feet and pushed her hand away, guiding his cock to her and thrusting deep.

Her muscles jumped and flittered around him as orgasm still rang through her body. Once he was inside her, he wasn't going anywhere fast. No, he took his time, loving the curve of her back, the way she felt against him—soft skin, round where a woman was supposed to be.

He made love to her, touching her deep but not nearly as deep as she touched him. This wisp of a woman owned him heart and soul and he couldn't remember what his life had been like before her, except that it had been colder and lonelier.

"Give me your teeth," she whispered, thrusting herself back at him.

With a groan, his resolve to continue to fuck into her until his knees gave quickly flitted away, replaced by the need to mark the smooth, creamy skin of her back in a place only he would see.

The sound she made when he did it shot straight to his cock and he came, her skin between his teeth, knowing he had the best thing ever.

22

Erin lay relaxed and perfectly still on the piercing table. "You sure you want to be in here?"

Todd jittered like water on a skillet. She knew he was torn between sexual excitement and concern. She also knew he wouldn't leave her alone with Raven, who would do the piercing. He seemed slightly worried about Raven, but not everyone understood her. Raven couldn't be defined or caught; she simply was. She was intensely loyal and loving, but as Brody had found out, trying to love her in return was difficult if you expected anything like a commitment from her. It simply wasn't who she was or what she was capable of.

"Todd, sit down right there. Don't speak. You can look at that magazine on the counter if you like." Raven didn't look up from putting on gloves and opening up the sterile pack with the piercing kit.

Todd exhaled sharply but sat without a word. Erin barely fought back a smirk. Raven could probably give Todd a run for his money in the domination department.

"Okay, baby doll, here we go." Erin closed her eyes, breathing deeply and relaxing as much as she could. Raven's hip touched her leg briefly. Cold liquid as the spot was cleaned.

Pain, white hot, seared her for a brief moment as she breathed through it and let it pass. That was gonna throb for a few days at the very least. Then the pressure of the bead against her clit and more liquid, the crinkle of plastic going in the trash, the tools going into a biohazard collector for the autoclave tinking against each other. And when she opened her eyes, Raven grinned.

"All done. You can look now, Todd."

Raven held a mirror so Erin could see the piercing. It was shockingly pretty, silver nestled there like a pearl.

"Wow. That's beautiful." Todd put a hand on her thigh briefly, his gaze shifting from the piercing to her face. "You all right?"

"Yes. It's good." She sat slowly after Raven helped her get her panties in place and her skirt down.

"Salt water soaks will help. No sex for three days. You can skip underpants at home. Keep it dry, or as dry as you can." Raven snorted, looking at Todd. "Two to three weeks and you should be fine."

Erin took the instructions Raven handed her and walked out. The sensation was already totally different.

"Let's go to your place, okay? I'll drive you to the airport in the morning."

"You don't have to do that." But he smiled prettily and she laughed.

"I know. I want to."

He took her back to his house and made her rest on the couch. He brought her a bowl of ice cream and handed her the remote too.

"I'm all right. The ibuprofen will kick in and I'll be fine."

"It's so fucking hot I nearly came in my pants just looking at it. God, I don't want to be gone for two weeks. I'm going to explode.

You'll explode! She just said no sex for three days. What will you do without me for the rest of the time?"

Erin laughed. "Todd, I'm perfectly capable of playing with my clit without you. I know how to make myself come. I doubt I'll want to be messing around in that vicinity for a while yet though."

He groaned. "You're going to kill me."

"It's not like you don't know how to jerk off. Sheesh. Too bad Ben won't be around. You and he could, you know, take care of each other. You'd have to give me all the details and if you wanted to take pictures or film it, that would be fine too. Just sayin'."

He laughed, sitting on the floor, leaning his head back to where she was nestled. "You wouldn't care? If I was with someone else?"

She grabbed a hank of his hair and pulled, hard. He yelped. "*Someone* else? That might get you maimed for life. But Ben isn't some random someone else. He's . . . he's ours, I suppose. No, I don't have any objections to you sexing it up with Ben. Ben digs you, he's a good guy, he's hot and he respects what we have together."

Todd turned, getting to his knees, and she fed him a spoonful of ice cream. "You know, I was planning on telling you that too."

She smoothed a hand over his hair. "Thanks, but it's only two weeks. I may hang out with him, but I want the first time I have sex after the piercing to be with you. And I don't know, I don't want him to feel weird, or you to feel weird, for that matter."

"Erin, you just said it would be fine."

"*For you.* I lost you before. I don't want to take chances. It's not worth it no matter how hot he is."

He took her hand. "Honey, I would absolutely not say this if it weren't true." He paused, blowing out a breath and turning pink in the bargain. She couldn't help but turn to mush every time he blushed, it was the sweetest thing about him. "It makes me hot to think about you and Ben together. Probably because I know him. I trust him and I trust you too. But watching you with him was one of the sexiest things I've ever seen. I don't want you to think I don't love you. God, do you think I'm a freak?"

She hugged him, kissing his cheek. "Todd, you're not a freak. You have a kink or five. That's good because so do I."

"I'm not one of those dudes who wants to have his wife fuck around and humiliate him, whatever they call that."

"Cuckoldry."

"How do you know this shit?"

"Porn Wikipedia, I suppose. I don't know, I just do."

He rolled his eyes and she laughed as he continued. "Anyway, it's sort of like having you in my own personal fantasy bank. I don't know all of why it turns me on, but it does. So if you wanted to make out with him or let him feel you up or jerk him off and then, you know, call me and tell me about it? It would make my trip so much better."

"Gosh, if you insist I jerk your best friend off after I let him feel my tits . . ." She sighed dramatically. "The things you ask of me. We'll see, Todd. Of course I'd tell you; I'd never do it without you knowing. But at this point I have no plans to go jumping on Ben's cock when you're gone." Despite the fact that his confession was seriously making her piercing throb—big-time.

"Before I go . . ." He licked his lips and she turned on the couch, putting her feet down and spreading her thighs after she got rid of her panties.

"Yes?" She carefully opened up enough so that he could see the piercing; she knew that's what he was asking, because his breathing hitched and he went for the buttons on his jeans. Now he was going to kill her. "I love how you look when you have your cock in your hand," she murmured. "It's very hard to keep my piercing dry when you do that."

He played with one of his nipples as he began the slow slide up

and down of fist over cock. His gaze fastened on her pussy the entire time, even after he came with a strangled groan.

She handed him her panties. "Use those."

He hung his head. "You're a fucking lethal weapon, Erin."

She laughed and settled back on the couch.

A few days later she caught Ben walking into the café at closing
time.

"Hey there, you busy?"

"I'm just about to close up and then I'm free for the day. Got
something in mind?" She put the chairs back in place after sweep-
ing and mopping and moved to the back, singing to herself as she
did so. "I have to wipe everything down. Take a seat. Have a cookie
if you like. I made snickerdoodles and they turned out awesome, if I
do say so myself."

"Oh, snickerdoodles!" He fell on them and grabbed two,
blushed and then stopped. She laughed and waved him on.

"Eat them all if you like."

"Score. I have two tickets to the Mariners game. Wanna be my
second?"

She paused. The crowds entering and leaving the game would
be hard to endure. But she loved baseball and she wanted to hang
out with Ben. "I'd love that. Give me a few minutes and I'll be
ready."

He smiled and relaxed a bit, leaning against the arched doorway.
"Can I help?"

She loaded the dishes quickly. "Nah. I do this like breathing.
It's not a big place, we have a limited menu and I keep up as the
day passes, so it's not that much to handle." She pulled the door
down and turned the handle. "There you go. Let me mop up in here
and I'll be out in a sec."

Ten minutes later she came out with her bag.

"I may come in here every day just to listen to you sing." He kissed her quickly—nothing sexual. Not really. But it still made her warm.

"Do you like motorcycles?" He pointed to a gorgeous Harley at the curb out front. "I ordered it three months ago. It just arrived and I'm dying to take it out on the open road."

"Oh, do I! I love them. But, um, I'm not sure I'm up to a long stretch on the open road right now."

He looked concerned as she locked up. "Are you all right? What's wrong?"

"Oh, I figured Todd would have told you. I got my clitoral hood pierced five days ago. It's fine now, the initial soreness has passed, but all that vibration right on it might not be the best way to spend a few hours. Once I'm all healed up, I fully expect you to take me on a long drive though."

He gulped hard; his pupils were large, swallowing the color in his eyes. "Your clit?"

She smiled. "Not the clit itself. Most people don't do that, you can get nerve damage. But the hood. A short ride to Safeco Field would be fine, but a trip on the open road sounds like more than I'd want to experience just now."

He laughed, still flushed. "How about I meet you at your condo in half an hour then? You can get changed for the game and then we'll ride over. Just to the park. I'll take it out tomorrow."

"Are you sure?"

"Of course."

"Okay, I'll see you in a few."

The night was warm enough she knew she wouldn't need the sweater she'd brought with her. His arm rested on the seat back behind her and it wasn't predatory or creepy. Being with Ben was nice; he kept the panic away and he smelled good.

"I know this place has sushi and stuff, but it seems wrong to not eat a few hot dogs. I can't help myself." She wiped the catsup from the corner of her mouth.

He laughed. "Even if you do put catsup on yours. That's a crime against nature you know."

"Oh god, you're a purist? I like catsup on my hot dogs and I put sugar on my tomatoes too."

He squeezed her shoulders and kissed her temple. "On you? It totally works."

She winced when the game ended and the people began to file out. He stood and she hesitated. Noticing, he sat down and took her chin in his fingers.

"Are you okay?"

"I . . ." She licked her lips and swallowed. "I don't do well in crowds when I get bumped around a lot."

He simply pulled her into a hug, tucking her head beneath his. "I'm sorry, gorgeous. I didn't even think."

"It's okay. If we can just wait a few minutes I'll be fine. It never used to bother me. Before."

So they sat, his arm holding her close, and waited for the crowd to thin.

Finally, they left, holding hands until she wrapped her arms around him as they rode back to her condo.

"You want to come up? I'm not going to be able to sleep for a while."

He looked her over and nodded.

He apologized once they entered her condo. "I'm really sorry about the game. I didn't think."

She kicked her shoes off and left her sweater and bag near the door.

"Truly, I had a great time. I promise. Two years ago I couldn't even have gone to a game with that many people. I don't know why it freaks me out so much. It's not like crowds are what killed my daughter."

"God, you're amazing." He shook his head.

"Meh." She shrugged and suddenly he was very close.

"I'm going to go. Because I want to kiss you and you're clearly uncomfortable with me like this." His words hung in the air.

"It's not that I'm uncomfortable with you. I'm not. You know I'm attracted to you and I know you know Todd is beyond fine with us being together while he's away."

She'd spoken to her man every day, even as they were driving to Yellowstone. Todd hadn't said *Hey, fuck my friend* or anything; he'd just said Ben had mentioned wanting to hang out and they'd talked for a while about things. *Things.*

She swallowed, the sexual tension in the air ramping up. She wasn't going to have sex with Ben. No matter how much Todd thought it was hot. No matter how much *she* thought it was hot. She wanted Todd to be there when she was with Ben again. It felt like Ben was *theirs*—not so much hers, not so much Todd's, but theirs—and because of that, she wasn't comfortable sharing all that with him when it was just the two of them. Maybe in the future it would feel all right, but it felt like betrayal to fuck anyone else.

But a kiss was another thing and his lips were soft and warm. She looked up at him. "I can't fuck you without him here. It feels wrong. I *know* he's more than all right with it." She slid a palm up the warm, very hard wall of his chest, up to cup his neck and pull him down to her lips. "But a kiss? I want that."

His arms went around her and his lips bridged that small gap and were on hers, stealing her breath. He kissed differently than

Todd. Todd, who was bold and sure and aggressive with his kisses. Ben was still sure, but he took his time, he wasn't aggressive; instead he listened to her body, waded into the kiss like a negotiation.

He was taller than Todd, so she had to stretch up and he had to bend down, but that only made the kiss more delicious.

He broke from her lips after a long taste, chest heaving a bit. Neither of them spoke. He wasn't used to thinking so hard about being with a woman, but this wasn't just any woman, and that was double-edged. He *liked* that she didn't just jump on his cock even though Todd was fine with it. He liked that she thought carefully about what it meant to be with him, even as need beat at him to have more of her.

"Come on, let's sit outside and stargaze." She stepped back and turned some music on. Pink Floyd's *Animals*. If the woman was any more perfect he wasn't sure he could stand it.

23

Todd looked up from his phone call to catch a pair of gorgeous legs walking down the stairs into the office. He'd returned home really late the night before and had called Erin to let her know once he'd woken up. He'd considered showing up at her place, but it was three in the morning and he knew she had to be up early to open the café.

So he'd crawled into his bed, lonely for her, and slept until Ben showed up with coffee and breakfast. Todd had to admit he'd loved how her voice sounded when he called. She was clearly thrilled to hear from him, which made him glad because he was sure as hell thrilled to know he'd be seeing her that day.

He stood, still on his business call, and she ran into his arms with a happy laugh.

"Gotta go," he said, hanging up and hugging her back. "You are a sight for sore eyes, honey. I've missed you so much."

She pressed against him tighter. "I can see that."

One-handed, he swept the top of his desk clean and laid her

down, pulling her shirt open as he did. "I've missed these, most definitely. But you're not wearing a bra to work now?" He arched a brow at her and she laughed, pulling at his pants to get them open.

"It's in my bag upstairs. I took it off when I got here. Along with my panties."

He froze. "The piercing." He breathed out slowly and pushed the hem of her skirt up; she spread her thighs and he saw it, glistening, resting against her clit. "Whoo, that's . . . Can I touch it?"

"Yes, god, yes."

He pulled her to the edge of the desk and her bare feet rested on his shoulders. Spreading her open, he touched the silver barbell and she whimpered.

"How does it feel with this"—he touched the bead at the bottom of the barbell—"sliding against your clit all day?"

"Most of the time I don't really feel much, but sometimes I'll move a certain way and it feels so good and I have to go in the back and finger myself."

He closed his eyes a moment.

Behind them, Ben tromped down the stairs and pulled to a stop once he saw what was happening. "Whoops! Holy shit."

Erin burst out laughing, until Todd leaned in and fluttered his tongue over her clit and the barbell. Then she moaned low in her throat.

"Should I leave?"

"Do you want him to leave, Erin?"

"I want your mouth back where it was," she said, sounding frustrated. "And no, of course not."

Todd shrugged—"You got your answer"—and went back to licking her clit. She tasted so good. He'd missed her so much he'd vowed repeatedly over the past two weeks that he'd never be gone from her side for longer than a few days. DJ had teased him about calling her so often because he'd had to head up the trail about a mile and a half from where they'd camped to get clear enough reception. It hadn't mattered; hearing her voice made it all worth it.

The jewelry made eating her pussy a new experience. He liked playing with it, flicking it, tugging, albeit very gently. Her clit was way more sensitive it seemed, or maybe it was his being gone for two weeks, since no one but her had touched it. He knew Ben hadn't, although according to both of them they had kissed a few times.

He opened his eyes to catch Ben straightening after a kiss. His cock was out and Erin's hand was wrapped around it. Todd's cock throbbed at the sight.

Gently, he sucked her clit between his lips, careful with the piercing, and she gasped and arched her back, shoving her cunt into his face as she came fast and hard.

He stood and kissed her belly. Ben's cock was right there, glistening.

"I've got to get inside you, but not on this desk, it's too low."

Both of them helped her stand on rubbery legs. Ben tucked his cock back into his pants and they went upstairs.

Todd liked the way she looked in his house. This business of having separate places was annoying and he planned to deal with that very soon.

"Let's lock the doors so we don't get any company. I have plans for you, Erin, and they don't include having my mother pop over to say hello."

"I locked up when I came in, but apparently Ben came in behind me." Erin looked at him over her shoulder as she locked the front door again.

"I'm gonna come in behind you again too," Ben said and Todd laughed.

Once the front windows were closed—being seen was hot; being seen by his mother, not so much—Todd dropped his jeans and pulled his shirt off.

"I love it when you look at me like that. Makes me feel like a superhero."

Erin laughed and pushed him to sit on the couch and then fell to her knees, clasping her hands at the small of her back once she'd tossed her shirt aside. He loved to see her that way; it drove him crazy.

He looked at her with a happy sigh. "You're so beautiful. God, I missed you."

Ben knelt next to her.

"Kiss her," Todd said softly, and Ben slid his fingers into her hair, tipping her head to take her mouth for a kiss. Erin's hand skimmed up Todd's thigh until she found his cock, grabbing it in a firm grip, pumping it a few times.

"Ben," Erin said softly once they'd broken the kiss, "help me."

Before Todd knew it, she'd bent over his cock, licking and sucking, and Ben joined her. Far from being uncomfortable, he nearly came as two tongues slid up and down over his cock, two tongues swirled around the crown of him. Funny how a guy who'd run from himself only ten years before could be turned on by this. But he was and he'd stopped questioning it.

She cried out around his cock when Ben slapped her bared ass.

"Goddamn, do that again. I love that sound she makes when my cock is in her mouth."

Ben moved behind her, flipping her skirt up, and before too long, the sound of his fingers dipping into her pussy wafted through the air as she moaned around him.

Ben brought those fingers to Todd's mouth and then everyone moaned as he licked them clean. Todd slid his fingers through Erin's hair as Ben left the room for a moment, and then he grinned when Ben came back carrying the crop.

Positioning himself behind her again, Ben flexed his wrist and the crop cracked against her ass. She cried out, still sucking Todd's cock furiously.

"Fuck, fuck, fuck. Erin, honey, you have no idea how hot it is when you make that sound around me like that. When you keep sucking on me even when Ben is whipping your ass."

"That's submission," Ben said, watching the pink lines rise on her ass. Todd had too light a hand, but Ben had a few years on him in the flogging and whipping department, so he knew just how much pressure and speed to use to elicit all the best sounds from a woman. And this one on her hands and knees, sucking Todd's cock, was a sight for sore eyes.

So achingly beautiful as she gave herself to Todd.

Ben used the crop several more times, creating a pattern on her ass and thighs so pretty he nearly shot in his jeans.

Todd pulled her back. "Wait, I want to fuck you. Can you take me? Is it okay?"

She nodded slowly and Ben knew she was edging into subspace. He helped her up and she straddled Todd, reverse cowgirl. She arched, putting her head back on his shoulder as she slid down his cock slowly.

"Oh, I've missed this so much," Erin said, feeling his invasion right up to her scalp. The heat of the welts on her ass rubbed the couch and Todd's skin, and when she opened her eyes, she caught Ben's gaze on her, roving hungrily from nipples to face to cunt.

Erin turned her head to kiss Todd, tasting herself on his lips.

"I love you."

"I love you too." Todd nipped her lip and she leaned forward, bracing her hands on his thighs.

"Come here, Ben, and bring your cock with you."

He made a show out of unzipping his jeans and shoving them down enough to free his cock. When he got close enough, she caressed it with her cheek and lips before taking him into her mouth to the root and back.

He groaned and Todd echoed it behind her.

Sex with the two of them always came close to nearly overwhelming her. They were both so masculine and dominant it stole her breath away and as much as Ben seemed to have no problems touching Todd—and wow, had that few minutes they both worked over Todd's cock been hot—he and Todd both put nearly every bit of their focus on her. What woman wouldn't like that?

One of Todd's hands palmed her nipple and the other found her cunt, already spread from the position she held over his cock. The piercing wasn't sore; she was happy about that. But she was nice and wet and filled with good stuff like serotonin and endorphins and she was on a sex high. He kept his fingers very gentle, just the lightest possible touch over her.

Ben found a rhythm and began shallow digs into her mouth as her nails dug into Todd's thighs. Both men groaned and she felt like a freaking goddess between them.

"Come, honey. I want you to come all over my cock." Todd leaned in and spoke in her ear. "Are you okay with Ben coming in your mouth?" He'd decreed that as a no-no before and she loved that he'd come far enough to change his mind. And to make sure she'd come that far too.

She hummed her assent and Todd nipped her ear. "You're so fucking perfect." Then to Ben, "You can come."

"In her?"

Such a comical conversation! But she liked that they both seemed to navigate the situation carefully and with their eye on keeping everyone happy.

"Yes. Blow down that pretty throat." As Todd said it, he slid his palm up for emphasis—to collar it—but a shiver ran through her and, totally unexpectedly, orgasm claimed her again.

She ground herself down onto Todd, listening to his groans, knowing he was very, very close. Ben's thrusts got deeper and faster, his fingers finding her nipples, playing with the rings until he gave a long groan and came.

With a kiss to his belly, she leaned back, resting her head on Todd's shoulder as he fucked up into her body. His thighs trembled with his effort to be gentle.

"I'm not going to break," she whispered.

"I know," he said through a clenched jaw, "but I like your new piercing. I can resist the urge to slam into you for another week or so."

He ended with a long groan and pushed up and into her, deep, as he came.

Gently, he set her aside and left the room for a few moments. She leaned into Ben's side, smiling at Todd when he got back.

"Tell me about your trip. I missed you."

He kissed her and settled her skirt back around her as Ben handed her her shirt. When she was dressed again, she turned sideways, her feet in Ben's lap and her body against Todd.

"I'm never leaving you for two weeks again. It totally sucked to be gone for so long. You're staying here tonight, right?"

She nodded. "I hate sleeping alone. You've totally spoiled me."

He put his chin on the top of her head. "Good."

Todd told them about the trip and about the payout he'd be getting for the shooting, which was nice and enabled him to pay off the house. He wasn't sure what they'd be doing with it. He'd also bought a ring at the family jewelers he'd driven past every day to work back when he lived in Boston. He'd spent part of that day on the phone with Brody and Adrian, along with his parents and siblings. He had plans for his beautiful little freak.

For the moment though, he had brought her back a present that didn't require a lot of fanfare. "There's a box on top of my dresser. It's for you."

She hopped up and raced from the room.

"I think she likes presents," Ben said dryly.

"Guess I need to give them more often."

She came out moments later, ripping the pretty wrapping off. And when she flipped open the top to the box she gasped, pulling the fine chain from the velvet inside.

"I knew you had a barbell so you couldn't use a chain on your clit piercing. But this one will hang between your nipples." He stood and went to her and she unbuttoned her shirt quickly. "We can't use a collar. It doesn't feel right for us and you obviously can't wear something like that at work anyway. But this, next to your skin"—he slid it through each ring so that it hung just so—"will remind you of me all day long."

She put her arms around him and looked into his face. "I think about you all day long as it is. I think my talents as a barista have worsened since you've come back into my life. It's beautiful and I love it. I love it when you mark me."

"Let's eat some dinner and we'll mark you some more afterward."

24

She woke up as Todd stretched and turned off the alarm. Erin buried her face in Ben's chest and he drew a line up and down her spine lazily.

"I have to get moving. I need to get to the café." She sat up and Todd pulled her back down to him.

"Stay."

"I can't. Ella will be waiting for me and I don't like to be late." She kissed his belly and he groaned. "Dibs on the big shower."

When she got out, she dressed quickly, glad she had a few changes of clothing at Todd's, and headed out into the kitchen where Ben had just finished some toast.

"Morning, gorgeous." He kissed her quickly and tugged on her hair. "I like the spiky thing you've got going."

"I have a rep to uphold and all. I'll grab something at the café. Tell Todd I'll call later, all right?"

"Sure. Erin, are you all right alone there? With this asshole trying to get to Ella, I worry about you."

"Aw, thanks. But Brody is right next door and so far, the creep has kept away from the café. Probably because of all the big, burly, scary-looking inked-up guys next door who'd smash a man into a greasy spot if he hurt a woman."

Speaking of Brody, her phone rang and the icon on the screen announced it was her older brother.

"Hey, I'm on my way now," she said by way of greeting.

"I was wondering what was happening. You rarely just leave the shop closed."

"Closed? Ella's not there?" Alarm seeped into her system.

"No. She didn't call either. I checked your voice mail when I saw no one was there. I just got in myself, that's why I'm only calling now."

"It's not like her to just not show. Okay, I'll be there in five minutes."

Ben touched her arm when she hung up. "Is everything all right?"

"Ella didn't show. Didn't even leave a message, which is totally not her style. She's very responsible. I've got to go."

"Erin, let me come with you. Or at least wait for Todd to get out of the shower so he can."

She clenched and then unclenched her jaw. "I'm fine. My brother is right next door. I don't need a babysitter. I'll see you later." She was out the door before he could argue.

The darkened windows of her café filled her with dread. She'd called Ella's house only to get her machine, called her cell and got a "voice mail full" message. Ella's mom's number was inside on the café's phone book, but she knew Brody would cluck at her if she went into the café first, so she breezed into the shop, waving at the other artists.

Brody grinned at her, kissing her cheek. "I love it when you indulge me. Did you get hold of her?" He unlocked the connecting door into the café and went in first. She rolled her eyes at his back.

"I didn't. Her voice mail on her cell is full. I left a message at her place. I'm going to call her mom now."

He turned off the alarms as she bustled to get the place open.

Once she'd dealt with the three customers who'd jumped from foot to foot to get their caffeine fix, she dialed up Ella's parents' house and nearly fell over when she found out why Ella hadn't been there that morning.

She grabbed the edge of the counter and Brody was next to her in moments. "What? Damn it, Erin, what?"

"Ella is in the hospital. Her ex tried to kill her last night." She gathered her stuff. "I have to go. She's at Overlake." Erin scribbled a note saying they'd be closed for several days and taped it to the front door.

"I'm coming with you." Brody reset the alarms and pulled her back through the door into his shop.

"Shut up. I saw the appointment book when I walked in a few minutes ago, I know you're slammed. I'm fine. I mean, I feel awful for Ella, but I can visit her in the hospital. I promise," she added when she saw the worry on his face.

"Erin."

"This isn't me trying to be the spunky heroine who refuses help for no apparent reason, okay? I'm fine. It's full daylight. I go over there all the time. As you may recall, my therapist is there and you made me start going back." He rolled his eyes at her. "It'll take me like twenty minutes tops to get there. I'll be all right and she will too, thank god. I promise to call Adrian or you or Todd if I need someone."

"That's not necessary." Todd stepped into the shop. "I'm right here and able to help with whatever has you looking so upset."

She wanted to groan when she caught the look passing between Todd and Brody, but she didn't have time.

"Fine." She kissed Brody's cheek. "I'll call you later to fill you in." She looked to Todd as she walked past. "You can drive if you like."

Todd followed her, opening her door before she could do it herself.

"What the hell do you think you're doing? You're obviously in trouble and you left without getting me out of the shower? Ben had to do what you should have."

"What? All I knew when I left your place was that an employee didn't show up for work. I'm the boss, welcome to my world. That shit happens all the time. I don't need you for that, for god's sake. You want I should get you to walk me through when the toilet in the bathroom overflows too? How about when the water filters on the espresso machine need changing and no one seems to know what the fuck to do?

"Ben didn't need to run and get you out of the shower for that. In fact, I told him not to. I am not some stupid, helpless person. I ran that café for three years before you came back to Seattle, thankyouverymuch."

"Where am I going?" He kept his eyes on the road.

"Overlake."

"Who's in the hospital and why?" He clenched his jaw, holding on to the steering wheel so tight his knuckles cracked.

"Ella. I spoke with her aunt a few minutes ago. Ella's ex broke into her house last night and attacked her. Beat her badly. That fucker tried to set her on fire! Luckily a neighbor heard and called the cops. She's in stable condition. The burns are worst on one of her legs. Her aunt said Ella covered her face, so there's one small light in the darkness." She sighed and put her head against the back of the seat.

"Do the cops have him in custody?"

"Yes. I don't know much more than that though."

He pulled onto 520 and headed east across the lake to Bellevue.

"Why didn't you call me?" Hurt pooled in his gut that she hadn't turned to him.

"Because I'd just walked in! I went to work like I always do and then no one was here and I found out why. It's been a grand total of about twenty minutes, so leave me the fuck alone. I don't owe you a minute-by-minute account of my fucking day, all right? Just because I let you call the shots in bed does not mean you control me. You need to get that right now. Something bad happened to me four years ago, but that doesn't mean I'm helpless." She'd raised her voice, which she did so rarely it alarmed him a bit.

"I'm sorry. Okay? I just worry about you. Domestic violence isn't something to mess around with. These abusers get touchy about other people in their victims' lives. I love you. I can't bear to think of you getting hurt. It's not because I don't think you're capable. I'm a protective man, Erin. It's who I am. I want to be there to make your life easier in all ways."

She blew a stream of air out. "I get that, Todd. But I cannot be managed or guilted. And I do not want to be wrapped in cotton and shielded. I have a life and I want to live it. I love you, but I don't want you to take over. I won't have it."

He wanted to though. He wanted to step in and take care of her, keep her safe and shielded from any and all threats. She couldn't know how much or she'd freak. Hell, he was a protective person in general; it's why he'd become a cop to start with. But with her it was more. She was his and he protected what was his.

Still, the last thing he wanted was to annoy or agitate her any further. She was upset enough by that point. Erin was strong, more than she gave herself credit for. But abusers were batshit crazy and he had no intention of letting her get in the middle of this mess.

He took her hand. "I'm sorry. I know you're capable. I just want to take care of you. Call Ben and tell him what's going on; he's worried too."

She made that snorting sound he knew meant trouble. "Call him yourself when we get there. And tell him I don't like tattle-tales."

Erin said little else to him on the drive over.

"I'm coming in with you. I don't care how mad you are," he said as he parked. But he said it to an empty truck because she'd already gotten out and moved across the lot toward the elevators at a furious clip.

Great. He didn't know Ella's last name and he'd just wander around aimlessly if he lost sight of Erin. He rushed to catch up, putting an arm around her to keep Erin at his side. She'd be protected whether she liked it or not. They would always need to work on their relationship; that's how relationships thrived and grew. This was something he hadn't understood when he was married. But he got it now.

Erin was his to protect and he would. He'd find a way to do it so she knew he respected her and her independence, but she had to understand it would happen.

He made a snorting sound of his own.

Two hours later, Erin's hands shook as she got back into Todd's truck. As much as she hated to admit it, she was glad he was there. If he hadn't been, she'd have needed to sit in her car a good half an hour before she could have driven anywhere.

Ella had been a mess. Barely conscious from the stew of opiates keeping the pain at bay. Her face purpled and swollen from the beating she'd endured. Her feet and legs wrapped up from the burns.

Ella's mother had filled them in on all the details. The ex was in police custody. There'd be a bail hearing on Monday. The cops would be able to show the guy had violated the protection order three times in the past sixty days, and hopefully he wouldn't get bail as he awaited trial.

Ella would recover. She'd walk again and hopefully find love with a man who didn't think killing her was the only way to keep her. Erin sighed heavily. What the fuck was wrong with people?

"You okay?" Todd asked softly.

She nodded. She'd been there in that hospital. In worse shape than Ella. And she'd survived and found love and happiness she'd never imagined holding in her life ever again. But the smell of the room, of the tape holding the bandages on, of the tubing, of the antiseptic—it brought things back and for a few minutes there, the walls felt very close.

But Todd had kept his arm around her and she'd felt better bit by bit. It still hung around her like shitty weather, but it would clear. Because it wasn't her life anymore.

Still, it was her friend's life, and she knew what that dark pit felt like.

"I just . . . Thank you for being there with me."

He looked startled and then he smiled. "Honey, I wouldn't have been anywhere else. I'm glad my being with you helped. I'm going to take you home, okay? Ben will get your car and bring it to your place. Are you up to seeing him? Or me, for that matter?"

She nodded again and he touched her neck but said nothing else.

25

"She's stable now. The burns are worst on her left leg and foot, but they said she'll be fine, although they're watching for infection."

Todd listened to her speak with Brody on the phone as he made tea for her. He needed to do something with his hands because he was torn between wanting to punch something and wanting to fuck her until she thought of nothing else.

"They didn't need grafts apparently... Yeah, I thought so too... Not much, she wasn't really conscious. They had her on a pretty major opiate cocktail," Erin continued.

Todd buzzed Ben up, relieved he'd arrived. He hadn't had much time to think about what had happened the night before other than to know he'd enjoyed it. Something had shifted; there was an easy sort of acceptance that Ben was part of whatever he and Erin had. He knew Ben cared about Erin and hoped between the two of them, they could keep her calm and stop her from thinking overmuch about what had happened to her friend.

He'd called a contact at the Seattle PD and spoken to him about

the case. The guy had several assault priors and had repeatedly violated the protection order. He also had two other ex-girlfriends in
his past who'd filed for protection orders, and the bastard, not surprisingly, had a history of stalking. Todd hoped it was enough to
keep him in jail.

"I'll talk to you later. I know you're busy, and Todd is here . . .
Yes, do you really think he'd leave me alone right now?" She
laughed and he smiled as he moved to her front door. "Love you
too."

He was letting Ben in as she walked out from her bedroom into
the main room.

"Hey, gorgeous," Ben said, moving straight to her to give her a
hug. "I know you're pissed I sent Todd your way, but suck it up.
We like taking care of you so you're going to have to deal with it."

She let Ben hug her, even as she made that little snorting sound.
It made Todd smile.

Ben kissed her forehead and stood back. "Here." He dropped
keys into her hand. "All delivered. I can call Cope to get him to
pick me up, or even cab it. I'm not too far."

"Shut up and stay," Erin said to Ben, touching Todd's belly as
she passed on her way out to the balcony.

"Guess you're staying or she'll kick your ass," Todd said in an
undertone.

Ben looked at him, serious for long moments. "Are you sure?"

"Do you want to be here?"

Ben nodded. "Yes."

"So be here."

Ben took his hand. Something passed between them and Todd
sensed the immensity of it.

"She needs you. I need you. You're still my best friend. That
hasn't changed, has it?"

Ben shook his head.

"I know you love her. I know you two have a relationship. But I love you, man, and I feel very deeply for Erin. My instinct just now was to kiss her on the lips. I want to be really clear."

Todd stepped to him and put his arm around Ben's waist. "Be here with us both. Be what she needs. She'll tell you if it's too much. I'll tell you if it's too much. But I don't want you to be half a person with us. I don't know what this means, but can it hurt to just let things go wherever they're supposed to?"

The rich scent of a clove cigarette caught his senses. She stood on the balcony, her skirt swirling in the breeze, designer sunglasses on, smoking.

"There are times like right now when she looks like she stepped out of a magazine ad," Ben murmured.

"It's hot."

Ben laughed and they went to her.

"I didn't know you smoked, gorgeous," Ben said as he took her free hand, kissing it.

"In times of stress. It's an old habit." She shrugged and Todd brushed the hair from her face.

"Seems like today's gotta be a time of stress."

"Yes, but not like you think. I'm not afraid this will happen to me. I mean, there was a time at the hospital . . . the smells, the sounds . . . I've been there and it wasn't pretty. But I'm *not* there now. This isn't about what happened before. Ella is my friend! I knew this guy was bad news. I convinced her to get a protection order and I paid for an attorney to go through the process with her and to help with the divvying up of their assets. They weren't married, but they lived together. She hoped if she was more than fair, if she gave him their car and most of their belongings, he'd go away. I knew that wasn't the reason he wouldn't let go. When people stalk you, when they obsess on you, it's not about fair. It's about control. This asshole controlled her with fear and he got off on it."

"She's going to be all right." Todd hated seeing Erin upset.

"Yes, on the outside. Thank god they never had kids." She shivered, and this time it was Ben who wrapped her in his arms as he stood behind her. Todd watched, wondering why it didn't bother him.

"Babe, it shouldn't have happened. I can't imagine hurting a woman that way. I hate like hell that you were involved in even an ancillary sense but I'm glad Ella has you as a friend."

She took a drag off her cigarette and Ben brought it to his mouth and took one too. The sight took Todd's breath away, so casual and yet sexy.

A phone rang inside and she sighed, easing from Ben's arms. She brushed her mouth over Todd's on her way past and both men watched her take the call.

A few moments later she hung up and turned to them. "Christ, when it rains." She tossed her hands up in the air, frustrated. "Jeremy is in town. He's at Adrian's. I need to go over and sign some paperwork. Would you like to go too?" she asked Todd. "You might speak with him about the security stuff, so we can pretend you want to do that when you really just want to see him for yourself." Erin fumbled through her stuff, sliding shoes on and smiling as she did it.

Todd laughed.

"You too, Ben, if you'd like," she called over her shoulder as she got on her cell and began talking to Brody about something

"This is the ex? The one she had Adele with?" Ben asked quietly.

"Yeah," Todd said.

"I'd like to take his measure."

"And hear why he's here so suddenly." Todd didn't like this little drop-in visit at all.

"You mind if I come?"

Todd turned to Ben and smirked. "Not at all."

Erin stood there, the annoyance that Jeremy had shown up so randomly, after her phone call to him the day before about business stuff, flowing away. Instead, her body heated as she watched the sparks fly between Ben and Todd and had to stifle the need to go to them and lick them both from head to toe. Something had changed between the three of them, between each of them as well. She liked it even as it made her wary. She enjoyed the interplay between Ben and Todd. Always had. And now that the sexual charge had filtered to the surface, it made her nipples hard and her breath come short. Todd had accepted the connection, the more-than-friends connection, between him and Ben. She loved how he openly accepted affection, even as he'd yet to really initiate more than a kiss or a caress with Ben. When that moment came, and Erin was pretty sure it would, she'd need to back off and let it unfold.

Ben turned to her first, surprised she'd been watching, but then his smile hitched up a notch when he noted her nipples.

"Let's go then. Get this over with so we can all relax." Todd looked at them both and laughed.

She drove, not wanting to deal with having to give directions. Plus she wanted to be in control right then as so many things in her life felt so distinctly *out* of control.

She didn't know why Jeremy had just shown up in Seattle, but she knew she didn't want him showing up at her condo or the café. She'd told him about Todd in detail the last time they'd spoken, which was just the morning before. She'd mentioned Todd before, but yesterday she'd told Jeremy straight-out that they were very serious. Erin was pretty sure that's what had brought Jeremy up there. She dreaded it from stem to stern. She didn't want to hurt Jeremy and she didn't want Todd to feel anxious.

"Todd, I love you. There's no need to feel jealous over Jeremy. You know that, right?" she asked as she punched in the code on Adrian's gate and waited for it to slide open.

"I know you do, honey. But I want to see this guy face-to-face. I want to see how he looks at you."

She did understand he'd want that. It was why she'd just told him, and invited him to come along. Todd was possessive and all manly-man and she knew he'd want to meet Jeremy. Funny, she had no desire to meet Sheila, the dainty ex-wife. And Ben had put his hands all over Erin, and Todd seemed not only unfazed but totally turned on. Men were a puzzle. But Todd was hers and she liked it that way. In the end, it would be good for Jeremy to see she'd moved on so he could too.

"This is some place." They got out and Ben glanced around the house and grounds that overlooked the water beyond.

She'd helped Adrian choose this house. He'd mainly given her the task of finding him a house in Seattle to keep her occupied and keep her mind off the nightmare her life had been. But the place had always given her a sense of peace. The entrance that faced the drive and the gates down the hill made up the back of the house. The front faced a bluff and Puget Sound. Big trees kept the lot cool and shady and flowering plants and bushes gave lots of color. Working in Adrian's garden gave her solace.

"I love it here. Our studio is downstairs; the control room has a wall of windows out to the sound." Erin walked to the door and then let herself into the house with a bracing breath. Moved down the hall to where it opened into the main, open room.

Jeremy had been sitting on one of the deep club chairs looking out the windows. She'd often found herself in those very chairs as Adrian puttered around. She was far lazier than her brothers were, so she lounged and they puttered. It worked.

He unwound himself, standing with a smile she still found beautiful. Jeremy was a handsome man. Elegant really, with his expensive haircut and his non-shine buffed manicure. He knew how to make the perfect pancake and cup of coffee. And he'd been a stellar father.

"Erin, you look beautiful as always," he said in that slightly East Coast drawl even years in LA couldn't erase totally.

She smiled, hugging him. "I'm surprised you're here. You didn't mention it when I spoke to you yesterday." She touched his arm and turned to Ben and Todd, standing there like contradictions to the man she'd just hugged. "This is Todd Keenan. He's the man I've been telling you about. And our friend, Ben Copeland. He and Todd run the security firm that'll be handling all my personal security for the shows I do."

Todd stepped forward, wearing a smile of a man who'd just been officially declared the winner, while still managing to look gracious. He shook Jeremy's hand without a hard squeeze.

"Good to meet you, Jeremy. Erin speaks well of you."

Ben followed with a handshake.

Adrian walked in before anything else was said and caught her eye with a *what the fuck* look of his own. He'd been surprised by Jeremy's visit too, it seemed.

Time to just deal with it. "Jeremy, let's take a walk." Erin headed to the French doors leading outside and Jeremy followed. The rest stayed inside.

"You look sad today," Jeremy said once they'd settled on a bench near the edge of the bluff the property sat on. "Is this guy making you sad?"

"No, not him. A friend was beaten severely by her ex. She's in the hospital and I've only just come back from visiting her. Why are you here, Jeremy?"

"You're in love with him, aren't you?"

She didn't look at Jeremy then. Instead she watched the water undulate, watched the boats, the seabirds, watched a ferry chug off toward Bremerton.

"Yes. I love him. I told you I was serious about him. You knew I'd move on. I know you will. That's how life works."

He sighed. "I miss you. I miss *us*. You never talked about me like you talk about him."

She turned to him, taking his hand. "Don't. I loved you very much. I still love you. I had the greatest joy in my life when we were together. We made a precious gift. But she was stolen and I lost part of myself. It's over, but that doesn't mean I didn't love you then and it doesn't mean I don't care about you still. This guy is the real thing and I'm sorry if you're hurt. I am, because I don't want you to be hurt."

Jeremy squeezed her hand and let go. "All right. I love you. I always will, and I'm sorry we lost each other after we lost Adele too. I wish I'd been better to you, given you what you needed. But you pulled into yourself like no one and nothing could touch you. God knows I tried. I failed." He shrugged his shoulders and looked very sad.

"You didn't fail. I just . . . I lost part of myself for a very long time. By the time I started to surface we'd fallen apart and I was *different*. I couldn't love anyone anymore and I didn't for four years. I failed. I failed her, I failed you. I failed a lot of people. But I'm working my way back to being human again. I'm happy. In love. It's good."

He smiled and shook his head. "Erin, you didn't fail and I guess I didn't either. It just wasn't meant to be, I suppose. I want you to be happy and that you're doing these shows just proves to me this guy is part of you coming back to live the life you were meant to. You were born to play live. I'm glad you're doing it. I brought some contractual shit I need you to sign and then I'm going to go back home. I just had to know. I had to know if there was even a small chance for us. I can see now the truth of it."

They hugged and she felt, for the first time in a very long time, that things were okay between them.

They went back inside and Erin tried not to smile at the way Ben scowled at Jeremy.

She signed papers and Jeremy gave her some forms showing the deposit of royalties into her account. She'd need to deal with her accountant now and she'd have to hire another part-time person to sub for Ella for the next several months at least. Erin had already assured Ella's mother she'd pay her insurance contribution and not to worry.

There was no way Erin would simply leave Ella to sink or swim. Her music and songwriting made her very comfortable, and it wouldn't hurt at all to continue to pay Ella a salary until she could come back. When she did come back, Erin wanted her on full-time so she could have days off.

"Okay, thanks. I'll get you copies of all this stuff. It was good to see you." He turned to Todd and Ben. "It was nice to meet you, Todd. Take care of her. I'll have the security guy at the label contact you in a month or so."

She hugged him.

"I'm just going to go now. See if I can't get on the next flight back."

"Stay, Jeremy. Don't rush off on my account." Erin didn't want him to feel chased off or kicked out.

"I need to get back. This was a spur of-the-moment thing and I have work to do back home. I need to call you soon anyway. I've received several offers I think you may be interested in."

Adrian grabbed her wrist as she started to leave, to stay her. "I'll walk you out, Jeremy."

"Come on, you guys want to see the studio?" she asked Ben and Todd. Ben's eyes lit up as he nodded.

She led them down the spiral staircase and through the doors into what she considered the heart of the house. She'd slept on the couch in the corner more times than she could count.

"Is everything all right?" Todd asked quietly.

"Yeah. It was hard for him, but he needed to see it. He'll be all right."

"This is amazing!" Ben looked around.

"It is, isn't it? We've done the last two CDs here. There's some postproduction stuff we've had to go down to LA to do a time or two, but I'd way rather record here. Once we recorded in New Orleans, which was awesome. But the studio was destroyed by Katrina. The new space is nice, I hear."

"It's not haunted though," Adrian said as he joined them. "The old one was magical. I was down in the new space to do some work with Mia Long, it's not the same. Ben, I don't think we've officially met, although we've seen each other in passing." Adrian offered a hand and Ben took it. "You two want to hear a track or two? Top secret and stuff?"

"No, it's okay! They don't need to." Erin wasn't sure why she was so nervous, but Todd and Ben were important to her.

"They want to." Ben rolled his eyes. "We'd love to," he said to Adrian, and Todd put his arm around her shoulders.

Todd listened to the tracks and fell for her all over again. Adrian did the singing—it was his CD after all—but she did backing vocals. He recognized the lyrics, knowing she'd written them a few months back.

He hadn't much liked the way Jeremy had looked at her, but he'd liked the way she'd looked back. Like a woman who cared about the guy but not at all the way she looked at Todd.

She blushed as she stood in his arms.

"This is amazing. This CD is going to fly off the shelves," Ben said to Adrian. "And you, that's some top-notch songwriting." He had turned to Erin and she grinned.

"I totally agree. I can't wait to hear this stuff live. The Gorge in the spring will be great," Adrian said.

"Long as it doesn't rain and shock me over and over. I hate that."

Adrian laughed, and Todd and Ben listened as the siblings began to trade stories about touring and recording. Todd liked their connection. Brody's connection to her was more paternal than brotherly. He had a way of taking her in hand that would have seemed dangerous coming from anyone else. But she and Adrian were friends as well as siblings.

Adrian had voiced his concerns to Todd some weeks before. Had laid it out that Erin needed stability and a man who loved her and would protect her while understanding she didn't need managing. He saw Todd as a man who would protect her but worried that Todd would try to control her, even if it was done for her own good.

That sort of honesty was refreshing and Todd had reassured Adrian he respected Erin as a whole person and understood she'd never allow anyone to manage her anyway.

They'd reached a place Todd liked to think was that of friends, and he appreciated her connection to her family.

"Can you guys stay for dinner? Brody and Raven are going to swing by when he's done with his last client." Adrian led them back upstairs. "I've got salmon and steaks for the grill."

"Yeah, that sounds good. Can you guys swing it?" She turned to Ben and Todd, who both nodded.

Todd took another step into her life, one more in a series that brought them closer each day. And Ben was there too, which meant something to him and Erin both, he knew.

26

They left Adrian's well after midnight. Ben had enjoyed watching Erin with her brothers and her friend Raven. She was softer with them, less guarded. He liked that side of her. Raven freaked him out a little and he could tell Todd wasn't a big fan either. She was free-spirited like Erin, but far more so. Brody was totally in love with her, that much was obvious, but Erin had explained that Raven just didn't commit to people that way. She loved many men and women, but Brody would never have what he wanted from Raven, so they were close friends who had sex and left it at that.

Personally Ben found it sad and he was grateful for the depth of connection he shared with Erin. And Todd. Even as he had no real idea what to call all they had, he just accepted it.

Hell, he liked all sides of Erin as he continued to get to know her, which led him into some really interesting places he wasn't sure he wanted to poke at too closely but knew he couldn't avoid forever.

"Where to, Erin? Back to your place? To mine?" Todd was driving Erin's car and she was snuggled into the backseat, making Ben take the front so he'd have more room.

"The café is closed until Monday. I can sleep in as long as I want, so I don't care," she said sleepily.

"Ben, you staying over?"

"If I'm invited. I don't want to intrude."

"We'll talk about this when we get wherever we're going," Erin said from the back. "I can't hear very well back here. I suggest my place because we can't be casually interrupted by fifteen friends, cops and assorted family members like we are at your place."

Ben had to laugh at that. She was right, and he liked the privacy of her condo.

Todd took them to her building and once inside her condo she motioned them back toward her bedroom. "Go on. I need a shower and then I want to snuggle in my bed."

She tossed her clothes as she went, until she was totally naked and the sight of her back and the high, muscled cheeks of her ass shot straight to Ben's cock.

"You two talk this over. I'll be back." She didn't even look over her shoulder as she closed the door to the bathroom.

Todd snorted a laugh. "I guess we have our orders. Ben, you're suddenly so, I don't know, hesitant? Uncomfortable? Not your usual self. I don't know what to say here. What's wrong? Do we make you feel unwanted or uninvited?"

The shower went on and moments later the scent of the grapefruit soap she favored carried into the room on a waft of steam.

Ben toed off his shoes and socks and put them in the corner. *What was wrong?* "I don't know where I fit now. Yesterday I knew. Today I don't. I've been second-guessing myself all day."

"Where do you want to fit?"

Ben looked at his best friend and thought about how to answer that question. They'd had a deep connection for as long as he could remember. And now it was *more.* Ben's mind shot back to the night before, when they'd kissed, when they'd slid together with Erin in between them. When he and Erin had shared Todd's cock. He'd always felt some level of attraction toward Todd, but they'd been so close he hadn't ever wanted to ruin it. Plus he knew Todd was basically straight, although Ben had had no idea all that kink lay beneath the surface. What started as a few fun experiences had intensified. His feelings, for both of them, had deepened.

"You invited me into your bed with Erin and I came into it knowing you two had a relationship. I accept that. But"—he licked his lips—"after last night, and after the last several times I've been with both of you and with her alone, I'm feeling some pretty intense things for you both. I want to fit into that. If I'm being totally honest, I want to be with the two of you."

Todd listened and nodded his head. The water in the bathroom shut off and Ben thought of how she'd look, the water glistening on her skin, of how she'd looked sleek and playful in the lake on the Fourth.

"So be here. Stop overthinking."

"What do you think? *You.* We've been friends for a long time. I don't want to ruin things and I need to know."

Todd stalked to him, stopping just a breath away. "It makes me hot all over and I don't know how to feel about it. I love Erin. You need to understand that. I love her and if it was anyone else in the universe I'd have told them to go. But it's not anyone else. It's you. I know you in ways I've never known another soul. At the same time I'm sort of bowled over by being intrigued and happy."

Carefully, slow enough to give Todd the chance to move away, Ben reached out to touch Todd's chest. "Bowled over because you think liking men is bad?"

Todd laughed, his pupils huge. "No. Bowled over because you're *ours.* You fit with us in some sense even if I can't define it. Your being in our relationship seems natural to me. I might be kinky, but I suppose I'm pretty traditional in a lot of ways. Possession and jealousy may seem old-school to some, but I guess I'm old-school, because Erin is my woman and I wanted to punch Jeremy's fucking face for looking at her today like he loved her."

Ben laughed then too because he'd felt the same way. "I know. I did too." He paused. "But you don't want to punch me? Because, I'll be totally honest with you, I want to rub up all over your woman as much as I want to be a part of her life every day. I'm well on my way to being in love with her. I already love you; I have for as long as I can remember. It hasn't been hard to take what we already had and to add to it."

"I don't want to punch you. And I don't think liking men is bad, by the way. I've just never actually liked one. Before now, that is."

Ben was aware the door to the bathroom had opened and he was concerned enough about Erin's reaction that he broke the moment with Todd to look toward her.

She leaned against the door frame, totally naked, her hair slicked back against her head, making her gorgeous eyes seem even bigger.

"Am I interrupting something?"

At the hesitation in her voice both men turned to face her fully. "No honey, not at all. Come here." Todd held out a hand and she walked over to take it.

She stood between them, looking up, and Ben realized that despite the size of her presence, she was smaller than both of them and scared. His heart squeezed.

"Don't look like that. You have nothing to be worried about." Todd's gaze roved over her face lovingly.

"You two have a connection I can't touch. You're close in ways I can't compete with. You've known each other your whole lives."

Her voice sounded so small.

Todd kissed her, collaring her throat as he did. "You don't have to compete. Erin, I'm yours. I love you with everything I am. I loved Ben before I met you, yes. He's my best friend, yes. But as it happens, you are now too. What I have with Ben doesn't threaten what I feel for you."

"I can walk out of here right now. Things can go back to the way they were before. I don't want that look on your face, Erin." Ben brushed a thumb over the curve of her cheek.

"What *do* you want?"

He knew now. He bent and kissed her, hauling her to his body as he invaded her mouth, loving her taste, loving the way she felt against him, all soft and female. He might be attracted to Todd, but Ben was *wild* for her on a completely different level. She was the center of their relationship. If they meant to pursue something, she and Todd both needed to understand that.

"I want you, Erin," he said as he tore his mouth from hers. "And with you, I want Todd. You both should know that while I like men too, it's *you*, Erin, you who would be the center here."

She put her fingertips to her lips and the gesture touched him. Christ, he wasn't *well on his way* to being in love with her. Truth be told, he'd started falling when he met her that first time, after she'd been painting. Each time he'd seen her since, it had been a few inches more into love. He'd shoved it away because Todd was his best friend and he'd never want to hurt either of them. Freed from that, now he could admit it—he was in love with Erin.

"What do you think, Erin?" Todd asked.

"I think many things." She took a step back and tossed herself onto her bed. "I think you both should be naked like me, first of all. I also think *Holy shit, two hot men!* I think we could make it work and I also think this is very complicated."

Todd crawled into bed with her and Ben took the other side. Both of them had to touch her, that much was clear, as their hands roved from her beautifully elegant collarbone down to her gorgeous nipples. Brief touches, caresses, it didn't matter.

"It can be complicated, yes," Ben agreed.

"Let's take this a step at a time then. Have some ground rules and take it as we go. Stop that! I can't think when you do that." Erin's voice had gone thick as Todd bent his head to take a nipple between his teeth.

Todd grinned up at her, totally unrepentant.

"Okay then. Ground rules?" Ben asked.

"No other women." She looked at them both. "I mean it and I don't care that it might seem unfair."

Todd laughed and Ben simply kissed her belly. The scent of her pussy tickled his nose, spreading through him like wildfire.

"Okay. Not that I'd been planning on it or anything. But I think we can all agree that it's just us three. No one outside." Todd nodded.

"I don't care if you two, you know, get it on when I'm not around. But I'd *like* to be around if I can because it's so pretty to look at. I might even be able to keep my hands to myself if I have to."

Ben laughed then and kissed her. God, she made him happy.

"All right. Same for us then. Although, you both know I like to watch." Todd went back for the nipple again and this time she didn't shoo him away, she arched.

"We'll keep the threesome thing quiet with Todd's and my families. You can tell your brothers whatever you want. I'll play best friend in public for a while anyway." Ben knew this part would be the most complicated.

"Enough rules for now. Someone needs to make me come," Erin said, grabbing Ben's hair in her fist and pulling him down to her mouth.

"Are you okay for fucking?" Todd asked and Erin hissed as she and Ben both looked down to see him lick the crease where leg met thigh.

"Even after last night my piercing is fine. Just don't get all gymnastic on me."

Todd laughed and shoved her thighs wide. Ben moved down her body, ignoring her pout.

"Stop looking at me like that," Ben said. "I'm sure if one tongue on your pussy feels good, two will feel even better."

"Oh," she said faintly, levering up on her elbows to watch as both Todd and Ben began to lick at her from different angles.

Unfuckingbelievable. Seriously, one minute she was dealing with loss and her life felt dark and she was pretty sure she'd never be as happy as she was before, and the next she had Todd. And now Ben was theirs too.

She fell back against the mattress and gave over to orgasm, letting it sweep through her.

Cracking an eye open, she was rewarded with the sight of Todd and Ben kissing, a deep, wonderfully sensual tongue kiss that left her breathless. They were so beautiful together, Todd more hesitant but clearly into it, Ben the more dominant in that situation.

She adjusted herself to watch, unable to not tug and pull on her nipples as desire ripped through her, even so soon after her last orgasm. Todd's head fell back as Ben moved his mouth to Todd's neck and then down to his left nipple.

This was like the best porno she'd ever seen.

Ben took Todd's cock firmly and began to jerk him off. *Holy cow!*

Todd brought his head up to look at Erin. "Oh fuck, look at you," he said in a strangled voice.

"Me? Uh uh, look at you two." She walked her fingers down her belly and found her clit. "You're so beautiful together like that."

"Suck me, gorgeous," Ben said, his voice all in charge and it shot straight to her pussy.

Leaning over, she pulled something from a drawer and then got to her hands and knees and crawled over to where they knelt near the foot of the bed. She dropped the tube of lubricant into Ben's hand and wended around Todd. Brushing her body against his, she braced one hand on Todd's thigh and licked down Ben's belly.

His cock was very happy to see her, if the way it twitched when she got near it was any indication. She paid extra attention to licking from sac to crown because he seemed to prefer that to just sucking. Every fourth or fifth time she took him into her mouth, tasting as much as she could before drawing off to lick again.

The rhythm set by the three of them undulated until Erin knew Ben was close. He thrust forward, held her shoulder and came with a gasp. Moments later, she felt Todd's muscles seize as he shuddered and came. Erin rolled to watch, making both men groan when she licked over Ben's fingers where he still grasped Todd's cock.

"Best Wednesday night ever," she said, falling back onto the pillows.

27

The heat of summer had eased into fall, and things had become stable, regular, strong between her and Todd and also Ben. She saw Todd daily and Ben at least four days a week. Her life was good.

She inspected her plants on the balcony as she watered them. It wouldn't be much longer before she'd need to put up her makeshift greenhouse out there to protect them from the weather. She heard the sound of her front door locks opening one by one and turned to catch Todd coming in.

"Hey there, I wasn't expecting to see you for a while. It's not even two." She put the watering can down and came inside, wiping her hands off on a nearby towel.

"I was just a few blocks away at a client's place and I thought I'd stop by for a kiss."

"Who am I to refuse such a request?" She tiptoed up and kissed him. "I'm glad to see you."

He smiled, hugging her. "Good. I like that. Here." He dropped a little gift bag in her palm.

"Wheee! Presents. I love presents."

He laughed. "I noticed."

Pleased, she dug into the bag and saw the box. Drawing it out of the bag carefully, she untied the bow and pulled out a square, velvet jeweler's box. *Holy Eddie Vedder*.

It cracked open with that sound only a ring box makes and there it sat. It wasn't huge. It wasn't showy. It was perfect. A square-cut diamond sat in the center, offset by a sapphire on each side.

"My mom says it's a princess cut. And since you're a princess, I think that's a sign. Erin." He got to his knees and took her hands in his. He slid the ring on her very shaky finger. "Will you marry me? You know I love you. I wasted ten years and I want to spend every moment from now until forever making up for being gone so long. I want to make you happy every day for the rest of our lives."

"I . . ." Her heart thundered in her chest. "Are you sure?"

He laughed. "So romantic. Yes, I'm sure. I was married before for all the wrong reasons. *You* are all the right reasons, Erin. I love you. I want a life with you. I want a future with you. I want to have a family—when you're ready of course. I just want us to be to-gether. No more sleeping over, no more trying to organize dates, because we'll live in the same place and be together every night. Not that I'm gonna phone it in or anything. You're made for me, Erin, and I was born to make you happy. Be my wife. Please."

She nodded as she fell to her knees. "Yes." They toppled when she threw her arms around him, but neither let go and Erin thought that was a very good sign.

She sat next to him on the plane just two hours later, slugging back a glass of champagne. "You know when I said yes, I didn't think you meant right now."

He just smiled and held her hand. The same serene smile he'd had on since he'd sprung the tickets on her five minutes after she'd accepted his proposal.

"I know, honey. But you're here and your suitcase is filled with tiny scraps of cloth you call clothing. Me, you, lingerie, some rope. The recipe for the best vacation ever."

She burst out laughing.

"Okay. But I told you I don't do any of that Cirque du Soleil stuff. It freaks me out. I don't care that they're suspended over fire hoops and doing the cha-cha backward while walking a dog on a giant rubber ball. In a diaper. It's fucking creepy."

He snickered. "Whatever you say. It's Las Vegas; there are plenty of things to do. I have some stuff planned, but after that, we have lots of time."

"Like what? What do you have planned?"

"I told you, it's a surprise. Erin, you do understand the word *surprise*, right?"

"You suck."

"Don't pout." He leaned in very close. "Or I'll whip your ass when we get there."

She shivered. "That's supposed to be a deterrent?"

"I'll whip your ass and I won't let you come."

"Oh. I guess I can wait."

She tried not to fret about the café. Brody and Ella, who'd returned to work on a very part-time basis, had assured her it was all taken care of.

"You sure Ben and Cope are okay taking over for a week?"

"Yes."

The flight was pretty quick and the blast of heat that met them as they stepped out to the taxi stand just outside baggage claim reminded Erin of the years she'd lived in Los Angeles.

"I'm such a weather pussy. The time I was in LA I absolutely melted. Let me hide in Seattle where we all whine when it gets over eighty-five for those two months a year."

"I hear you." He loaded them into a limousine she hadn't seen coming. Once they'd settled and pulled away from the curb, Todd turned back to her. "I missed Seattle so much when I was in Boston. I really wanted to move back. Boston is a great city in a lot of ways though. It's similar to Seattle. Great beer, it's a food-loving town, lots of water. Some of the best bookstores I've ever been in. The traffic is fucked."

She laughed. "I've been to Boston many times. I liked it there, but I'm glad you came back to Seattle."

The hotel was gorgeous. The Bellagio was one of her favorite hotels in the world. Elegant, luxurious and a perfect counterpoint to all the noise and chaos to be had on the Strip.

"You have good taste. I love this place."

"Good."

"Ah, Mr. Keenan, welcome." They were given key cards and a bellman took their luggage up.

"Honey, I'll be up in a second, I just need to check on our reservations for tonight. By the way, you've got a spa treatment in"—he checked his watch—"forty minutes. I'll walk with you. I have one too."

The room was beautiful. Fresh flowers, a basket of fruit and cheeses and a hella big box of chocolates were waiting for them. Score. She tipped the bellman and kicked off her shoes, before opening the box and selecting a chocolate or three.

Todd came up just a few minutes later and she'd changed into a flirty sundress and sandals.

He handed her a sheaf of parchment paper that she unfolded, and as she read, she realized it was their wedding invitation. For that evening.

"This is . . ."

"Please don't be mad. I just knew you'd overthink and find reasons to wait and everyone would want to butt in and it would be political and complicated and I wanted you to have a fairy tale because no one deserves it more than you." He took a deep breath.

She was beyond touched that this big, forceful, arrogant, pushy, dominant man who held her hand through the therapy sessions he'd begun attending with her once a month would plan such a beautiful thing.

For the two-dozenth time that day alone, she threw herself into his arms and rained kisses on his face. "I just figured we'd go to the Elvis Chapel or whatever. You're the best, Todd Keenan. I love you."

"Thank god you're not mad. Brody and Adrian are here. My parents, siblings, Ben and Cope. Raven too. I asked Jeremy. He sends his best wishes, but understandably he's not here. We had a good talk. I think he's a good guy. Ella is back in Seattle with Hype from Brody's shop running your café in the mornings. She said it was her present to you."

She burst into tears and he looked worried for a moment, until she blubbered that they were good tears.

"What am I going to wear?"

"Raven came down yesterday with Adrian. They've picked out four dresses for you to choose from. They're in the spa where they'll do your hair and makeup and all that stuff. We'll say our vows outside and then we'll all have a lovely dinner. Tomorrow we'll hang with everyone and then you and I are on our own for a honeymoon. Come on, you have lots to do."

She took his hand. "Is Ben okay with all this?" She loved them both and while she wanted to be married to Todd very much and knew she sure couldn't marry both of them, the last thing she wanted was to hurt Ben.

"Ben helped me plan it all, so he's more than okay."

"All right. But here's my wedding present to you. I've been considering buying the condo next to mine. It's bigger, two stories, with the bedrooms upstairs. Move in with me and you can work from there. That condo has a much bigger balcony; it's like a deck actually, with a hot tub and stuff. I could create a lovely garden out there."

Todd knew this part would be hard. He loved her condo. It was private and central to most everything. But he loved his house too. He hated the idea of selling it.

"My place is near the zoo and the lake. It's closer to the café than your condo."

She chewed her lip. "It's so *exposed*."

"We can talk to people about just dropping by." He laughed.

It looked as if she was going to cry again as she shook her head. "Not that. I don't care so much about that." She tried to walk away, to pace, hiding her face with her hair, which was currently a honey blond with fiery red tips.

He caught her, holding her tight for a moment. "Hey. Share with me. This is more than giving up one place over the other. Tell me."

"My place is thirty-two floors up! It has a doorman and security cameras. You can't even get to my floor without a key card or an access code I change every week! It's *safe* and I can sleep at night and not be afraid. I . . . At your house, I hate when you leave to go get something or if I get there and you're gone. I hate going inside. It's at ground level. It has all those windows. The basement windows! Anyone could get in. I can't. I just can't."

Oh fuck, what a dumbass he'd been. It hadn't even occurred to him.

"God, I'm stupid. I'm sorry. Of course I'll move in to your place, although I'm a bit uncomfortable about you buying something so expensive for me."

"It's for us, really. I mean, my place is huge already, but now we'll have space for you to work from home too. Plenty of room for a nursery and stuff when the time is right."

She looked up into his face, and he loved her so much it nearly hurt. He wanted children with her and that she'd consider it after what she'd suffered meant a lot.

"I know I'm asking you to give up more than I am and Cope will have to come into downtown every day, which will suck for him. The place next door comes with three parking spots, though. I mean, obviously it'll take some planning and coordination. The permits take a while and the contractor told me it would take months to get the connecting wall down and arched. We'd have to talk about what you wanted and if you wanted it and, oh man, I'm just babbling."

"Let's go get ready for our wedding. We can talk about all this stuff tomorrow." He smiled and led her out of the room.

After being massaged, manicured, pedicured, facialed (in a non-porn way) and hairdone, Erin slid into the dress she'd chosen. Clearly Adrian and Raven knew her well because each dress was perfect in its own way.

The one she chose was a soft pink, floor-length gown with a V-neckline and off-the-shoulder spaghetti straps. The bodice fit snugly and the skirt was organza and was close to her body, but still felt feminine and flowy.

Her hair was pinned up with flowers and she chose not to carry a bouquet.

"You look so beautiful. I don't think I've ever seen you like this before," Brody said as he came into the room where she waited to go to the ceremony. "You glow like magic." He kissed her. "I'm so honored to walk you down the aisle today. Todd is good people."

"I think so. Look at me in a fucking pink wedding dress with a train! Who knew? Also, thank god I'm not on my period, 'cause this dress fits like a glove but last week I'd have looked like a sausage."

Brody laughed. "Aw, now, you look spectacular. You deserve a happily ever after."

Adrian would be her dude of honor and Todd's father would be his best man.

"Ready?"

Erin nodded, and they walked down a hall where she blushed as hotel guests saw her and *ooh*ed and *ahh*ed. And then she *ooh*ed and *ahh*ed herself when double doors opened up to a courtyard lit by dozens of candles. She walked down the steps toward Todd, who looked beyond edible in a dapper tuxedo.

The ceremony was a blur. Todd had been happily surprised when Brody handed her the ring she'd sent him out in search of. For two hours, he'd sent her pictures via cell phone as she'd been prettified for the ceremony, until he'd found something she knew was perfect immediately.

Lorie hugged her and kissed her cheeks. "Welcome to the family! We're so happy for you two. Next month won't you let Dean and I throw you two a reception? For all our friends and family who'll want to meet you?"

Erin was touched and accepted. They'd eaten a spectacular meal and had laughed and talked until the wee hours of the morning, until she and Todd finally staggered back to their room, where rose petals had been spread on the bed and the bathtub had been filled just right.

"Damn, if you want to quit the security business I think you'd have a bright future as a wedding planner."

"I already have a bright future," he said, tossing his jacket to the side.

She tutted at him and hung it up, then moved to him again to undo his cuff links and to unbutton his shirt.

"I love French cuffs. They're so elegant and glamorous." She drew his shirt off and hung it as well.

"That dress . . . You look like a goddess, Erin. I lost my breath when I saw you come out those doors. It's perfect. You're perfect. I love you so much. I've never been happier than I am right this very moment."

"Let me try to make you even happier," Erin said, reaching for him.

28

Todd took a shower and watched her sleep for a while after he got out. *His wife*, nestled in the blankets, her hair covering her face, a leg poking from the covers in a long, creamy expanse.

What a lucky man he was to have her, to have those big hazel eyes looking up at him with such love and trust. They'd made love and fucked and made love again until after the sun had come up.

He heard a light tap on the door and when he peeked, he saw it was Ben. Todd smiled as he let him in.

Ben had helped with the planning, knowing that Erin would be another man's wife. All the while, loving her. Todd and Erin had talked, in between bouts of sex, about turning part of the second condo into a living space for Ben so he could be there with them. As they'd sealed their relationship officially, they'd both understood they wanted Ben to be a more established part of their lives too. More important, they wanted him to feel and understand they desired him to be theirs full-time and not just when it fit into their schedule.

"Hey, is she still sleeping?" Ben asked as he came in.

"Yeah. I, um, tired her out. We didn't get to sleep until dawn. You could have come with us, you know. I know Erin told you that."

Ben grinned. "I expect there will be times when I want to have her all to myself and I figured your wedding night would be a time you wanted that."

"Go wake her up. We're supposed to meet everyone for a late lunch before they all go back home tonight."

Ben quietly stalked to the bed and Todd admired the way he moved. He'd been close to Ben for most of his life and he'd grown closer to him over the last months with Erin than he'd ever been before. It wasn't that Ben was male or female; it was that Ben was Ben. That's what made him appeal so much.

Logically, Todd knew it was weird. He knew he should be jealous and territorial, but he wasn't. Erin had enough for both of them and they certainly had more than enough for her. Both of them loved her, wanted her safe, and in turn, cherished her. Ben didn't have that history Todd had with her, but they were building their own memories.

Todd didn't know what to call it; he only knew it worked.

Ben drew her close as he got into the bed. Warm and sleep-soft, she came willingly, snuggling into him with a smile, her eyes still closed.

"Morning. Mmm, you smell good. Like coffee. I need it."

He laughed. "You know the way to make a man feel wanted."

She smiled, her mouth against his neck. "We missed you last night. You're staying this week, right?"

He swallowed. He'd wanted her to ask. When they'd planned it, he and Todd, Ben had been truly happy for both of them. But he wanted Erin to want him too, wanted her to ask him to stay with them. It would take some planning with Cope, who knew what was up and thankfully never judged. But there was no way he'd turn down the opportunity to be with them both this week. Far away from home in a city that wouldn't bat an eye at two men squiring one woman out on the town.

"I'd love to."

"Mmm, good." She opened her eyes and looked at him. "I need a shower and to brush my teeth." She scrambled over him, getting him all worked up, and kissed Todd quickly on her way into the bathroom.

"I told you that you were welcome," Todd said, grabbing the phone to order up some coffee.

"I wanted her to ask."

"I'm moving into the condo when we get back." Todd told him about the way Erin had reacted to moving into his house and Ben's gut tightened.

"I fucking hate that she's scared. God, I wish I could rip this fucker apart with my bare hands." The way she sometimes winced at loud noises or jumped when someone surprised her broke his heart.

"Get in line. Ben, we'd like it if you'd consider moving in. She's buying the condo next door to hers and remodeling. Apparently it's huge. You can have your own space, but we talked about taking the master in the other place and knocking out a wall between it and the adjoining bedroom to make one giant bedroom. For all three of us." Todd got up when room service brought coffee. Erin emerged from the bathroom, looking ridiculously pretty in a little dress and with her hair pulled back. She wore just a tiny bit of makeup and, as always, Ben was aware of how naturally beautiful she was.

She fell on the coffee, giving Todd a kiss and settling on the couch next to Ben.

"I heard you two as I was getting dressed. We don't want to

pressure you, Ben. But we want you to know we want you with us. We're going to have an office space for you guys and you can have your own rooms too. I expect we'll all need that from time to time. Everyone needs space that's just theirs alone."

Ben took her hand. "I love you, Erin."

She blinked back tears and smiled. "What a lovely present. I love you too. I know this is odd and people won't understand. I'm not sure I do, but I love you. *We* love you. Whatever you decide, you have a key card, so I want you to come and go as you please. I don't want to pressure you or rush you or whatever. "

"Gorgeous, this last year has been a lot about unexpected happenings. I figured eventually I'd find the woman for me and I'd marry. But the woman for me is married to someone else. Luckily, I love him too and he's willing to share. If you two are okay with it, I'd love to move in. More than love it." He shrugged, speechless at how fabulous he felt.

She bounced happily and he laughed. "Yay! I have a meeting with the contractor next week so you can come and we can talk about what we'd like to do."

"I should have known you'd already put this into the works." Todd smirked.

"I didn't know you'd be asking me to marry you and carting me off to Vegas! But I hoped we'd be able to live together and didn't want to pass up the opportunity when the people next door moved out and sold. I'm forward-thinking." She crossed her arms over her chest, and Ben hugged her, kissing her neck until she laughed and relaxed.

She swung around, straddling him. "I'm not wearing any underwear. Don't you think you should do something about that?"

In moments he had his pants undone and his cock out.

She leaned in and spoke in his ear, her breath sending shivers down his neck. "I want you in me naked. It's time. We've been careful and tested. Give it to me."

Across from them, he heard Todd groan and get up to walk behind the small couch he and Erin were on.

Ben swallowed hard and, without much finesse, thrust up, into her, and nearly died at how she felt. She made a needful sound, low and deep, and squirmed on him as he banded her waist with his arm and held her so he could control the pace.

"Open up." Todd spoke from where he stood behind Ben and soon the wet sounds of Erin's lips wrapped around Todd's cock began to echo against them. Her fingers dug into his shoulders to hold on and keep her balance.

Ben licked up the side of her neck and loved the soft sound she made in response. She rocked against him, grinding her clit against his pubic bone.

"That's the way, gorgeous. So wet and hot, you feel better than I could have imagined. And you have to know I've imagined a lot."

She laughed, Todd's cock still in her mouth. Ben leaned his head back in order to watch the way her mouth worked Todd. Fuck, that was hot. Her eyes were open, locked with Todd's. One of Todd's hands cupped her cheek gently, reverently.

Yes, it was complicated. No, Ben had no idea how he'd even begin to describe what they had to anyone other than Cope and maybe a very few others. He didn't know what they'd do about kids when they came along. But he knew he cherished this with everything he was. He'd protect it with his life, and he'd love Erin until he drew his last breath. What they had was special and wonderful. He knew how lucky he was.

One of Todd's hands landed on Ben's shoulder and squeezed as Todd groaned. Ben watched as Erin closed her eyes a long moment before opening up again and turning to Ben.

"Your turn." Erin waggled her brows at Ben.

Todd laughed and kissed the top of Erin's head and then Ben's before moving back to watch the two of them with a lazy smile.

"Should I play with your clit, gorgeous?" Ben whispered into her ear and she nodded, leaning her head on his shoulder.

The cool, slick surface of the barbell met his fingers as he began playing his fingers against her. The corresponding tightening of her cunt around him told him she was as close as he was.

"I can feel so much more this way," he managed to get out in a strangled whisper.

"Me too," she said, nuzzling into his neck and kissing him. He pressed a bit harder and her teeth grasped the meat of his shoulder as she came all around him.

It was too much, her body hugging him like liquid fire. He pushed into her one last time and came for what felt like fifteen minutes.

She kissed his mouth, tasting of herself and of Todd too. He tasted her, taking what she gave like the gift she was.

"Okay, now we have to go eat with everyone. First dibs on the bathroom," she called as she pulled up and off his cock and ran into the bathroom.

Ben crowded in with her, liking to watch as she touched up her lip gloss and finger-combed her hair again. She was a bundle of contradictions, incredibly feminine but with an edge. Ink on her back, rings in her nipples, funky hair and rock and roll written all over her. Somehow, on her, all those edges and contradictions combined to make the kind of person who drew your attention when she walked into a room.

That she loved him seemed a miracle.

"I know how you feel," Todd said as they let her out into the hallway first. "Every day, at least five times a day I have the same thought."

"Am I that obvious?"

Todd shrugged. "With us, yes. But I haven't seen you slip in public. It may happen one day, but whatever. We're adults and we can make our own choices. If and when it comes, we deal with it."

"You boys want to stop whispering and get over here? The elevator is here."

"As my lady commands," Todd said and they went to her.

29

"How's the construction going?" Ella asked when Erin arrived to work.

"The contractors are awesome. Turns out they're related to Ben and Cope, so the project is ahead of schedule right now. They should be done with the basic stuff by Thanksgiving. They've already torn out the wall between the condos and have finished the arching and all that jazz. Now they're working on the office space for Todd's and Ben's apartments. They'll start on our master bedroom when they're done with that. It's all very noisy and dusty, but I can't wait to see the finished project."

She began to stir the soup for lunch. A new recipe she'd gotten from Todd's mom. Pumpkin.

"Who knew pumpkin soup would taste so good?" Ella murmured as she took a spoonful and sighed.

"Lorie Keenan is no slouch in the kitchen, let me tell you. We went over for dinner a few weeks back and she made fresh pasta. Butternut squash ravioli! My parents died when I was twelve, but I remember enough to know my mom never made butternut squash ravioli."

Erin turned and checked on the sandwiches. She had two different kinds of panini, veggie and black forest ham. Panini were a bit time-intensive due to the toasting, but worth it.

"I've decided to take the promotion and I was wondering if you'd be willing to go with me to all the trial stuff," Ella said in one long stream of words.

Erin started to answer, but customers came in and the lunch rush began in earnest. And thank god, because she wasn't sure what to say. Of course she wanted to support her friend through the process. It was a horrible process for the victim, because she wouldn't be able to be in the courtroom until after she testified, so all this stuff would be happening and it was about Ella's life, but she couldn't be there.

At the same time, Erin's hands shook at the thought of going through a trial again. Administrative buildings in general gave her a stomachache for days.

But in the end, Ella needed her; she'd reached out, and there wasn't any way Erin could say no.

Once the initial rush passed, she leaned back and Ella exhaled. "Wow, I can't believe you did that alone every day."

Erin laughed. "I don't normally do panini, and today is particularly busy for some reason, but yeah, I'm so grateful you're going to take this promotion. I think Dave will appreciate more hours too, since he's only working part-time. He and I spoke last week about it and he said he could easily take on another fifteen or so. And that means actual days off for me."

Ella nodded with a grin. "I expect Todd would like that."

"Yes. He wants to go on trips and stuff and now it's possible. Can you stay after we close today? Then you and I can talk about some of the ideas I've got for staffing and the future?"

"Definitely."

"And of course I'll go through the trial stuff with you." Erin hoped she sounded more sure than she felt.

Ella hugged her. "Thank you. Really. I know it's hard for you. My mom will be there and of course my advocate, but I feel totally lost in so many ways. You're so strong and so calm. I need that."

Todd walked in and looked at Erin, of course knowing something was up. He had that way about him.

"Hello there, beautiful wife. Take pity and feed me?"

She rolled her eyes. "Go sit. I take it Cope will be joining you too?" she asked as she turned and put a panini in the press and began to ladle some soup into a bowl.

"Of course. You know he likes to come in here and flirt enough to make me annoyed."

Ella laughed as she got coffee for some customers.

Cope came in as she was putting the food down. Once she did, he swept her up and kissed her smack-dab on the lips. Erin couldn't help but grin at him. He did it purely to poke at Todd, like any other little-brother type would.

"Your mother must have a hell of a lot of gray hair from you boys," she said as she walked away.

"But I'm so cute!"

"He is," Ella said in an undertone. "Sort of scary with that face he gets sometimes. Ben too. But they're all so nice to look at."

"You should see the rest of them. Todd's brothers and all the assorted fathers, cousins and other cop types who show up at barbecues and stuff. It's like porn for women."

"I have noticed more cops in here on a regular basis. I like it." Ella took a deep breath and Erin understood her. At least Erin's attacker was in prison. Ella's was out on bail, which had to be terrifying.

"They take my being Todd's wife and Dean's daughter-in-law

very seriously. It's amusing to look out there and see all our funky people mixing it up with the cops."

"It's a hotness buffet in there at least three days a week," Ella agreed.

Closing time came and Erin locked up but didn't shoo Todd and Cope out. She and Ella cleaned up and then went to a table of their own to spread out a calendar and some new menu ideas Erin had.

She wanted to keep the hours they had; that much made sense. She might make more money with dinner, but really, she didn't want the hassle and she sure didn't want to work more. She liked the income from the cafe. It wasn't a lot, but was enough to keep everyone's salary paid and to pay for more hours from her employees so she could take time off.

But she wanted to be there less and she wanted weekends off so she could be with Todd and Ben. That meant not only hiring Ella on full-time, which she'd just done, but bringing Dave on for more hours so Ella could have days off too.

They planned and agreed on hiring a third part-timer to supplement the hours. Ella was smart and organized and had a good business mind, and she wanted to make something of her life. Erin sure couldn't argue with that goal.

When they finished, Todd was still there but Cope had left. They walked Ella to her car and then Todd turned to Erin, kissing her.

"Tell me."

"She asked if I'd go through the trial stuff with her. I'm okay, just a bit shaken."

"I'll come too. Or Ben. One of us will be there with you both. I don't like this asshole being out on bail."

"You don't have to come, but I'd be lying if I said I wouldn't appreciate it. As for that asshole being out, me neither. Anyway, I'm going every day until she testifies and then she'll be able to attend as well. It shouldn't be a really long trial. They're not charging him with attempted murder. That fucker. First-degree assault along with unlawful imprisonment because he wouldn't let her leave when she tried. And there's this other thing, interfering with reporting of domestic violence, because he yanked her phone from her hand and stomped on it. Then there's violating the protection order and other random stuff. It seems to me that the prosecutor is gunning for the asshole. Which is nice. King County has good laws. Some other places, not so much."

"Even if he's convicted, I don't know how much time he'll serve, Erin. It might not be a lot. I want you to be prepared for that." Todd's brow furrowed.

"I know. She's got an advocate from a local domestic violence advocacy organization who's been working with her for months now, since before the attack. The woman has been really good about walking Ella through the process."

"I'm driving you home." Todd got his stubborn face on and she put her hand on his arm.

"No. I'm fine. Just a bit shaky, but not as bad as I would have thought. This isn't me. It's her, and that takes part of the pressure away. That sounds horrible, god."

He kissed her gently. "That sounds human."

"Go back to work. I'll see you in a few hours. We'll have dinner, everything will be fine."

He sighed but let her go and she blew him a kiss as she drove away.

The condo was, of course, filled with workers who'd be there another two hours or so. She waved and headed through the plastic sheeting back into the hall and into her work space.

She closed the door and put on her headphones and began to write. Despite this stuff with Ella, Erin had never been more productive with songwriting.

Creatively she was on fire. Not only was she writing songs, but cooking and canning too, and Lorie was teaching her how to knit. It was a rebirth of sorts and Erin loved it. The fear remained, coiled down deep, but the edge of it dulled, and she wondered when it would wisp away like smoke instead of being a lump in her gut.

Ben came home, glad it was after five and the construction people had gone. The quiet was welcome after a day in which he'd dealt with one client issue after another.

The condo was slowly beginning to feel like home. He'd moved in right after they'd all returned from Las Vegas, and aside from a few struggles between him and Todd for time with Erin, things had been smooth. Just then it was a matter of finding his place in their relationship. He'd known Todd pretty much all his life, but with Erin, it was new. He wanted more of her, needed more, and had to work to not be greedy or hurt when he saw the easy way she and Todd had. Although, she gave Todd a rasher of shit on a regular basis. She might fall to her knees for sex, but everywhere else, no one pushed her around. That part was amusing, he had to admit.

He heard her singing as he moved down the hall. Not wanting to disturb her while she worked, he kept on to the master bedroom and changed from his work clothes into a T-shirt and some ratty jeans. He had a room that was his. He often worked there in the evenings or in the early part of the day instead of going straight to their office, but he slept in the master bedroom with Erin curled into his side and Todd bracketing her other side.

As he looked out the windows over the city, he thought about how happy he was. In truth, even when he'd been in his relationship with Caroline and Greg, he'd always felt lonely. Funny, he'd often thought it would alleviate the loneliness, that extra person. It wasn't as if he'd been ignored or felt left out by the other two, but looking back, he realized he'd never truly invested himself with either of them. He went through the motions, had had some great sex, learned a lot about his desires and how to express them, but he hadn't really learned about himself and what he needed emotionally.

But something about Erin was different. He connected to her in a way he never had with anyone before. He felt steady, stable and, for want of a better word, *understood*. Together with her and Todd, he felt like a whole person.

"Hi there."

He turned to see her in the doorway, looking soft and relaxed in a tank top and yoga pants. He loved those pants of hers. They clung to her ass like they loved it nearly as much as he did.

He opened his arms and she was in them in just a few steps. The weather had gotten cooler and fall was waning, but the condo was nice and warm from a day of afternoon sun, so her body was warm and she smelled of sunshine.

Once he'd touched her, he felt better, wrapping his arms around her and breathing her in.

"Mmm, you feel good. Did I bother you? I heard you working."

She tiptoed up to kiss him, setting his hormones on fire. "I'm good. I finished a song I've been working on for two days. I just e-mailed the sound file to Adrian. You have a message on the machine, by the way."

He put an arm around her waist and walked out with her to the living room where the answering machine was.

Caroline.

He sighed and turned to Erin, surprised by her facial expression. He reached to touch her, hating that she looked worried. "I'm not going to see her. Not without you and Todd, and probably not at all. I told her about you."

She looked up at him, and he sat, bringing her along with him, settling her into his lap.

"Are you all right?"

She swallowed. "I think so. I believe you. I mean, look, this is all totally foreign territory. I never expected to love anyone the way I love Todd, to be married. But then you came along. You were unexpected on a whole different and yet so wonderful level." She touched his lips. "It's sort of beyond me to try and define it, so I don't, other than to love you both. I wonder if it'll be enough for you, but a call from your ex isn't going to send me over the edge. I'm really okay."

"Caroline is someone I'll always care about. She's a kind person. Good-hearted. But when we were together, while I was happy, I didn't love her. Not the way I love you. Not the way I love Todd. I was in a nice relationship. I learned a lot about communication and how to work with an extra person in a romantic situation. But when she got her job offer I was never tempted to leave with her. And I haven't really spoken to Greg, our third, since Caroline moved away."

She snuggled into his body. "You don't need to tell me all this. I know you love me."

"I know I don't need to. I want to. I want you to know you come first. Before Todd, before anyone. Before with Caroline, I never felt settled. I was lonely. I'm not lonely anymore. You are more than enough. You're everything. We'll work through things as they come up. I love you, Erin."

She smiled against the skin of his throat. "Good. I love you too. I'm sorry you were lonely, but I know what that is. I'm glad you don't feel it anymore. And I'm glad you told me all this. I do feel better. So call her and talk a bit. I'm going to start dinner."

He caught her before she stood fully and brought her back to his lap, finding her mouth and giving her a long, lazy kiss.

She sighed happily when he released her and he liked that very much.

"Tell me about your day. I'm not calling anyone just now." He stood and went with her into the kitchen and did the tasks she assigned him as he drank a beer and listened to the smoke of her voice.

She told him about the trial and he frowned, but knew good and well that once she'd decided to do something, she would do it, and he'd just have to deal with it. He liked that Todd had insisted on one of them being there with her during the trial though. Smart man.

"How do you feel about it? About going back into a courtroom?"

"Panicked. Nauseated. Freaked. But I need to do it. She's my friend and she needs me. I feel like everything I've experienced, this past year especially, has been for a reason. Todd coming back into my café, meeting you, getting married, this trial. I need to do this because I'm supposed to. I know that sounds all woo-woo and stuff, but there it is. I'm meant to face my fears, I'm meant to overcome them. Each time I beat something back, I get stronger and"—she paused, hanging her head—"and I want to not be scared anymore. I want to be who I was."

She tried to hold back the tears; he saw her struggle and, in the end, she simply turned to him and let him wrap his arms around her, hugging her tight. That she'd turn to him this way made him want to cry, but also made him feel like they'd reached yet another important place in their relationship. She trusted him with her good stuff as well as her bad.

"You will never be who you were before, Erin. You've gone through things people shouldn't have to experience. But you *are* claiming your life. Every day since I met you, you've been grabbing your life back with both hands. I'm proud of you, and Todd and I will be there every step of the way."

"Thank you."

"Don't thank me. It's my job."

The keys rattled through all three locks Ben had carefully locked behind him when he'd come home. She didn't disentangle herself from him immediately and a part of him settled that much more.

She kissed him. "I'm so glad you love me."

"You always know to say the exact thing I need to hear right when I need to hear it."

She smiled. "Good."

"Hey, you two," Todd called out as he ditched his shoes and other crap near the front door. Erin's back was rigid under Ben's palm until all three locks sounded.

Todd came toward them, touching Ben's arm and kissing Erin while she was still in Ben's embrace. She made no move to leave and Todd made no attempt to take her.

"Evenin', honey, you feeling better?" Todd pulled back, and Ben handed him a beer when Erin went back to work slicing up vegetables.

"I finished a song and snuggled with Ben. I'm much better now. You should call Cope and invite him to dinner. He comes around a lot less now that you both live here, and I'm sure he misses that." Erin put the vegetables aside and began to mince garlic. The scent painted the air, making Ben's stomach growl.

"Yeah, good idea." Todd grabbed the phone and in a few sentences, his brother was on the way over for dinner.

Erin would wait until Cope arrived to toss the prawns into the vegetables. She made a quick orzo salad and grabbed a bottle of wine and some sparkling water, slicing up limes to serve with it.

Ben and Todd were discussing some client or other; most of what they were saying was just a sexy male rumble from several feet away.

Her life was normal even as it was unusual. Then again, it had never been usual or typical, so really, what was two men instead of one? She smiled to herself; it was lucky when both men were smoking hot, protective, dominant and loving, but she'd had many exceptional experiences in her life, so this was another she was grateful for.

Cope showed up all noise and clomping boots. She smiled as he kissed her cheek and handed her a box of chocolates from Dilettante. The men cracked open beers and laughed, at ease with one another and she watched while tossing the prawns briefly with the veggies.

"You know, you're welcome to drop by here too." Erin slid the prawns and veggies over the orzo and put the platter on the table. She knew how close the three were and the last thing she wanted was to come in between them. She liked Cope and wanted things smooth for the brothers and for Todd too.

"I just didn't want to get in the way." Cope actually blushed and Erin laughed.

She put out the bread she'd picked up at the Market on her way home and the cheeses she'd bought for them. "We don't have sex every waking moment, you know."

Ben choked. "Erin's right. You're welcome here. God only knows what would happen to you if you had to fend for yourself for dinner. You'd waste away."

They all sat and began to eat. Todd watched her, smiling from under his lashes, and she knew he was amused.

Cope began speaking as he ate. "So I got in touch with the guy from the label's security team. They sent their security plan—which is really good, by the way. I've got a schematic of the venues and entry and exit plans. We can carry concealed in both places. I'll be the liaison. They assured me they would handle Erin's security just fine."

Ben and Todd's heads both snapped up, eyes glittering, and she felt instantly better. They wouldn't let anything happen to her. Neither would Cope. She patted Cope's arm before refilling Ben's plate.

"And you told them, what?" Ben asked.

Cope rolled his eyes. "What do you think? I told them we appreciated the offer, Erin was sure they would do a fine job, but she'd contracted with us and that was how it would be. If they had a problem, they could speak with Jeremy. They backed off quickly."

"Thank you, Cope." Erin said and he grinned at her.

"You're like my sister-in-law twice over, I got your back. We've all got your back. And you feed me, which is a plus. In case you haven't noticed, you fill in all the blanks. I like to look at pretty women. Check. I'm hungry. Check. You know, the basics. Too bad you settled on Ben. I'm clearly the hotter of the Copeland boys."

She burst out laughing and Ben just rolled his eyes as the phone rang.

"I got it." Ben got up and went to answer. From the way he tightened up and then put the phone back into the cradle moments later, she knew it was the ex. The woman she tried not to wonder about but couldn't help herself.

He came back to the table, looking her straight in the eye and smiling. He wasn't hiding anything. She felt like each time they shared a few moments like they had earlier that evening, they got closer as they learned each other. Erin knew what it was to be surrounded by people and yet still be lonely. Even when she was with Jeremy she'd been lonely. It was only for those glorious years with Adele that she had felt right. And then it went away and she was cast adrift, even as she had people who loved her in her life.

Because of that, she understood why Ella had stayed with her ex as long as she had. Even when it wasn't perfect, sometimes it was better than being alone. Or it felt that way until you were alone long enough to realize nothing was worth being hurt by someone who claimed to love you.

"You okay?" Ben asked quietly.

"Yeah. Just thinking." She squeezed his hand. "Caroline?"

He nodded. "I said we were eating and I'd call her later. Are you upset?"

"No. Really, I promise. I'm curious about her of course. But you're not hiding anything and we're okay. I was just thinking about what it meant to be lonely even when you're surrounded by people."

He nodded, understanding. And she knew Todd did as well. Each of them had been that way and they'd all finally found each other and held on. It worked. Thank goodness.

They chatted as everyone cleaned up. Cope stayed until eleven or so and ambled out with hugs and a laid-back smile.

"I think he feels better now. Knowing he's welcome. I've told him that and I know Ben has. But hearing it from you made a difference." Todd kissed her. "Thank you for making a place in our lives for him."

"I like Cope, silly. Of course I would."

Her cell rang and she saw it was Adrian. "I'm going to work for a while. I expect he wants to talk about the song I sent over earlier." She kissed him and blew a kiss to Ben, who was on the balcony.

Ben lit a clove cigarette and inhaled, letting the aromatic smoke fill him, affect his senses, before blowing it out again.

"Is everything okay?" Todd said, pulling a chair up and leaning back. The sky was clear and beautiful.

Ben nodded. "She's had a rough day. Caroline called. I'm getting ready to call her back."

"She has, but she'll be okay. She knows we're here for her. What's this about Caroline?"

"She's in town. She called earlier and left a message on the machine. Erin and I talked. She's curious but not worried."

"And what about you? How do you feel about your ex calling you out of the blue and being here in Seattle?" Todd wasn't sure how *he* felt about it.

"The breakup wasn't bad. I don't hate her. There's no resentment. I care about her, sure. But there's nothing for anyone to worry about. You and Erin are my present and my future. I told Erin that too. Wanna be here when I call?"

Todd snorted and stood, kissing Ben quickly. That sort of intimacy had grown over the last months until it had become natural.

"Ben, you don't need a chaperone. If you did, I wouldn't want you in our relationship. I'm going inside. Erin will be working for another hour or so and then I'm going to jump her."

"Good idea. I'll meet you in an hour."

30

Erin smoothed down her blouse and took a deep breath. Todd saw the shaking hands and his heart ached. But he knew she needed to pull herself together without help from him, so he forced himself to sit and watch her get ready.

Today would be the opening arguments for Bill Richman, Ella's ex. Todd had taken the day off and would sit with Erin the whole time. Ben had wanted to go, but their client load had grown enough that it wasn't possible for both of them to have the day off.

It had led to an argument of sorts, stressing Erin out until she'd tossed a coin, made them each choose a side and announced a winner. After that, she'd gone into her office and slammed the door, turned up her amp and played the bass for an hour.

Todd had been hurt that they'd caused her any upset, but at the same time, that little fight had released a great deal of tension. That they'd survived it and were all three still strong meant a lot to him. They could fight and it didn't mean anything in the big picture.

The realization had made him relax a bit more, even as Ben pouted so much that Erin had babied him and made his favorite breakfast that morning.

"You ready to go? You look very businesslike today." Todd stood as she turned and grabbed her bag.

"Ready? Hell no. But I'm gonna do it anyway." She took his arm and held on for dear life as they walked to the King County Courthouse rather than mess with traffic.

The cool morning air did a world of good for them both. She perked up, her color came back as they walked and he felt better seeing *her* feel better.

She hadn't been overly specific about her own trial experience. Just that it had been horrible. He knew enough that he could fill in the details for himself.

The metal detectors loomed ahead and she froze.

He spoke to her softly, rubbing a hand up and down her back. "It's for everyone's safety. In the nineties a man came in with a gun and killed his wife and her pregnant friend in the hallway outside the courtroom where their divorce was being heard." It had been a fucking horrible day. He'd been a relatively new cop and was in the courthouse to testify in another case when it had happened. It had been one of the events in his time as a cop that'd hardened his resolve against domestic violence.

She took a deep breath and straightened, walked through the metal detectors and waited patiently until she got her bag back and he joined her.

The wait outside the courtroom seemed interminable, but finally they went inside and she chose a seat near the back but on the aisle. He wanted to sit on the end, wanted his body between her and anyone who walked past but she shook her head hard, white-lipped, and he realized she needed to feel like she could get up and leave anytime she wanted.

He put an arm around the back of the bench, touching her but not holding her.

Erin hated the nausea, but she fought it. Fought it like she fought the memories of sitting in that courtroom in LA, of being cross-examined and having to relive every fucking moment of that day. She'd held on, just barely keeping from crying. She'd waited until she got back to Adrian's and then she'd withdrawn into a world of prescription medicine and too much booze. Adrian and Brody hauled her out of bed every morning and shoved her into a shower.

If anyone deserved praise for support it was her brothers. They cleaned up her sick, ferried her to court every day, held her hand, kicked her ass and generally were her anchors in a storm that rocked the foundations of her life.

She'd been smiling at the memory until Bill walked in with his attorney. Shortly after that, Ella's mother came in and sat on Todd's other side.

That first morning was mainly procedural stuff, but the opening arguments pissed her off. She didn't blame the defense attorney; that was his job. And despite the fact that Erin wanted to run Bill over with her car, she believed everyone deserved an able defense. Still, listening to this bullshit about mistakes and differences in *perception* really made her angry. At least Bill wasn't claiming he was crazy like Charles Cabot had.

When they dismissed for lunch, they dismissed for the day due to scheduling conflicts, but Ella was expected to testify the following day, so at least she could be there after that.

Erin hugged Ella's mother good-bye, shot a glare at Bill, who gave her one back until Todd stepped beside her and sent Bill the scariest look she'd ever seen on his face. He put his arm around her and she relaxed into his body.

"Let's go. I'm taking you home."

"No, I need to go to the café. You get to work. Really, I'm all right."

He hustled her out and they walked back to the condo, where she could grab her car. He was stoic the whole time and she knew he was thinking on a way to get her to stay home.

Managing two bossy men like Ben and Todd was a full-time job. They always wanted to take over, to do things for her, to spare her, but she liked to do things herself. She appreciated the support, but man, did they work her nerves some days.

She headed to the elevator, and Todd got that smirky smile until she hit the P button for the garage. Then he sighed and crossed his arms over his chest.

"You know, you can give yourself a fucking break every once in a while. Is it too much to ask that you go home and rest? Why do you owe the world anything right now? You're being stubborn for the sake of being stubborn."

"You know, you can give *me* a fucking break every once in a while. I went to court today because Ella asked me to. She's working for *me* right now in my café. I'm going over there to talk to her and while I appreciate your protective nature, I'm getting miffed at this point and you need to back off."

"You're not the only one who's miffed, Erin."

Oh no he didn't.

She flapped a hand at him and went to her car, slamming inside. He moved to the passenger side and she flipped the locks. If he rode with her, they'd continue this stupid fucking fight and she'd want to shove him out an airlock.

"Erin," he said warningly.

"Go to work, Todd. Thank you for coming with me today," she said as she started her car and drove away.

She waved through the front window of Brody's shop as she walked past and he blew her a kiss. She laughed and went through the door of the café. Things were jumping, and she immediately moved to the coffee bar and began pulling espressos until the crowd thinned.

"My mom came by."

Erin looked at Ella and nodded. "She give you the recap?"

"Yeah. *Perceptions?* Like I mistook him kicking my door in and hitting me with the iron I'd been using as an attack? How could he sit there with a straight face?"

Erin hugged her friend. "You'll testify tomorrow and tell the truth. They've got your medical records, pictures of what you looked like, all the times he violated the protection order. It's going to be all right."

"The prosecutor is really nice. She walked me through what it's going to be like. It's bad, isn't it?" Ella asked.

Erin exhaled hard. "It's not the most pleasant thing. But you'll survive it. You've survived worse and you're here now. He will be there, watching you, and they'll try to shake you up too. But you need to try to focus and remember that you living to tell the tale is your best revenge. *Justice* is your best revenge. And when they try to make you look like you were wishy-washy and how could he know if you really meant him to go away and you liked it rough or whatever, you have to stay focused. Just be honest. Think about what you say and don't let them rush you. And remember, this is about him, not you."

"You're so awesome. I know it was hard for you today."

"It was worth it to see his face when your mom and I glared at him. Todd sent him an uber-mean face too."

"I'm glad Todd was with you. He's so good."

"He is." Even when he was a controlling, protective butthead.

They worked side by side until it was closing time and then cleaned up.

"You want me to go home with you?" Erin asked as she locked up the front door.

"No, I'm good. I'm heading to my parents' for the afternoon and then I'll spend the night there. We'll go to the courthouse first thing."

They hugged and Ella got into her car. Before Erin could get to hers, Brody materialized with a concerned look. "Hey there, you doin' okay?"

She hugged him. "Yeah. I'm good. It was weird. Flashback in a big way about the whole metal detector thing. It smells the same in the courthouse. I need to go home and scrub it off my skin."

"Wanna tell me why Todd called here to ask if I'd check on you?"

She told him about their argument and he laughed. "You're both perfect for each other. You're outnumbered with Ben. Lucky for you, you've got enough spine to push back when they push you. And they push because they love you and want to take care of you. I have to stop myself half the time too, and I'm your brother." He shrugged.

"I know. I'm not mad at him. I just need to process this and go about my business. Honestly, if I'd gone home and stopped for a few minutes I'd have dwelled. I don't need to dwell. I need to keep moving. Like a shark, you know?"

He kissed her forehead. "Yeah, like a shark. That's you. Don't forget dinner at Palomino on Saturday."

She closed her eyes and prayed for patience. Label people were in town, and she'd promised Adrian she'd go and play nice.

"Yeah, can't forget that. I should take Ben too. I hate leaving him out of this stuff."

"So bring him. The label people won't care. As for life in general and living in an alternative relationship? We need to have coffee or a drink to talk about that one, Erin. You know I'm fine with it. Adrian too. But Ben's folks don't seem to be the kind to easily accept that he's in a threesome with you and another dude. I know you want to show him you care as much about him as you do Todd, but you know you have to remember how it will blow back on them too. You're a fucking musician; no one cares what you do. They're not."

"I know. Don't think I don't. I'm not in the mood for *it's not fair* right now. I'm going home. I love you."

"You know where I am if you need me to kick some ass."

She rolled her eyes and went home.

"Ms. Keenan?"

Erin looked up at the doorman calling her name. It was hard to get used to being called Keenan, but it made Todd happy and it gave her another level of anonymity, so that worked too.

"Yep. What's up?"

"You have a visitor." He pointed to a statuesque brunette waiting near the front doors. She knew who it was before the woman introduced herself

"Caroline, am I right?"

The smile faltered a bit. Erin really wished this had happened another day. She usually went straight up to her place, but of course she had to stop by the mail room. *Damn.*

"Yes. And you're Erin."

"Ben's at work." Erin checked her watch.

"I know. I thought we could talk."

Erin sighed heavily. "About what?"

"Just things. I thought perhaps it would be good if we talked without Ben."

"Oh no. I don't do that. You could have called; you know the number. Instead you're here in my lobby when you know Ben is at work. That makes me very uncomfortable. I don't go around Ben."

"Will you have a cup of coffee with me? I promise to be quick."

"I'm really not trying to be rude, but what's your angle here? I've had a crappy day and I'm not in any mood to dance around the subject. Ben is mine, I'm not giving him back, and I don't plan to share him with you. Is that what you needed to know?"

"He said you were blunt."

"Caroline, I know he cares about you. I know you were together for several years. If you're trying to be my friend, asking me to do something Ben doesn't know about isn't the way to do it."

"I'm not trying to get him back. I just thought we could be friends."

Erin was so tired. "As I said, you're going about it entirely the wrong way. How would you feel if you were in my shoes?"

"I'd want to size up the competition."

Erin laughed. "That might be true if I thought you were competition. But Ben's not a prize to be won. I'd never play with him like that, and if you would, you weren't worthy of him. To be quite honest, at this point, I can safely say we're not friends. Mission accomplished."

"So you'll stop Ben from seeing me?"

"Is that what this is about? I haven't stopped him from doing anything. He's an adult. What is your deal? Seriously? I mean, Ben cared about you once. He still does, from what he tells me. There must be some redeeming qualities about you. But I'm really failing to see them right now."

"Erin? What's going on?"

She turned to see Ben approach.

"I don't know. I was just asking Caroline that right now, but she seems unwilling to answer me clearly."

"Maybe we should all go upstairs." Ben put his arm around Erin's waist.

That was the last thing Erin wanted. She just wanted to go and take a bath, not play some passive-aggressive games with an ex-girlfriend.

At the same time, she didn't want to upset Ben, so she sighed long and tired and walked toward the elevators.

Once inside she turned to Caroline. "Not to be rude, but as I said, I've had a very crappy day. Why don't you talk to Ben and deal with whatever is bothering you. I'm going to take a long bath."

She tried to turn and go down the hall, but Ben was on her in three steps. "What is wrong? Did she say something?'

"I'm not having a good afternoon. I don't want to deal with this. I don't have the energy. I spent the morning in an assault trial. I got into a fight with Todd. I went to work, dealt with my friend who was upset. Came home and your ex is waiting in my lobby wanting to talk to me behind your back. I'm very tired and I need to be away from people right now. Deal with her and get her out of my house."

He touched her cheek, drawing his thumb over her lips. "I'm sorry it was a shitty day. I'll be there in a few minutes."

"Bring liquor and be naked."

He grinned. "Of course."

Ben watched her retreat into their bedroom and close the door. He took a deep, calming breath and turned back to Caroline, who was busily taking in the place.

"What's going on? I thought you went back home. Why are you here?"

"I wanted to see her. Is that a crime? I'm back in Seattle to check on my dad. They're taking the cast off his hand and so I was downtown and I had the address."

"It's not a crime, but it's not normal. You're a bit past the wanting to check out the new woman stage, aren't you? In any case, I don't like that you've gone behind my back."

"She said that too. I like her. She puts you first. I'm going to go. I really didn't mean to upset her. It sounds like she had a bad day. I should have called first. She's right. Do you think we could have dinner before I go back home? Bring Erin and Todd too, if you like."

"I don't know. Caroline, you don't understand her at all. She'd never stop me from having dinner with you if I wanted, but she takes our relationship really seriously. If she feels you've tried to go around that, you may have done permanent damage here."

"I'm sorry. I was here and I just, I missed you. I wanted to see her with my own eyes, this woman you speak of like you never did of me." She looked up at him and he shook his head.

"Get out. You don't get to do this."

"I wasn't coming on to you. I wouldn't do that. Not to you and not to her. We were close once. I miss that."

He went to the door and opened it. "You need to go. I'm not joking. I understand what you did. I understand why you did it. But it's not okay. I love her. I love what we have together and she gets me like no one else. Not you, not Todd, not Greg, not my family—*no one* has accepted me and understood me like Erin. I choose her well-being over anything else. You have to go."

She looked sad, but she nodded and went into the hallway. "I am sorry. I really didn't mean to cause all this upset. I just wanted to check her out, see if I had any competition should I want you back. Stupid, I know. But I'm sorry." She raised a hand and walked away.

He shut the door, not watching her a moment more. Only seeing the lines around Erin's eyes.

He knew about the fight. Todd had shown up, really pissed off,
and they'd talked it over. Ben had left work in his hands and decided to come home a little early. The workmen would be packing
up next door in a few minutes, but they'd leave through there anyway. He and Erin were alone, and that's what counted.

He grabbed a bottle of tequila, a big bottle of water and a shot
glass, and headed toward their bathroom.

Her eyes were red-rimmed and his heart broke. He took his
clothes off, settled in behind her in the tub and poured her a shot.

He took one himself and put his arms around her. He didn't say
anything for some minutes. She needed the silence, he knew.

Instead he massaged her shoulders and scrubbed her back. He
rinsed her and she turned, on her knees.

"Baby, I hate to see you so sad," he said before she brushed her
lips across his.

"I'm all right. I just needed the silence for a while. I just needed
to not be responsible for anyone's anything. Thank you."

He stood, helping her out and then drying her off. She patiently
let him take care of her before taking his hand and following him
into their bedroom.

"How about a fire?"

She nodded as she got into bed and he hit the switch. Instantly,
the room lit with a golden glow.

"Takeout?" He looked at the clock. "Todd will be leaving in a
few minutes. I can have him stop on his way home."

She nodded again and he went to the phone. Todd heard the request, asked if she was all right and sounded relieved when Ben said
yes. He said he was leaving then and would be home as soon as possible.

Ben turned back to her and slid into bed, holding her.

Finally, he spoke. "I'm sorry you had a shitty day. I'm sorry about the fight with Todd and I'm sorry about Caroline."

"It was a stupid fight with Todd. He wanted me safe and got all macho. I needed to be alone and pushed him away. He got snitty, I got bitchy. It's fine, I'm sure. You all wouldn't stay around if you couldn't handle bitchy."

He smiled. "Plucky. Sassy. Independent. Not bitchy. Not most of the time. Although you hog the chocolate gelato when you're PMSing."

"As for Caroline, I don't have a problem with you having dinner with her or whatever. I don't like this *let's talk without Ben around* business. She barged into my life at precisely the wrong time and she wouldn't just spit out why she was here, although I have a good idea."

He kissed her forehead and adjusted his body to look into her face. "Yeah? And what's that?"

"Ben, Ben, Ben. So very pretty but not very sharp sometimes. Your little Caroline wanted to see me so she could gauge how easy it would be to maneuver back into your life. Now, she may not really want you back. She left you easily enough before. I'm sorry, but it's true. Stupid cow. But she's one of those girls who may not really want that piece of cake but they don't want anyone else to have it either. For all her talk about being poly and oh so progressive and free, she's full of shit. And I'm in the music industry, I can spot someone who's full of shit a mile away. She wanted to talk to me to propose a little foursome action. Oh, she'd invite us to a club like the Spot or something, a way to get us all into position, and she'd make her play. Only, the thing she misses is that it takes more than big tits to be yours. If that was the case, you'd *be* hers."

She slid a hand up from his belly to his heart. It was disconcerting to hear her be so frank and be so fucking right all at once.

"You see, I *know* you. I know you deep inside. I care about all of you. I want to understand you. I'm not with you for your magical cock, although I do enjoy it. I'm with you because you're like a wish come to life. She didn't love you. Not really. But I do, and because of that, she'll never have you the way I do. I'm not jealous, I'm just annoyed she wasted my time and yours."

He kissed her, feeling laid bare before her.

"You have Todd. You'd have been happy without me." And there it was. She'd pulled his deepest fear from him without asking, without prying. Because he trusted her.

She looked at him carefully, not jumping to answer and deny off the bat. "Yes. I do have Todd, and yes, I'd have been happy without you. I *was* happy without you. But that was before you stepped into our lives and now that you're here, I *wouldn't* be happy without you. It's not Ozzie and Harriet, but it's us and it works."

She knew just what to say. He was defenseless. If she wanted to hurt him, she could do so very easily. But he knew she wouldn't. That last bit he'd been holding back, that small knot of fear, of feeling on the outside, loosened and fell away.

He rolled on top of her and she opened to him easily, wrapping her legs around his waist as he slipped inside.

"Already wet."

"We've established I like you." She smirked up at him.

"Good. But if this is how you are with everyone you like, I'm concerned." He set an easy rhythm.

"Ah, but I don't like too many people. You're safe. My pussy's virtue is safe."

"I love you. It doesn't matter what Caroline wanted today. She can't have it."

She arched, rolling her hips to take him deeper. "I love you too. And I know."

He laughed and continued to fuck into her until a pretty flush built from her breasts up her neck. He bent to lick, tasting salt and woman against the heated column of her throat.

"Would you like to come?" he murmured, kissing up her neck, stopping just below her ear.

"Yes." She swallowed hard and whimpered when he swirled his tongue in that supersensitive spot.

"Touch yourself."

She reached in between them, and he felt her forearm muscles cord as she began to work her clit. He wouldn't be long once she started this. First it was ridiculously hot and made him want to blow every time she did it, and second, her cunt was utterly irresistible when she climaxed. Hot, wet and tight, those inner muscles rippling around him until he couldn't take it.

But really, it was the intimacy they'd shared that had pushed him so far to start with.

When she gasped and her eyes went desire-blurred, he felt his own orgasm rush from the tips of his toes and fingers straight to his balls and deep into her body.

He'd just kissed her and rolled off when Todd came home.

"I'm going to clean up really quick," she said, rolling out of bed. "I'll be back."

He watched her pretty, naked ass as she hurried into the bathroom.

Todd smelled the sex when he got to the doorway. He was hungry for her, hungry to reconnect and to know she was all right. Hungry to know *they* were all right.

"Hey," Ben said from the bed, looking every bit as satisfied as he should.

"Hey, yourself." Todd dropped the pizza and antipasti on the bed. "I'll grab us something to eat on and be right back."

Before he'd reached the hallway though, Erin came out of the bathroom, naked and disheveled, looking beautiful and sex-tousled. She saw him and smiled, coming into his arms and everything was all right again.

"I'm sorry," she said as Todd held her. "I know you were just looking out for me."

Todd snorted, kissing the curve of her cheek. "You stole my thunder. I'm sorry too. I know I pushed your buttons at a time you were most likely to react."

"Mmm," she hummed as he kissed down her neck. "I'm starving." She eyed the pizza box and he hurried to grab the plates and some cream sodas, which she took from him and began to pass around as he got naked too.

Sitting on their big bed, naked and laughing, they ate dinner and made more good memories to ease away the bad.

31

In the month following the trial and the guilty verdict, their lives smoothed again as they moved toward Thanksgiving. The Keenans and Copelands always had a giant celebration, and so of course they'd all go to that. This year Brody and Adrian would also go, which meant Mercy and Marianne would be there too, because what young girl would miss the chance to have dinner with Adrian Brown?

Erin awoke to a cock tapping her lips and Todd looming over her. She kept her eyes closed and opened to him. The way they needed her touched something deep within her.

He groaned in that grumbly, morning way, entirely satisfied male, and it hardened her nipples.

She concentrated on the head and crown, fisting around the root. The room was cool and dark and she heard Ben shift and the soft exhale as he must have opened his eyes to take in the scene before him.

The bedding rustled as he moved to them and his hands found her belly and it was her turn to moan when he gave her mound a light slap, not hard but the way she liked it.

"Wait a sec," Todd said, flipping on the bedside lamp. "Now I can watch you eat her pussy."

Ben chuckled as he found his way between her thighs and began to lick, slow and steady.

"I love it when you make that sound with my cock in your mouth," Todd said, idly tugging on her nipple rings. She arched, digging her heels into the bed as Ben slid his tongue into her gate.

Todd collared her throat and her entire body shuddered in response. Her eyes fluttered closed as she concentrated on Todd's cock and Ben's mouth on her cunt.

More. She needed more and Todd knew it. He slid his cock into her mouth deeper, keeping his rhythm up.

"Your mouth is so hot. I'm close. So. Fucking. Close."

One of her hands had burrowed into Ben's hair and the other still held the base of Todd's cock. She let go of Ben and dipped down, past his mouth, wetting her fingers with her own juices before moving them up to play against the supersensitive skin of Todd's anus.

He stuttered a moan as she pressed just inside, stroking. He hardened impossibly more and came, exhaling hard.

Erin had just started to come when Ben reared up, flipped her over, pushed her knee up near her chest and entered her from behind. Her nipples pressed against the blankets and the echoes of her climax rippled through her, ebbing and flowing with each thrust and retreat of his cock.

She let her muscles go and took him into herself over and over until he leaned down, kissed her neck and came.

Afterward, she rolled over, pushing the hair from her face as she caught her breath. "My! That's certainly a way to wake up."

Todd's cell phone rang and he muttered a curse as he rambled from the room to grab it.

She went up on her elbow to look down at Ben. His hair was

getting long and he probably needed a cut, but she really liked it this way. Brushing a fingertip over one of his nipples, she loved the way his lips parted and he sucked in a breath.

"What are you thinking? You have such a wicked look on your face."

"I was thinking how much I liked your hair now. I love how it curls up where it touches your neck. Sort of sloppy and loose but sexy. And also how hot it would be if you pierced this nipple right here." She underlined the sentence with a flick of her tongue, and he laughed.

"Then I'll do it." He shrugged. "I can't let my hair get any longer than this, I'm sorry to say. Our clients like me more clean-cut. But no one is going to see my shirt off at work."

"They'd better not." She stretched, well aware he watched her. "I've got work to do. The work next door on the upper floor should be done by the end of the day, so I need to cook for the Thanksgiving feast all day today and then get ready to move our stuff into the new bedroom tomorrow."

"I'm surprised you don't want to move tonight." Ben swatted her as she moved toward the bathroom.

"I'd love to, but they only painted in there two days ago and I want to give it one more day to dry and for the smell to dissipate," she called out before shutting the door.

When she came out, teeth brushed and cleaned up, Ben had left, so he'd probably used the other bathroom. She rustled through the dresser and found clothes and pulled them on.

In the living room she rounded a corner to catch Todd jam a finger on his phone to disconnect a call.

"Is everything okay?" she asked, following him out into the kitchen.

"I need to go deal with a client." He sighed. It was an unofficial holiday, the day before Thanksgiving, and she knew he'd wanted to stay home all day and laze around alone with her and Ben. But she also knew what it was to run a business.

"Here in downtown?"

He nodded.

"Go. It's still early. I'm going to be around all day cooking anyway. Go deal and finish." She shrugged and hopped up on a bar stool.

"You want some help?" Ben asked him, putting a hand on Erin's shoulder to stay her, before moving to make the coffee.

"Nah, thanks. It's Harris. You know how she is." Todd kissed Ben's temple and then put his arms around Erin, pulling her back against his body as he stood behind her. "I have to go, reset her system, explain it to her yet again and then I'll be back. No use you having to deal with her."

"*Hmpf.* She likes looking at you. Tell her your wife will scratch her eyes out if she touches. A little eye candy won't hurt though. Look at you." Erin laughed, entangling her fingers with his.

"Ha. She's in her seventies. Not my type."

"I believe the proper answer is *anyone but Erin and Ben are not my type.*" Erin smirked his way.

"You two keep me busy enough I don't have time anyway." Todd kissed the top of her head. "I'm going to shower and get over there. Text me if you need me to bring anything home."

He disappeared and the workers showed up next door.

"I'm going to be glad when they're finished." Ben pulled eggs from the fridge. "Sit. Let me make you breakfast for a change."

"Thank you." She smiled at him and watched him work.

Todd left and, within minutes, Cope showed up.

Ben let his brother in, and Cope rubbed his hands together at the sight of food on the table.

"You have radar." Ben frowned, but Cope shoved past and gave Erin a hug before sitting at the table.

"I like to smooch up on your woman. Plus," he said, shoving two pieces of bacon into his mouth at once, making Erin wince, "Mom is coming by today. Just thought I'd warn you."

"She's never dropped by here before. I'm seeing her tomorrow. What's the deal?" Ben asked, pouring another cup of coffee since Cope had stolen his.

"She's invited a *friend* for you for tomorrow."

Ben and Erin both froze.

"What?"

Cope laughed. "What? Come on, Ben. She wants you to be married. She wants grandkids. She had her hopes pinned on Caroline and then she moved. You haven't found anyone suitable to breed with. So there's some daughter visiting a neighbor"—he snickered—"and she's coming tomorrow."

"This is insane."

"It's what moms do, Ben. Just flirt and make her happy." Erin didn't want any discord between Ben and his family. Having such a big secret was difficult.

"Tell her you're gay." Cope looked up from shoveling food into his mouth.

"Then she'll hook me up with nice single boys from the neighborhood." Ben glared at Erin. "And I'm not pretending to be interested in some random woman when the one I'm in love with is four feet away. It's stupid."

"Yes, it is." She moved closer, to touch him. "But what are you going to do? This will only get worse the longer you go unmarried. We're going to have to find a way of dealing with it in the long term, but let's get through tomorrow first."

Cope reached out and squeezed Ben's forearm. "Hey, I'm sorry, man. I just wanted to give you a heads-up and get some food. I didn't mean to upset you."

Ben sighed and kissed Erin's forehead. "Eat. You're right. We'll get through tomorrow and the holidays and then we'll figure out what to do."

"I'm going to start cooking. Take your mom next door to your rooms." Erin shrugged, getting up. "It'll be a nice tour and she can get you alone."

"I'll just stay here to help lick the spoon." Cope grinned, looking like a miniature version of Ben.

"Don't lick anything else."

"As if."

The two brothers bickered as Erin began to chop the vegetables for the stuffing and tried not to think about what a difficult thing Ben faced.

She was laughing and sipping her second cup of coffee when Todd came through the door, talking loudly to none other than Annalee Copeland.

"Look who I found downstairs." Todd looked around quickly, relieved nothing naked was happening, and ushered her in.

"Hello, Mrs. Copeland. Can I get you a cup of coffee?" Erin called out from her place in the kitchen.

"This is such a big, lovely place!" Annalee, all nearly six feet of her, came in and gave Erin a hug. Her hair was dark like Cope's, but they both had her blue eyes. She was a seamstress and had a small shop in Ballard that her family had operated for two generations. Erin liked her a lot. She was open and generous, funny like Lorie, and she loved her family.

"Andrew, what are you doing here?"

Erin laughed, pouring a cup of coffee for Annalee, who thanked her.

"Free food, Mom." He shrugged, and she rolled her eyes at her son before looking at Erin.

"He was already at my house to eat breakfast first thing."

"That was before I went on my run."

Annalee sighed. "I raised them all to cook, goodness knows."

Ben came through from the rest of their newly enlarged place. He smiled when he saw his mother. "Hey!" He hugged her. "Fancy seeing you here."

"I haven't seen you in a while and I wanted to see this place. Lorie said the renovations were finished?"

"I just had dinner with you on Monday." Ben put his arm around her shoulders.

"Still."

"You want a tour?"

Her face lit up. "Yes. Show me the place."

Cope stood. "Me too. I haven't seen the office space yet."

"Come on then." Ben looked back at Erin, who smiled, and he wondered just what he would do about the situation brewing. He'd lived with Caroline, and as far as his family knew, Greg was a tenant who lived in their mother-in-law unit. But this was different. They knew Todd and Erin were married. They knew Todd. He wasn't sure how to broach it, not that he hadn't thought about it nearly constantly.

"Wow, they've done a great job." Cope turned around as he took in the space.

"The expanded kitchen is here." He pointed to a state-of-the-art kitchen with marble counters, fridge drawers and all the bells and whistles you could imagine. "We'll all move here and they're going to rehab the rest of the apartment next. Erin will keep her music room and expand into the bedroom next door. The kitchen in there will be removed and that entire living space will be a media room with a home theater. There'll be a library back where the master bedroom is now and a guest room."

He had to admit the renovations had gone exceptionally well and their new living space was more incredible than he could have ever imagined. He did get the occasional twinge at how much it all cost and what a large portion of it all Erin paid for, but she'd been so excited and then had given him and Todd the *if it were reversed, you'd want me to take it* speech. So they'd given in but volunteered to pay for the new furniture.

"Our living room will be small for now until they're done next door."

"Where's your room going to be?" his mother asked with perceptive eyes.

"Here." He opened up French doors leading to a small living area with a couch and a television and into a bedroom with an en suite bath. They'd moved his bedroom furniture into it the day before, and he'd dashed in to rumple it a bit before his mom came in.

"Wow. Do you need a roommate?" Cope asked.

He snorted at his brother.

"This is very nice, Ben. Not as big as your old apartment or even your house with Caroline. Aren't you a little old to rent a room in someone's house? How are you ever going to find a woman if you live here?"

"I like it here. I love the building." He ushered them out and across the apartment to another set of French doors. "This is our office space." The workmen were nearly finished with it. "We'll all work in this space instead of having to lease space downtown." He backed out, waving at the workers.

"The main bedrooms are upstairs. A master and a room just off of that that can be a nursery someday, along with another bedroom." The place was huge and he loved it. They'd all worked on the plans together, made their future together.

"Oh! You'll like this, Mom." He led them outside to the very large deck. "Erin had them build a modified greenhouse. The hot tub is in there, so the heat stays in, but the walls slide back for when the weather heats up too."

"This is all very extensive and expensive. I guess when you're a rockstar you can do that." His mother smiled tightly.

"Cope, I need to talk to Mom."

His brother's eyes widened a moment. "Are you *sure* about this?"

"Yes."

"Okay then." Cope left them alone on the balcony, and he took his mother into the greenhouse, where it was still very warm.

"Spit it out, Mom."

"Ben, this isn't right for you. You're hanging on to Todd and his wife as a way to keep from moving on. You're hiding from your future. I know this breakup with Caroline was hard. You've been different in the year since she left. But you can't think living here is going to solve that."

"I appreciate that you love me and want me to be happy. I wasn't happy when things ended with Caroline, but not so much because she left. I wasn't really that happy when I was with her. I seem different because I'm happy now. Can you just trust me on that?"

"Are you gay? Because if you are, that's okay. We love you just the same."

He smiled. "No, I'm not gay. I do like men, but I like women too. More than I like men, but anyway, this is not a conversation I really want to have with you."

"So you're bisexual? Then you have lots more options!"

He laughed. "Mom, truly, I have never been happier than I am right now. Never."

"I see the way you look at her," she said quietly and he knew.

"Who?"

"Erin. She's a lovely woman and I like her, but she's not for you. No good can come of you living here. You can't love your best friend's wife. Todd has been like a brother to you. Don't betray him like this. You don't want to be that person."

He exhaled long and slow. "I would never betray Todd. Or Erin, for that matter." He moved to look out over the city. Typical November Seattle weather; the rain spattered on the glass as he gathered his thoughts. "I have to tell you something, but I need you to know before I do that Dad would never understand. If you tell him, or Lorie or anyone else . . . What I'm going to tell you, it could hurt people. I'm asking you to keep this secret, and I know that's not fair. But I'm asking anyway."

She sat on the chair near the hot tub. "You can tell me anything. You know that."

"I *am* with someone right now. With two someones."

She blinked at him. "What do you mean? You're dating two people and they don't know about each other? Is one of them a boy? I know your dad is old-fashioned, but I could work on him and we could get him to accept it in time. I know we could. He loves you no matter who you love."

He'd lucked out in the mom department. "You're amazing, Mom, but you may not be so happy to help when I tell you the rest. I'm with Erin and Todd. The three of us are in a relationship. A committed relationship. I love Erin very, very much, which is why you see me looking at her the way I do. And Todd, he's been my best friend for as long as I can remember. I live here because this is our house. I wouldn't live anywhere else."

She got pale. "I don't understand. They're married. So they keep you like a pet? To service them when they get bored?"

"Mom! Do you think I'd ever allow that? Do you think Todd would ever do that to anyone? I know you don't know Erin very well, but she would never do that either. Obviously we can't all three be married, but I consider Erin my wife too."

"What about children? How will you do that? Have you even thought of this?"

"You know her child was murdered four and a half years ago, right?"

She nodded.

"She never considered having children again until Todd, and then me. If and when they come, they'll be mine and Todd's both. Legally, they'll be his because he's married to her, but we've spoken with an attorney about how to handle power-of-attorney and medical issues. That sort of thing. It's not perfect, but I've never been happier. Not ever."

His mother stood. "I don't know what to say. You're an adult and I love you. That won't change. You're right that your father would definitely not understand. Hell, I don't understand. I also don't like Erin very much right now."

He grabbed her hand. "You can't understand how it was for me before. I can't explain it except to say I was alone and lonely and Erin makes me feel whole and loved. I know this is strange. I know it's hard to accept, but don't be angry at Erin for making me happy."

She squeezed his hand. "I have to go. Your secret is safe with me. You can always talk to me, Ben. But I need to think. I'll see you tomorrow, I guess."

He walked her out, and she didn't look at Erin as she left. "Hey, Cope, why don't you take Mom home?"

Cope looked back at Erin, kissed her cheek and waved at Todd before meeting their mother and walking her toward the elevator.

When Ben got back, Erin looked stunned.

"You told her."

He nodded.

"She hates me."

"She doesn't." He moved to her, but she stepped back.

"She wouldn't even look at me! We're supposed to go over there for dinner tomorrow and you told her? Without even talking to me first? They know you. They know Todd. You're both family. I'm not. Oh my god, what must she think about me?"

"I had to tell her, Erin."

Todd stayed where he was in the living room but listened intently.

"She thought I was hiding from my future because I was living like a twenty-year-old in my best friend's basement. She said she saw how I looked at you and how she worried I'd betray Todd. I had to tell someone the truth. I hate living a lie. I have this beautiful, wonderful thing and I wanted my mother to understand that. Is that so wrong?"

She sighed, the rigidity in her back relaxing a bit.

"I only told her once she promised not to tell anyone," he explained to them both. "And she won't."

He walked another few steps, all his tension falling from his shoulders when she allowed him to hold her. "Please don't be mad. I had to tell her."

"I'm not mad. But I'm worried they'll all hate me."

His heart ached. "She doesn't understand, but she doesn't hate you."

His mouth found hers and took it. Claimed it because she was his and he'd said it out loud. Erin wrapped her arms around his neck and held on as he possessed her, giving herself to him, soothing him even as that submission enflamed him.

"They're nearly done next door." Todd spoke softly and Ben pulled back.

"She won't tell your mother," Ben said to Todd.

"I know. And I understand why you did it. I know how hard it is for you to have to pretend to be the best friend while I get to be her husband in public."

Erin just watched them both, her men. Christ, this was unexpected. She didn't blame Ben for wanting to be in the open with his mother, but she cringed to think about spending the entire day with them all tomorrow and pretending his mother didn't think she was the whore of Babylon. She'd never been ashamed of her sexuality before, but for the first time she felt embarrassed at what his mother might think. Yes, it was someone else's hang-up, but that someone was important to her because she was important to Ben.

"Bread is rising. That'll take a while. Stay out of everything in the fridge in here. If you're hungry, go next door. I'm going to take a bath over in our new bathroom."

Both men looked at her lecherously.

"*Alone*, you perverts."

She gathered her clothes. She'd moved her bath stuff up there a few days prior. Important things first. She went up the stairs and headed down the hall. The new space was perfect and she loved it. The bathroom was a work of art. The sunken tub put her old one to shame. She'd hung up sconces and lit the candles in them, turning on some music and starting the water.

The bath was the place she'd always gone to think and escape her troubles. Even as a kid she'd done it, in the tiny bathtub they'd had in the house she'd grown up in and the apartments Brody could afford.

Now *she* could afford giant tubs and bathrooms the size of the shithole apartment they'd had in Hollywood.

She took some of the scented oil she hoarded zealously and poured it into the water and the scent of blood oranges hit the air. She'd found the stuff while in Italy and had charmed the woman who owned the small apothecary in the hill town into sending her some. A batch or three would come at random. Whenever Bartolla thought of it. But always when Erin had needed it.

Erin disrobed, slid into the silky, heated water and closed her eyes to think about everything that had happened in the last year.

She couldn't fault Ben even though she wished he'd spoken with her first and had chosen a better time than the day before Thanksgiving. Annoyance and embarrassment surged through her and she had to breathe in deep again to find her center, to calm down. She realized she had a freedom neither of them had. Total acceptance from her family. And Todd was her husband. Everyone knew it and accepted it. But Ben had to hide and she understood his pain.

They'd started down this twisty path and she had to accept the consequences. She just hoped it didn't end up hurting Ben or Todd, because she was pretty sure she couldn't survive that.

She sighed and let it go. It would happen the way it happened, and in truth it was up to Ben and Todd to tell their families or not. How they might perceive her was small in comparison to how the men felt about hiding. The problem was how interconnected the Keenans and the Copelands were, but again, that wasn't something she could do anything about except support Ben and Todd.

God, this bathtub was heaven.

There was a tap on the door and she smiled. They'd given her a good half an hour. Frankly, that showed a lot of restraint. The water was beginning to cool anyway. She was sure they'd danced around out there nervously, starting up the stairs and then going back down a dozen times.

"Yes, you can come in," she called out, and the door opened, admitting two very lovely looking men. She stood up and enjoyed the way they watched.

"Are you mad at me?" Ben asked, handing her a towel.

She moved to him, cupping his face with her hands. "No." Tiptoeing up, she kissed him quickly, but he didn't want quick. His arms slid around her and held her tight as he turned the kiss into something else entirely.

He broke the kiss and turned her into Todd's arms, where she followed happily, enjoying the difference in his kiss.

"We knew this would happen at some point," Todd said when he pulled back.

She shrugged. "Really, I'm not the one to decide this stuff. My brothers are fine with it. I don't have to hide it. Ben has the biggest burden here. You and Ben have to deal with the fear of your families finding out. I don't have that. I will support whatever you decide."

She grabbed her sweater and pulled it on as they watched her hungrily. The testosterone level in the room made her sweat more than the heat from the water had.

"Come on. We can't start anything right now. The workers are still here and I have bread to bake."

"I'm going to die of a toxic overload of semen."

Laughing, she hopped up on the counter. "I just sucked your cock a few hours ago, Todd." She pulled on one thigh-high stocking, warm cashmere, a present from the man looking at her like a very bad wolf.

He stepped to her, and her gaze snagged on the movement of his hand as he popped his jeans open and pulled his cock out, fisting it a few times.

"Perfect position. These cabinets are perfect for this. Open up."

She scooted to the very edge and put her heels on the counter next to her hips. Yay for yoga!

Ben swore softly as she exposed her pussy to Todd, waiting for him to fill her.

Todd tested her readiness, groaning when he found her wet. The fat knob of his cock brushed against her and pressed inside quickly. The pleasure at being filled by him shot up her spine.

"Doesn't matter when you took me last, Erin. I *always* want you."

She looked into his eyes, eyes that held only her, and the swell of love nearly made her cry. "I love you," she whispered.

"Thank god," he said as he fucked into her body fast and hard. It wasn't finessed, it wasn't slow and seductive. He wanted her and he took her. Nothing was sexier.

She held on to the edge of the counter. Ben stepped forward and reached between them, finding her clit, and she sucked in air at how wonderful it felt.

Todd turned and Ben leaned forward. As always when she watched them together, she wanted to melt into a puddle. They kissed each other differently than they kissed her. With each other they were harder, rougher and yet neither tried to dominate the other. They saved that for her. *Wheee!*

The kiss broke and Ben was on her in moments, her hair in his grasp, pulling her head back to kiss her neck. She had to let go of the counter as he bent her back, his fingers still working her clit.

Overwhelmed, she held on to his shoulders and wrapped her legs around Todd's waist. Shivers wracked her as she came, and a few breaths later, Todd's cock jerked inside her as he followed.

Ben stood and Todd helped her upright and down off the counter. "I just got all cleaned up and you've sullied me again," she joked, and Todd didn't look abashed in the slightest.

She pulled on her skirt, zipped up the side and turned back to Ben, who leaned against the counter where Todd had just fucked her.

"Hmm, what about you?" she asked in her best purr.

Todd moved close and pulled the front of Ben's jeans apart. Erin blinked. Todd was easy enough with kissing and the occasional fondling with Ben, but he hadn't initiated sexual contact in this way, at least that she'd seen.

"Bring me the lube, honey. Let's take care of this."

Erin moved quickly to the drawer that held all manner of things, condoms and lube primarily, and pulled out the Boy Butter. "He likes to get jerked with this," she said in Todd's ear, but loud enough for Ben to hear.

She didn't do anything other than watch, not wanting to break into the moment between them. She caught Todd's eyes in the mirror every once in a while when she could tear her gaze from his hands sliding, one after the other, up and off Ben's cock, over and over. Ben's eyes went half-lidded and his breath quickened and shallowed.

"Harder," Ben said to Todd, his voice desire-rough.

The muscles in Todd's arms corded as he angled his wrists differently to fist over Ben's cock harder. Ben leaned back and began to thrust up into Todd's grip and the sounds of male grunting and groaning made her sway as a flush built from her gut outward.

When Ben came, she was transfixed by his facial expression, feeling like a voyeur.

She moved slow like honey to clean Ben with a warm, wet washcloth.

Todd smiled as he looked her up and down. "I'm a really lucky man. A woman wearing a tight sweater and a short skirt with thigh-high stockings is going to bake bread for me. A hot man to share her with. It's good to be me." Todd winked as he dried his hands off.

32

Lorie *ooh*ed and *aah*ed over the bread and other things Erin had brought, and Annalee studiously avoided her. It made Erin want to throw up, but there was nothing to be done about it.

The Keenans' home was filled to the gills with people, absent, thankfully, the neighbor girl Annalee wanted to fix Ben up with. At least she'd listened on that.

Joe brought home his new girlfriend, and Liz had a date too. It was warm, the air smelled good with food and spices, and the sound of family filled the air. Erin surveyed it all with a smile, happy to belong to something so wonderful.

Todd came up behind her and wrapped her in his arms. "Hey, gorgeous. You doing all right?"

"More than all right. This is good. The best Thanksgiving I've had in a really long time."

"Good. God, you make me happy." He kissed her cheek and she snuggled back into him, watching the Wii boxing match taking place in the family room.

"Must make your dad happy to whack the crap out of Joe like that."

"God knows I've wanted to more than once," Todd murmured into her ear.

She laughed.

"Erin, your bag is ringing," Mercy called out from the other room.

"Crap, should have turned it off," Erin said, extricating herself from Todd's hold and heading to her phone.

But a 213 area code on the number stopped her in her tracks. She took the phone and went out on the front porch.

"Hello?"

"Erin Brown?"

"Yes," she answered warily.

"It's Detective Emery."

And just like that her legs gave out and she slumped to the deck.

"I'm sorry to bother you on Thanksgiving, but"—he sighed—"I was notified late yesterday that Charles Cabot is getting a parole hearing next month."

She shot up from where she'd been crouched. "What?" she yelled. "Parole? He had a twenty-seven-year sentence. How can he possibly get parole? He killed my daughter. Goddamnit!"

"I'm so very sorry, Erin. You know I am. If I had anything to say about it, he'd be dead. But I don't and he's getting a hearing. They're going to want to hear from you. Can you come down to testify?"

Her legs went away again and she sat with a hard thump on the front steps. It rained on her, but she didn't care.

"Listen, I know it's a bad time. You're probably just getting ready to eat some turkey and pumpkin pie. I wouldn't have bothered you, but I felt you had the right to know. I'll give you a few days. You know where I am. Give me a call by Tuesday, all right?

I'm sorry, Erin. I am. But, damn it, we need you there. We need you to stand up and tell the board what this man has done to you."

She thanked him for telling her and hung up before putting her head on her knees and giving over to tears.

"Where's Erin?" Todd asked Brody, who shrugged.

"Dunno. I haven't seen her in a while. Is everything all right?"

"She was here and then she took a call." Todd looked around but didn't see her.

As he walked through the front entry, he glanced to the left and saw her through the windows, hunched over, sitting on the front steps in the pouring rain. Panic held him for a moment.

He turned to see Ben had just walked into the foyer. "Down the hall in the linen closet. Towels. Hurry," he told Ben as he moved to the door.

Todd rushed outside.

"Erin? Honey?"

She turned, and it was obvious she'd been crying. She turned her back to him, trying to wipe her eyes, but the rain simply made that task impossible.

"You're scaring me. What is it?"

Ben came out, and they each took an arm and brought her inside to where others had gathered in the hall. Ben toweled off her hair and Todd took a hand. His heart thundered. He hadn't seen her this upset since the day in June when he'd broken into her apartment on the anniversary of Adele's death.

Brody pushed his way through and took her upper arms. "What is it? Tell me!"

"Cabot is getting a parole hearing," she said, snapping from her tears. Her hands gripped the front of Brody's sweater, her eyes bearing a haunted look that tore at Todd's heart.

"Okay, everyone out," Todd's mother ordered before she pressed a tumbler into Erin's hand. "Drink it."

Erin gulped it down and coughed.

"That's the way. A little Jameson will get you warm. Go into my closet and grab a sweater," she told Todd's dad, who sent a look of condolence to Todd.

She bent in front of Erin. Todd had managed to get her sitting on the upholstered bench in the front hall. She began to shiver. Ben wrapped a dry towel around her.

His mother took Erin's hands. "This is the bastard who killed Adele?"

Erin paled, which Todd couldn't believe was possible, as she'd already been paler than he'd ever seen her. She nodded and Brody sat on the floor, leaning his head against Erin's side.

Adrian sighed and sat on her other side.

"We'll go down there and testify. We can do that too, right?" Brody asked. "He can't get away with this. They have to know what it's been like since."

Todd's mother brushed a hand over Erin's forehead, pushing her hair back from her eyes. "Erin, sweetie, why don't you change into some dry clothes and lie down for a while? Then you'll wake up and eat and we'll work out how to deal with this. Of course we'll *all* do what we can to support you."

Alarm gripped Todd's gut. Erin had sort of disappeared into herself. He'd never seen her this way. He looked at Ben, who also wore a haunted face.

"Not again." Her voice was a bare whisper. "I want to go home. I want to be alone for a while," Erin said, her voice flat and empty.

Todd's mother turned to him, standing. "Take her home. I'll get you some food to take with. You call the doctor if she's not livelier in a few hours, do you hear me?"

"*No.* Todd and Ben, stay here with your family. Brody or Adrian can take me home. Or I can go myself. I need to be *alone*." Erin spoke, but her eyes didn't have their usual warmth. She wasn't even pissed that they'd all been coddling her. That in and of itself was worrying.

Todd cut his gaze to Brody, who returned his concern.

Brody stood. "Okay, Erin. Let's go, baby." He wrapped her in another towel and Adrian grabbed her purse. "Stay here. No use your day getting ruined. I'm just going to give her a Xanax and tuck her into bed," he said to Todd.

"The hell," Ben spoke from next to Todd with such vehemence Lorie looked at him askance.

Annalee approached and put her arms around Erin, kissing her cheek. "Let them give you comfort. You need it." Erin roused a bit and more tears came.

Lorie nodded, looking slightly confused.

Renee came forward with several bags of food, DJ at her side. "What can we do?"

Todd was so grateful for these people, every last one of them.

"Brody, it's okay, I've got her." Todd took over, and Brody nodded, approval in his eyes.

"Honey, let's get you home. We'll tuck up into bed, eat turkey and you can wear your flannel jammies."

She nodded absently when he'd been hoping for a smile. Ben came up on Erin's other side.

"Get her home. Call me later and let us know she's all right," his mother said.

"I'll make some calls," his father said. "We'll make sure this bastard stays in prison."

Grateful for all the support, Todd hugged them both and took the bags of food.

Ben had deposited her in the car and traded off with Todd, rushing back to say good-bye to his family.

Brody stood at the car door, kissing her forehead. He looked up at Todd. "You call me if you need anything. *Anything*, do you understand?"

Todd nodded. "Of course. I'm just going to get her home and tuck her into bed. Get some Xanax into her and go from there. We'll get hold of her therapist too."

"We have to go down there and testify." Adrian grabbed his arm. "Adele was special. This man took that. He has to pay."

Todd blinked back tears as he nodded. "I know."

Ben came out and got into the car, moving to her immediately. Todd nodded at Erin's brothers. "I'll talk to you both tomorrow."

In the car on the way home she resisted when they tried to get her out of her wet clothes. Todd just turned the heater up and Ben held her tight. She didn't say anything. She didn't cry. She just rested in his arms and that alarmed him.

When they got home, she pushed away once they got inside. "I need to be by myself."

"Tough." Todd shook his head, frustrated. "You don't live by yourself. We come with the deal now."

"You don't get every part of me." She went upstairs and they followed.

In short, jerky movements she pulled her wet clothes off. Like an automaton, she went into the bathroom, turned on the taps to run a bath.

"Take something, damn it." Ben held out a pill and a glass of water.

"I won't."

Her spine straightened and Ben felt a bit better at the sight. If they had to make her mad, so be it. Anything was better than despondent.

"Don't be stubborn, Erin. Just take it. You'll feel better."

She got into the bath, and slid all the way under for so long Ben began to lean to yank her out when she surfaced.

"I'm not taking anything like that again. I can't think straight when I take the pills. I need to think straight."

"Do you? Right now?" Todd knelt next to the tub and squirted soap on the loofah and began to pass it over her back. "You can't just give yourself a fucking break for one day?"

"What do you know about it?"

Ben pulled his clothes off and got in with her. She groaned in frustration.

"You boys are smart. You know what *I want to be alone* means! But you're still *here*."

"We're not going anywhere. You're hurting and we love you. Let us in." Ben took her hand, kissing her fingers.

"And you're right. I don't know about it. I can't unless you share," Todd said.

"Some things hurt coming out."

Ben heaved a sigh. He ached for her.

"I know they do, gorgeous. But once they're out, they can't poison you anymore."

"I don't want pills. I lived in a narcotic haze for nearly a year after Adele was killed. I'd go to the trial and relive that day over and over. Like a twisted version of *Groundhog Day*. And I'd come home, take pills, wash them down with booze and pass out. I could *not* deal. But I went every day because I wanted Charles Cabot to have to see me. The pills ate me up, the booze ate me up, the rage that my baby was murdered and left to bleed out on the street ate me up." Her voice shook and her eyes held fire. "I'll never do that again. I have to be aware. I have to because he can't get out. It can't happen."

Todd met Ben's eyes over her shoulder and tears shimmered there.

"Nothing will ever happen to you. We won't allow that. You have to know that. This building is safe. We'll escort you to work every day if we have to. He can't touch you." Ben needed her to understand.

She shot up, sending water sloshing over the edges of the tub. "It's not that!" she screamed. "I don't care about that. I wish he had killed me instead."

Todd shook his head hard. "No. Damn it, no. Don't go down this path, Erin."

"He can't be out and living a life when Adele is in a coffin. I can't bear it. She was everything. Beautiful and loving and she did nothing wrong. She was light and love and he stole that. He dirtied it and ruined it." Her face crumpled and Ben stood to gather her to him. "He got twenty-seven years and it's only been four. She'll never see another birthday and he might be getting out."

"Let's get you out of the water and into some pajamas. We'll get the fire going and lie in bed. Okay?" Ben picked her up and she clung to him. Todd wrapped her in a towel, and they headed into the bedroom, where Todd turned on the fireplace.

Erin sighed when Ben put her down. She grabbed the towel and dried off, hung it up before rustling to find panties and her pajamas. They'd been right about that one thing. She wanted the comfort of flannel and hoped it would chase away the chill that had settled back into her bones.

"I'm getting some mulled cider and making plates." Todd looked back at her and narrowed his gaze. "You, in bed."

"Bossy," she muttered, but did it and felt some comfort at the scent surrounding her. *Their* scent.

Ben sat across from her. He'd put on snug black boxer briefs and she couldn't help but feel that zing that existed between them.

"Erin, I understand and *respect* that you want to remain clear-headed here." He paused and she knew he was being very careful with his words.

"Don't. Just say it. I'm not made of glass."

He smiled. "You're fucking scaring me. Okay so, she's gone. He took her from you and it can't be taken back. I'm sorry, so sorry that this happened, but wishing yourself dead in her place won't change that. The only option you have right now is to go down there and testify before the parole board."

"Exactly." Todd walked into the room holding a huge tray of food and a stack of plates. "My mother went a little wild." He smiled. "Eat. Leaving the cider in the Crock-Pot downstairs was an awesome idea. Drink it. I added some Jack."

She picked among the food, not really having an appetite, and Todd took over, heaping potatoes, turkey, stuffing and green beans on a plate.

Fire left a trail down her throat after she took a sip of the cider. "Yeah, just a bit of Jack." She coughed.

It was quiet for a few minutes until they'd eaten, and Erin had to admit she felt better for it.

"I know you're scared." Todd met her eyes as he spoke.

Her skin crawled. "I shouldn't be. I should rush down there and set up a tent outside the parole board in protest."

Todd closed his eyes and finally got it. "You can't feel guilty for being afraid. Erin, he stalked and terrorized you. He nearly killed you and he killed your daughter. Of course you're afraid."

Ben brushed hair from her face. "That's what he relied on. He built it up over time. That's what stalkers and abusers do."

"It doesn't mean you didn't love Adele. It doesn't make you a bad mother. It doesn't make you a bad person."

She burst into tears again and Todd moved the food out of the way so he and Ben could hold her.

"Let it go. We've got you. We won't let you fall." Todd kissed her cheek, tasting the sadness of her tears.

"Baby, let us help you make it through," Ben said and it just made her cry harder.

When she'd reached the stage of hiccups and what had to be a really disgusting runny nose, she sat up and took the hankie Todd held out to her.

"I'm scared," she finally said. "But I'm sick of it. There's nothing else to do but stand up and face him. For myself and for Adele."

"I'm proud of you. And we'll be right by your side when you do this."

"I need to call Jeremy. He would have called if he heard. Emery said the hearing was next month." She scrubbed her face with her hands.

She dialed Jeremy's parents' house, knowing he'd be there.

"Hello, Sue, it's Erin. I'm sorry to bother you, but I need to speak with Jeremy, it's important."

33

Ben pushed his parents' front door open with his foot, his arms full of packages. Erin and Todd came in behind him.

His mother came in, wearing a nervous smile, wringing her hands. She saw Erin and smiled, going to her.

"You ready for this?"

Erin took a deep breath. "Which this do you mean?"

His mother smiled. "Going down to the prison, and I suppose this here too."

"Both things scare the heck out of me. But I love Ben and I'm here to support him. As for the parole board, I'm trying not to think on it too much, but there'll be so many family members there I think I'll be okay." Erin took Ben's mother's hand. "Thank you for asking. I know this is . . . difficult for you. Hard to understand. I'd expect for you to resent me."

Annalee shook her head. "My boy is a grown man. He's capable of his own decisions. I can't promise it'll be easy. But I love him just the same and if you're his choice, I can live with that. Took me a while, I admit. But I watch him and he's happy. A mother can't ask for more."

"Ben?" Cope came out and saw them all. He dropped a kiss on Erin's cheek and nodded at his brother and Todd. "He's out back, working on a new bench for the front porch."

"Let's go."

"With all those tools? Are you sure?" Annalee asked nervously.

The point was moot anyway as Bill came through the back door. "Any coffee for a man frozen to the bone?"

They all went into the kitchen. Bill Copeland had definitely passed his genes on to his sons. He was as tall as Ben, and broad. Dark hair liberally salted with gray and piercing blue eyes marked his features. He had a cop's countenance, wary, watchful, but open all the same. Ben knew he had that look, even when he hadn't been a cop for three years.

"Hey, Dad." Ben waved. It wasn't that Ben didn't think his father loved his sons. He knew their dad loved them. But Bill Copeland was not demonstrative. The hugs and kisses came from Mom and that's how it was. Ben had never seen his father cry and Ben could count on two hands the number of times he'd told his boys he loved them. Bill was a man of few words. A family man, even if he didn't kiss scraped knees.

"Hey there, son. Didn't expect to see you today. Is someone sick?" Bill looked around. "Erin, is everything okay with the hearing? They didn't move it up without telling you, did they?"

Ben liked that his father cared for Erin and for a moment he considered just not saying anything. But the circle of people who knew had gotten wider, as Lorie now knew. DJ wasn't speaking to them at all. The others hadn't heard yet, but it would only be a matter of time.

Erin had asked them both to reconsider doing this before Christmas, but had supported them in the final decision.

"Dad, I need to tell you something."

Erin got off the plane at LAX, her heart thundering in her chest. It was a week before Christmas and she'd been dreading this for the past month.

Todd was in front of her and Ben behind. Cope had gone ahead and she was torn between wanting to laugh at the whole exercise and being comforted.

Adrian took her hand as they moved toward baggage claim. "It's gonna be fine," he murmured.

"Either way, I'm going to do this."

Jeremy sent two limos to take them to the hotel. They'd all leave for the prison the following morning.

"This is the life," Ben joked and she laughed, albeit tightly.

"It's a good perk, I admit."

"They'll probably take it out of my contract," Adrian said. "Nothing's free."

She shrugged. He was probably right.

"You can afford it."

He brightened and leaned forward to snatch the sunglasses from her nose. "You're the one wearing Versace shades. Hell, I'm wearing thrift store jeans and a T-shirt I've had since high school."

"That's because you're cooler than me. I have to pay for it."

"There she is," Brody said softly.

"Sometimes I lose myself," she said back.

"But we always find you."

She smiled and squeezed his hand.

The hotel was understatedly elegant, a quality she appreciated. Jeremy had met them for dinner, along with his parents. Stilted and awkward wasn't an adequate way to describe it. The amount of grief at the table made her want to choke.

They trudged up to their rooms, but once the door was closed, Ben locked it, looked to Todd and nodded. Both men turned their attention to her.

"Naked and on your knees."

They turned and went into the bedroom.

With trembling hands, she obeyed. The sex in the last several weeks had been as frequent as usual but softer, more gentle, with each man speaking sweet words. With the stress of finding out about the hearing and then of telling their families, things had been more rushed.

Seeing this side to her men once again made her heart thunder as her body readied for them.

The chain Todd had given her swayed as she got to her knees.

Some minutes later they both returned, shirtless but still wearing jeans. Her pulse jumped at the sight of them. At the gleam of the ring in Ben's left nipple, at Todd's very flat belly with the tattoo bearing their initials marking the hollow at his hip.

Their lips were swollen and she wanted to moan at the image of them kissing as she'd waited there, patient and on her knees.

Todd approached with a blindfold that he put over her eyes gently, tightening it against the light. And just like that, her skin came alive as she lost her sight.

She heard the steps on the lush carpet as they circled her, and the dull thud and scent of hemp. *Rope.* Her lips opened on a gasp.

The heat from Ben's body buffeted her back as he helped her to her feet. "I need you a little farther in the room. Two steps forward."

She trusted him to guide her and then felt Todd's hand, splayed across her belly, just above her mound.

The shock of an openmouthed kiss on her collarbone.

A hand on her shoulder, urging her to kneel, this time on a pillow they'd put down for her.

The rasp of the rope as it made the first seductive contact against her upper body.

'Round and 'round it went. Around her body. Circling her arms. Binding her wrists. Between her legs, snug against the slope where leg met body, opening her cunt. Between her breasts and around to her back again.

She lost herself in the sensual array of the binding. The scent of rope and male arousal, the feel of fingertips contrasting with the rough hemp.

Her breathing grew deep and slow as her blood thrummed with the heady brew of hormones the rope always brought.

"So beautiful." Ben spoke against her ear and she shivered.

And then the slither.

She heard the sound of the tails of the flogger, which Todd had grown to love. Leather on leather. She saw the move in her mind's eye as he turned it in his hand. The low creak of the handle echoed in concert with her panting.

Her clit throbbed, extra-sensitive since the piercing. The cooler air of the room caressed her flesh as they moved, stirring the air.

She wasn't expecting the first strike from the flogger, just barely touching her nipples. Absently, she thought about how good Todd had gotten with it.

Again and again, until her body heated with the blood rising to the surface. She wasn't hurting, just hypersensitive.

Ben against her back, the texture of his jeans as he put his calves just outside hers.

"Shall I make you come?" he asked, licking up the side of her neck to her ear.

She swallowed hard, trying to find words. Instead she managed to nod and he chuckled.

Arching. Her back arched as she pulled against the ropes, toward where Ben knelt behind her.

Struggling against disorientation and loss of balance, until she remembered they'd catch her and she relaxed.

Until Todd shoved her thighs apart and his mouth found her pussy. A desperate moan surfaced as her fists opened and closed, wanting to touch the silk of his hair, to hold him to her.

Wave after glorious wave of pleasure rolled through her, sending her far away from herself even as the ropes, even as Todd's hands on her thighs, even as Ben's hands on her arms, kept her anchored.

She was picked up and carried, carefully; placed on a bed, still kneeling.

The blindfold was removed and she saw their actions reflected in the mirror opposite the bed. Tousled, flushed, nipples dark and tight. Wanton and desirable. Desired.

Tears stung her eyes when she found Todd's gaze. He looked at her as if she were precious and she felt it. Ben's eyes sparked with his desire for her, his concern and love.

"Not the time for tears," Todd said, tossing the flogger in the open suitcase. "Just pleasure. Tonight is about us helping you forget the bad and remember the good in your life from now on."

Ben easily untied the rope, slowly bundling it as he unbound her. She still bore the furrows where it had lain against her skin and she found it beautiful in the same way she found the marks from Todd's bites beautiful.

When Ben had finished, he put the rope away and each man took a wrist and massaged it where the ropes had gripped. Strong, capable hands on her, making the pain fade.

"Thank you."

Todd smiled, just the barest lift of one corner of his mouth. "We're not done yet. Not by a long shot."

"Oh."

Ben chuckled and kissed the inside of her wrist.

"Can I touch you?" she asked both of them.

"Yes." Todd moved closer and she went to his waistband. She got off the bed to remove his clothes and then followed suit with Ben, and at last they all stood naked and her heart raced at the sight.

They turned back to the mirror she'd seen herself in minutes before and she took them in. Tall and masculine, hard lines of jaw, the defined muscle of pecs and biceps. Todd with a bit more hair on his chest than Ben. Ben who stood two inches taller. Beautiful and masterful and all hers.

Still facing the mirror, she took a cock in each hand and gave an experimental pump or two. And lost herself in them once more, trusting they'd catch her if she fell.

Todd had watched her all that day. Had witnessed the slow drain of her vitality and color, but she hadn't given up. At the dinner with Jeremy and his parents, they'd spoken, albeit haltingly, of Adele. Todd had felt like he truly knew her through it. Felt her loss, or the edge anyway. Erin's grief was deep; he knew they only saw the briefest outline of it.

He and Ben had decided to exorcise her of the day in the way they knew best, with a little bit of pain and a lot of pleasure. They'd help her lose herself in the sea of endorphins and serotonin and reinforce that they'd be there as her safety chute.

She looked so damned beautiful, her eyes now half-lidded and sex-blurred. Her skin an enticing shade of pink, still marked in places where the rope had held her tightest.

He continued to watch in the mirror as she turned and fell to her knees once more, drawing him and Ben hip to hip.

And then he had to look down as she brought their cocks close and licked and sucked each one and both at once as she could. The sensation of her tongue and hands as his cock slid along Ben's nearly made Todd lose his mind.

Her eyes fluttered closed, her lashes fanning against the uppermost ridge of her cheeks. Drawn by need, Todd traced over the sweet hollow just below her shoulder, on her back. Nestled within a bower of ivy her brother had inked around it. The drawn pucker of the scar Charles Cabot had given her had faded, but the memories hadn't. She had one more on her thigh and each time Todd saw them or touched them, he sent up a prayer of thanks that she was alive to bear them.

"Enough," Todd said roughly, pulling back from the sweetness of her mouth. "I want to come inside you."

Ben moaned. "I want to come in your mouth."

"I know a way we can make that happen." Todd sat on the bed, scooting back just a bit. Erin followed, knowing what he wanted.

She straddled him, her back to his front, and sank onto his cock, hard and fast instead of her usual slow, seductive way. Todd sucked in air and counted to a hundred to keep focus.

Ben hummed his satisfaction and stepped forward so she could take him in her mouth again and the three began to move. Thrust, suck, thrust, like a machine with three moving parts, until it became smooth and singular.

Ben knew he wouldn't last long, not given the way she'd been after he tied her up. So pretty and vulnerable yet strong beyond imagination, Erin was the most precious thing he knew.

He loved being with her this way, as Todd was inside her, as they all shared one another. What a gift his life had become each and every day. It lessened the pain of the estrangement he now had with his father, gave him enough hope in human nature that he'd someday not have this gulf there.

He wondered at her, at the miracle she was, as he sifted his fingers through the softness of her hair. Hair that was currently chocolate brown. He'd simply accepted that she'd come home with a new hair color or a new piercing, even a new sex toy for them all to try.

Pleasure rushed from the soles of his feet and out his cock as she palmed his sac and played her middle finger against his perineum in just the right way to push him over the edge.

Then he knelt and kissed her as she ran her fingertip back and forth over his nipple with the ring.

Behind her, Todd groaned and she gasped into Ben's mouth as he found her clit, squeezing it between his fingers and bringing her off right on the heels of Todd's climax.

Todd pulled her up and off and they tugged her into the bathroom, where they'd laid out all the accessories she'd need for a long soak, and she blinked back tears as she hugged them both.

34

They all got up before dawn and trudged out to the waiting limos. Erin was grateful she didn't have to drive as she tucked in, settling between Ben and Todd.

She wore a suit, as did the men. Brody had combed down his normally wild hair and Adrian looked stylish and handsome. Of course Ben and Todd were beyond handsome in their suits, but they wore *cop* like cologne and she took comfort in it.

The trip to the prison would take them east for about two hours, so she settled in for the drive. No one spoke much, but they all glared at her until she drank her juice and ate a muffin. Then they forked over the coffee and she held on to it like a lifeline, trying not to think of what she would be facing.

That fateful day she'd had everything one moment and nothing the next. She wanted the parole board to know that. She'd brought a folder with pictures in it.

She was lost in thought until Ben sat up straighter and she looked out the window to see the industrial hulk of the prison walls.

Detective Emery was there and, to her surprise, he hugged her. "I'm glad you're here. Listen, chances are he won't get parole today. I want to repeat that. But you being here makes a difference. I know it's hard, and I'm glad you have your husband and your family with you."

Jeremy came up with his parents and Emery said hello to them as well.

"Shall we?" Emery motioned and they moved through the gates into a holding area, where Erin's bag was searched. She left her cell phone and most of her belongings behind before they moved through another set of fenced-off sidewalks to an outbuilding.

Her hands shook and nausea swamped her. She stumbled and Todd put an arm around her.

"Buck up. We're here for you. You *will* make it through. Do this for Adele. Do it for yourself." Todd kissed her cheek, and she nodded, numb.

"We'll wait out here until they call us. There's another hearing going on right now," Emery explained. "This board is a good group. Due to the nature of what Cabot was convicted of, they'll let you all speak. Erin should go first. Jeremy, you should sit with her and then speak right after. Then the uncles and grandparents. I'll speak as well, and we have the psych report, which isn't rosy."

Erin nodded, in a daze, but clung to reality by her fingernails. She would do this, damn it.

The hallway smelled much like every other government building she'd ever been in. The scent settled in her nose and she knew when they got back to the hotel she'd need to shower for a long time to rid herself of it.

Finally they were called in and she stopped short when she caught sight of Charles Cabot sitting there in an ill-fitting suit. He hadn't changed much since she saw him last, also in another ill-fitting suit on the last day of the trial.

His eyes lit up when he recognized her and Ben stepped into his line of sight without reacting otherwise.

"Hold on," Jeremy said softly. "Don't let him win. This is for her."

She nodded, jerkily, and they sat. She barely heard the board speak, but she did listen attentively when Cabot spoke about his remorse and how he'd found his calling and wanted to help troubled youth.

Brody forcibly unclenched her fists and handed her a handkerchief because her palms were bleeding where she'd dug her nails into the flesh. He'd help youth? How about by not killing them?

She heard her name and Ben squeezed her shoulder and Todd kissed her cheek as she and Jeremy got up to sit at a table facing the parole board.

She thanked them for allowing her to speak and then she began to place the pictures of Adele on the table, from ultrasound to the picture taken in the morgue. Her hands shook, but she kept going.

"This is Adele and she was my baby. Charles Cabot stole a life, a future filled with possibilities. I won't see her get on the bus to kindergarten. I won't see her lose her first tooth. I won't watch her graduate from high school and college. We won't ever argue about curfew and how much lip gloss she can wear. I won't see her marry and I'll never hold her children. I gave birth to this person and she is not here now for *one* reason, and that's Charles Cabot and his instability. His selfish lack of control cost my child her life and has made me look over my shoulder ever since."

And then she did the thing she needed to do, for herself. She looked Charles Cabot in the face, holding his attention long enough to let him know she would not let his attempt to get around the system this way go unchallenged.

Her eyes broke away and she went on, just speaking from her

heart and careful not to look at Cabot again. She'd made her point, to herself and to him, and to look again would only give him what he wanted.

Jeremy spoke, and Erin heard the catch in his voice as he talked about what Adele's birth had been like for him. How he'd taught her to swim and how her first word had been *no*. He spoke of how the attack had not only nearly killed Erin and ended the possibilities of Adele's future, but how it had torn their relationship apart and kept Erin off stage.

Detective Emery spoke, and then Brody and Adrian, followed by Jeremy's parents. The pictures of Adele stayed on the table until they were all finished speaking and the board dismissed them while they deliberated.

"I've won," she said quietly to Ben.

"What do you mean?" He held her hand.

"No matter what they decide, I did it. I walked in there and I stood up for Adele. I looked him in the eye and let him know I wouldn't let this pass. If they parole him, I will fight it. If they don't, I'll be back when they hear this again."

Todd heard it and knelt in front of her. "I'm so proud of you. You kicked butt in there."

"I couldn't let him own any part of me anymore. He doesn't get my fear. He can't control me with it. That doesn't mean I won't be afraid; I can't help it. But it means I can push it back and fight it off."

"With our help." Todd kissed her forehead and pushed to stand again.

He paced and Ben sat holding her hand. Jeremy excused himself for several minutes and came back red-eyed but more steady. Brody looked off into space and Adrian spoke quietly to Emery.

It wasn't an exceptionally long wait before they were called back in and the parole board unanimously rejected Cabot's request for parole and agreed to rehear the case in three years.

Erin exhaled, putting her head in her hands and swallowing back emotion. Standing straight, she held her back and head up high and thanked the board before walking out.

35

The night air was warm as the sunset rendered the grassy knoll on the hill facing the stage a riot of oranges and pinks.

Erin walked out with Adrian, and the sound of the crowd going wild at seeing her there bolstered her, fed her, made her smile.

She adjusted her strap and began to play, laying the beat, enticing Adrian's voice to join, enticing his guitar to play with hers. And he did. The song caught her, and then another, until she'd given in and let it carry her. It had been a very long time, but it felt good and right that she be there.

Stage left, her family stood. Her mothers-in-law, Brody, those brothers-in-law who were still part of their lives. Most important, Todd and Ben watched her, smiling, understanding what it meant for her to be there.

She tipped her head back and looked into the sky, looked up at the stars and sent out thanks. She wasn't that woman she'd been eleven years before, playing small clubs, having a hot affair with a cop who had big issues with his sexuality. She'd changed and there were still parts of her inside that were broken. She still jumped at loud noises and hated crowds. But the part where her music lived thrived and unfurled, filling the stage, freeing her in the way only that one thing could.

She had a past filled with bad things and a future filled with joy. In the balance, that was really all anyone could ask for.

Adrian broke off for the bridge and they fed off each other like they had for so many years before the darkness came. But it was there, like it had never left, and instead of tears, she only had laughter.

AUTHOR'S NOTE

This book is solidly rooted in music. Erin is a musician, it's how she views the world, it's who she is. It marks time in her life. It's about moments and tragedies and, in the end, it's about rising above and surviving.

"Outshined"—Soundgarden
"Is There a Ghost"—Band of Horses
"Sunday Kind of Love"—Etta James
"Inside and Out"—Feist
"Creep"—Radiohead
"Gong"—Sigur Rós
"Saeglopur"—Sigur Rós
"Glosoli"—Sigur Rós
"Change"—Deftones
"Way of the Fist"—Five Finger Death Punch
"Clubbed to Death (Kurayamino Mix)"—Rob D.
"Untouchable Face"—Ani DiFranco
"Marrow"—Ani DiFranco
"Fountain"—PJ Harvey
"Victory"—PJ Harvey
"Sheela Na Gig"—PJ Harvey

"A Place Called Home"—PJ Harvey

"Open Your Eyes"—Guano Apes

"Run and Run"—The Psychedelic Furs

"Run"—Kittie

"Inside Job"—Pearl Jam

"Rearview Mirror"—Pearl Jam

"Blood"—Pearl Jam

"No Way"—Pearl Jam

"Lazy Eye"—Silversun Pickups

"Awakening"—The Damning Well